Couples Therapy

JUN
2011

Couples Therapy

Michelle Larks

www.urbanchristianonline.com

Urban Books, LLC
78 East Industry Court
Deer Park, NY 11729

ISBN 13: 978-1-60162-788-9
ISBN 10: 1-60162-788-2

First Printing June 2011
Printed in the United States of America

10 9 8 7 6 5 4 3 2 1

This is a work of fiction. Any references or similarities to actual events, real people, living, or dead, or to real locales are intended to give the novel a sense of reality. Any similarity in other names, characters, places, and incidents is entirely coincidental.

Distributed by Kensington Corp.
Submit Wholesale Orders to:
Kensington Publishing Corp.
C/O Penguin Group (USA) Inc.
Attention: Order Processing
405 Murray Hill Parkway
East Rutherford, NJ 07073-2316
Phone: 1-800-526-0275
Fax: 1-800-227-9604

JUN - 2011

Couples Therapy

A Novel

By

Michelle Larks

Couples Therapy is dedicated to the women in my life:

My Mothers, Mary and Jean

Sisters:
Patrice, Sabrina, Adrienne, Donna, Catherine, and Rolanda

Nieces:
TaShawn, Tonisha, Cathleen, Stephanie, and Nicole

And Daughters:
Mikeisha and Genesse

I love all of you so much. I am so blessed to be a part of all your lives.

Acknowledgments

As always, I give thanks to my Father above. I thank Him for the many blessings He has bestowed upon me, especially during trying times. I know firsthand that the Lord truly can make a way out of no way.

To my mothers, Mary and Jean, thank you for always having my back and for listening to and encouraging me.

To my daughters, Mikeisha and Genesse, Ma loves you.

To my siblings: sisters Patrice, Sabrina, Catherine, and Rolanda; and brothers Jackie, Marcus, Roland, Darryl, Wayne, Michael, and Rodney, Big Sis loves you.

To my nieces and nephews, I am so proud to be your aunt and equally proud of you, the next generation. Continue to do the family proud.

Special kudos to Joylynn Jossel, my editor at Urban Christian Books. Thank you for the opportunity again to speak my literary voice. Tee C. Royal, my agent—a big thank you.

A special shout-out goes to Friendship United Methodist Church. I miss you!

I'd also like to express my gratitude to the fellow authors who have lent me a helping hand along the way, and who check on me from time to time: Francine Yates, Sheila Peele-Miller, Dyanne Davis, and Nicole Rouse.

I'd like to give a big thanks to the bookstores that allowed me to sign in your establishments and stocked

Acknowledgments

my books on your shelves, the libraries that invited me to participate in your author events, and the book clubs that invited me to your book club discussions—I had a blast. Thanks also to the book reviewers who have reviewed my books. Your feedback has been invaluable.

Most of all, I'd like to give a special thank-you to the readers who have supported me over the years and who e-mail me from time to time to say how encouraged you are by my books, and for asking, "When is your next book coming out?"

To my husband, Fredrick, thank you for picking up the slack when my head is over the computer, and for your unwavering support and love.

Chapter One

Meesha Morrison sat upright and scooted against the edge of the royal blue-and–gold-upholstered love seat that paid homage to her sorority, Sigma Gamma Rho. She and her church club, the Helping Hands, were gathered in the dark, wood-paneled recreation room of her seven-room Georgian brick home located in the Chatham community on the South Side of Chicago.

The tall, full-figured, thirty-five-year-old had an upturned nose and slanted hazel eyes that seemed luminous against her caramel complexion. Meesha reached up and smoothed the sides of her reddish brown shoulder-length hair that was pulled back into a ponytail. She impatiently uncrossed and re-crossed her big, shapely legs while waiting for the women to settle down so the meeting could commence. Meesha was focused, detail-orientated, and driven by nature. She had served as president of the Helping Hands for the past five years.

One of her hands fluttered to her throat, and almost unconsciously she unfastened the top button of her crisply pressed white cotton blouse. Meesha then pushed up her shirtsleeves over her elbows as if she had a momentous task at hand.

Sucking her teeth in frustration, Meesha leaned forward and abruptly rapped on the glass top of the pine cocktail table positioned in front of the sofa.

The buzz of conversation that hung in the air continued to drone despite Meesha's valiant attempts to get the attention of her sisters in Christ. She brushed a few cookie crumbs off the black, stonewashed stretch denim jeans that hugged her lower limbs.

Meesha loudly clapped together her dainty, French manicured hands. She then cleared her throat and said in a forceful, louder tone, "Ladies, can I have your attention please?" She stood and walked to the other side of the room and turned off the CD player that had been playing Kirk Franklin's latest CD.

Regina Cole, Meesha's best friend, who looked like she could have been Meesha's sister, was an outgoing, pleasingly plump, honey-colored sista with deep dimpled cheeks that any grandmother would love to pinch. She sipped from a glass of iced tea. A bit sloshed out of the glass onto the pumpkin orange sweat suit she wore with matching tennis shoes.

She hastily dabbed at the stain with a napkin that she removed from around her neck and cocked her head slightly to the left. Her long auburn weave swayed gently from side to side. She looked at Meesha and shrugged her shoulders guiltily. "Sorry, your guacamole dip is to die for. I got a little distracted. . . " Regina, affectionately nicknamed Reggie, sat the glass on the table, and gave Meesha a thumb's up sign and her undivided attention.

"Goodness, Reggie, control yourself. The food isn't going anywhere," Meesha teased her friend as she fought to keep a smile from her face. She picked up a sheet of paper off the table. "I e-mailed everyone a copy of the agenda a few days ago. Anyway, I'd like to discuss the main subject that we've been talking about for the past three months."

"My bad." Reggie's voice squealed as she apologized. She put her hand over her chest. "Madame President, you have the floor and my full attention. Please proceed." She jauntily saluted her friend, then picked up the pitcher of tea off the tray next to her chair and replenished her glass with the sweet brown liquid.

The babbling in the room ceased. The committee members' eyes honed in on their leader.

"Now, as I was saying," Meesha said in a tone that was a tad bit dramatic. She paused and then said, "I think now is the perfect time to approach Reverend Dudley about my idea for offering couples' therapy at the church. I want to make sure we're all in agreement with my proposal before I set up a meeting with Pastor. I'd like to contact him within the next week or so. I want to feel him out and get his thoughts on the subject."

"I don't know." Natalie Dozier, or Natty, as her family and friends called her, looked at Meesha dubiously. The older, mocha-colored woman's eyes looked twice their normal size because of the tortoise shell bifocals perched on her nose. "Just the words 'couples' therapy' sound so . . . I don't know." She pursed her lips in concentration and then snapped her fingers. "I know what I want to say, so far out there."

Meesha sat the paper on the cocktail table; then she walked over to one of the end tables and picked up a folder. She removed the papers and passed them out to the committee members. "Ladies, I'm going to give you a few minutes to read the recommendation that I plan to present to Pastor." She waved the swatch of papers in the air. "Then we'll discuss it when you're done."

Crystal, the youngest member of the group, was chocolate-colored with a pretty baby face. She reached over the side of the chair and picked up her burgundy Coach bag. She rummaged inside it and pulled out a pair of silver, wire-rimmed reading glasses. Crystal pushed the glasses on her nose and squinted as she read the sheets of paper in her hands.

Reggie snickered as she flicked a strand of hair back over her shoulder. "You need to see an ophthalmologist, sister, get a prescription, and then go buy yourself a pair of glasses that you can read out of instead of those fake ones from Wal-Mart."

Crystal frowned and waved her hand dismissively at Reggie, ignoring her fellow committee member's comment. She laid the paper on the floor next to her chair, then rose from her seat and walked across the room to the wooden teak bar, which spanned the length of the multi-roomed basement. Crystal put a couple of pieces of chopped carrots and broccoli florets along with a dollop of ranch dressing on a Dixie paper plate; then she returned to her seat and sat down. Crystal shifted her body in the chair in an effort to get more comfortable. After she settled on a spot, Crystal dipped a carrot in the white, creamy dressing, put it inside her mouth, and began to read the document that Meesha had distributed.

Meesha glared daggers at her best friend because of her comments to Crystal and shook her head disapprovingly. Reggie hastily placed her plate of Swedish meatballs and deviled eggs atop her lap, then she picked up the paper Meesha had passed out and scanned it. She mouthed to Meesha as she nodded her head, "Okay, I'm reading it now."

Meesha returned to her seat and sat down. The room was quiet save the sound of the women flipping the pages of the paper that Meesha had prepared for them. Fifteen minutes had elapsed before Meesha faced the group with her arms folded across her chest. She stared at each woman, one by one, and then said, "Are you ready now?"

Gayle's smooth, oval-shaped, café au lait-colored face crinkled with uncertainty. The secretary of the group for six years and counting, she waved her hand in the air. "I don't know Meesha," she sighed, holding up the proposal. "I agree with Natty. What you're trying to do seems drastic. And anyway, what makes you think that couples in our church are going to spill their personal business to a therapist?"

"I can think of several reasons why they would," Meesha responded as she held up a manicured finger, "but the most important one is that the state of marriage in the African American community is under siege. It's eroding quicker than scrap metal left out in a rainstorm. Lack of communication is drastically affecting the traditional family as we know it. And that, my sister, is why," Meesha responded ardently. She squared her shoulders resolutely as if she was about to do battle in a Middle Eastern nation. She lifted her chin a notch.

Natalie's salt-and-pepper hair was twisted in an untidy French roll. Wisps of curls crept along the nape of her neck. She nervously smoothed the hem of the denim skirt she was wearing. "Meesha, I'll defer to the data you've provided us," she remarked. "But it's been my experience that Black men are even more averse than women are to talking about their problems. How are their wives, assuming you get anyone to participate, going to sell the idea to their husbands?"

Meesha nodded, "Good point, Natty. I ask that you trust me. I've thought of all kinds of scenarios." She stretched one finger in the air. "First, I think having Reverend Dudley's support behind us is half the battle. Two, Black people might not want to discuss their problems in public, but I feel if Reverend Dudley stresses the importance of how therapy could help our spiritual beings and save families in the long run, then I think the members of the church will be responsive and use the resource we're offering to them."

"What you're saying is fine in theory, but who do you really know who would be willing to participate?" Natalie asked. Her perfectly arched eyebrows rose upward. She wrote notes on the index of the paper.

"Ladies, where is the love?" Meesha clucked her tongue and shook her head from side to side. "I feel like I don't have your support, and we're the committee presenting the proposal. If we as a group can't reach an agreement on this matter, then how can we expect the church membership to?" Meesha complained, waving her hands in the air. "I have all the logistics worked out. I told you that my old college roommate and friend Zora Taylor is moving to Chicago in January. Her bio is on the last page of your handout."

Meesha continued speaking. "Zee counsels children and couples. Her credentials are impeccable. She received a master's degree in psychology from Johns Hopkins University, and she has a Ph.D. The Academy has an opening for a guidance counselor, and Zee has applied for the position."

"What does that have to do with what you're proposing?" Gayle asked with a befuddled expression on her face. "Did I miss something?" She put a potato chip dripping with guacamole dip in her mouth and chewed it.

"I'm glad you asked that question." Meesha smiled at Gayle and folded her arms across her chest. "We can kill two birds with one stone. Zee, praise the Lord, is a Christian. She will meet with couples once a week, free of charge, as part of her salary for the school."

"Why would a doctor want to work for a church school as a guidance counselor? Isn't that like taking a step down?" Crystal asked skeptically.

"Everyone isn't motivated by titles and money. Zora has exceeded all of her academic and professional goals. She's looking for a change of scenery and, most of all, she's on board regarding my proposal," Meesha explained. "I'd like us to stay focused on the task at hand."

"Don't you think you're getting ahead of yourself?" Reggie asked. She sat the empty plate on the tray and rubbed her hands together. "She hasn't even gotten the position yet."

"Girl, I prayed and we all know God answers prayer." Meesha looked upward and then back at her committee. She said fervently, "I feel very strongly that Zee will be offered the position. She's already completed two interviews with Pastor and the school's steering committee."

"So you've talked to her already about what you're trying to do? And she's in agreement with this?" Natalie asked, sounding somewhat skeptical.

Meesha replied ardently, "This is my dream we're talking about here. I admit, it could be the social worker side of me hoping against all hope that the church will adopt the committee's resolution to implement therapy for couples. I feel very strongly about the need for therapy at the church. It's like God has called me to do this as my ministry. It doesn't hurt that Nichole Singleton was able to persuade Pastor to start a Gambler's Anonymous outreach group for the church last year. This tells me that our minister is open-minded to new suggestions."

Regina cut her eyes to the left and the right. "I'm not one to gossip," she whispered, "and I've never attended any of the meetings, but I heard that Nichole had a little gambling problem herself. Maybe Pastor approved her suggestion because she's his goddaughter."

"Girl, I heard the same thing," Natalie chimed in. "How she nearly lost her husband because she couldn't stay off the gambling boat." Natalie dipped her head. "Of course, we don't have any way of knowing whether the rumor was true or not."

"Let's not get sidetracked from the issue at hand," Meesha chided the women. "Churches as a whole haven't offered a support group for couples experiencing marital issues, short of talking to the minister. I know what I'm proposing is a radical theory. Still, I feel strongly that offering marital counseling in a group setting is needed in the church."

"All I can say is that you have your work cut out for you. You're my best friend, and I'll support you. But it's going to be a hard sell," Reggie proclaimed. She stood up. "Can I turn the CD player back on now? I brought the new Vickie Winans CD with me. I'd love for everyone to hear it. It's the bomb."

"I'd prefer you wait until after we're done. We need to take a vote on the proposal," Meesha stated firmly.

"I don't think we need to take a vote, Meesha. If you feel this strongly about the idea, then as your committee, and friends, we're one hundred percent behind you," Natalie said. Her cell phone chirped. She scooped it out of her purse. "Give me a minute." Natalie stood up and walked toward the powder room.

"We still need to take a vote for our official records," Meesha remarked. "We'll wait for Natty to finish her phone call."

The group looked in the direction of the staircase as Imani, Meesha's eight-year-old daughter, clattered down the basement stairs. "Mommy, it's almost time for me to go to my dance class. Are you almost done with your meeting?" The little girl's chocolate-colored, heart-shaped face was a replica of her mother's, except for the pouting expression that marred her pretty face. Cornrows danced about her shoulders. Imani was thin as a rail and full of nervous energy.

"I'm in the middle of a meeting, young lady, and we still have a ways to go. Where's your daddy? I thought he was going to take you to class?" Meesha asked her daughter with a sinking feeling in the pit of her stomach.

"Daddy left," the little girl informed her mother. The corners of her mouth were turned down dramatically as she hopped from one foot to the other. "He said to tell you that he couldn't take me to class and that he had to go to the office. Mommy, I can't miss my class. The recital is next month," the little girl whined.

Reggie rose from her chair and walked to her goddaughter. She patted the top of Imani's head. "Why don't you go back upstairs and get your stuff together, honey. I'll take you to class."

Imani clasped her hands together and looked up hopefully at her mother with widened eyes. Meesha nodded. A smile brightened the young girl's face. She turned and ran back up the stairs.

Reggie turned to Meesha and said in a soothing tone, "We're almost done here. I'm pretty sure the vote will be unanimous." She looked at Gayle, who nodded as she stared at Meesha with concern in her eyes.

Natalie returned from the powder room in time to catch the tail end of the conversation. She returned to her seat. "What did I miss?"

Reggie continued speaking to Meesha. "Why don't we vote after church service tomorrow? It shouldn't take anymore than what, fifteen minutes?"

"Mommy," Imani yelled from the top of the basement stairs, "I got my stuff. It's time to go."

"I'll be upstairs in a moment," Meesha replied just as loudly to daughter. She turned to the committee.

"That's a good suggestion, Reggie. Let's meet in the Garden of Eden conference room tomorrow immediately following the eleven o'clock service."

"I pass by the dance studio on my way home. I can drop Imani off if you'd like," Natalie suggested to Meesha and Regina after Gayle explained Imani's dilemma. "I know that the studio is out of your way, and it's only three blocks from my house."

"Good suggestion," Reggie said, nodding. "That's fine with me if it's okay with Meesha."

"Yes, that will give me time to straighten up here and then I'll pick her up when class is over," Meesha replied. "Thanks, Natty."

"Sure, it's no problem." Natalie picked up her purse and put the handout from the meeting inside it.

Meesha said a quick prayer before the women departed for home. A few minutes later, Imani returned downstairs wearing her red down, fake fur-lined parka with her pink dance tote bag slung over her shoulder. "Mommy, I'm ready to go."

Meesha bent over and retied the strings of Imani's jacket. "Mrs. Dozier is going to drop you off at class. I'll pick you up when class is over."

Natalie donned her black sable coat and put the matching hat on her head to fend off the hawk, as Chicagoans call the city's wintry wind. The meeting took place on the second Saturday in November 2007. Natalie removed her car keys from her Dooney & Bourke bag. "Come on, young lady. Let's get going. I don't want you to be late."

Imani put her arms around her mother's waist. Meesha bent down and kissed her daughter's cheek. "I'll see you later."

"Bye, Mommy." Imani waved to Meesha. Her hands were encased in black mittens.

The committee members began putting on their coats and preparing to depart. They walked upstairs, hugged one another, and then left. Meesha locked the door and stood in the brightly lit foyer indecisively.

Meesha was mortally wounded upon learning that Edward left to go to work even though he knew that she was hosting a meeting. Unbeknownst to Meesha's family and friends, and especially Edward, Meesha had a hidden agenda for proposing couples' therapy. She had already invisibly penciled in herself and Edward as session participants. Edward's work hours were driving Meesha crazy and creating discord between the couple. She felt like she was raising the children alone. Meesha wanted Edward to share the load as he had promised when they married.

Meesha wiped a tear from the corner of her eye. She went to the kitchen and removed a plastic bag from the pantry, then returned to the basement to tidy the room. She put plates, cans, and cups inside the garbage bag. Then she folded the tops of the bags of chips and screwed the tops back on the condiments. When she was done with her chores, Meesha turned off the light in the basement and returned upstairs. She checked the time, noting she had about forty minutes before she had to leave to pick up Imani from her class.

Meesha went downstairs to retrieve her notes. She returned upstairs, walked into the den, sat on the sofa, and pored over the papers again. She planned to talk to Reverend Dudley soon. The state of her own marriage might depend on the minister's yea or nay to her proposal. Meesha reached over the cocktail table, picked up the cordless telephone, and speedily dialed her mother's number.

Sabrina Deavers answered the telephone after the second ring. "Hello?"

"Hi, Mom, it's me. I don't need you to babysit the kids after all. Edward and I planned to take the kids to Chuck E. Cheese's after Imani finished dance class. Then we planned a date night. Our plans are off because Edward went back to work."

The older woman could hear the pain in her daughter's voice. "I'm sorry, baby. I know you were looking forward to a night alone with Ed. Why don't you and the kids come over here anyway and have dinner with me and your dad? You know I love seeing my grandchildren."

Meesha pushed her bangs off her forehead. "Not tonight, Mom. I'm not in the mood. I just wanted to let you know that my plans have changed and that I'll see you in church tomorrow." Meesha listened to her mother ramble on for a bit. She then bade her mother good-bye before the women hung up the telephones.

Following her conversation with her mother, Meesha decided to go pick up her six-year-old son, Keon, who had gone to the movies with a classmate and his mother. Meesha massaged the sides of her head, then walked to the foyer, removed her coat from the closet, and slipped it on.

She took her purse off the dining room table, exited the house from the back door and went into the garage. Meesha entered her vehicle and clicked the remote to open the garage door. She drove down the alley and made a left turn onto the main thoroughfare. The tires of her olive green Ford Explorer screeched in anger. Meesha gripped the sides of the steering wheel so tightly her fingers ached. Her brow was furrowed with tension lines, a telltale sign of the upcoming, unpleasant discussion she would have with her husband.

Chapter Two

A few weeks later, Nichole Singleton waddled back to her seat in the choir stand after singing the last notes to a rousing rendition of "It Is Well With My Soul." The young woman's stomach protruded awkwardly from beneath her choir robe, but her face glowed with happiness. She and her husband, Jeffrey, were expecting their first child the following month, and Nichole's demeanor radiated pure joy, which flowed through in her singing.

Outbursts of joyous hallelujahs and hearty shouts of amen reverberated throughout the sanctuary of the Christian Friendship Missionary Baptist Church. The choir's organist, Latrell Monroe, played soul stirring music as the church members waved their church bulletins in the air.

When the music and the shouting died down some, the ushers collected tithes and offerings. The females wore white uniforms and the males dark suits and white shirts. At approximately 1:30 P.M., the congregation rose to sing "God Be With You Till We Meet Again." After the last note ended, Reverend Calvin Nixon gave the benediction, indicating church services had concluded for another week.

Meesha gathered her possessions and rose from her seat. She wore a soft, wool lavender-and-black plaid skirt suit with a black turtleneck and matching lavender pumps, which gave her an air of authority. She looked from left to right for the Helping Hands committee members, but the church had been packed that Sunday morning and she couldn't find hide nor hair of any of them. Imani and Keon were in the lower level of the building attending children's church. Meesha picked up her coat and draped it around her shoulders. She greeted various church members as she maneuvered her way to the conference room where she'd scheduled the committee meeting. There had been a virus outbreak in Chicago a few weeks earlier, and several committee members had been stricken with the flu, so Meesha had rescheduled the previous committee meeting.

When she walked inside the room, Meesha removed her coat and laid it on the back of an empty chair. Biblical scenes and scriptures were taped to the wall. Meesha took a folder out of her briefcase and laid it on the table.

Reggie looked fetching as she walked into the room next wearing a burgundy suit trimmed with gold. "Girl, I tell you, Reverend Nixon preached a powerful sermon this morning," Reggie said breathlessly as she walked over to Meesha. "That man is getting better all the time at preaching the Word. He's fine too." She took off her coat and sat down in one of the gray metal folding chairs. Then Reggie reached up took off the hat she was wearing and finger-combed her hair.

"Yes, the sermon was very stirring," Meesha agreed. She looked up to see Natalie, Crystal, and Gayle strolling into the room. The women, like Reggie and Meesha, were dressed in their Sunday best, clad in power suits appropriate for any corporate boardroom.

"I talked to Reverend Dudley yesterday and asked him if he could spare us a little time to discuss our proposal this morning." Meesha looked at her watch. "He should be here any minute. Are we all in agreement with the proposal?"

"Yes," Regina said, holding up her hand. She made a motion that the proposal be accepted.

"Definitely," Gayle seconded the motion. The vote was unanimous. Gayle dutifully added notes to the steno pad that she removed from her oversized purse.

"Then we're set." Meesha looked around the table at her friends and took a deep breath. She sighed in satisfaction. "If you have other plans, then feel free to proceed with them. I can meet with Pastor alone since his appearance was a last-minute decision," she informed the women.

"I'll stay," Reggie volunteered, nodding her head. "If two of us are available to talk to him, then we'll provide more of a united front."

"I wish that I could stay, but I'm having my in-laws over for dinner. In fact, I have to run now." Natalie glanced at the watch on her slender wrist as she stood and slipped on her coat. "Call or e-mail and let me know how the meeting went."

"I've got to run too," Crystal added and rose from her seat. "Josh and I are meeting some friends for lunch. Let me know how things went too."

"I can stay," Gayle announced. "Three are better than two." She laid her pen down on the table.

"I will let everyone know how the meeting went. I'll e-mail you this week," Meesha responded. Crystal and Natalie departed. Meesha's throat felt dry and her hands were clammy. She thought, *Lord, please put the right words in my mouth so Reverend Dudley will understand what I'm trying to accomplish.* She nervously scanned her notes one more time.

Reggie, in the meantime, pulled out her checkbook and began balancing the figures. Gayle called her husband, who was at home with one of their sick children, to tell him she would be late returning from church.

"Ladies, good morning," Reverend Dudley said as he walked into the meeting room. He looked distinguished wearing a black double-breasted suit with a gray shirt. Following on his heels was the church's assistant minister, Reverend Calvin Nixon. He wore a dark brown suit with a pale yellow shirt, which contrasted nicely with his light brown skin. His hair was short on the sides, with natural waves on the top; his moustache appeared to be newly trimmed. The minister was medium tall with a muscular build from his regular workout regimen.

Meesha, Reggie, and Gayle stood up and said in unison, "Good morning, Pastor."

"Ladies, please have a seat," the minister instructed the women. The men sat at the table. After exchanging a few pleasantries, Reverend Dudley requested a copy of the proposal, and Meesha handed him a sheaf of neatly stapled papers.

"If you have any extra copies, would you please give one to Calvin?" the minister requested, scanning the first page of the neatly typed proposal.

"Sure." Meesha passed a copy to Reverend Nixon. She was grateful to have had enough foresight to print additional copies.

"Thank you, sister," Reverend Nixon replied. He looked down and began reading.

Meesha held her breath as Reverend Dudley put on his glasses and read the proposal.

After he finished perusing the document, Reverend Dudley pushed the glasses up over his forehead. "This is interesting and informative data, Meesha." Reverend Dudley folded the papers together and looked at the young woman. "What I'd like to do is study this a little bit further. I like what I see. While I can't promise your idea will be approved as a viable program for the church, I'll certainly give it consideration. Why don't you schedule a time to meet with me later this week with Roslyn? I'll call or e-mail you within the next day or so if I have any questions." The minister turned to Reverend Nixon. "What do you think, Calvin?"

"I don't think I've seen or heard of anything like this before, certainly not in any churches today. It's an interesting concept. I agree we should meet with Sister Meesha for further clarification of some of the points she's raised," Calvin offered.

"How does your schedule look this week?" Reverend Dudley asked Calvin.

"It's pretty clear," Calvin answered after checking his BlackBerry.

"I brought Calvin with me today because he's my new project liaison. If the board decides to accept your proposal, he will work with you to help bring the project to fruition," Reverend Dudley informed Meesha.

Meesha expelled a long breath. "So do you think the project has merit?" She looked at both ministers. "You think we should move forward?" Beneath the table, she crossed her fingers.

"Oh yes, it definitely has merit," Reverend Dudley nodded.

"Thank you, Pastor," Meesha gushed enthusiastically. "All I ask for is an opportunity to try to present the ministry to the church membership."

The men stood. "Have a glorious day," Reverend Dudley said. "Don't forget to see Roslyn before you leave."

"Have a blessed day," Reverend Nixon said with a sober expression on his face.

The men and Gayle departed the room.

Regina stood up, did a little dance, and then pumped her fist in the air. "Part one is over and in the books. I'd say that went quite well."

"Let's not count our eggs before they're hatched. Still, I have a good feeling about the meeting. I'm prayerful that God will help make the group a reality." Meesha had a satisfied expression on her face.

"Where's Ed?" Regina asked Meesha as she put on her tan coat and matching hat. "I didn't see him in church this morning."

"He had to work again," Meesha wailed. "I don't know what to think. He's never home. When I question him about how he's MIA, he says he's working on a top-priority project."

Regina rubbed her friend's arm. "I know it's tough, but you knew when you married Edward that he was a go-getter. His eyes have been and will always be on the prize."

"You're right, I knew that," Meesha sighed. "But I counted on him making time for me and the kids, and he hasn't."

"It could be worse. You could be with one of those brothas who don't work at all."

"I know what you're saying, Reggie." Meesha twisted her lips together. "Still, there has to be a balance in life. A time to work and a time to play, you know? Like the passage in Ecclesiastes. Edward's agenda includes work and more work. He promised to spend time with the children and me yesterday. Lately, it's a rare occurrence when he doesn't go to work, and you know how things turned out a few weeks ago. Our private time together didn't happen at all." Meesha was visibly upset.

"Yesterday was supposed to have been family day again," Meesha scowled. "Then I planned to spend some one-on-one time with my husband. We'd planned to take the kids to an arcade after Imani's dance class. I went to Blockbuster and rented Denzel's movie *Antwone Fisher* for the two of us to watch. Ed skipped out after we took the kids to the arcade."

"Well, you did spend some time together," Reggie consoled her friend. "Girl, you better support your man. You know if you don't there are hundreds of women out there who will," Regina observed as she wrapped her thick, black knit scarf around her neck.

"I don't mind supporting him, but he never seems to come home at a decent hour anymore. Ed didn't get home until close to midnight last night. So you tell me, where is the balance in our lives?" Meesha rubbed her tired eyes, moaning dissonantly.

"I didn't realize things had gotten so bad, Meesha. Why didn't you tell me what's been going on?" Regina pulled on her gloves and picked up her purse off the table.

"I kept hoping things would get better, but they haven't." Meesha shrugged her shoulders helplessly.

"No wonder you're so gung ho about the therapy group." Understanding dawned in Regina's eyes. "Oh, my God, you're planning to be a part of the group, you and Ed, aren't you?" Her hand flew to her mouth.

"Yes, you hit the nail on the head." Meesha nodded smugly and folded her arms across her chest. "That's why I know Zee will have at least one couple to counsel, me and Ed."

"If Ed can't make time for you and the kids, then what makes you think he'll make time for seeing a marriage counselor?" Regina asked caringly, though her eyebrow rose skeptically.

"He doesn't have a choice," Meesha said passionately. "I can't continue to stay married to him under these circumstances." She stuffed her hands inside her pockets.

"Wow, that's a big step, Meesha." Regina's eyes widened. "Are you sure about what you're doing?"

"As sure as my name is Meesha Mechelle Morrison. Edward and I need a change, something to shake up the marriage. I need my husband to realize just how important his family is to him."

"Hmm, girl." Regina's eyes narrowed. She reached over and squeezed Meesha's arm. "I'll keep you in my prayers. I hope for your sake that Pastor and Calvin approve the plan. What if they don't?" Regina couldn't resist asking.

"Then we'll have no choice except to see a marriage counselor. I thought it would be easier for us to meet with Zora in a group setting. She's a Christian, and that's important to me. I'm hoping she can help us work on our issues from a spiritual standpoint."

"I got your back. Maybe we should see if Roslyn is still here and go ahead and make that appointment to see Pastor this week."

"Good idea." Meesha snapped the briefcase shut and tied the belt on her Burberry coat around her waist. She and Regina left the room and headed to Reverend Dudley's office. Roslyn sat at her desk outside the minister's office.

The secretary flipped the pages of the minister's appointment book. Her finger tracked the scheduled appointments. "Pastor is free on Wednesday at three o'clock in the afternoon and then at six o'clock. Can you meet him at either of those times?"

Meesha took her Palm Pilot out of her purse. She removed the stylus, then scrolled to her calendar and selected Wednesday. "Yes, I can. I'll be here promptly at three o'clock."

"Good." Roslyn neatly penciled the appointment in Reverend Dudley's book. "I'll check with Reverend Nixon to see if he's available."

"Thank you for your help, Roslyn. I appreciate it."

"No problem, sweetie." Roslyn flashed a smile at the two women. "How are those adorable children of yours doing?" she asked Meesha.

Regina said, "I hate to break up the party. I have to go, Meesha, and check on my parents. I'll talk to you later today or tomorrow."

"Okay," Meesha replied. The friends hugged each other, and Meesha turned back to Roslyn after Regina left. "My children are doing just fine. Imani has a dance recital coming up soon, and Keon just joined the Boy Scout troop here at the church. Their grades were very good the last marking period."

"That's excellent," Roslyn raved. "So many children are out of control today." Her voice dropped conspiratorially as she winked at Meesha. "Good parenting skills make a difference, and exposing your children to Christ at a young age."

"That's for sure. I try to keep them busy in extracurricular activities too. I'd better get out of here. The kids are still at children's church, and I know they're wondering where I am." Meesha put her purse strap on her shoulder.

"I'll see you Wednesday. Have a good day." Roslyn looked behind Meesha. A group of church members stood patiently in line waiting to talk with the church secretary.

Meesha's lips curved into a tiny smile as she left the office and went to gather her children. Part one of her plan was in the books. Now the rest was up to Pastor Dudley and Reverend Nixon; most of all it was in God's hands. She sighed as she thought about how she would present the idea to Edward. All things in their time was her motto.

Chapter Three

Deacon Kenneth Howard was a light-skinned, freckle-faced bear of man. He had a wide girth, broad shoulders, and an engaging smile that displayed neat rows of pearly white teeth. Kenneth held the arm of his petite wife, Beverly, as they walked cautiously on the ice-covered walkway to their four-bedroom, gray, brick Cape Cod-style on Eightieth Street and Martin Luther King Drive. As they neared the house, Beverly and Kenneth could hear loud male voices.

The good mood Kenneth had been in after leaving church deflated like a burst balloon. He pursed his lips like he'd bitten off a piece of spoiled fruit. His smile turned into a frown when he noticed that his stepson, Amir, hadn't shoveled the sidewalk or the pavement outside the silver chain-link fence as Kenneth had requested before he and his wife left for church that morning. Amir was a sharp thorn in Kenneth's side. Kenneth considered the twenty-seven-year-old, soon-to-be twenty-eight years old, a moocher who had his mother wrapped around his pinky finger. After turning eighteen, Amir abandoned attending church on a regular basis, usually visiting only Mother's Day and Christmas services.

Beverly's hands flew out as she slipped on a patch of ice. Kenneth tightened his grip on her arm, breaking her fall. "What the dickens! What is all that noise coming from our house? It sounds like a party is going on in there." He and Beverly walked slowly up the slick stairs. Then he pulled his house key out of his coat pocket, unlocked and pushed open the white aluminum storm door.

Amir and five of his friends sat in the couple's usually neat-as-a-pin off-white living room. The royal blue velvet sofa seemed to groan under the weight of two oversized young men. Amir and his crew were gathered around the family's fifty-two-inch, high definition television watching the Bears football game.

Sweating cans of beer created rings on the top of cocktail and end tables because Amir had forgotten to use the coasters. Bags of spilling potato chips, popcorn, nachos, and other snack food were partners to the alcoholic beverages. The young men had carelessly dropped some of the snacks on the dark blue shag carpet.

Kenneth stalked to the closet in a huff, hung up his coat, and pulled his hat off his short Afro. He glared toward the living room, fuming as he helped Beverly remove her coat and hung it up in the cedar closet.

Beverly jumped slightly when she heard her husband slam the closet door. "Now, Kenny," she whispered uneasily as she patted his arm, "take it easy, honey. Don't forget what Dr. Hoffman said about stress and your blood pressure."

Beverly didn't look her age. She was in her late forties, but could have passed for thirty-five. She was no bigger than a minute with a cute, heart-shaped Hershey chocolate-colored face. Beverly had large light brown eyes and a slight overbite. The only hint of her age was her silver gray hair, which she wore styled in a short cut, an easy to maintain hairdo. A few lifelines, as she called them, adorned her attractive face.

Amir was short in stature with a thin frame. He was dark skinned like his mother, and average-looking with a charming smile. Amir ran his hand through the twists in his hair. He glanced from the television and looked at his parents momentarily. "Oh, what's up, Mom and Dad? I didn't expect you back so soon. How was church?" His eyes flew back to the television as he scratched his scalp.

Kenneth gritted his teeth. "I thought I asked you to shovel and put salt on the pavement this morning before your mother and I left for church? Your mother nearly fell outside when we walked to the house." He pointed to the young men whose eyes were glued to the television set. "Who are these people, and why are they in my house?"

"These guys?" Amir pointed to each man and introduced them to Kenneth and Beverly. "They're just my boys: Leonard, Khamal, Brian, and Otis. Dudes, this is my Moms and Pop. We're watching—" Amir's attention shifted back to the television screen. One of the Bears running backs scored a touchdown, tying the score with the Minnesota Vikings. The young men hooted and jumped from their seats, exchanging high fives.

"Where is your sister?" Beverly asked her son, glancing uneasily at Kenneth. She stood motionless behind her husband.

"She's here somewhere." Amir didn't look at his mother but continued to stare at the television screen.

Unlike her brother, the Howards' daughter, Tracey, did attend church on a regular basis. She had stayed home that morning to take care of Amir's son, Jalin, who had an upset stomach.

"I thought Jalin didn't feel well when we left for church this morning. You and your friends are making so much noise. I hope you're not disturbing him," Beverly said as she stole a peep around her husband's bulky body.

"Naw, he's all right. He just ate too much junk last night," Amir replied, his eyes still glued to the television set.

Kenneth loosened his tie. His jaw quivered with rage. He walked into the living room, picked the remote up off the table, and powered off the television. "The party is over. If your last name isn't Howard, then you need to get moving." He walked over to the front door and opened it.

Beverly shook her head as she walked down the hallway to her daughter's room.

Amir jumped up off the couch and walked over to Kenneth. "Dad, why did you do that? The game is almost over. There's only two minutes left in the fourth quarter." He picked up the remote control from the table to turn the television back on.

"I wouldn't recommend doing that." Kenneth shook his head at Amir. "The last time I checked the mortgage statement, it read that this house belongs to me and your mother. Our home is not a restaurant or a bar. If you want to watch the game, then I suggest you go somewhere else." Kenneth looked at Amir intently, daring his son to turn on the television.

Otis, a dark-skinned mountain of a man with a huge baldhead, looked almost homeless in the long-sleeved Bears T-shirt and dingy jeans he was wearing. He stood and picked up his green fatigue jacket from the side of the sofa. "Hey, my brother," he said to Amir in a deep voice. "It's no problem. We can go to my house and finish watching the game there."

"By the time we get there, the game will be over," Amir replied testily. "Come on, Dad. Let us at least watch the last few minutes of the game, and then we'll go."

The other young men stood up and prepared to depart. They weren't immune to the hostility that hung heavily over the room like a veil. They quickly donned their jackets.

Otis and Brian picked up the two remaining six packs of beer from the floor. "Amir, we'll holla at you later. We'll probably go to my house and watch the second game," Otis informed his friend. The men gave one another some dap and left the house.

Amir's eyes smoldered with rage as he glared at his father. He walked to the closet and removed his Bears jacket.

Kenneth stared at his son and said angrily, "Where do you think you're going? Aren't you keeping your son this weekend?"

The young man looked fiercely at his father. "Mom can watch him, or Tracey. I'm outta of here." He turned to open the door.

Before Amir could reach for the doorknob, Kenneth had stepped in front of the door. He growled at his son, "Your mother and sister are not your personal babysitters or servants." Kenneth's face shimmered with disgust as he pointed his finger in Amir's chest. "Jalin is your son and your responsibility. What you need to do is to stay here and watch him yourself and shovel the snow like you said you would."

"Whoa, watch yourself, old man," Amir muttered under his breath. He held his hands up and then dropped them to his sides. His hands unconsciously had curled into fists.

Beverly, rushed back into the room and stood between the two men, trying to diffuse the situation. She touched her husband's shoulder tentatively. "Kenny, it's no problem. I can watch the baby. I told Amir that I'd help him take care of Jalin this weekend. Please calm down," she cajoled.

Kenneth shrugged from his wife's contact. "Look, I know you mean well, Bev, but this is between me and

Amir." He looked at his son and said, "Amir, I'd advise you not to leave here this afternoon."

Amir glowered at his father. "I'm sorry, Dad, but I want to spend some time with my boys. I won't be gone too long." He glanced at his watch. "I'll be back around six thirty, as soon as the second game is over."

Kenneth became livid, and splotches of red suffused his cheeks. "If you leave here, Amir"—he pointed to the door—"then don't bother to come back. I've had enough of you sponging off your mother and me."

Amir pulled a skullcap out of his jacket pocket and pulled it over his head. "I know how you feel about my staying here. You've already told me that a million times. Right now, I don't feel like listening to you busting my chops. I'll be back in a few hours to get Jalin. I'm out of here." He turned and walked out the door.

Kenneth looked like he was suffering from an attack of apoplexy. His eyes bulged out of their sockets. The veins in his neck throbbed ominously.

"Kenny, please calm down. Getting upset with Amir won't do any good. I'll talk to him when he comes back."

"You make sure that you do." Kenneth looked at his wife and shouted, "If I don't see any improvement in his behavior soon—and I mean soon—then he's out of here, job or no job. He's got to go."

"Oh, no. Don't say that." Beverly's eyes widened as she took a step backward and held out her arms, pleading with her husband. "He doesn't have any place to go, Kenneth. What kind of parents would we be if we put our only son out of the house and he doesn't have a job? Honey, please try to calm down."

"It's too much, Bev. Both of our children are still home with us. They're both darn near thirty years old and still live at home. I don't know—If things don't improve around here quickly, then someone's going to have to leave, and I'd hate for it to be me." Kenneth snapped his mouth shut and went to the bedroom to change clothes.

Beverly stood in the middle of the living room wringing her hands together. She closed her eyes and prayed that Kenneth was just blowing off steam. Beverly didn't relish having to choose between her children and her husband. In her mind, Amir was just going through a tough time, as he always did. Beverly, as usual, remained hopeful that her son would find a job the upcoming week. She said, "Lord, please stop by here today and help my family."

She then turned and went into the bedroom she shared with Kenneth. Her husband had taken off his shirt and laid it on the bed. He removed a black flannel shirt from the chest of drawers in a corner of the room and put it on. After he changed into a pair of jeans, Kenneth informed Beverly that he was going outside to shovel snow.

Beverly just nodded, not trusting herself to speak. Tears gathered in her eyes, and her hands flew to the side of her cheeks. When Beverly heard the back door open and shut, she walked over and sat on the edge of the bed. A sob escaped her lips, and she folded her face inside her hands. Beverly sniffled a few minutes, wiped her eyes, and said, "Lord, I just prayed for my family at church today and asked that you put love in Kenneth's heart for Amir. Then we come home and this happens. I just can't bear it, Lord. I need you to stop by here." Beverly sat with her head bowed a little while longer before she rose to change into a two-piece lilac lounging outfit, from a cream-colored suit and a matching turban, which complemented her complexion.

There was a knock at the bedroom door.

"Come in," Beverly said in a falsely bright tone.

"Hey, Mom. Are you all right?" Tracey asked her mother. "Jalin and Rhianna are taking naps. Actually, Daddy was wrong about Amir pushing the kids on me. Amir had asked me earlier if I'd watch Jalin until you came home from church. He said that then you'd take care of him. I don't mind taking care of my nephew. I don't like to see Daddy so upset." Tracey sighed loudly. Rhianna is Tracey's three-year-old daughter.

"You and me both," Beverly replied wearily. "I'm going to warm up dinner."

Mother and daughter walked into the kitchen, where they immediately began taking pots and pans out of the pine cabinets. Beverly had decorated the kitchen in soft beige tones with splashes of red. A small island dominated the center of the room. Instead of a traditional kitchen table, a rectangular wooden table with bench seats was positioned next to a large window covered with red curtains.

"Maybe I should find my own place," Tracey said, glancing down at the floor. "I hate to put you and Dad through any trouble. I was trying to save money for a year before I moved out." The striking-looking, cocoa-colored young woman was about five feet, five inches tall and thickly built. She wore micro braids pulled off her face in a clasp on the top of her head. Tracey had moved back home after her husband, Rick, refused to get help for his gambling problem. His habit had caused the couple to lose their home and end up in bankruptcy. They had been divorced for six months.

"I don't think your father has a problem with you staying here. But your brother is a different story altogether," Beverly sighed.

Tracey smiled and reminisced. "I remember Daddy saying lots of times that when Amir and I grew up and left home, he planned to retire and buy an RV so that you two could travel and see the United States. I guess that would be hard to do with me and Rhianna living here, and Jalin here every other weekend and sometimes during the week. I don't think this is what Daddy had in mind for his older age."

Beverly nodded at her daughter. Tracey was correct; traveling the USA was Kenneth's plan for his and Beverly's golden years. The couple had been married for over twenty-five years. The marriage was Beverly's second. She had married young, and Amir was the offspring of her previous marriage.

Beverly turned on the stove, then took a foil-lined pan with a roasting chicken out of the refrigerator. "You know your father; his bark is worse than his bite. He's old enough to know that life doesn't always go as we plan. I love having you and your brother staying here with us. Truthfully, I never wanted you to leave in the first place. I think he was a little upset with me because I went a little over my budget when I went shopping with my sisters yesterday. I think he took his frustrations out on Amir."

"Daddy obviously doesn't share your sentiment about us being here. You'll have to show me what you bought after dinner." Tracey took bottles of oil and vinegar out of the pantry. "Are we eating in here or the dinning room?"

"In here," Beverly answered as she took another dish out of the refrigerator.

"I'll set the table," Tracey offered. She wore one of Kenneth's old black-and-red checked flannel shirts with a red turtleneck and black jeans. The young woman walked to the dining room and removed three white plates trimmed with gold from the cabinet. After she placed the plates on the table, Tracey went back to the cabinet and returned to the kitchen with three crystal goblets in her hand. Tracey put the glassware on the table.

"Mom, do you think Dad is really going to put Amir out of the house?" Tracey paused as she took napkins out of a kitchen drawer and folded them.

Beverly turned on a burner to boil water for gravy. She shivered. "I hope not, but I don't know. Your brother may have messed up big time." The older woman shook her head tiredly.

The front door opened then closed loudly. Kenneth took off his shoes and laid them on a brown mat in front of the door. He hung his black jacket on a bronze coat tree and walked to the kitchen at the rear of the house.

Beverly was warming up a pot of cabbage, and the aroma of the vegetables and the macaroni and cheese bubbling in the oven permeated the room.

"Mmm, it smells good in here," Kenneth remarked. He walked to the refrigerator and removed a can of tea. Kenneth greedily gulped it down. "How soon will dinner be ready?"

"Give me another fifteen minutes or so," Beverly answered as she stirred the pot of gravy.

A little girl and boy who appeared to be around four years old burst into the kitchen from the hallway. "Granny and Papaw, you're home," the little girl said; then she sneezed.

"Bless you," the adults said automatically.

Tracey's daughter, Rhianna, was dressed in bright yellow OshKosh bibbed corduroy overalls with a long-sleeved white turtleneck. She wore small white and untied pink sneakers on her feet. She had a tiny gap between her front teeth , and two Afro puffs were smashed against the sides of her head.

Hey, Rhianna. How is Granny's baby?" Beverly exclaimed. She bent down and kissed the top of the little girl's head. "Are you hungry?"

Rhianna nodded her head and then smiled. "Yes."

"Me too, Granny, I want something to eat," Amir's son, Jalin, added. He walked over to Kenneth and held his arms up. The nearly four-year-old boy wore blue jeans, a green hooded sweat top, and white Nike sneakers.

Kenneth picked up his grandson. "Hey, Jalin. Were you a good boy while your Granny and I were at church?"

The little boy's hair was styled in cornrows with a short ponytail at the base of his skull. "Uh-huh." Jalin vigorously bobbed his head up and down.

"No, he wasn't, Papaw," Rhianna whined and poked out her lips. "He hit me. Right here." She touched her arm.

"You know boys shouldn't hit girls, don't you, Jalin?" Kenneth scolded the child. "I hope you told your cousin that you were sorry."

"I did." Jalin dropped his head, clearly abashed. "Auntie Tracey made me.

Tracey cut a homemade roll in half, quickly dabbed butter on each portion, and laid the halves on two napkins.

Kenneth put Jalin down and took his grandson's hand. They walked over to Rhianna, and Kenneth grabbed her hand. He led the children to the table and sat them in their blue and yellow booster seats. He wiped their tiny hands clean with moist towelettes from a box Beverly kept on the sand-colored marble countertop. Tracey sat the rolls on the table, and the children picked up the mouth-watering bread and began eating.

After Rhianna ate the last bite, she licked her fingers and said to her mother daintily, "More please."

"Not so fast, little girl. Dinner will be ready in a minute, and you can have another one with dinner," Beverly said to her granddaughter. She dipped her pinky finger in the gravy and tasted it. She nodded with satisfaction and then washed her hands.

"Where's my daddy?" Jalin leaned forward in his seat and looked toward the living room.

"He went out for a bit. He'll be back soon," Kenneth answered. The older man felt his son should be having dinner with his son instead of running the streets with his no-good, lowlife friends.

Beverly shrugged her shoulders helplessly. In her mind, she could hear Kenneth's thoughts. "Tracey, I've finished warming up the meal. Why don't you go ahead and fix plates for the children."

"Okay, Mom." Tracey reached into an upper cabinet and got two plastic plates. One had a picture of Sponge-Bob Squarepants on it, and that plate belonged to Jalin. Rhianna's plate had a picture of the Cheetah Girls on it. After she put food on the plates, Tracey cut the cabbage and roasted chicken into tiny pieces, and sat the plates on the kitchen table.

Beverly took kid-sized eating utensils out of a drawer and laid them next to the children's plates.

Jalin happily picked up a couple slivers of chicken with his hand.

"Uh-uh, young man," Kenneth scolded. "I'll bless the food when your grandmother and auntie sit down. Then we can eat."

"Kay," Jalin said, grinning shyly at his grandfather.

Five minutes later, the family bowed their heads and held hands as Kenneth blessed the meal.

The food tasted so good that Kenneth forgot about his threat to Amir. It would be postponed to another day.

Chapter Four

Douglas Freeman was trying his best to avoid a verbal confrontation with his wife, Julia, so he kept his eyes focused on the road as he drove south on Michigan Avenue on the way home from church. Doug's slightly gnarled, pecan-hued fingers fiddled with the radio dial. He turned to WVAZ 102.7, which was airing old school songs on a show hosted by Chicago's own Herb Kent, "The Cool Gent."

A longtime member of the powerful Trustee Board of Christian Fellowship Church, Douglas was a six foot five, gangly, brown-skinned man. His face was framed by a cloud of wooly white hair, and his features resembled Nelson Mandela's. Douglas wore gold wire-framed glasses and had a scholarly look about him.

The owner of a snow removal/landscaping company and part owner of a florist business with his brother, Douglas found marital bliss later in life. He was close to fifty-five years young, ten years his wife's senior. The pair met when Douglas and his brother supplied the floral arrangements for a local fashion show where Julia was modeling.

Julia immigrated to the United States from South Africa with her family when she was ten years old. She had been a successful local model before she married Douglas twenty-one years ago. The tall, take-charge American's steady wooing tugged at Julia's heartstrings, and within two years of meeting the couple wed.

Julia's features and six-foot-tall frame boasted of her proud African heritage. She had thick, lush lips and large doe-shaped eyes. Julia's face was a rich mahogany brown with high cheekbones and a tiny mole on her left cheek, giving her an exotic look. She volunteered at the church tutoring the youth in French, which she learned during her modeling days in Europe. She was employed as a director for the Catholic Charities organization.

From the corner of his eyes, Douglas glimpsed Julia's leg, covered in beige-colored hosiery, which matched the shirt she was wearing, bouncing up and down as her foot tapped on the floorboard of the automobile to a melody only she could hear. Julia had been sighing audibly since they'd left church.

"Do you need to make any stops before we go home?" Doug peeped over at his wife and then back out the windshield.

"I'd like to go out to dinner, if you don't mind. I don't feel like going home just yet," Julia pouted. She pressed a button on the side of the door, and her window lowered and then rose back up. Julia's cheeks were taut with tension. She pushed a dark ringlet of hair off her face. Julia still maintained a trim figure.

"Not again, Doll Baby," Douglas sighed. Doll Baby was his nickname for his wife.

"I just don't feel like going home yet. We haven't spent much time together, just the two of us, for a while. So I thought it would be nice if we went out for dinner. Not anyplace fancy, just someplace in the neighborhood." Julia unknowingly chewed the tangerine-colored lipstick off her lips.

"Your not wanting to go home wouldn't have anything to do with not wanting to spend time with Brandon and Erin, would it?" Douglas asked his wife. He moved into the right lane of traffic, then turned and drove south toward Ninety-fifth Street. After conferring, the couple decided to dine at the Applebee's restaurant located near Evergreen Plaza Shopping Center.

Fifteen minutes later, Douglas and Julia sat inside their car in the restaurant parking lot. Douglas turned to his wife and asked, "What is all of this really about, Jules?"

"I never could fool you, could I, Doug?" she remarked ruefully, dipping her head forward. "I don't feel like being bothered with Erin right now, and listening to her complaining and whining about how much the pregnancy has changed her body or any of that nonsense." She held out her hand.

Douglas pulled Julia's brown-gloved hand inside his black leather-encased one. "We've been over this a million times. I know you're disappointed that Brandon married Erin and she's not of our race, but, Doll, there wasn't really anything we could do about it. Kind of like when you decided to marry me instead of the African wholesale merchant your father intended for you to marry." Douglas's eyes twinkled at the thought.

Julia pulled her hand away from her husband's grasp. She wrinkled up her nose like she smelled something unpleasant. "At least we're the same color, but Erin is just so common-looking. She acts like she's Black or something. I really dislike White people who try to act Black, and like low-class Blacks at that. I tell you, Doug, this is not the future I envisioned for our son when he was born." Julia's eyes sparked fire.

"I know, dear," Douglas said as he tried to placate his wife, "but we couldn't choose a mate for Brandon. I know we thought his future would be sports, playing pro basketball one day. When he was awarded the scholarship to Tennessee State University, we assumed his life was set," Doug mused. "Apparently that's not what the Lord had in store for him."

"In a way you're right, but Brandon messed up beyond belief. Not only did he come home with a White wife, he doesn't want to go to school and now he aspires to be a rapper. If I hear one more boom, boom from the basement, I'm going to snap. I feel like our only child has taken leave of his senses. And I don't want them living with us. We should have given them one of the apartments in the building we own." Julia looked away from her husband uncomfortably.

"Try to be fair, Jules. Erin is pregnant with our first grandchild and she's having a rough pregnancy, so we need to keep an eye on her. Brandon did the right and moral thing by marrying Erin. We have no choice except to let them live with us until they settle down. Brandon is going to a local college next semester, and Erin wants to go to cosmetology school after the baby is born. Let's just support them, and in time they'll be fine."

"They could have stayed with her folks in the Ozarks, or wherever she's from. God help me, Doug, I am so disappointed with our son. Plus, how do we know that Erin is really pregnant by Brandon? He could have continued going to school, but nooo, he didn't bother to tell us he was failing classes in addition to impregnating that redneck." Julia sighed dramatically as she shifted her body in the seat.

"We'll have to take Brandon's word that he is the baby's daddy. Don't worry, Doll. The Lord will see us through." Douglas leaned toward Julia and wiped a tear from her face. "We'll have to lean on the Lord, as with anything else in life, and allow Him to direct our path," Doug smiled. "Personally, I'm glad they're in Chicago and we're near for the birth of our first grandchild." Douglas peeped at his wife out the corner of his eye.

Julia's chin was propped on her right hand. She turned and glanced unseeingly outside the window. Snow had been steadily falling all morning, and the temperature was mild that November Sunday afternoon, in the low-thirties. There was no hint of the blustery winds that Chicago was known for. Occasionally the sun played peekaboo with the clouds.

"I am also disappointed with myself. I feel like I'm being mean-spirited and a bigot where Erin is concerned," Julia admitted, still looking outside the car window.

"Why are you acting that way?" Douglas asked his wife curiously. "This type of behavior is out of character for you, Jules." His eyes searched her miserable face.

"I don't know why. I've asked myself that same question over and over again since Brandon called us three months ago and said he had a surprise for us. I thought he meant he got all A's in his classes during the school semester. Boy, was I totally wrong." Julie's lips twisted into a grimace.

"You need to figure it out, what's bothering you. Then you will probably learn why you're so hostile toward that girl," Douglas advised his wife.

Julia nodded. "I know you're right, but Erin makes me physically ill. I have flashbacks of living in Africa. She's so pale-looking, Douglas. I think I could have accepted another race—Italian, Hispanic, or Indian. But that girl—" Julia's hand fluttered to her throat—"she's just so White."

"Are you trying to punish Brandon for not living up to your expectations? Or Erin because of her color and your experiences in South Africa?" he asked his wife kindly.

"I don't think so . . . maybe a little of both. I'm such a terrible person." Julia moaned and threw her hands helplessly into the air.

"I think, like you said, you're disappointed with Brandon's choices and you don't know how to get past your feelings," Doug suggested.

"Hmm, maybe you're right. Don't try to psycho-analyze me, Douglas. I'm still hungry." Julia's stomach made a grumbling sound.

"Let's order takeout for us and the kids," Douglas suggested diplomatically.

"Do we have to?" Julia lamented. She loudly sucked air between her teeth.

"Yes, we do." Douglas nodded. He got out of the car and walked around to Julia's side to open her door.

Forty minutes later the couple departed the restaurant. They were headed east toward their home. Soon Doug drove his black Mercedes-Benz sedan slowly into the driveway on the right side of their spacious, two-story Beverly home with the green-and-white-striped awning.

"I'll have to shovel and put down salt later. I didn't know we were having a winter storm today, did you?" Douglas asked Julia as he backed the car slowly down the driveway.

"I think I read something about one in yesterday's newspaper," she replied, gathering the bags of food. Several minutes later, the couple walked inside the house.

Julia gasped with disgust when she saw the kitchen was still in the same state of disarray as it had been before she and Douglas left for church. The couple had attended Sunday School at nine o'clock and left the house early. Erin had assured Julia that the kitchen would be clean when the older couple returned from church.

Blotches of scrambled eggs and grease from bacon speckled the top of the stove. The kitchen sink was still full of the dishes that Erin had sworn she'd put in the dishwasher the night before. The beautiful yellow and green designer kitchen Julia had copied from an issue of *House Beautiful* magazine resembled a pigsty. Her mouth constricted with anger.

Douglas laid a hand on her arm and warned Julia, "Let it go." He set the white paper bags of food on top of the glass kitchen table.

Brandon walked up the basement stairs, opened the door, and entered the kitchen. "Hey, what's up, folks? I see you brought food back with you. Did you get something for me and Erin?" He and Erin lived in the basement, which had been hastily renovated into an apartment for the couple. Brandon was a pretty boy, tall like his parents and lean. He had a smooth, chocolate-colored, unshorn baby face with long curly lashes framing his eyes. He inherited his mother's high cheekbones and wore his hair styled in short twists.

Julia glared at her son, then turned abruptly on her heel and stomped up the stairs to her and Douglas's bedroom.

"What's wrong with her? Is it that time of the month?" Brandon asked his father in a kidding tone of voice. He walked to the table and peeped inside the bags.

"I think she's a little put out with the state of this room." Douglas clued in his son as his arm swept around the kitchen.

Erin walked into the kitchen from the basement. She massaged the lower portion of her back. "I'm sorry, Papa Doug, for not doing the dishes. I felt a little nauseated last night. I think it might have been from the pickles and ice cream I snacked on after dinner." Her oval face, framed by dark and blond micro-braids, reddened. She was hefty in size, and at best could be described as a pleasant-looking young woman before becoming seven months pregnant.

Now Erin's nose had spread wildly out of control across her face. Her jutting stomach was the focal point of her body. She walked to the sink and turned on the water to rinse the dishes and place them in the dishwasher.

Fifteen minutes later, Julia had changed her clothing and returned to the kitchen. She was dressed casually in a pair of jeans with a lime-colored sweater. She rolled the sleeves over her elbows. "Never mind, I'll clean up," Julia said to her daughter-in-law after she turned the water off. "Why don't you all go ahead and eat. I'll eat later."

Douglas had walked down the hallway and hung his coat in the closet. When he returned to the kitchen, he said to Julia, "We're going to sit down and dine together as a family. Brandon and I will clean up the kitchen after we finish dinner."

Julia scowled at Douglas. She walked to the kitchen table and took the food containers out of the bag from Applebee's.

Douglas had ordered steaks for the evening meal along with baked potatoes and steamed oriental vegetables. Erin, trying to be helpful, took a pitcher of pink lemonade out of the stainless steel refrigerator.

"Would you get glasses out of the cabinet?" Julia asked her son as she prepared a plate for Douglas. She laid the plate on the table and began fixing plates for Brandon, Erin, and herself.

"Oh, sure," Brandon replied. He hopped out of his seat, removed four glasses from the cabinet over the sink, and sat them on the table.

Erin felt guilty about not cleaning the kitchen as she had promised. She took cutlery out of the cabinet drawer and laid it on the table. Julia sat at the table as Erin filled the glasses with lemonade and passed one to each family member.

Douglas prayed over the food. "Lord, thank you for the food, which has been prepared for the nourishment of our bodies. Amen."

Julia glanced at her daughter-in-law and asked, "Shouldn't you be drinking milk instead of lemonade?"

"Oh, I'm fine, Mama Jules," Erin reassured Julia as she spread a napkin over the top of her stomach. "I'll drink some milk later." She deftly sliced the steak into bite-sized pieces. "How was church service this morning?" She looked questioningly from Douglas to Julia. "I just love the choir at your church. That Nichole Singleton and Maya Nelson can really sing. I wish I had their voices."

"It was fine," Julia answered her daughter-in-law. "Our assistant minister, Reverend Nixon, preached a fine sermon. It's too bad you two couldn't get out of bed and join us," Julia said sharply. Secretly she was glad that Brandon and Erin's church attendance was sporadic. She was ashamed of her daughter-in-law's appearance and race. Julia knew the gossipers at the church had a field day with Brandon's predicament, especially since Julia had laid it on thick to her friends and associates at the church about Brandon's scholarship.

"I wanted to go to church with y'all, but your grandbaby just wouldn't let me get any sleep last night," the young woman said shyly as she patted her belly.

"That doesn't excuse you, Brandon. You haven't been to services much since you came home from school." Julia looked away from her son. "Would you pass me the A.1. sauce?" she asked Douglas.

Erin snatched the bottle before her father-in-law could get it and handed it to her mother-in-law. "Let me," she said to Julia.

Douglas wiped his mouth with a white paper napkin. "Don't you have a doctor's appointment this week, Erin?"

"Yes, I do, Papa Doug. I was hoping Brandon would be able to go with me, but he has an audition at the same time."

Douglas frowned disapprovingly at his son and laid his napkin on the side of his plate. "Shouldn't your priority be to go with your wife to her doctor's appointments instead of that music foolishness?" He picked up his fork and began to eat the vegetables.

"It's not foolishness," Brandon protested as he shook his head. "I have an audition for a gig, and with the baby on the way we need all the money we can get."

"I guess your priorities are different from mine. I always made time to go with your mother to her doctor's appointments when she was pregnant," Douglas added.

"You and Mom's situation was different from mine and Erin's," Brandon said affably. He put a helping of baked potato dripping with butter into his mouth.

"That's the truth," Julia muttered under her breath.

"Did you say something, Mother Jules?" Erin asked in a honeyed tone of voice.

"No, not at all. The food is tasty," Julia answered, changing the subject.

"Well, maybe you can take Erin to her appointment, Julia. What do you think?" Douglas asked his wife.

Julia's fork clattered into her plate. "Who me? I can't possibly take her. I have an important meeting at work."

"It's at four o'clock in the afternoon. I was going to ask if I could borrow one of your cars." Erin looked hopefully at Julia.

"We only have two cars, Erin." Julia looked at her daughter-in-law as she shook her head. "And both Douglas and I need ours."

"That's okay then. I can take the bus." Erin looked pale. She jumped to her feet. "Excuse me, I don't feel too well." She made a beeline to the powder room, which was located off the kitchen to the right.

Douglas looked at his son and said, "Don't you think you should assist your wife?"

"Naw, I don't think so. She's probably puking her brains out. What can I do for her?" Brandon continued eating his meal.

"I think one of us should take Erin to her appointment," Douglas began.

"The topic is not up for discussion," Julia snapped. "Erin is Brandon's responsibility, not ours. I'm not taking her anywhere, not this week or any other week." She rubbed her forehead. "I don't really have an appetite. I'm going to lie down. I'll finish eating later." She stood up and walked upstairs to the bedroom.

Douglas and Brandon could hear the basement door opening and closing. Erin had gone downstairs. She'd heard her mother-in-law's comment, and she was too embarrassed to return to the kitchen table.

Brandon glanced at the basement door and then at his father. He sighed. "Mom really doesn't like Erin much, does she?"

"I wouldn't say that," Douglas hedged, not wanting to hurt his son's feelings. "She's still trying to get used to you not going to school and now being married. Your new situation has been a lot for your mother to absorb."

"I know, Dad, but I feel like she isn't even giving Erin a chance. She's rejected her because of her color," Brandon protested.

"Watch yourself, boy," Douglas warned his son, holding up his hand. "I wouldn't say your mother is prejudiced. She's mainly disappointed with the choices you've made."

"And those choices include Erin, don't they?"

"To a small extent they do. Just give her time. By the time the baby gets here, your mother will be back to her old self again."

"Somehow I doubt that. I don't think life will ever be the way it used to be." Brandon leaned back in his seat and pushed his empty plate away from him.

"Maybe you should go check on your wife, son. I'll load the dishwasher and put up the food. Maybe your mother and Erin will finish dinner later."

Brandon stood up to his full six feet, six inch height. "I guess you're right. . . . I'll go see what's up with Erin. Are you sure you don't want me to help you in here?"

"I'm positive. Go see about your wife, and when you're done, why don't you shovel the snow? I'll handle things in here."

"Okay, Pop." Brandon stood up and walked to the basement door; then he turned to face his father. "I hate it that Mom doesn't care for my wife. And Erin knows it too. She thinks Mom hates her."

"I'm working on your mother, son. That's all I can do. I'll see if I can talk her into taking Erin to the doctor's office. If not, I may take her myself."

Brandon's eyes lit up and then the brightness dimmed. "You know how Mom is; she can be stubborn. She rarely changes her mind once she's made it up about something."

"Let me see what I can do." Douglas rose from his seat and took a box of aluminum foil out of the pantry. He wrapped foil around his wife's and daughter-in-law's plates and put them in the refrigerator.

"Thanks, Pops." Brandon walked downstairs and closed the door behind him.

Douglas was nearing his breaking point. He wished everyone in his family could just get along. Douglas briefly considered Julia's suggestion that he give the kids one of his rental apartments, but he didn't want Erin to be alone at this time. He made a decision to call Reverend Dudley the upcoming week and get the minister's opinion on what could be done to alleviate the tension in the house.

Douglas put the plates inside the refrigerator. Then he walked over to the dishwasher, opened the front-loading door, and began putting the soiled dishes inside the appliance. He put dishwashing liquid into the detergent slot and turned on the appliance. "I've got to do something about the family before we fall apart. Lord, we need your divine intervention in this house," Douglas spoke aloud before he went into the living room to his reclining chair and opened the thick Sunday paper and began to read it.

Chapter Five

The following week, early on a Tuesday morning, Reverend Dudley sat inside his office at church. He turned over the last page of Meesha's proposal, quickly read it, and placed it on the left side of his desk along with the other pages. Then he removed his glasses and rubbed his eyes.

The minister pressed a button on the side of the telephone. "Roslyn, can you get Reverend Nixon on the line for me?"

"Sure, Pastor. Give me a minute." A few minutes later, Roslyn's voice sounded on the intercom. "Reverend Nixon is on line one."

"Thanks, Roslyn." Reverend Dudley pressed the button for line one and then activated the speaker. "Calvin, how are you doing today?"

"Blessed by the Holy Spirit. How are you feeling, Pastor?" Reverend Nixon replied.

"Ditto, son. Say, the reason I was calling is to see what you think about Meesha Morrison's proposal." He stacked the papers together neatly and paper clipped them.

"Sir, I find it very intriguing. You can tell Sister Morrison spent a lot of time and thought in preparing it."

"What do you think, son? Should we add it to the Trustee Board's agenda for the next meeting?" Reverend Dudley pulled a handkerchief out of his pocket, took his glasses off his face, and wiped them.

"I think we should, Pastor. I also like the fact that Sister Morrison has found a counselor for the program without the church having to spend additional money."

"Zora Taylor has proven to be a great find. I think she'll be a great asset for the church and the school." Reverend Dudley placed his glasses back on his face.

"If you don't mind me asking, Pastor, where is Ms. Taylor in the running for the new guidance counselor? Is she the leading candidate?" Reverend Nixon asked. He was employed as a stockbroker for Goldman Sachs. At that moment, his secretary walked into his office and handed him a bundle of papers.

"Yes, she is. The committee loves her credentials. She has a strong church background. Her mother is an evangelist. Roslyn is preparing an offer letter for Ms. Taylor as we speak."

"Well, good then. I'd say we're headed in the right direction. That is, if Ms. Taylor accepts the position." Calvin glanced at the papers his secretary, Suzette, had handed him.

"Russell Jamison, the president of the school board, has talked to Ms. Taylor. We should call her Dr. Taylor. He indicated that she's prepared to move to Chicago by early next year if we make her an offer. So we're confident that she'll accept the position."

"In that case, I think we should talk to Sister Morrison as planned and get the proposal on the agenda for next week's meeting so the board can vote on it." Calvin switched the telephone receiver from one ear to the other.

"I agree with you, Calvin. I'll talk to Sister Baldwin, the committee secretary and ask her to add the proposal to the meeting agenda. I'll call Sister Morrison and ask her to join us for the meeting."

"That sounds good, Pastor. I'll talk to you later."

Calvin placed the receiver in its cradle, while Reverend Dudley pressed a button to disconnect the call.

A week later, at seven o'clock Thursday night, Meesha paced a well-trod path outside the church's Mount Sinai conference room like she was an expectant father at a hospital waiting for his wife to give birth. The Trustee Board was meeting to vote on the Helping Hand Club's couples' therapy proposal.

Regina looked up at her friend from a chair across the room. Regina paused from grading papers for her third period algebra class. "Girl, would you sit down. You're making me dizzy."

Meesha smiled wistfully and sat down on a seat next to Regina. "I guess I am overreacting a bit." She smoothed out a pucker on the gray skirt she was wearing. The silver bangles she wore jangled on her wrist.

"What happened to, 'This is my calling'?" Regina imitated Meesha good-naturedly. "You need to just chill out and let the Lord, Pastor, and Reverend Nixon handle things in there for you." The young woman pointed to the closed door as she tried to calm her friend's nerves.

"I don't have to tell you how important the therapy is to me." Meesha gulped and ran her fingers through her hair, then picked a loose thread off the sleeve of her fuchsia sweater.

"Well, I'm not worried about anything. I know the Trustee Board is going to accept the proposal. You did a good job preparing the documentation, Meesh. Now it's in the board's and God's hands. The proposal will benefit our members, so why don't you just relax." Regina squeezed Meesha's arm.

"You're right. I just have so much riding on this." Meesha nibbled on a hangnail on one of her fingers.

Regina wrote an X next to one of the answers on her student's paper. She continued checking the answers; then she looked up from her work and asked Meesha, "How are things with you and Ed?"

Meesha glanced at the closed door and dropped her eyes to the floor. She fingered the gold cross around her neck and sighed. "Not much better. I'd say things are at a standstill for now. I've expressed my feelings many times about the number of hours Ed works. He just tells me to bear with him, how things are crazy because of a new version of software being rolled out and that his workload will lighten soon. I had to ask his mother to watch the children so I could attend the meeting this evening. There was a time when he would have been at church right beside me sweating the decision instead of you."

"Well, his explanation makes sense to me. Why can't you give him the support he needs?" Regina looked down and wrote a comment at the top of the paper.

"Because he said the same thing a month ago—no, let me make that three months ago—and things haven't changed yet. He's coming home later and later." Waves of pain filled Meesha's eyes. She blinked back tears.

"You don't think he's having an affair or something, do you?" Regina looked at Meesha with concern in her brown eyes.

An image of Edward flashed in Meesha's mind. Her husband was an attractive, chocolate-brown man with a slim build and clean-shaven head. Edward had droopy bedroom eyes that the women at their college, including Meesha, loved. "I really don't know what to think, except that I'm tired of carrying the load by myself. I get the kids ready for school, fix their breakfast, help them with their homework, and then prepare dinner. By the time I get in bed and read Scripture, I'm exhausted."

"I know the work situation is tough on you, Meesh. You and I both know that life has a way of flipping the script, turning our lives upside down, but trust in the Lord, give it over to Him, and in time this too shall pass."

"I hear you, girl, but right now my faith is being tested mightily, and I feel so out of synch. The only time the kids see Edward at a decent time is on Fridays. He manages to come home from work by six o'clock, but it's not enough. If Edward doesn't agree to counseling, then I think we'll have to separate, so he can decide what his priorities are."

Regina pointed her red ink pen at Meesha. "You know we always hear about how sistas want a good man. They desire a BMW, a Black Man Working." Regina shrugged and nodded her head. "You know what I mean—a man who has a decent job, owns a car, and most of all, is a good provider. Girl, you have all that and more. Are you willing to throw your life away over Edward working too many hours?"

Meesha crinkled her nose distastefully. "It's not that cut-and-dried, Reggie, and you know that." She thrust her finger at her friend. "My issue is about the quality of our life. You don't understand that because you've never been married."

Regina's face dropped. She was obviously bothered by Meesha's remark about her marital status. She opened and then closed her mouth. "I'm going to let you get away with that comment only because I know how stressed out you are."

The door to the meeting room opened and closed. Reverend Nixon walked into the foyer. He wore a beige cashmere sweater with a charcoal gray shirt and dark slacks. His expression was stoic, not giving away a clue as to what transpired inside the room. "Sisters, the board has reached a decision. We'd like you to join the meeting."

Meesha's legs wobbled as she stood up. Her body trembled slightly. Regina gathered her papers together and put them inside her briefcase. She gave her friend a cheering wink. "It's going to be all right. Keep the faith." She held up two crossed fingers.

The two women, along with Reverend Nixon, walked into the room and sat down at the table. The six men and four women who made up the Trustee Board greeted Meesha and Regina.

Reverend Dudley noticed the look of consternation on Meesha's face. He dipped his head encouragingly at the young woman.

"I know you've been on pins and needles for the past few weeks, Sister Morrison, so let me put your mind at ease," the minister joked. "Christian Friendship Church has decided to accept the Helping Hands Club's proposal to institute couples' therapy at the church beginning next year, tentatively in February 2008."

Thank you, Lord. Meesha breathed a sigh of relief. "That's wonderful news, Pastor." Her voice was gay as her eyes swept the room. "I'd like to thank everyone on the board for your vote of confidence."

"Dr. Zora Taylor will be joining the academy next month as guidance counselor. Dr. Taylor feels that with the assistance of your club, Meesha, she should be ready to start with the first round of couples by mid-January or early February at the latest. Is that enough time for the Helping Hands to implement the program?" Reverend Dudley asked. He sat back in his seat at the head of the rectangular table with his fingers folded into a triangle.

"Yes, sir," Meesha said. "Zee and I have had conversations about the best way to put the program into operation, so I can safely say half the work is already done."

Sister Eveline Baldwin raised her hand. "I'd just like to say that I find this grassroots approach to marital counseling most enlightening. These are difficult times that we live in today, and maybe therapy is the mechanism that can help couples committed to trying everything within their and God's power to keep their marriage intact."

"Zee and I were thinking about offering sessions to newly engaged couples as a future project," Meesha added, looking at Reverend Dudley hopefully.

"I was thinking along those same lines," Reverend Nixon interjected as he nodded his head. "It's easy enough for couples to get married, but once the hard work kicks in, that's where couples have a problem keeping it together."

"Thank you for your comments, Sister Baldwin," Meesha said. "And you're correct, Reverend Nixon. The idea has weighed heavily on my mind. I see a lot of couples in marital chaos as part of my job, and I feel it's time the church did more to help."

"I minored in clinical psychology in college, so I'll help in any way I can," Reverend Nixon volunteered.

"That would be great. I know there are other members of the church in the health field. Perhaps they'd be willing to volunteer time as needed," Meesha suggested as she held out her hand.

"The idea seems to be spawning other ideas, and that's the beauty in having professionals on staff as part of the school and church family," Regina chimed in. She brushed a stray lock of hair off her face.

The president of the Trustee Board, Alonzo Miller, asked in his deep, booming voice, "Does anyone know if we will have any potential participants for the first session? I'm worried about how well the proposal will be received by the membership. Black folks can be closemouthed about their business." He tugged at the ends of his tie.

Meesha inhaled sharply as Regina nodded encouragingly at her friend. Meesha replied, "I'm almost sure that my husband, Edward, and I will be one of the participating couples." She clasped her hands together on top of the large, gleaming maple table.

The board members looked at Meesha with interest. Douglas thought it took a lot of heart for Meesha to literally put her business on the table.

"I had a call from Deacon Kenneth Howard the other day," Reverend Dudley announced. "He's interested in more information about the program."

"Wow, that's great," Meesha said in a relieved tone of voice. "I'm surprised that Brother Kenneth inquired. Usually women are the ones to initiate therapy."

"Kenneth is a good friend of mine. One thing I can say about Kenny is that he's open-minded to new suggestions or techniques. So you may have two couples already. We'll just need to find a third one and you'll be set."

Zora and Meesha had decided to limit the number of participants to three couples to keep the group small and intimate, and to work within the eight-week counseling time frame.

"What do you think about me making an announcement in church Sunday? Do you think that would help?" Meesha offered as she leaned forward in her seat.

"Sure, I think that's a good idea. It definitely won't hurt the cause. I have a young couple in mind. I'm going to make a call and get back to you by the end of the week, Sister Morrison," Reverend Dudley interjected.

"Thank you, Pastor. You don't know how much I appreciate your approval and all your help." Meesha's smile was as bright as a hundred-watt light bulb.

"The vote on couples' therapy concludes all the items on our agenda for tonight. I move that the Trustee meeting be adjourned and we get home," Brother Miller suggested.

"I second the motion," Reverend Nixon added.

Reverend Dudley bowed his head and prayed for the attendees to have a safe journey home. The meeting was officially closed. Everyone began putting on his or her coat.

Reverend Nixon turned to Meesha. "I'll be in touch with you Saturday so we can work out the logistics, if you're available."

"I'm available, and if I wasn't, I'd make myself available. Zora plans to move to Chicago next month. I'll help her get settled and then both of us will be available to work with you."

"Thank you, sister," Reverend Nixon said. "Be careful driving home. You be careful too, Sister Regina." Reverend Nixon told the women good night; then he left the room to return to his office.

"We will," Regina and Meesha said at the same time.

Regina looked at Meesha and smiled. "Didn't I tell you that your worrying was for naught? All you had to do was wait on Jesus, wait right here, like the song says. God came through again."

"You're so right." Meesha hugged her friend. "God is good all the time."

"All the time God is good," Regina finished Meesha's sentence.

"Amen," the friends echoed. They gathered their belongings and walked arm-in-arm as they exited the church.

Chapter Six

The following Sunday, after concluding his sermon, Reverend Dudley opened the doors to the church, extending an invitation for people to become members. Two people responded to the invitation, walking down the middle aisle and following Roslyn to her office.

Reverend Nixon strode to the dais. He pulled the microphone toward his face, and it made a crackling noise. "Sisters and brothers," he said as he raised his hand, "could I please have your attention for a few brief minutes? Sister Meesha Morrison has a special announcement that she'd like to make this morning."

Heads turned Meesha's way as she rose from her usual seat in the center row, near the middle section of the pews. Edward looked at his wife in surprise. She stood and quickly smoothed the sides of her black A-line dress, which was topped with a lacy ecru collar. Meesha wore a multicolored velvet jacket, and a pearl bracelet adorned her wrist. She wore pearl earrings to accessorize her outfit.

She walked to the podium. "Good morning, church," Meesha said as she adjusted the microphone. "Didn't Reverend Dudley satisfy our spiritual appetites this morning?"

Shouts of amen resounded through the church. Members clapped their hands. Meesha's expression became serious. "As most of you know, my name is Meesha Morrison, and I've been a member of Christian Friendship

Church since I was a teenager. I am the president of the Helping Hands Club, and I've served in that capacity for five years. I won't go into detail regarding the various stewardship projects that my organization has implemented for the church. There is a new ministry we're putting the finishing touches on, and it's near and dear to my heart. It's kind of on the level of the scholarship fundraising program we instituted a few years ago."

There was a smattering of applause from the congregation.

Meesha's eyes lit on Edward, who stared at his wife curiously before she continued speaking. "Today, I'd like to announce an exciting new ministry that the Helping Hands Club plans to implement at the church called Couples' Therapy." Meesha turned her head to the left side of the sanctuary. "I've been employed with the Department of Children and Family Support Services, which most of you call DCFS, as an assistant director of my district here in Chicago. In my ten years of service as a social worker, I've seen some truly horrific situations and the slow deterioration of the African American family. The number of families in crisis is staggering for our ethnic group. It's time for the church, Christians, and for us as a people to step up to the plate and staunch the bleeding. The future of our families is at stake."

The congregation nodded receptively at Meesha. She cleared her throat and glanced at Edward, who looked questioningly at his wife. "Reverends Dudley and Nixon have pledged their support of the program, and Reverend Nixon will play a prominent role in the ministry, which my committee has dubbed Couples' Therapy. The sessions will last eight weeks, and enrollment is open to couples in the church who are in need of a Christian and unbiased therapist to help repair the rough patches in your marriage.

"Dr. Zora Taylor, my former college roommate, has accepted the school position as guidance counselor, and she will perform double duty as the therapist for the group. There is a nominal fee associated with the program to help offset administrative costs. We want everyone with a need for counseling to be able to participate.

"Dr. Taylor has performed magic in her private practice, and she has a high success rate for helping couples and families. She is here at church today. Dr. Taylor, would you please join me at the podium?" Meesha gestured for Zora to join her.

Zora was a light-skinned, attractive, medium-sized woman with a deep cleft in her chin, dark brown eyes, and large, sensual lips. She had wavy light brown hair that was parted in the middle and flowed midway down her back. Zora had been sitting next to Meesha. She wore a beige and black flowered dress with a black lace shawl draped carelessly over her shoulders. She stood up and walked to the podium.

"Reverend Nixon, will you join us?" Meesha turned around and nodded at the minister. He laid his Bible on the chair and stood by Meesha's side.

After Zora stood at her friend's other side, Meesha with outstretched arms announced, "Church, I'd like to introduce you to the facilitators who will play a pivotal role in the formation of the newest ministry, Couples' Therapy."

She smiled at Zora and Calvin and then resumed talking. "I'd also like to put my money where my mouth is. My husband and I will be one of the first couples to participate in the sessions. I hope any of you who are feeling shy about baring your soul before church members will put your fears aside. Any information you divulge during the sessions will be kept in strict confidence. With that said, if anyone is interested in more information regarding the program, please see any member of the Helping Hands Club. Regina, Gayle, Crystal, and Natalie, would you stand?"

The women stood, waved their hands, and then sat back down.

"Thank you," Meesha responded to the round of applause that greeted her at the conclusion of her speech. She and Zora left the dais and returned to their seats.

Following the benediction, Edward stood up without waiting for his wife and quickly raced away from the sanctuary. Several church members strolled over to Meesha and Zora. After Meesha made introductions, the members shook Zora's hand and warmly welcomed her to the church. Meesha reached inside her tote bag and distributed handouts to the members who expressed an interest in the sessions.

Regina walked over to the women. She thrust a few sheets of paper into Meesha's hand. "I wrote down a few names and numbers of people who wanted more information."

"Good," Meesha nodded with satisfaction. "The response has been better than I hoped for."

"Girl, Edward looked like a deer caught in headlights when you made the announcement that the two of you were one of the chosen couples," Reggie laughed. "I know there's going to be drama at your house this afternoon."

"Well, I did kind of take him by surprise. I didn't really discuss it with him first," Meesha admitted. She nervously twisted her wedding ring on her finger.

"I need to buy myself a bag of popcorn and come to your house to see the *Meesha and Ed Reality Show*." Regina nudged Meesha's arm with her elbow.

Zora's eyes widened dramatically when she spied the guilty look on her friend's face. She threw up her hands in mock horror, "Tell me what I just heard isn't true? Please don't tell us that you didn't bother to talk to Edward first?"

Meesha shrugged her shoulders helplessly. "Hey, a woman's gotta do what she's gotta do. Ed is going to kill me, but"—she flung out her arms—"I can handle it."

Zora shook her head and tsk'ed. "I guess your motives were pure, but the implementation was definitely sloppy." She folded her arms across her chest. Zora had flown to Chicago for the weekend to begin her pre-move chores. The number one item on her to-do list was to seek housing, followed by an appointment with a local mover.

Douglas walked up to the trio of women, removed his hat, and held out his hand to Zora. "Dr. Taylor, my name is Douglas Freeman. I am a trustee here at the church. On behalf of myself and my wife, Julia, I'd like to welcome you to the Friendship family."

"Thank you, Brother Freeman." Zora smiled as she shook Douglas's hand. "Friendship already feels like home. I worshipped at Mt. Zion Baptist Church in Tempe, Arizona, and I'm going to miss my church home. I'm sure I'm going to enjoy worshipping here. Meesha has told me wonderful things about Friendship Church. What can we do to help you?"

"Actually, I wanted one of those applications for therapy." He looked around and leaned his tall body down toward Zora. Douglas looked like he was evading nosy eyes and ears. He whispered, "I don't need one for me and my wife. It's for our son, Brandon, and his wife, Erin. Meesha, Pastor said he mentioned them to you as possible participants."

"He sure did. I plan to call Brandon this week." Meesha pulled an application from the folder and passed it to Douglas. "Here you go. How are the newlyweds doing?"

"I ought to be ashamed of myself for misspeaking in the house of the Lord. The application is really for me and Julia. The kids haven't decided if they want to participate." Douglas lowered his voice. "My wife and I are having major disagreements regarding the kids' situation. I've come to terms with all that has happened, Brandon marrying out of our race, and he and Erin becoming parents at a young age, but my Julia is still struggling over all the events. I think it would help her to talk to other people and get advice from another point of view."

"Well . . . " Meesha said slowly, "we don't have many interracial couples in the membership. I don't know how much help we'd be." She looked at Zora, silently signaling for help.

"Don't worry, Brother Freeman," Zora said in a soothing tone of voice. "We can help you, your wife, and your son and daughter-in-law if any of you choose to attend the sessions. Let me put your mind at ease. I've had experience with the type of situation you've spoken of. My family struggled with acceptance issues when my brother married an Asian woman. Some of my family members were initially averse to his choice of a mate. They eventually came around, with counseling and prayer."

"The kids are going through an adjustment period too." Douglas looked miserable. He put his hat in his other hand. "I think my daughter-in-law pictured herself married to an up-and-coming NBA star. Instead, she's married to a UPS driver with aspirations of becoming a rap star. I know things haven't exactly turned out the way she thought they would either."

"I'm sure we'll be able to provide support for any of your family members, whoever decides to attend," Zora said, dipping her head toward Douglas.

"From what I could tell from Sister Morrison's speech, it sounds like you're going to head up this venture."

Zora nodded in agreement with Douglas's observation.

His eyes traversed the stragglers in the sanctuary to see if Julia was nearby. He knew she would pitch a fit if she knew what he was doing. "I think the program would be more effective with a man's point of view as well as a woman's."

Reverend Nixon walked up and caught the tail end of Douglas's statement. "You're absolutely correct, Brother Freeman. I couldn't help but overhear what you were saying. I will definitely be assisting Dr. Taylor. So if issues arise that need a male perspective, I'll be more than happy to help in any way I can."

Zora nodded approvingly. "Thank you, Reverend Nixon. I think your participation will be a win-win for the church membership and the ministry."

Douglas put his hat back on his head. "Thank you. I've got to run. I know Julia is wondering what's taking me so long. I'll be in touch with you soon, Meesha. Have a blessed day and week everyone."

"You too, Brother Freeman." The four people bade him a blessed week.

"Wow! That was surprising," Regina commented as she wrapped her scarf around her neck and put on her coat. "I guess you never really know what goes on behind closed doors. Well, I'm out of here. I'll call you, Meesha." She made a phone motion with her hand next to her ear. "Reverend Nixon and Zora, good luck. It sounds like your work is cut out for you."

"Okay, Reggie, I'll talk to you later," Meesha said. She picked her coat up off the pew.

"Have a blessed week," Zora said to Regina.

"I guess I'd better go and face the music," Meesha said, slipping black leather gloves on her hands.

"I'm sure everything will turn out fine for you and Edward. Call if you need me." Zora patted her friend's arm.

"Oh, I meant to ask you, would you like to have dinner with me, Edward, and the children?" Meesha asked Zora.

"No, I have an appointment with a realtor in Hyde Park and then I'm going to lunch. I might as well use my time wisely before I return to Arizona on Tuesday. My appointment with the realtor is in less than an hour. You go ahead and handle your business, sister." She smiled and shook her head at Meesha.

"I will. Take care of yourself." Meesha looked at the minister. "Reverend Nixon, enjoy the rest of your day."

"I plan to," the minister said after stealing a quick, I-like-what-I-see peek at Zora.

Meesha and Reverend Nixon walked out of the sanctuary. Zora closed her briefcase and put on her beige wool coat. She pulled a brown and beige striped knitted hat over her head, then walked to the church parking lot. She was surprised to see the majority of the church members had departed. There were very few cars still in the lot. She glanced down at her watch. *I guess it's later than I thought. I'd better get a move on if I'm going to meet Mrs. Dean on time.*

Zora got inside the automobile she rented from Hertz and put the key in the ignition. She shivered from the northerly wind that caused the silver gray Pontiac G6 to sway. The car didn't start. Zora pumped the gas pedal and turned the key again. The car still didn't turn over. *Darn it. What am I going to do now?*

A spate of panic flooded Zora's chest. She clutched the steering wheel tightly and looked up to see Reverend Nixon standing at the car door tapping on the window. Zora opened the door and sighed with relief. "I'm glad to see you. It looks like everyone has left already."

"Do you need help, sister?" Reverend Nixon asked. He turned up the collar of his coat against the chill and bent toward the open window.

"I guess so," Zora nodded. "The car won't start. I don't know what's wrong with it." She shrugged her shoulders helplessly.

"Why don't you scoot over and let me take a look?" Calvin suggested.

"Sure." Zora swung her body over to the passenger side of the car.

Calvin tried starting the car a couple of times to no avail. Then his eyes traveled to the dashboard. The needle for the gas capacity was at E. He pointed to it. "I think I see what your problem is."

"Darn it," Zora moaned as she rolled her eyes upward. "I meant to fill the gas tank on my way to church and was running a bit late. "Reverend Nixon, could you please take me to the nearest gas station?"

"I heard you mention to Sister Morrison that you have an appointment. Why don't you let me drive you there? The nearest station is about five miles from here. You'll lose time if I take you to get gas and then come back and put it in the car for you."

"I'd really hate to put you out of your way." Zora felt unsettled by the minister's closeness, though the console separated them. Her hands trembled slightly.

"Not a problem. Please call me Calvin." The minister turned to Zora and smiled, displaying a mouthful of capped, dazzling white teeth.

"Okay, Calvin," Zora replied, taken aback by the minister's incredible smile and dimpled cheeks. Reverend Nixon suddenly looked younger to Zora. She had originally surmised incorrectly that he was at least ten years older than she was. The grin on his face told her different. He looked closer to her age, maybe a few years older.

The Joop cologne emanating from his toned body was working her sense of smell too. His hair looked like he'd recently visited the barbershop, and his thin moustache was nicely trimmed over his thin lips. His black leather shoes shone like a new penny. Zora thought, *Hmm, Reverend Nixon's got it going on.* She wondered why Meesha hadn't told her about him. Meesha had said that one of the assistant ministers would be playing an active role in the therapy, but she'd left out a couple of things.

"Sister Taylor, would you like me to take you to your appointment?" Reverend Nixon repeated, looking over at the indecisive look on Zora's face.

"Reverend Nixon, I mean, Calvin, it wouldn't be fair for me to intrude on your free time. I know you have things to do on the weekend like most working people." Zora's mind shied away from the idea of spending any more time with the young minister.

"Actually, it wouldn't be a problem, Zora. I was on my way home to prepare my Sunday meal, and that sums up my plans for today," he informed her, waiting for Zora to make a decision.

"In that case, I'll take you up on your offer, but only if you allow me to treat you to lunch," Zora replied gratefully. With a little luck, she wouldn't be too late for her appointment.

"It's a deal," Calvin nodded. "My car is over there." He pointed to a black BMW sedan.

"Thank you." Zora removed her purse and briefcase from the backseat.

Calvin took the keys out of the ignition, handed them to Zora, and then exited the car. He walked around to the front passenger side of the car and opened the door. The two walked together to his vehicle and got inside.

After he turned on the car, Calvin waited for Zora to tell him where the real estate company was located. Instead, her eyes roved the rich maroon interior of the car. She noted the car was neat as a pin.

"Where to?" Calvin asked Zora with an amused expression on his face.

"Oops, I forgot to mention that. We're meeting Mrs. Dean at Metro Pro Realty Company." She gave him the address.

The two chatted about real estate during the drive from the church to Hyde Park. Outside the car, the wind continued to howl, and the snow floated from the sky. Inside the vehicle, Reverend Nixon made it his mission to learn more about the academy's new guidance counselor. She definitely piqued his interest.

Chapter Seven

Meesha entered Edward's black Cadillac Escalade following the church service. It didn't take a rocket scientist to deduce that her husband was less than pleased with her announcement to the church about their participating in the therapy sessions. She glanced at Edward, and the vein on the left side of her husband's throat teemed with anger. Meesha could literally hear Edward gnashing his teeth.

She was in no hurry to undertake a war of words with Edward after they arrived home. So when Imani and Keon asked their parents if they would stop at McDonald's for Happy Meals on the way home from church, Meesha was more than happy to comply. Doing so would be a reprieve before the inevitable showdown between wife and husband.

Twenty minutes later, when the family walked inside their home, Edward hung up his coat in the closet and made a beeline to his and Meesha's bedroom without saying a word to his spouse.

"What's wrong with Daddy?" Imani asked her mother matter-of-factly. Her thin arms were folded over her chest, and she stood on the balls of her feet as she watched her mother help Keon remove his outer garments.

"He's probably tired from working yesterday," Meesha replied after hanging her son's jacket on the coat tree.

"Daddy must always be tired because he's always at work, isn't he?" Imani asked her mother. Meesha ignored her daughter's comment.

Imani and Keon, with McDonald's bags in tow, headed to the kitchen table to enjoy their treat.

Meesha followed behind them. "When you finish your meal, change clothes and double check your homework. I'll look at it after you're done," Meesha instructed the children as she ran her hands over her tousled hair.

"Mommy, can I play on my PS2?" Keon asked his mother hopefully. Then he popped a French fry inside his mouth.

"Not until after I've checked your homework. If I don't find any errors, then you may play for a little while," Meesha absently answered her son.

"Mommy, I have a spelling test tomorrow. Would you help me with the words?" Imani asked her mother as she rose from the chair, walked to the drawer, and removed a butter knife. When she returned to her seat, the girl cut the hamburger in half.

"I will. Just make sure you study first." Meesha folded a dishtowel that was lying on the countertop and hung it on the towel rack. She wrapped her arms across her chest and glanced uneasily toward the bedroom.

"Do you want some of my food, Mommy?" Keon asked as he pushed the container with chicken nuggets to his mother. "I like the honey barbeque sauce. It's my favorite." He put a nugget inside his mouth and chewed it. He was the spitting image of his father, but with Meesha's hair and skin coloring. He was chubby and cute as a button, with missing front teeth and tiny glasses on his face.

"No thanks, baby. I guess I'll go change clothes and figure out what I'm going to cook for dinner." Meesha smiled at her children, then walked down the hallway to the bedroom.

When she reached the closed door, Meesha hesitated before she walked inside the room. Edward sat stiffly in his favorite brown corduroy lounging chair, holding the remote control unit in his hand. The television was tuned to an old movie, *Claudine.*

After Meesha entered the room, Edward's face became red, and he compressed his lips tightly together. "What do you mean by pulling that stunt in church today?" He glared at his wife.

"I don't know what you're talking about," Meesha replied matter-of-factly. She walked to the closet and removed a pair of jeans and a blue button-down shirt off their hangers. Meesha slipped off her dress and pantyhose, then quickly put on the jeans and blouse. She slid her feet into a pair of fuzzy pink house shoes and put the hosiery inside the dresser drawer.

"If you think I'm going to marriage counseling at the church, then you're sadly mistaken. There isn't anything wrong with our marriage," Edward snarled.

Meesha removed an earring and put it inside the jewelry box on her dresser. As she removed the other one, she turned around and looked at Edward incredulously. She put her hands on her hips. "Speak for yourself. There's been a lot wrong with this marriage for a long time. I've asked—no, let me correct that—begged you to reassess your priorities, but you refuse to. The topic isn't up for discussion, Edward. We either attend the sessions, or we go our separate ways."

Though Meesha took a hard stance, she was suddenly frightened by the look in her husband's eyes. Edward's body seethed with resentment. He clenched and unclenched his fist. "Who are you to give me an ultimatum? I admit that I've been putting in many hours at work lately. However, I do it for our family and because my job requires me to. It's not like I'm running around on you or anything. What part of that don't you understand?" His eyes narrowed with something akin to loathing.

Meesha felt like her head might spin on her neck like Linda Blair's in the movie *The Exorcist*. Her voice was icy cold as she spoke. "You must think you're talking to one of your flunkies at work. I'm your wife. What I do understand is that those two children in the kitchen haven't spent any quality time with you in months. At your insistence, I signed Keon up for peewee football. You asked me to do that so the two of you could spend quality time together, but instead of going to games with him, you're working. So now, I'm the one forced to take him to practice and games, which, by the way, he doesn't enjoy.

"When was the last time you made it home from work in time to have dinner with your family, Ed? Do you even know?" Meesha's lips trembled with anger, and her body quivered from frustration. She was outdone that Edward had the nerve to look at her angrily, like he didn't have a clue what she was talking about. She shook her head sadly.

"Is that what this is about, Meesha?" Edward asked with incredulity throbbing in his voice. "We knew as I climbed the corporate ladder that sacrifices would have to be made, and this is one of those times. When the project is completed, I expect a promotion to vice president and a generous bonus from my job. We can take a vacation, babe, just me and you. Heck, with the money I'm going to pull down, we can even take one with the kids. I'm not going to any therapy sessions. The subject is not up for discussion." Edward picked up the remote he had sat on the side of the chair and changed the television channel.

"You don't get it, do you? You think I don't understand how corporations work? There will always be
another hot project. It doesn't end with just one." Meesha raised her voice slightly then dropped it, mindful
that the children were down the hall. "If you don't go
to those sessions with me, then you need to move, go
somewhere, until you come to your senses." She pointed
to the door. "I'm not going to stay in a marriage where
my feelings aren't ever put first, or raise the children by
myself. I suggest you think carefully about what I'm asking." Meesha spun on her heels, stalked out of the room,
and went downstairs to the basement. Tears spilled
from her eyes.

The house was unnaturally quiet when she returned
upstairs after getting her emotions under control.
Meesha assumed the children were in their bedroom
doing homework as she had instructed them to do. She
walked into the den and sat down heavily on the brown
and beige couch with her hand over her eyes. Her disappointment mounted because Edward didn't even try
to make amends for his behavior.

Several minutes later, Imani walked into the room
and put her arms around Meesha's neck. "What's wrong,
Mommy? Are you sad because Keon is playing on his silly
PlayStation and not doing his homework?" She held a
piece of paper in her hand with her spelling words on it.

"No," Meesha replied, wiping her eyes quickly. "I
was thinking about something sad and got a little
teary-eyed." She motioned for Imani to sit on the sofa
with her.

"Are you ready to go over my spelling words with
me?" She handed her mother the list.

Edward walked into the room with a hangdog expression on his face. He walked over to the sofa and

said, "Why don't I help you, Princess?" He reached for the spelling list.

"Can you, Daddy?" The smile on the little girl's face lit up the room like sunlight. She looked at Meesha. "Is it okay, Mommy?"

"Yes, it is," Meesha smiled dolefully. "I can start on dinner. Since you're in a generous mood, Edward, why don't you make sure that Keon does his homework too? I'm sure he can use some help with his math problems."

Edward was taken aback by Imani's asking Meesha if it was okay for him to help her with her homework, like he needed his wife's permission. His face became drawn as he realized how far out of the family loop he'd been.

"Why don't you relax, Meesha? I know you've put in a lot of time with your church projects and holding down the fort here at home. Why don't we go out to dinner?" Edward felt helpless and put his hands inside his pockets.

Meesha didn't miss the byplay on Edward's face. She imagined he was embarrassed by Imani's question. "Sure, I need a little downtime. But don't think for one minute, Edward, you're off the hook. My request still stands."

"Hooray, we're going out to dinner. Wait until I tell Keon. Daddy, can we go to Red Lobster? Me and Keon like to see the fish and turtles in the tank." Imani flung out her arms and pirouetted gracefully around the room.

"Come on, Miss Ballerina, let's see how well you know your spelling words." Edward turned from his daughter to his wife. "Meesha, we'll talk later." Edward frowned at Meesha's sad, unsmiling face, and took Imani's hand and led his daughter out of the room as the girl stared at her father with pure adoration on her face.

After the family returned home from dinner and settled in for the night, Meesha decided to put off pressing
Edward about attending the sessions. She wanted him
to make the decision on his own. The children were in
bed, and the couple lay in bed with their backs facing
each other.

Meesha traveled back in time. She remembered how
Edward used to hold her in his arms and how they reasoned out their problems together. She thought, sadly,
that an insurmountable wall had sprung between
them. Meesha was totally clueless as to where her husband's animosity arose from.

Edward's cell phone vibrated on his nightstand. He
sat up in the bed and reached for the phone. "Hey, Mac.
What's up?" he asked. He listened for a minute and
then covered the phone and whispered to Meesha, "I
have to take this call. It's work-related. I don't want to
disturb or bore you, so I'll take the call in my office." He
got out of bed and walked out of the room.

Meesha couldn't believe that one of Edward's co-
worker's had the audacity to call at that hour of the
night. She peered at the clock on the nightstand and
saw that it was after eleven P.M. She lay in the bed becoming more furious each moment she waited for her
husband's return.

After Edward didn't return to the bedroom in what
Meesha considered a timely fashion, she got out of
the bed, put on her bathrobe, and rushed to Edward's
home office in the basement.

The door was slightly ajar, so Meesha stood behind it
and eavesdropped. Edward spoke in low tones, so Meesha moved a little closer and turned her ear to the door.

"I don't know what to tell you . . ." Edward stopped
talking for a minute. "My wife is going crazy, and now
she's pressuring me to go to marriage counseling. I

don't know how much more of this I can take. I feel
like I'm being pulled in two directions. She knows that
work is a high priority. Sometimes I don't know about
Black women; they just want too much."

Meesha felt like she'd been sucker punched. Her
stomach dropped to her feet. *I'll show you how a Black
woman acts.* She walked back upstairs. *Edward Morrison, you will go to those sessions with me, or I'll see you
in court.* Meesha groped for the handrail to the stairs.
Her eyes were so filled with tears, she could barely see.
Meesha returned to the bedroom and lay in the bed
wondering if her marriage was in more trouble than she
thought.

Chapter Eight

Tuesday morning the aroma of frying bacon wafted down the hallway from the kitchen to the bedroom that Beverly and Kenneth shared. The aroma tantalized Kenneth's sense of smell and caused his stomach to growl loudly.

Faint chords of a melody streamed from the clock radio that sat on Beverly's nightstand. It was tuned to one of his wife's favorite gospel stations. Kenneth lay in the bed with his eyes closed listening to the Mississippi Mass Choir sing "God Will Fix It."

With a lot of coaxing on his part the night before, Kenneth managed to talk Beverly into taking the day off work. It seemed playing hooky from work was the only way the couple could spend quality time together. Kenneth had asked Beverly not to prepare breakfast since he planned to take her out. He knew Beverly would ignore his request and prepare the morning meal for Amir. That was the way she was.

He clasped his hands behind his head and thought about how his conversation with his wife was going to proceed. He and Beverly had been married a long time and weathered many storms, but the issue of their children left them strongly divided. Beverly's spending habits were spiraling out of control. He'd found a couple of bags from Macy's department store stashed under his worktable in the garage.

Kenneth knew the best way to approach Beverly about their participating in the couples' therapy group at church was with caution. He closed his eyes and practiced his speech to Beverly in his head.

Downstairs, Amir stumbled into the kitchen. He was bleary-eyed and dressed in jeans that looked like they hadn't met an iron or washing machine in a long time. His T-shirt was full of holes. Amir's eyes widened in surprise at the sight of his mother still home at that time of the morning. It was ten o'clock, and Beverly usually left the house at nine o'clock to go to work.

"Hey, Mom. Whatcha doing here?" Amir greeted Beverly.

"Your Dad and I are spending the day together," Beverly explained as she reached inside the cabinet and removed a coffee mug. "Would you like a cup of coffee? I fried bacon too," she told Amir. He nodded. She turned on the microwave and heated the bacon and eggs. When the food had warmed, she handed it to Amir and poured him a cup of coffee.

"Thanks. Man, if Dad is going to be home today, he's going to ride my behind." Amir sat down on a kitchen chair and rubbed his forehead.

Beverly pulled the belt of the pink chenille robe she was wearing tighter around her waist. Then she poured herself coffee and sat down at the table across from Amir. She put two spoonfuls of sugar inside her cup and stirred it. "Well, son, what do you have planned for today?" Beverly queried Amir, peeping at him over her coffee cup. She knew from his reddened eyes and constant yawning that the answer would probably be nothing.

"Well, I ain't feeling too good this morning." Amir rubbed his brow and then put another forkful of eggs in his mouth. He swallowed and flashed a weak grin at his mother. "I probably hung out with the fellas a little longer than I shoudda last night."

Amir, as he always did when asked a question he didn't want to deal with, deftly changed the subject. He chewed a piece of bacon and then asked, "Did Keisha pick up Jalin on time like she said she would Sunday? She's getting on my nerves. Every time I turn around, she wants money for something." His mouth gaped open, and he put his hand over it.

"Yes, she picked Jalin up on time," Beverly answered. "She wasn't happy that you weren't here. Keisha said she'd been trying to reach you, and you were ignoring her calls. She needed money to buy Jalin new shoes. I gave her the money."

Amir had finished eating. He wiped his hands on the napkin Beverly had put next to his plate. Then Amir rubbed his eyes and sipped the last drop of coffee. He looked up and said to Beverly, "Thanks, Mom, for giving Keisha the money. I don't know what she expects me to do. I don't have a job. I can't do nothing."

"Maybe today would be a good day to look for a job," Beverly said forcefully as she sat her mug on the table and looked into her son's face, giving Amir her full attention. "You know we'll support you in everything you do, but your dad isn't happy about your not working. One of these days he's going to make good on his threat to put you out of the house, and there won't be anything I can do to stop him. You know we'll give you money to help out with Jalin's expenses, if you need it. It would be nice if you did chores around the house to offset the loans, but you won't. You need to pull your weight around here." Beverly looked expectantly at her son.

Amir picked up the mug, and placed it in one hand and then his other. "I ain't the maid around here. And the money you and Dad give me don't cover nothing but a couple packs of cigarettes and my cell phone. If I didn't feel so rotten, I would look for a job today. For real, Mom, my head is hurting me so bad that I think I should wait until tomorrow to try to find a job," Amir said impatiently. He stood up and said, "I'ma lay back down." He rubbed his stomach. "I don't feel so good."

"Okay, suit yourself. I think you're making a mistake." Beverly shook her head sadly. "Your father's patience is growing thin. The doctor has warned him to watch his pressure. Kenneth and I aren't getting any younger." She pointed her finger at her son, "I want you to think about what I've said and do the right thing. I try not to bother you too much. I know it's hard for a Black man out there, but you need to try to find a job and spend more time with Jalin. He adores you."

"I will." Amir reached across the table and patted Beverly's hand. Then he stood up, walked around the table, leaned over, and kissed his mother's cheek. "I promise I'll look for a job tomorrow. If I feel better, maybe I'll go pick up Jalin from pre-school this afternoon. That'll probably stop Keisha from yapping her gums." He walked over to the stove, picked up a strip of bacon, and put it inside his mouth. "Do you have any Tylenol?"

Beverly watched him openmouthed, stunned by his actions. "There's a bottle in the medicine chest in the powder room. Oh, I almost forgot, there's something else that Keisha mentioned. She feels if you aren't working that you could babysit Jalin while she's at work. She says that would save her a little money."

"I ain't no babysitter neither," Amir snorted as he wiped his hands down his pants. "I don't mind keeping the little fella sometimes, when she has something to do or he's sick. But on a regular basis? Naw, I don't think so." He shook his head and winced.

Beverly frowned and tightened her lips. "Jalin is young, and before you know it he'll be a teenager. I want him to have happy memories of his childhood. There's nothing wrong with you watching Jalin, and Rhianna too for that matter, if Tracey and Keisha need you to." The older woman suddenly looked tired. She rubbed the area between her eyes.

Amir looked down at the floor, feeling abashed. He softened his stance. "Okay, I'll think about it, Mom. I'm going back to bed. I'll talk to you later." He walked down the hallway to the powder room and then to the basement.

Beverly stood up, removed the mugs and plate off the table, and sat them inside the sink. She took the dishrag from the sink and wiped drops of coffee Amir had spilled from the table. After she rinsed out the dishrag and hung it on the towel rack, Beverly walked down the hall to her and Kenneth's bedroom.

Kenneth had showered and dressed, and was sitting on the side of the bed. He looked at his wife with an appalled expression on his face. "Bev, I listened to you and Amir's conversation, and that boy has got to go. He has you wrapped around his little finger, just as he did when he was a kid. You should have stood up to him. You and Tracey are like his servants. I bet he didn't even take his utensils off the table, did he?"

Beverly blushed as she walked into the room. She waved her hands in the air. "You can't say I didn't try to talk to him, Kenny. He's still growing and trying to find himself." She went to the walk-in closet, opened the door, and began pushing clothing back and forth along the rack.

"He's almost thirty years old, and he still lives at home. You're enabling Amir, not allowing him to grow up." Kenneth leaned over and put on his socks.

"I am not enabling him," Beverly's voice quivered and rose an octave as she turned from the closet to face her husband. Her hands flew to her hips. "Children don't mature at the same rate. I admit it's taking Amir a little longer than others, but in time he'll be fine. We'll just have to continue to love and support him."

"A lack of love and support is not what's wrong with that boy. It's your spoiling him. You told me how he nearly died when he was a child before I met you Bev, but you've got to let go and cut the apron strings. Otherwise, Amir will be sponging off us the rest of his life. And I've worked too hard for anybody to use me." Kenneth stood up, tucked his shirt inside his jeans, zipped his pants, and fastened a black leather belt around his waist.

Beverly removed a pair of black jeans from a hanger and a tangerine-colored wool sweater. "Of course I can never forget how Amir nearly died when he was five from rheumatic fever. His heart was damaged, and he's not physically fit. Therefore, it's taking him longer to find the perfect job. You are just hard on him because he's not your son." Beverly had been married before she married Kenneth.

"Humph," Kenneth grunted. He got down on all fours and pulled his shoes from under the bed. "That boy has passed all his physicals since he was ten years old. How long are you going to let him hang that excuse over our heads? And you're wrong; I'm harder on him because he needs someone to discipline him. He's lazy."

"Well, he did have dizzy spells when he worked at the factory," Beverly retorted defensively. She sat on the other side of the bed and began dressing. She had showered earlier that morning. "It's not like he was making that up."

"He was hung over from drinking like I bet he is now." Kenneth held out his hand as if imploring his wife to see the situation his way. "Don't you remember he went out drinking with his buddies the night before he lost his job and how Amir was still hung over when he left to go to work? That escapade is the reason why he lost his job."

"No, I haven't forgotten," Beverly snapped. "Still, the dizzy spells were due to his heart condition, not drinking," she volleyed back stubbornly. "Look, Kenny, I didn't stay home to argue with you about Amir. Can we give it a rest?" She stood up and walked into the attached bathroom to style her hair and apply makeup on her face.

"Sure, we can give it a rest for now, but at some point we're going to have to come to a decision about what to do about Amir. Also, we need to talk about your new purchases that I found in the garage. Your spending is getting out of control again." He walked into the bathroom and kissed Beverly's cheek. "Now, hurry up, beautiful. You know I hate when we fight about Amir. Let's go out for breakfast. We can even do some early Christmas shopping, that is if you left any money in the bank. I want to spend a stress-free day with my best girl."

Beverly looked at Kenneth gratefully. She suppressed a sigh and smiled weakly at her husband. "That sounds like a plan." She watched Kenneth walk out of the room, looked upward and said, "Lord, I know this is not the end of our discussion. Why can't Kenny see things my way? God, please help us find a solution to Amir's problems. In Jesus' name I pray. Amen."

Kenneth put on his jacket and walked out the back door. He realized that his work was cut out for him. But he hoped in the long run Beverly would come around and see things his way regarding therapy. He'd talked to his buddy, Douglas, yesterday. Doug told Kenneth that he planned to approach Julia about attending the therapy sessions, and suggested Kenneth and Beverly do the same.

Kenneth wondered how his friend was faring with presenting the idea of therapy to Julia. As he walked to the garage to warm up the car, Kenneth thought he had his own battles to fight and he counted on God to help him. He was asking, as the Bible instructed, and Kenneth hoped the Lord would give. He started the car so it could warm up and waited for Beverly to join him.

Chapter Nine

Julia and Douglas sat cozily together on the wooden bench in the waiting area of an Olive Garden restaurant. The square, black remote paging unit Julia held in her hand lit up.

Douglas and Julia rose from the bench, walked to the podium, and followed the young, college-aged girl as she led them to a booth in the rear of the dining room. She handed the pair menus and removed the extra silverware. Then she said as if by rote, "Your waiter will be here shortly to take your orders. Enjoy your meal."

"Thank you," Douglas murmured after he pulled a chair from the table for Julia.

She took off her black ranch mink fur coat and laid it on the empty chair next to her seat. Then Julia removed her hat, finger-combed her curly hair, and sat in the chair.

Douglas was busy perusing the menu. "Do you want an appetizer?"

"Give me a minute." Julia sat her purse on her lap and opened the menu. A few minutes later, she looked up and answered Douglas. "I think I'd like mozzarella sticks. What about you?"

"I have a taste for calamari. Will you share an order with me?" Douglas continued reading the menu.

Julia nodded as she dropped her eyes. A few minutes later, she remarked, "I think I'll have Chicken Fettuccine Alfredo for my entree."

"Sounds good. I'll have the manicotti." Douglas closed the menu. He picked up Julia's and laid it on top of his.

Attendance in the restaurant was sparse. It was four o'clock P.M., and the dinner crowd had yet to arrive. Douglas picked up a water glass and eyed it to make sure it was clean.

A young man carrying a pad and pencil walked to the table. "Hello my name is Gordon, and I'll be your waiter this evening." He recited the specials for the day. Then the waiter opened his pad and asked the pair, "Are you ready to order?" He glanced at Douglas and then Julia.

Douglas recited both orders to the young man. The couple requested iced tea as their beverage.

"I'll be back shortly with your appetizers," the waiter informed them as he collected the menus and then left the table.

Julia looked around the restaurant, then back at her husband. "It looks like we got lucky and missed the crowd. That's good because I have a million things to do when we get home." She crinkled her nose.

"I thought the two of us having dinner together alone would be nice. Plus it gives Brandon and Erin some time alone."

"Hmm. Since she's pregnant, I think we should thank God they won't be getting into any further trouble." Julia lifted her nose in the air.

"They're married, Jules. Erin is our daughter-in-law. I know you're not crazy about her, but at least give her that respect," Douglas said in a lulling tone of voice.

"I don't have to give her a darn thing." Julia held out her hand toward Douglas. "Isn't it enough that she and Brandon are living with us? And our boy was supposed to be at college preparing for a career in the NBA. Instead, he's working at a UPS warehouse loading packages in a dead-end job like someone who doesn't have any options." She snorted. "And he had the nerve to knock up a White girl. Please." Julia had a tinge of rancor in her voice as her eyes flashed anger at Douglas.

"I understand where you're coming from, Doll, but what can we do about it now? What's done is done. We can only move forward," Douglas responded.

The waiter returned to the table and sat two tall glasses of iced tea atop it for the couple. "I'll be back shortly with your appetizers," he said and departed.

Julia opened three packets of sugar and sprinkled the tiny white particles into her glass. She took the wrapping off a straw, put it inside her glass, and stirred the sugar.

Douglas picked up his spoon and stirred the sugar he'd poured into his glass. Then he sat the spoon on the side of the table. "I don't want to sound like I'm criticizing you, Jules, but I think you should lighten up on your treatment of Erin."

Julia's eyes hungrily followed a biracial girl who looked to be between five and eight years old. She walked inside the dining room, swinging her arms back and forth as she walked hand-in-hand between her parents. They were a White and African American couple who appeared to be in their late twenties or early thirties.

The little girl wore a mischievous expression on her caramel-colored face. She was missing her bottom middle teeth, and her eyes were turquoise. Her sandy brown hair was styled in two braids with a part that spanned down the middle of her head.

Douglas looked up at Julia, then his eyes followed the same path his wife's had taken. "She's a very attractive little girl, isn't she?" Douglas commented as he unfolded his napkin and spread it across his legs.

"Uh, what did you say?" Julia brought her attention back to her husband. The waiter walked down the aisle with the couple's appetizers atop a dark tray. He sat the plates on the table. "Can I get you anything else?"

"No, we're good for now," Douglas murmured. After the waiter left, Douglas blessed the food and said to Julia, "Let's eat."

Julia put portions of food on the small plates for Douglas and herself. The couple dug in and ate.

They conversed about their workday. Julia took a sip of tea, sighed, and said, "That's good." Then she placed the glass back on the table. "So, what's up, Doug?" She looked candidly at her husband. "I know you have some type of hidden agenda for suggesting we have dinner together. I've been very civil to Erin this week, so I know you're not going to lecture me about that again." Julia tugged at the hem of her beige and brown striped skirt. She wore a chocolate and off-white blouse with gold accessories.

"Well, Doll," Douglas began saying, "I wanted to talk to you about the therapy program the church is offering."

Julia's eyebrow arched upward, but her expression was impervious. "What about it?" she asked impatiently, glancing at her fingernails. She was eager to try a French manicure with pink tips instead of white. She decided to call her nail technician the following day to see if Cherese could fit her into her schedule. Julia took another sip of tea and looked at her husband.

Douglas stole a glance at his wife and said tentatively, "I think we should participate in the sessions."

Julia sputtered. The tea she had sipped had gone down the wrong way. She picked up her napkin and coughed inside it. Her eyes shone luminously, and she said in a hoarse-sounding voice, "Say what? Come again?"

"As I said, I think couples' therapy could help us. Maybe there are some techniques or something we could learn to help us deal with the kids' situation," Douglas repeated forcefully.

"And why is that?" Julia asked as she placed the napkin on the table next to her cup, pulled a tissue out of her black leather purse, and wiped her eyes. "We don't have any problem with our marriage, and I'm doing better dealing with Erin. Or at least, I'm trying to."

"We don't per se, Doll." Douglas held up his hand apologetically. "But you are having problems dealing with Erin, and if you can't change your feeling toward the girl, then your behavior will affect our grandchildren in the long run."

Julia just stared at her husband wordlessly for a few seconds. She wore a hurt expression on her face. She balled up the tissue she held in her hand and tossed it across the table at Douglas. "I can't believe that you think we need therapy because of a few issues I have with that girl," she blustered as her eyes radiated anger at her husband.

Douglas deftly deflected the pink tissue as he raised his right hand and caught it. "That girl, as you call her, is our daughter-in-law and the mother of our first grandchild." He spoke earnestly, putting the tissues inside his jacket pocket. He extended his hand across the table and took Julia's in his own. His eyes pleaded with his wife to understand his position.

"I'm working on adjusting my attitude toward Erin," Julia sniffed, "give me some time. Rome wasn't built in a day."

"I know, Doll, but she's having complications with the pregnancy." The waiter returned to the table with warm bread for the couple. He sat the basket on the table between Julia and Douglas. "Your orders will be up shortly," he said, then left the table.

"What kind of complications?" Julia asked. She removed her hand from Douglas's, folded her arms across her chest, and pierced Douglas with a frigid stare.

"She has high blood pressure, and the doctor has recommended bed rest and no stress," Douglas replied after he dipped a piece of calamari into the red sauce and put it inside his mouth.

"When did she tell you this?" Julia asked. "She just went to the doctor, when? A few days ago?"

"Since Brandon couldn't go with her to her appointment, I took her myself. It just doesn't seem right, Jules, that our pregnant daughter-in-law has to ride the bus to her doctor's office for an appointment."

"Oh," Julia's eyes dropped. "Doug, I told you that I couldn't take her to the doctor. I had an important meeting at work. Maybe I can go with her next time." She sipped the glass of tea and sat it back on the table. "I still don't see why we need therapy because of my feelings about our daughter-in-law. If anything, I think Brandon and Erin would benefit from those sessions more than us. We don't have any issues with our marriage."

"Erin had an ultrasound during her appointment, and the test showed that she's having a girl." Douglas couldn't keep a smile off his face. "I know I've been telling everyone that I was hoping for a grandson, but really I prefer a granddaughter since we have a boy."

"How nice," Julia murmured. She picked up her purse from the empty seat next to her, pulled a piece of paper out of it, and began reading it.

Douglas stared at his wife with a frown on his face. "I wasn't done talking to you, Jules. Can I have your undivided attention?"

The waiter returned to the table carrying a tray that held their entrees. He placed the plates on the table. "Can I get you anything else?"

Both Douglas and Julia shook their heads.

"Then enjoy your meal." The waiter walked away from the table, satisfied that he had done everything possible to receive a bountiful tip from the couple.

Douglas and Julia closed their eyes and dropped their heads. "Father, thank you for this meal that we are about to partake in. Please use it to nourish our bodies, and, Lord, bless the cook," Douglas added.

Julia whispered, "Amen," after Douglas blessed the meal. She picked up her fork and knife, sliced her food, and began eating.

For a time Julia and Douglas didn't converse as they dined. Thoughts raced through their minds. Douglas knew Julia would be averse to the idea. Still he was determined to persevere and refused to back down. He felt Erin's medical condition put the life of their first grandchild at risk. He silently prayed the Lord would help him find the right words to convince Julia to agree to his suggestion.

Twenty minutes later, Julia pushed her plate away from her. "The meal was good. With all the fancy restaurants we have in Chicago, there's something about the Olive Garden and Applebee's that I like from time to time."

"Me too," Douglas agreed. "Do you want dessert?"

"No," Julia protested. "I'll probably have to exercise three days to get the pounds off I packed on today." She smiled at Douglas.

"I think I'll have a slice of cheesecake. I'm not watching my weight like you are," Douglas teased his wife.

"That's because your metabolism is different from mine. I don't think you've gained much weight since we've been married." Her hands swept down. "On the other hand, I can't say that about myself. I'll definitely have to work out."

"Stop fishing for compliments, Doll. You look better to me than the first day I met you. Now you have curves." Douglas wiped his mouth with the napkin and signaled for the waiter to come to the table. He ordered a slice of strawberry cheesecake. Julia ordered coffee.

"I'll be back shortly," the waiter promised.

"Julia, we've been blessed to have a good marriage. We're coming up to our twilight years, or at least I am. And I'd like to continue enjoying life, going to church, and spoiling our grandchildren. I need you to work with me. I haven't made many demands of you over the years. You're a smart, loving, independent woman. I just want us to stay on the course we set out on when we married."

Julia listened to Douglas speak. Her elbow lay on the table, and her head rested on her hand. She knew in her heart that Douglas had been a good husband. He'd always supplied their financial needs, and he listened to her and encouraged her many endeavors. She suffered a miscarriage after having Brandon and ended up having a hysterectomy, and not once did Douglas complain.

While Julia bemoaned their fate, she remembered Douglas saying after her surgery that the Lord had blessed them with one child, and there were so many people who couldn't have one at all. He said he was content with their blessing. She shook her head and brought her attention back to Douglas as she listened to him present his case.

Julia knew the right thing to do would be to support her husband. After doing some quick soul-searching, she held up her hands. "Okay, Doug. I cede, but I have one request. If the people in charge of the program will agree, I'd like Brandon and Erin to join us."

"Praise God." Douglas's eyes lit up like stars in the night. "I was hoping the Lord would put it on your heart to agree to participate. I know the committee emphasized there could only be three couples per session. Still the Lord moves in mysterious ways, His wonders to behold. I will talk to Sister Morrison tomorrow and see what she says. Thank you, Jules. I love you, and I know the Lord has only good things in store for our family."

"I love you, too, and you're right, the Lord has blessed us tremendously. I will go to the sessions, but only if the kids can participate," Julia announced emphatically. She thumped the top of the table.

Douglas held up his glass and motioned for Julia to do the same. "Here's to opening ourselves up to the possibilities of what God can do."

Julia touched Douglas's glass. "Here, here. Amen."

The following morning at ten o'clock, after Douglas had assigned his crew's snow removal route for the day, he leaned back in his chair in his office. Douglas opened the desk drawer and pulled out a list of the church members' telephone numbers. His finger scrolled down the page until he found Meesha's cell phone number. Douglas picked up a Bic pen and wrote the number down on a slip of scratch paper.

Douglas called Kenneth first to see if his friend had luck getting Beverly to attend the sessions. Kenneth said getting Beverly to participate in Couples' Therapy was painful, like pulling teeth without Novocain. He chuckled and said he'd kept the pressure on Beverly until she decided to join the therapy.

After Kenneth and Douglas ended their conversation, Doug closed his eyes, bowed his head, and prayed.

"Father God, I give all praises to you. Sometimes we mortals don't always understand why things happen the way they do. Like Julia, I struggle to understand how our son ended up with Erin. Father, you said we don't have to understand why things happen the way they do, but know that you are in control, and that all mercy and grace comes from you.

"God, I feel you put it strongly in my heart to do what I can to ensure my family prospers and remains mindful of the things you want us to do as your children. Lord, keep your mercy shining upon my wife, my son, Erin, and the new baby girl you're going to bless us with. Lord, thank you for putting the idea of therapy in Sister Morrison's heart. Let the new ministry be an instrument in helping couples who need edification of your word and strengthening of their marital bonds. In Jesus's name, I pray, Father. Amen."

Douglas opened his eyes, picked up the telephone receiver, and quickly dialed Meesha's number. He expected to get her voice mail. Douglas assumed Meesha was busy at work. He was quite surprised when Meesha herself answered the telephone.

"Good morning, Brother Freeman. How is your family doing? And how may I help you today?" Meesha asked after Douglas identified himself.

"We're doing fine and blessed by the Lord, Sister Morrison. Say, I have a proposition I want to run past you."

"Then by all means, let me hear it," Meesha replied. Butterflies fluttered inside her tummy. She hoped that neither he nor any of his family members had changed their minds about participating in the sessions.

"Julia and I are interested in participating in Couples' Therapy. As I explained to you and Dr. Taylor, we're having a crisis of sorts at home, and I feel the sessions would benefit all of us."

"Well, that's good news," Meesha said as a grin tugged at the corners of her mouth. "Brother Freeman, you have my undivided attention."

"My son and daughter-in-law are having problems adjusting to marriage, and complicating matters for them is a baby on the way. Julia and I also are having a hard time adjusting to the hasty marriage and the baby on the way."

"Okay," Meesha said with a puzzled look on her face. "What can we do to help?"

Douglas took a deep breath and exhaled loudly. "I know my request is a bit out of order, but I was hoping the committee would consider adding another couple to the sessions. I know three couples is the limit, but I'd really like all four of us—Julia, Brandon, Erin, and myself—to participate."

"Wow," Meesha relaxed her body against the back of her chair. "I never saw that one coming."

"It is a bit irregular," Douglas admitted. "I think this would be perfect for my family, especially since Dr. Taylor has dealt with issues facing interracial couples."

Meesha nodded. "Maybe your family could meet with Zora as a family unit outside of the therapy sessions. Maybe that type of setting would be more appropriate."

Douglas took off his glasses and laid them on the desk. "I know where you're coming from, Sister Morrison. I beg to differ in this instance. I think the sessions would be the ideal place for this type of dialogue to take place. Surely Julia and I can't be the only couple facing interracial relationships within the family. The discussions might help someone else in the future, and what better place than the house of the Lord to discuss how people can improve their marriages and relationships in general."

"Hmmm, you have a point, Brother Freeman. All I can do is present the information to Dr. Taylor and Reverend Nixon since they will be facilitating the meetings."

Douglas picked up the ink pen off the desk and twirled it in his fingers nervously. "Then that's all I can hope for. I just ask for the opportunity to present our case. I don't have a problem with seeing a therapist, and I think it's easier to open up knowing that the therapist is a part of our church family."

"Well, some people believe that it's more difficult for people to open up, knowing that the participants are church members, people you may know and socialize with."

"I disagree, Sister Morrison. For me it would be easier," Douglas said definitely. "Would you please present my request to Dr. Taylor and Reverend Nixon? I know the Lord will put it on their hearts to agree to my entire family attending the sessions. Um, Julia says she will only attend is if the kids attend too."

"Okay." Meesha bit her lip to keep from laughing. "I understand now."

"I don't want my family to end up in counseling later in life, especially the new granddaughter we have on the way. That's why I'm so insistent about the kids participating, sister. So will you please consider my request?"

Meesha couldn't help but be swayed by the emotional request that flowed across the telephone from Douglas. He sounded like a man on a mission. "Brother Freeman, I can't speak for Zora and Reverend Nixon, but I'd like to do what I can to get your request approved. Give me a couple of days to run your request by them, and I'll get back to you soon."

Douglas covered the base of the telephone. He looked above and mouthed, "Thank you, Jesus." He removed his hand and said, "Sister Morrison, that's all I can ask of you. The Lord will work it out. I look forward to hearing from you. Have a blessed day."

"Thank you, Brother Freeman. You too have a good day, and I will be in touch with you shortly. Good-bye"

Douglas hung up the telephone. He had a strong feeling that things would turn out positively.

Meesha clicked off the cell phone and sat it inside the charger on her desk. The committee in all their planning and wisdom had never considered the possibility that more than three couples might want to participate in the sessions. The subject had never even come up for discussion. Zora decided to limit the participation to three couples because she felt any more would present a timing issue for the hour allotted for the sessions.

A smile covered Meesha's face as she reminisced about her conversation with Douglas. Then her face drooped as she thought about Edward. She wished her husband was as open-minded as Douglas. Edward hadn't given her a yea or nay as to whether he planned to attend the sessions or not.

She refused to entertain the thought that Edward wouldn't. Her stomach felt queasy as she contemplated that she might have to make good on her threats to actually take the children and leave him.

Chapter Ten

Open warfare had been declared in the Morrison household, that is when Edward bothered to come home. He began arriving home from work later and later, further worrying Meesha. The children had long stopped asking when their father would be home.

Meesha felt like Edward worked longer hours to retaliate against her demands that he attend therapy. Conversations had become all but nil between the couple. Meesha never knew when he was coming or going. Most of the time she was asleep when Edward arrived at the house in the wee hours of the night and asleep when he left for work in the morning.

As Meesha sat at her desk at work, she wondered aloud, "Lord, what am I doing wrong regarding my marriage? I've tried to follow your will, and my husband has always been the head of the household. Lately he's been missing in action. I don't know how we've managed to come to this place of no compromise. Lord, I ask that you help us and get us back on track. We need you, Father, to help us raise our children and try to be the best Christians we can be. In your son's name, I pray for strength, Lord. Have mercy on your child. Amen.

Meesha's hand shook as she picked up her cell phone. She closed her eyes and then opened them as she punched in Edward's work number. Her body trembled when Edward's secretary, Deidre, answered the telephone.

"Hi, Dee, is he available?" Meesha held her breath waiting for Deidre to answer.

"Hello, Mrs. Morrison. Yes, he is. Please hold on for a moment. I'll get him on the line."

While Meesha waited for Edward to pick up the line, she willed her hand to stop shaking, but it didn't.

"Yes, Meesha, what can I do for you?" Edward asked in a disinterested tone of voice. His eyes darted to the computer screen in front of him. He wished he had instructed Deidre to hold all his calls.

"Hello, Edward. And how are you?" Meesha couldn't contain a tinge of bitterness from spreading to her voice.

"I'm all right, just in the middle of something. What do you want?"

Edward's cold voice pierced Meesha's heart, and she regretted calling him. Her eyes filled with tears. "I just wanted to see how you're doing. I haven't talked to you all week."

"I've been busy. The project is consuming everyone's time, not just mine," Edward informed his wife. The telephone receiver was cradled against his neck as he entered sales figures on the PC keyboard.

"I assumed that, Edward," Meesha replied acerbically. "It would have been nice if you had discussed it with me as you have in the past. When I wake up in the morning, you're gone, and then when I go to sleep at night, you're still not home. I am not sure what to think anymore."

"Well, I know how you feel," Edward replied. "Kind of the same way I felt when you stood up before the church and announced our business. Payback isn't pretty, is it?"

Meesha counted to ten in her head before she replied. Her voice was tight as she stated, "Our marriage is not negotiable, nor do I ever want to hear you refer to it as something you want to get revenge against."

"I didn't mean it that way. Sorry." Edward sounded chastened.

"Thank you." Meesha sounded mollified. "I really need to talk to you, Edward. It's important. If you want me to, I can come by your office. You have to take a break sometimes."

Edward ran his hand over his head. "That won't be necessary. I'll come home from work at my regular time, but I'll need to return to the office after we finish talking. As I said, the project I'm working on is very intense." He clicked the save icon on the monitor.

"How about having lunch together?" Meesha asked, knowing the answer to that question.

"No can do. I'll be working through lunch. We have a team meeting scheduled. I will see you this evening. That's about the best I can do today," Edward informed his wife.

"Somehow, I don't think that's the case, but I'll take what I can get. I'll see you later." Meesha ended the call.

"Yes, I'll see you then." Edward disconnected the call and then quickly dialed another number. When the person he called answered the phone, Edward said, "Hi, Mac, it's me. I won't be able to meet you as planned. Meesha just called and she wants us to have dinner." Edward listened silently for a few minutes.

"I know we had this planned for a while, but if I don't meet with Meesha, she'll keep harping on the issue, or worse, come here to the job and cause a scene. I'll call you this evening after I'm done at home. Okay, catch you later." Edward hung up the telephone and closed the spreadsheet he'd been working on and brought up a new one.

Meesha twirled her seat around to face the window behind her. She was assistant manager of her work district. Her office was decorated tastefully for a social worker employed by the state of Illinois. In reality her workspace was only a little bigger than a cubbyhole. She came to the office the weekend after her promotion and painted the dingy walls white. Meesha purchased a red-and-gold-trimmed Persian area rug to adorn the floor. She'd bought several prints and placed them on the wall. The furnishings included an old wooden desk that she'd restored and a matching bookcase filled with textbooks. A gray steel filing cabinet sat in another corner of the office, and it contained her case files. She glanced at the bookcase where pictures of her family were displayed.

Meesha looked at the ticking clock on the wall, and the time was just past eleven o'clock. She knew Regina had just dismissed her third period class and had a planning period, so Meesha removed the phone from the charger and dialed Regina's cell phone.

Her girlfriend promptly answered the telephone. "Hey, Meesha. What's up?"

"I swear you sound more like those teeny boppers everyday. I'm good, How are you?"

"I'm fine. I have a tutoring session scheduled soon. What can I do for you?"

"I was hoping you could pick up the children from school for me. The king of the castle has decided to honor me with his presence this evening. I hadn't mentioned to you that Edward hasn't been home on time since I gave him the ultimatum of attending the sessions with me. When we came home from church the Sunday I made the announcement, we had it out. He tried to make amends by helping the kids with their homework. That lasted all of a day; since then he's been working nonstop. He claims it's because of the project, but I wonder. I called him at work a little while ago and told him we needed to talk. So for the first time in a long time, he's coming home on time."

"That's good," Regina said. "You two need to iron out your differences, and I guess that's why you want me to pick up the children, so you can have some privacy." A student peeped inside the classroom from the open door. "Hold on a minute, Meesha." Regina lowered the telephone away from her face. "Give me a moment, Clark," she told the young man at her door, "then I'll be ready to start."

"Okay, Ms. Cole." Clark walked a few steps to the left and stood next to the door.

"Meesha, I'm back. Sure, I'll pick up Imani and Keon from school. I'll take them to dinner and call you before I bring them home. I don't want us to interrupt an intimate moment."

"Thanks, girl. I really appreciate it. I don't want any interruptions either. Edward and I haven't been intimate in a while. Anytime you need a favor you know who to call." Meesha expelled a loud breath, clearly relieved.

"No problem. You know I love spending time with my godchildren. Good luck talking to Ed. I'll talk to you later."

"Thanks, Reggie. I'll call the school to tell them you're going to pick up the children. I owe you."

"I know, and one of these days, I'm going to cash in some of those favors," Regina informed her friend. "Enjoy the rest of the day. Like the song says, Jesus will work it out. I'll say a prayer that you and Edward resolve your issues. Bye, girl."

"Good-bye. I'll see you later."

The women ended the call. Meesha pressed a button on her work telephone to route her calls to voice mail. She scrolled through her e-mail calendar and saw that she had only one appointment that day. She stood up and walked out of her office and down the hall to talk to her manager about leaving early. That way she could go to the store and pick up Edward's favorite dishes to prepare for dinner.

Several hours later, Meesha stood at the almond-colored stove in her kitchen. Her eyes flew to the clock on the upper portion of the range. Edward would be home in an hour. She walked rapidly to the sink, turned on the faucet, moistened the dishrag, squirted a few drops of Palmolive dishwashing liquid on it, and wiped down the stove. She turned the jets on the stove on low. Then Meesha wiped her hands on the dishtowel, dimmed the light in the room, and walked to her bedroom.

She went to the closet and pulled a black dress off the hanger, laid it on the bed, and strode to the bathroom, where she quickly took a shower. As she showered, doubts clouded Meesha's mind. She knew something was bothering Edward outside of the job. The two had been together since their junior year of college, and Meesha had always been attuned to her fussy husband's moods. *Lord, let Edward open up to me about whatever is bothering him. Please help us work it out,* she prayed.

Meesha dried her body with a peach-colored towel and rushed from the bathroom to the bedroom to dress. When she was done, Meesha looked at her reflection in the mirror and tried to quell the fears that played ping-pong inside her stomach. Though she'd gained weight after the birth of the children, Meesha thought she still looked attrative. She hadn't ever been a small size even as a child. She reassured herself that Edward knew he was getting a big girl when he married her.

She sat on the stool to her vanity and twisted her hair into a French roll, then applied makeup to her face. When she was done, she put on the two-carat diamond earrings Edward had given her as an anniversary gift last year. Then she dabbed a few drops of Escada Pacific Paradise, on her wrists, her neck, and behind her ears.

After putting away the clothing she'd worn that day, Meesha departed from the bedroom and walked down the hallway to the dining room. While the food was cooking, she'd set a formal dining table. She stopped by the local florist and bought a bunch of daffodils to decorate the large mahogany table.

Meesha stepped away from the table and nodded her approval. "Oops, I forgot the candles," she reminded herself. She walked to the cabinet, opened the bottom drawer, and removed a pair of rose-colored candles to match the mauve-colored room. Meesha put the candles inside the brass candleholders. "That looks better," she said as she nodded her approval. "Now I'll check the food."

She walked into the kitchen and took the lid off a pan and turned the asparagus spears that were steaming. She had broiled lamb chops and prepared a pasta salad to round out the meal. An Eli's cheesecake chilled inside the refrigerator along with a bottle of Sutter Home White Zinfandel. "Now, all I have to do is wait on Edward to put in an appearance and we'll be set." Meesha left the kitchen and walked to the living room. She searched through a stack of CDs until she found one of Edward's favorite David Sanborn CDs. She quickly put it inside the CD player and turned on the music

Meesha hummed to the melody as she returned to the kitchen to turn off the stove and oven. She returned to the bedroom and lined her lips with lip gloss. Meesha preened at her reflection in the mirror. Then she closed her eyes and prayed the Lord would help save her marriage. She prayed she and Edward would be able to discuss and put their differences aside to rectify their ailing marriage. Meesha twisted a curl on the side of her head and returned to the living room to sit on the couch and wait for Edward.

Several hours had elapsed and still she had not seen hide nor hair of Edward. Meesha became uneasy and kept glancing at the gold watch at her wrist. It was now eight o'clock, and Edward still hadn't come home.

The temperature had dropped, and the house had become cool. Sitting by the window in the dimly lit living room, Meesha rubbed her bare arms briskly. Her chin rose defensively in the air and then dropped to her chest. Meesha slowly brought her hands to her face and began sobbing aloud.

She stopped several minutes later and sniffed. She stood and walked into the kitchen. The food on the stove was cool. Meesha snatched up the telephone and aggressively punched in the number to Edward's office. The telephone rang until the call was routed to voice mail. Meesha called his cell number and immediately his voice mail message played, like he had turned the phone off. Meesha threw the cordless telephone on the counter, turned on her high-heeled feet, and flounced out the room to the bedroom.

The telephone rang. Meesha snatched the cordless telephone off the base. "Hello, Edward? Where are you?"

"No, this isn't Edward, it's me, Regina. I wanted to know if this was a good time to bring the kids home or not? We've been watching movies this evening. I was going to bring them home after we finished watching *The Little Mermaid*. Edward didn't come home? Oh, no. I'm sorry, Meesha." Regina commiserated with her friend.

Meesha cleared her throat, which was clogged with unshed tears. "No, Reggie, Edward didn't come home. I was about to change clothes and call to tell you I'm coming to get the kids. I wanted to give Edward a little more time." A sob escaped her mouth.

"Don't worry about it, girlfriend. The kids can spend the night with me since its Friday. We're having fun. I'll bring them home in the morning. I'm sure there's a good reason why Edward hasn't come home. He probably had an emergency at work," Regina said in a calming tone of voice.

"I wish I could believe you," Meesha replied. "But I called his office and cell phones, and for reasons unknown to me, Edward isn't answering my calls. I am very upset to put it mildly." She wiped away a tear that had trekked down the side of her face.

"Try to calm down. I have the kids. Edward has to come home sooner or later, and when he does, I know you two will sit down and get it together." Regina looked toward her den. "Uh-oh, your children are calling. I have popcorn in the microwave, and they said it's ready. Call me back if you need me, and try not to worry too much."

"You're probably right. I'm overreacting. Edward has been late before. I'll see you in the morning. How about meeting at IHOP for breakfast? My treat," Meesha asked as she removed bobby pins from her hair. She'd slipped her feet out of her shoes.

"Okay, Meesha. I'll see you in the morning. Duty calls," Regina quipped. "Your children are impatient. Try not to worry."

Meesha sat the telephone on top of the nightstand. She stood up, unzipped her dress and removed it from her body. She walked to the closet and put it back on a hanger. Then Meesha took her cotton pajamas off the hook on the closet door and put them on.

When she was done, Meesha removed Edward's robe from the hook opposite the wall where her pajamas hung. She put the robe to her nose and inhaled. The material smelled slightly of Edward's cologne. Tears sprang to Meesha's eyes as she put the robe back on the hook.

She left the room, went into the den, and removed a folder from her tote bag that contained papers from work and church. She removed her notes for Couples' Therapy from the desk and laid them on the table in front of the sofa. She then walked into the kitchen and fixed herself a plate of food, put it inside the microwave, and then stashed the leftovers in the refrigerator while she waited for her plate to warm. The microwave beeped, indicating the meal was ready. Meesha took a 7UP out of the refrigerator, and sat at the table and ate dinner. Then Meesha returned to the den to keep her mind occupied with busywork. Later she retired to the bedroom.

By ten o'clock, Edward still hadn't come home or called. Meesha covered her mouth to suppress a yawn. She picked up a folder from work, opened it, and began reading the document detailing her latest case, making notes on the side of the paper.

Later, the sound of the back door in the kitchen opening and closing startled Meesha and roused her from a light sleep. She sat up and smoothed her hair away from her face. Meesha stood up as Edward walked into bedroom.

Husband and wife faced each other wordlessly for a few minutes. Meesha folded her arms across her chest. She took a deep breath and said simply, "Where have you been, Edward?" Other thoughts she could have verbalized bounced around her mind. *Does he think I'm stupid or something? I know he could have called me.* Meesha's faced paled. *I can't bear it if he's messing around with another woman.* Meesha shook her head slightly from side to side as she made an effort to pull her mind away from those depressing thoughts.

"I'm sorry, babe. An emergency came up at work, and I couldn't get away before dinner. Please forgive me." He held up his hands, and the sleeves of his black trench coat strained against the sides of his arms.

Meesha bucked her eyes at him wildly. She wanted to scream, *You're a liar*, but held her peace. "Why didn't you call to tell me, Edward? I've been waiting for you all afternoon."

"I wanted to call you, but Mr. Torrance flew into town today without warning. He arrived at the office after I talked to you and called an emergency meeting. There simply wasn't time to call," Edward replied smoothly. He glanced down at the floor, preferring to look anywhere except his wife's face. He knew disappointment, resentment, and probably something close to hatred might be reflected in her eyes.

Meesha didn't miss how Edward refused to meet her gaze, and her stomach bounced up and down. She knew her husband was lying to her. Meesha moistened her dry lips. "Edward, when you left your office and passed Deidre's desk to go to the meeting, did it ever occur to you to have her call me and tell me about the change in plans?"

Edward looked directly at Meesha, and he was shocked by the hurt that shone from his wife's resplendent eyes. He moved toward her, and Meesha stepped back from him. "Honestly, before I went to the meeting, I thought about asking Dee to call you. Honey, I was hoping the meeting would end by quitting time. Come on, Mee-sha," he pleaded as he moved closer to her and made a motion to take her in his arms.

Meesha sidestepped her husband and said dubiously, "Edward, we have a problem. I've been trying to tell you that for weeks. You are in denial and refuse to admit something is wrong. Is there another woman? Are you tired of me? Have I gotten too fat for you?" Her bottom lip quivered.

Edward protested, "Of course not." He still wouldn't meet Meesha's eyes. He looked down at his wrinkled blue shirt and rolled up the sleeves. He looked directly at Meesha. "Don't be foolish. I care about you. I'm here, aren't I? This new project has tied up all of my time. I just told John this morning that after this project is done how I want to take time off work to spend with you and the kids." Edward smiled at Meesha uncomfortably.

"That's assuming you still have a wife and children to come home to once the project has been completed," Meesha shot back. Her lips clamped shut.

Edward loosened his paisley burgundy and yellow tie, and rubbed his eyes. "I'm tired. Let's finish this discussion in the morning."

"No," Meesha stamped her foot. "You know when I married you and we took our vows at the church, in God's house, that marriage is for better or worse. And, Edward, worse has gone on for too long. It seems like nothing matters to you except your job. What about me and my feelings?"

Edward looked startled at the fury on Meesha's face. "Whoa, you know I have to work to support our family. You knew I was ambitious when we took our vows. I am this close," he held up two fingers with a tiny space between them, "to attaining my goal. Why can't you just go along with the program?"

"Why, you ask?" Meesha screamed. "Because there has to be balance in life. Everything can't be about one person's needs. You know that, Edward." She shook her head sorrowfully. "We're not teenagers, learning each other's wants and needs. We've been together for over ten years. I know how you like things done and vice versa, and I didn't sign on for me to be doing everything here at home without any help from you."

"Why can't you just support a brother? We'll be set for the rest of our lives. When the new software is rolled out, we'll have money to send the children to college. We can even move from the city if we choose to." Edward pointed at Meesha. "Your problem is that you can't adjust to change. Nothing stays the same in life. You have to roll with the punches."

"You just don't get it, Edward." Her eyes widened incredulously. She waved her hands in the air. "I'm tired of living like this. You obviously have a problem. I don't know what it is, but I'll tell you this: you either go with me to the sessions, or you can kiss me and your family good-bye." As soon as the words left Meesha's mouth, she regretted them. Zora had told her over and over how both parties had to agree that a problem existed and to work together for a change to occur. And here she was threatening to leave Edward if he didn't participate.

"You know I don't take too well to threats," Edward said. He put his hand to his mouth, stifling a yawn. "We're both tired and don't want to say anything we'll regret. Let's pick this up in the morning."

Meesha walked to the bed and removed the pillows and comforter. "Yes, you might be right. Let's finish this discussion in the morning, and I suggest you think carefully about everything I've said. That is, if your precious job doesn't call and you have to rush out of here in the morning." She turned and quickly exited the room, trying to keep the tears in her eyes from falling. She quietly closed the door behind her.

Edward sat on the side of the bed. One part of his mind told him to get up and go talk to Meesha. The other part urged him to let her go. If the discussion continued in the same vein, one of them might say something they wished they could take back. He knew how hard it was sometimes to take back words spoken in the heat of anger. He'd been guilty of that shortcoming.

He walked to the bathroom, stood at the sink, turned on the faucet, and splashed water on his face. Edward noticed fine, spider-like lines etched on his face. The day had been a difficult one for Edward because he had to deal with multiple problems at work. He wondered why a man couldn't return to his castle and not listen to complaints. Edward felt that after the software installation was rolled out to his company's clients, things would return to normal at home. He turned on the faucets in the shower and began stripping off his clothing.

Edward soaped his lean frame and let the water cascade over his tired body. His mind fluttered between maintaining his pride and attending the sessions with Meesha. Maybe it would get her off his back. He wondered why he couldn't have married a patient woman, and how the timing wasn't good for him to have any problems or distractions at home. Edward knew he needed to concentrate on doing his part to make sure the customers were satisfied with the software upgrade so he could collect his bonus. It would be close to a quarter of a million dollars—more than his father made in his lifetime at his government job.

After he finished showering and drying off, Edward slipped on his navy blue and green robe. He towel dried his head, wiped the steam off the mirror and walked back to the bedroom. Edward laid his tired body on the bed and sighed. Several minutes later, he was asleep.

When a half hour elapsed and Edward hadn't come out of the room to talk to her, Meesha worked herself into a fit of resentment as she tossed and turned on the daybed in the guest bedroom. Meesha pushed the comforter aside and walked briskly back to her bedroom. She pushed open the door and found Edward in the bed fast asleep, snoring. "It's on," she proclaimed as she walked back to the guest bedroom.

Chapter Eleven

On Thursday, February 6, Reverend Nixon and Zora were placing literature and handouts on the table in the middle of the Adam and Eve meeting room at the church. The first Couples' Therapy session would commence in thirty minutes.

Zora peeped at her watch. "I would have thought Meesha would have been here by now. The meeting starts soon," she said to Calvin.

He looked at Zora reassuringly. "I'm sure she's on the way. The program is her baby, and knowing Meesha the way I do, I don't think she'll miss it. Do you want me to put more chairs around the table?"

"Yes," Zora said absentmindedly. She was worried about Meesha. "I mean no. I think we should sit in a circle." She pointed to the front of the room. "Sitting in a circle will make the meeting more intimate."

"It might also make it more intimidating," Calvin observed. He held up his hands. "You're the boss, it's your show."

"Hmmm," Zora mused as her eyes darted back and forth between the table and the empty space where she suggested Calvin place the chairs. "Let's try the circle. We can always change later if the couples have a problem with the seating. I want people to be comfortable because I know if they aren't, it will make our job more difficult."

"Okay, I'll set up the chairs." Calvin smiled at Zora and began moving chairs from the table to the empty space in the front of the room.

"Thanks, Calvin. I appreciate all your help." Zora smiled back.

Meesha rushed into the room. "Good evening, Reverend Nixon. How are you doing, Zora? I see you two have already gotten started. Sorry I'm late."

Zora saw the tense look on her friend's face and tried to put her at ease. "We still have time. You're okay. How are you doing?"

"Girl, my house is like a battle zone. Edward and I are really going at it—when he's home, that is. I think he's deliberately staying away so he won't have to deal with our problems."

"Hopefully, Calvin and I can do something about that. Keep the faith," Zora told her friend as she gave her a thumb's up sign.

Calvin accurately sensed the women needed to talk. "I'll be back in a minute," he said and departed from the room.

Meesha took off her coat and laid it on the table. "What do you need me to do?" she asked Zora. She could tell as her eyes scanned the room that Zora and Reverend Nixon were nearly finished preparing for the meeting.

"Why don't you put out the pastries I bought and start a pot of coffee? I bought hot chocolate too."

"Good idea," Meesha replied. "I'll go to the kitchen and grab some paper cups along with the coffee and hot water. I'm praying the meeting goes well."

"It will. Just calm down and let me and Calvin handle things." Zora tried to ease Meesha's fears that Edward would miss the meeting.

The trio finished setting up the room, and twenty minutes later Julia and Douglas walked into the room along with Erin and Brandon. Julia held her nose in the air, and her unsmiling face indicated she was attending the session under duress. Erin looked traumatized, like a doe caught in headlights. She wore elastic-waistband blue jeans with a smock top that barely fit over her growing belly. Douglas walked over to Calvin, Zora, and Meesha, looking resolute and unconcerned about his wife's funky attitude. He was determined to save his family from heartache down the road.

"Good evening," Meesha greeted the couples. Doug introduced her to Erin and Brandon.

"Take off your hat," Julia instructed her son. "Trust me, I taught him better than that," she said to Meesha as she rolled at her eyes and sighed loudly at Brandon.

Brandon removed the White Sox cap he wore and stuck it inside his back pocket.

Julia frowned at the chairs. "Are we sitting there?" she asked Meesha.

"Yes, we are," Zora answered. "Follow me. We have refreshments for you to snack on and literature for you to take home and read."

Kenneth and Beverly walked into the room. Though she still wasn't feeling the sessions, Beverly came out of denial long enough to realize that if she and Kenneth didn't come to a meeting of the minds soon, her family unity could be destroyed forever. Plus, she was afraid Kenneth might actually leave her. Beverly and Kenneth greeted everyone genially, removed their outer garments, placed them on the back of the seats, and walked over to the refreshment table to get cups of hot chocolate.

Meesha sat down in the aluminum folding chair and folded her hands on her lap. She kept glancing at the doorway, expecting Edward to walk in any minute, but he didn't.

Everyone ate the cookies and crackers, and sipped their beverages. Finally the meeting began. Calvin asked everyone to stand so he could lead the group in prayer. They stood and clasped hands.

The minister bowed his head and prayed. "Father, we come to you this evening asking that you bless the new endeavor the church has decided to undertake. Sometimes, Lord, we have to be open to new experiences and continue to trust in your unchanging hands. Bless Sisters Zora and Meesha, and the couples gathered here tonight. Teach us through your Word, Lord, how to be better husbands, wives, sons, and daughters. Father, shower your blessing upon us tonight and every night that we meet. Amen."

The group echoed, "Amen," then sat down.

Zora looked around the circle at everyone and smiled. "I'd like for everyone to introduce themselves." She took a deep breath. "I'll go first. My name is Zora Taylor. I was born and raised in a small town near Mobile, Alabama. During my freshman year of college at Southern Illinois University in Carbondale, I met a woman who became my roommate and my closest friend, Meesha." She looked at Meesha and smiled. "And we've been close friends since then. I decided I needed a change of pace and scenery, and after talking to Meesha about her new ministry, I applied for the position of guidance counselor at the church and returned to Illinois. So far, I'm enjoying my new experiences, and I joined your church last Sunday. The weather is going to take some getting used to after the mild temperatures in Arizona." She grinned at the group, who reciprocated.

"After I graduated from SIU, I attended medical school at Johns Hopkins University and majored in psychiatry and received a medical degree and later-received a Ph.D. from the University of Arizona. In addition to teaching part-time, I own a joint practice with several partners in Tempe, counseling families and children. I'd like to think I've helped a lot of people overcome adverse situations during my career."

Most of the group listened to her with interest. Brandon played a game on his cell phone until Julia caught him and gave him the evil eye. The door to the meeting room, which Calvin had shut when the session began, opened and Edward strolled in. He brushed snow off his coat and said, "I apologize for my tardiness. I had to work overtime."

Meesha's heart overflowed with thankfulness. *Thank you, Jesus.* She pointed to the empty seat next to her and mouthed to Edward, "I saved a spot for you."

Edward walked to the chair, took off his coat, and laid it on the back of the seat.

After Edward was settled, Zora continued speaking, making eye contact with everyone. She gestured with her hands as she spoke. "I was raised in a Christian household. My mother is an evangelist. I also minored in theology in college. For a time, I thought I might want to go into the ministry, but psychiatry has been a better fit for me. I consider counseling my calling and hope in the future to roll this program out to other churches.

"What I'd like to accomplish during the sessions is a dialogue of sorts, and to discuss scripture to help strengthen your marriages. Everything that's said in this room will be confidential. Reverend Dudley has volunteered to come in to talk to us if requested. But enough about me. Now who wants to go next?"

One by one, every person in the circle told Zora and Calvin a little about themselves. Erin remarked that she wasn't exactly sure why she was there. "My in-laws," she looked apologetically at Douglas and Julia, "insisted Brandon and I come." Julia sucked her teeth when she heard Erin say that and Douglas patted her arm.

Zora picked up her notes off the floor next to her chair. "Today we're going to spend time getting to know one another. Next week we'll get down to the nitty-gritty. I have a question for you. When you hear the word therapy, what immediately comes to mind?"

Meesha said, "I think of the healing of a disability."

Zora nodded. "That's probably a clinical definition. What about you, Julia?" She sensed correctly the older woman didn't want to be there, and Zora wanted to get her involved.

"I think therapy implies someone is nuts," Julia answered tersely.

"Yeah," Brandon added, nodding his head. "Someone sick who has to see a headshrinker." He made a circle around the side of his head. Doug shot him a disapproving look. Brandon threw his hands up in the air in surrender. "We're in church, Pops. I thought we should keep it real."

Everyone laughed, including Zora. "He's right, Douglas. We should be truthful." The mood lightened.

"I think therapy is a waste of time," Julia said with an edge in her voice. "A family should be able to resolve their problems as a unit." She waved her hand impatiently. "Ministers are counselors too. We can go to them if we have problems."

"That's true," Zora nodded, "but sometimes it helps to discuss problems in a group setting, so people won't feel they are alone when they experience trials in life. Other times people are incapable of solving their problems because they are too close to the situation."

Julia cocked her head to the side. She nodded as if conceding the point Zora had made.

Erin raised her hand hesitantly.

"Please feel free to share your thoughts with us, Erin," Zora said encouragingly to the young woman.

"My family didn't believe in therapy. My daddy called it mumbo jumbo. I just want to say I'm glad, in a way, that my father-in-law suggested me and Brandon join the group. I don't have any friends in Chicago, and coming to the meetings gives me something to do besides go to my doctor's office," Erin said shyly.

"Kenneth, what do you think when you hear the word therapy?" Zora asked the older man.

"I think of therapy as a healing power from God. I've always been a firm believer in trying new methods to solve problems. God is the master creator, and since therapy exists, it should be used," Kenneth proclaimed in his deep voice.

"Okay, what about you, Beverly?" Zora asked.

"I haven't bought into the idea. I agree with Julia, a family should be able to resolve issues or go to our minister." Beverly glanced at Kenneth. "I will try to keep an open mind to all this," Beverly promised.

"Edward," Zora said, "you've been quiet. What do you think?"

"I think of therapy as something my wife is forcing me to do." Edward glanced at Meesha with a serious expression on his face. Meesha glanced down at the floor, feeling mortified at her husband's truthful admission. Her cheeks warmed.

"Everything you've said is the same reaction that I get from most people who enter into therapy the first time." Zora nodded at the group. Her left hand swept around the circle. "Your feelings are normal. I hope by the end of the sessions some of you will have a different outlook on the benefits of therapy. What we're going to do is groundbreaking, and most importantly we're going to approach our sessions from a spiritual standpoint. The good thing is that we're going to help one another. We have many resources in this room, and all of you share a need to improve the quality of your life or you wouldn't be here, duress or not." She smiled. "With my help and Reverend Nixon's, we're going to do everything humanly possible to help you overcome some of the issues you face."

With gentle prodding from Zora and Calvin, the group continued the discussion. The facilitators fielded questions, and half an hour later everyone seemed to be more comfortable with one another. Before long the session was about to end.

Calvin rose from his seat, walked to a table, and removed a sheaf of papers. He returned to the circle and handed the papers to Meesha. "Would you take one and pass the others around?"

After everyone had taken a sheet, the couples glanced at the page and then up at Calvin. "This is your homework assignment for next week. I'd like you to bring it back with you next week." Calvin's eyes fell on Brandon. "And I'd like it filled out, please."

Brandon groaned. "Man, I might not have time to complete it." He stretched his long legs out in front of him. "I have a couple of auditions. I'm going to be a rapper."

Julia rolled her eyes. "Much to me and his father's chagrin." She shrugged her shoulders as if to say, Doug and I have nothing to do with his plan.

"I think it's cool," Erin added to the conversation. "Just think, when Brandon hits it big, we can move out to Cali and hang out with the stars." She rubbed her belly.

"See what I mean," Julia complained. "These kids today have unrealistic expectations. Brandon needs to settle down and finish school." She cut her eyes at her son. "That should be your priority along with your wife's well-being." She pointed at Erin. "And your child's."

"At least he has aspirations," Kenneth snorted. "Our son, Amir, seems content to loaf in our basement for the rest of his life, while Beverly and I help raise his son, at least this son. We think he has about three other baby mamas."

"Kenny," Beverly said in a warning tone. She put her hand on his arm. "That's not true. Amir just hasn't found himself. He's still young. Give him time."

Wow, Julia thought. *Someone has it worse than us.* She glanced at Kenneth, then at Beverly, and then back at Reverend Nixon.

"I hate to break the meeting up," Calvin said, holding up his hand. "You're opening up with one another and that's good. We have the program mapped out and need to follow the guidelines for you to get the full effect of the therapy. We'll get into the specifics of your issues over the next few weeks. I have another meeting to attend, so we're going to have to close this one now. Shall we stand?"

Everyone stood up. Calvin bowed his head and said, "Father, due to your grace and mercy we've gotten off to a good start, and I thank you. We know you can make a way out of no way, and when our way seems dim, you'll step in and guide us. Father, keep us safe as we leave for our homes, and we know you'll be with us next week and the ones to follow as we seek to grow spiritually and draw these couples closer to You, so that they may strengthen their marital bonds. Amen."

Calvin told the group, "Don't forget to complete your assignment. I'll see you next week," then he left the room.

The meeting had officially adjourned. The women chatted with Erin about the baby, while the men talked about the Bears and whether Chicago's football team had a chance of making it to the playoffs. Shortly afterward, everyone prepared to leave.

After Edward put on his coat, he said to Meesha, "I'm going to warm up my car. If you give me your keys, I'll warm yours too. I'll wait for you outside."

Meesha shook her head. "My mother drove me here, so I'm riding home with you." Edward left the room and went outside. Meesha looked at Zora. "I think everything went very well, don't you?"

"Yes, I'd say we're off to a good start. Praise God," Zora said. "I sense Julia and Beverly were holding back, but I'm sure by the time we start to get down to business, with the Lord's help, they'll open up. I was glad to see Edward made it to the session, although I detected a bit of hostility on his part."

"If he wants to stay married to me, he had to come; he didn't have a choice."

Zora patted Meesha's arm kindly. "I know your heart is in the right place, but be careful, my friend. Edward has to buy into the validity of the sessions and not because you coerced him into doing so."

Meesha looked tired. She rubbed her forehead. "I know you're right, Zee, but I'm at my wit's end. I've been praying and reading Scripture, and nothing seems to help. I love Edward, but I can no longer play second fiddle to his career." She zipped her coat and put a scarf over her head.

"I hear you, but you know what we're supposed to do with our problems, don't you?"

"What do you mean?" Meesha asked wearily. She put the strap of her purse on her shoulder.

"Turn it over to the Lord," Zora said. "When I'm feeling down and in need of solace, I recite First Corinthians 16:13–14." Zora closed her eyes. 'Watch, stand fast in the faith, be brave, be strong. Let all that you do be done with love.'"

Meesha shook her head vehemently and clasped her hand over her breast as if she was mortally wounded. "You don't know what I had to go through to get Edward to attend the meeting. God forgive me, I was ruthless and didn't take any prisoners. Zora, what am I doing?" Meesha asked in a hollow tone of voice.

"It will be all right, girlfriend. Take your burdens to Jesus and leave them there," Zora said. "I'll pray for the Lord to give you strength."

The women walked to the parking lot. Meesha got into the car with Edward, and they waited for Zora to leave, then departed for home. The tension in the car was thick enough to cut with a knife.

Meesha peeped at Edward. It was obvious he wasn't happy since the vein in the side of his neck pulsated like a beating heart. She closed her eyes and laid her head against the headrest. "I think the meeting went well considering it was the first one."

Edward didn't respond. His car phone rang. Meesha looked down at it and saw the name Mac. He pressed the ignore button and the call went to voice mail. Edward looked in his rearview mirror and changed lanes.

Newly fallen snow blanketed Chicago. The city looked like an Alpine town.

"Thanks for coming to the meeting, Edward. I mean it," Meesha said meekly.

"Well the suitcases you had packed and sitting near the door when I left this morning were a strong indication that I didn't have a choice in the matter," Edward remarked as he glanced at Meesha and then back out the windshield. "Where did you think you were going? And why would you go to such lengths to ensure I come to the meeting?"

"Because I love you, Edward, and I used any means necessary to make sure you came to the meeting. I keep telling you that I'm tired of being in a marriage alone, and I'm not backing down on that fact. I will either be with you and we'll be partners in this marriage as we promised to do on our wedding day, or I'll go my way. I need you to give me and the kids more of your time, or I'll go stay with my parents." Meesha sat up in her seat and looked at Edward. She pulled the hem of her dress over her knees, and her body shook.

"Woman, why can't you understand that I'm in the middle of critical negotiations and software rollouts? Our future rides on a successful outcome of the company's new venture. I don't see why you don't understand how important my job is to me, and everything that I do is for you and the kids."

"I don't think so, Edward." Meesha snorted indignantly as she pointed her finger at Edward. "I think you're just feeding that ego of yours. What's the point of you earning a six-figure salary and bonuses if you can't be there to enjoy it with us? Keon had a play Monday, and you told him that you couldn't make it. Do you know how your absence made him feel? Do you even care?" Meesha folded her arms against her chest and glared at her husband.

Edward said impatiently, "I couldn't get away from the office twice in one week. I could either make his play or the session tonight. I'm not a total cad, Meesha. My priorities are straight. I need you to work with me and stop nagging me. God, I feel like I can't breathe sometimes. I am under enormous pressure at work to succeed. Why can't you just be quiet sometimes and let me have peace? The last thing I want to hear when I come home from work is you nagging me about something I should have done and didn't."

Edward had turned the car onto their block and steered the car in front of their house. Meesha swallowed back tears. She felt like David fighting Goliath when it came to dealing with Edward. She noticed Edward hadn't shut off the car. "Aren't you coming in?"

"No, I have to go back to the office," Edward replied, looking out the window. He refused to look at his wife.

"See, this is what I mean," Meesha snapped. She removed her seatbelt and got out of the vehicle. By the time she unlocked the front door, Edward had pulled off and was heading down the street.

She went inside the house, into the den, and put on a happy face when she greeted the children and her mother. Sabrina was babysitting the children while the couple attended the meeting. It was Sabrina's suggestion that she drop Meesha off at the church. Sabrina hoped time alone after the meeting would help the couple work on their problems. By the time Meesha returned home, Sabrina had given the children baths, and they had on their nightclothes. Meesha talked with them for a while, and then sent the children to their rooms to go to bed.

Meesha's mother asked her daughter where Edward was, and Meesha explained with a scowl on her face that he had returned to work. After her mother left to go home, Meesha went to check on the children and then into her bedroom. She closed the door, got down on her knees beside the bed, and looked upward. "Lord, what ticks me off is how Edward refuses to work with me. He could have stayed home with me. As much as I complain about not having quality time with him, what does he do but go back to work? What am I going to do now? Help me, Jesus."

Her forehead creased with wrinkles, and her eyes closed tightly together. Finally, she rose from the floor and prepared for bed. Tomorrow was another day. Before she fell asleep, Meesha consoled herself with the thought that at least Edward had come to the meeting.

Chapter Twelve

Douglas and his family were nearly home after their first Couples' Therapy session. Julia, Brandon, and Erin stared blankly out the car windows into the starry night, while Douglas kept his eyes firmly on the road, checking for patches of ice. "I enjoyed the meeting. I thought it went well. What about you all? What do you think?" He glanced in the backseat through his rear-view mirror and then back at the road.

"It felt like being in school to me," Brandon commented. "I meant to ask Miss Zora if me and Erin could work on the questionnaire together as a team."

Erin yawned. "It was fine." She looked at her husband and shook her head. "I don't think answering the questions together is an option, or else Miss Zora would have said so." Her mouth gaped open again, and she quickly covered it. "Oh, I'm sorry. Excuse me, I'm tired."

Erin had a Southern drawl, which Julia called a redneck accent when she was alone with Douglas. Julia ignored the fact that traces of her African heritage were apparent in her speech when she became excited or agitated.

"What did you think, Doll?" Douglas asked Julia.

Erin giggled from the backseat. "I just love to hear yo' daddy call your mama Doll. I think it's so sweet." She caressed her stomach. "Since Brandon and I are having a girl, maybe we could call her Baby Doll instead of Doll

Baby like Papa Doug calls you sometimes." She inhaled loudly. "She kicked me hard that time. Feel it, Brandon." She guided Brandon's hand to her abdomen.

"That was a sharp kick," Brandon nodded. "Maybe she'll be a jock like me and my Pops."

Julia rolled her eyes, silently mimicking her daughter-in-law. Then she said to her husband, "Oh, I don't know, Doug. I'm still not comfortable with the whole thing. I still don't see the sense in discussing your business in public."

Douglas reached over and patted Julia's leg. "Give it time and you'll see why." He made a left turn into the alley and parked the car in their garage. Everyone trudged silently through the newly fallen snow to the back stairway and into the house. Douglas opened the door and turned on the light in the kitchen. "I guess one of us will have to shovel the snow," he said to Brandon.

Julia and Erin removed their coats and placed them in the hall closet.

"I'll do it," Brandon volunteered. He went back outside to the garage.

"Well, I'm going to bed," Erin said to Douglas and Julia. "I feel so wiped out. Good night." She walked to the basement door and opened it. "I'll see you in the morning," she told the elder couple.

"Are you feeling all right?" Douglas asked the young woman solicitously as he removed his coat and hung it in the closet. "Maybe you and Brandon should sleep upstairs tonight."

"No, Papa Doug, that's all right. I don't want to put you and Mama Jules to no trouble. I feel okay, just sleepy."

"Okay, if you're sure then. The option is available any time you want to sleep up here." Douglas nodded at Erin. "Good night."

Julia and Douglas heard Brandon walking outside and then the roar of the snow blower. "I would have thought he would have shoveled and not used the snow blower. There's not that much snow outside," Douglas observed as he and Julia walked to their bedroom.

Julia went to her vanity and sat in the white cushioned seat. She took a couple of cotton balls and a pad out of the box on top of the mirrored vanity, and began removing makeup from her face. Douglas went to the walk-in closet, removed his clothes, and changed into a pair of pajamas.

After Julia had removed the makeup from her face, she took a gold clip from her hair and spongy curls sprang free. She had a disturbed look on her face when she turned around and looked at Doug. "Why did you tell Erin that she and Brandon could sleep up here?"

Doug walked over to Julia and kissed the top of her head. "You're tense. Relax. Your body feels like a piece of stone." He caressed the top of her shoulders and then began massaging them. "Because she isn't well, Doll, and I'm worried about her. It wouldn't hurt us to keep a closer eye on her. God knows Brandon is completely clueless about what lies ahead for him. I can picture him fainting in the delivery room."

The two chuckled. Then their mood turned somber. They were both thinking about their deceased baby girl. Julia had been pregnant with a daughter they named Nia two years after she gave birth to Brandon.

One minute, Julia was doing fine, and then a few minutes later, blood began spewing from her body like a geyser. Her blood pressure shot up dangerously high, and Doug had to call 911. He was frantic with worry. Losing the baby was one of the low points of the couple's life. Afterward, Julia was diagnosed with preeclampsia. The main symptom is heavy bleeding, high blood pressure, and certain complications can cause death to mother and child, if the placenta deattaches from the uterine wall. Julia and Doug's baby girl was stillborn, and Julia had an emergency hysterectomy.

Douglas and Julia had planned to have three children. Julia felt guilty after Nia's death and kept her feelings bottled up, whereas Douglas relied on his faith in God to get through the crisis. Every year on Memorial Day, they placed flowers on little Nia's grave. They laid her to rest with Doug's deceased relatives.

A tinge of guilt rushed through Julia's being when she realized that perhaps her husband's actions toward Erin were prompted by past events. She turned around and took Douglas's hands in her own. "I'm so sorry, Doug, that we couldn't have more children. Maybe we should have adopted." She dropped her head.

"I told you everything that happens is a part of God's plan. He decided to bless us with Brandon, so how could I have any regrets? I just think we should be careful about Erin's health and try to be more considerate of her feelings. Her parents haven't called her once since she moved here."

"I'll try, Doug. I promise." Julia stood up and flung her arms around Douglas's neck. His arms snaked around her waist. The two stood together that way for quite some time, lost in their memories. Later they retired to bed.

In the basement, Brandon sat on a chair in a partitioned-off area away from the bedroom. He called the room his recording studio. He had the best equipment money could buy, having used most of his salary to purchase the digitized system. Douglas felt Brandon should pay a stipend for living at home, but Julia disagreed, feeling it was obscene to charge their only child rent. Brandon looked like an alien wearing the headphones on his head. His body swayed to the beat of a recording that he'd made.

Erin waddled into the room and sat down heavily on the sagging couch. Brandon didn't see her enter. She called his name, and finally stood up, walked in front of him, and waved her hands. Brandon took the headphones off. "What's up?"

"I feel lonely and want to talk," she answered morosely, flipping a long blond braid over her shoulder.

Brandon flipped a switch to turn off the music; then he and Erin walked over to the couch and sat down. "Dang, girl, you getting big as the Goodyear blimp," he teased.

"Brandon," Erin wailed as her face reddened. "That's not funny. What did you really think about the meeting tonight and why do you think your mom wanted us to go?" She held out her hands and looked at her fingers, which resembled sausage links to her. "Yuck," she said, dropping her hands. "My hands and fingers are so fat."

"Oh, you can talk about yourself, and I can't?" Brandon joked. He lifted a braid off her neck and dropped it.

"What's up with your mom?" Erin repeated. She was determined not to let Brandon change the subject.

"Hmm." Brandon squinted his eyes, then rubbed his chin thoughtfully. "Truthfully, I think she did it to punish us."

Erin did a double take. Her mouth dropped open as she stared at her husband. "What do you mean punish *us*? No, the truth is that she wants to punish *me*. That's what I think. Your mother hates me." She folded her arms on the top of her abdomen.

"No, my mom is a living testament to the saying 'misery loves company.' My dad tries to keep the peace, and he pretty much lets her have her way. Whatever Mom wants she gets. I bet Mom didn't want to go to those sessions and Dad forced her hand, so now we all have to suffer with her."

"So everything is my fault, isn't it?" Erin sniffled. She rubbed her nose. "Your mother hates me."

"No, that's not true. It just takes her time to warm up to people," Brandon fibbed. "Dad just wants us all to get along, and he feels if someone else besides him tells Mom that, then it will work out better for all of us in the long run. Mom, well, she's just Mom. She has some funny ways. I think it's because she was born in Africa."

Erin began crying. "Oh, Brandon, yo' mama hates me. I have just totally wrecked your life. She probably hates the baby too." She covered her reddened face. Her hormones had kicked into high gear.

Brandon took her hands away from her face and drew her into his arms. "Naw, that's not true. I think in a way Mom is looking forward to being a grandma. Whatever issues she has aren't your fault." He clumsily patted her back. "Come on now, Erin, don't cry. You're supposed to stay upbeat and positive, so we won't have a sad, crying baby. At least that's what Grandma told me. Please don't cry." He held his wife in his arms and tried his best to comfort Erin, who sobbed nonstop. Later she returned to their bedroom, and Brandon continued mixing his rap tape.

At the Howard home, Beverly and Kenneth were lying in the bed watching *CSI: Miami*. Kenneth knew Beverly was itching to talk to him, and she was waiting for the show to end in five minutes.

As soon as the credits started to roll, Beverly let loose with a mild tirade. "Kenneth Howard, if you ever embarrass me by talking about our children like that, I'll . . . I'll . . ."

"You'll what, Beverly?" Kenneth had a stern look on his face as he tried to hold in the torrent of laughter that threatened to spill from his mouth. He put his hand over his mouth to hide a smile. Beverly always looked cute to him when she was upset. She looked like a spoiled child.

"I don't know what I'll do. Kenny, I felt so humiliated, like I'm a bad mother or something." She moaned dramatically as she rolled her eyes upward.

"Truthfully, the problem we have in the house isn't about you or me, Bev. It's past time for Amir to have grown up and assumed responsibility for his life. I do know that if it was left up to you, he'd still be your baby with rheumatic fever the rest of his life, unable to do for himself because he knows you'll take care of him. You need someone besides me to tell you about your son."

"It was unfair of you to talk about him like that in front of strangers," Beverly shot back. "He was sick when he was a baby." Beverly poked her lips out. She rose from the bed and walked to the dresser and took a plastic bag of pink foam curlers off the top of it. When she returned to the bed, Beverly sat on the side, leaned across the nightstand, and opened the top drawer to remove a comb and brush.

"Wait a minute." Kenneth scooted over to where Beverly was sitting. He took the brush from her hand and positioned his body behind his wife. With gentle strokes, Kenneth brushed his wife's hair.

Beverly melted against her husband's chest. It felt good to her to spend quiet time with Kenny. Beverly realized her husband was a good man, but he was like a bulldog when it came to Amir. Beverly surmised that Kenneth was ashamed of their son's shortcomings and that he couldn't love Amir unconditionally. She remembered how reserved Kenny was with Amir when he met the boy for the first time when Amir was five years old. He and Kenneth just didn't mesh well at all.

Beverly had doubts about the relationship between her beau and son during the couple's courtship, but Kenneth hung in there and wooed his ladylove. Eventually Amir came around.

Then a few months into Kenneth and Beverly's marriage, when Amir was five years old, the boy became ill with rheumatic fever. During and after his recovery period, the dynamics of the household changed. Beverly became like a lioness protecting her child, and the results were dire as far as Kenny was concerned. He watched his wife slave over their son day and night. It seemed if Amir snapped his fingers or coughed, Beverly went running. It didn't help that Amir later developed asthma.

When Amir was eight years old, Kenneth caught the boy faking an illness. Amir was in his bedroom dancing about the room whooping it up. When Kenneth confronted the boy about his duplicity, Amir's eyes grew wide as saucers; then with an angelic expression on his face he calmly walked back to the bed and laid down.

Amir explained in a grave voice that a miracle had occurred and that God had healed him like in the Bible stories his mommy read to him. Then he began shedding crocodile tears and screamed for Beverly. She ran into the room and found Amir clutching his chest. He said it felt tight. Those words sent Beverly in a mad dash to the bathroom for Amir's inhaler and later she called her son's pediatrician.

Later when Kenneth tried to tell Beverly what he had seen, she immediately took her son's side. Though Kenny loved Amir, after that night he never really liked him much.

Kenneth reached out and massaged Beverly's scalp. She flattened her body against his and purred like a kitten

"Mmm, that feels good," she murmured. "If you weren't employed by the post office, you could have worked in a hair salon, Kenny," Beverly said softly. "I admit Amir has some problems, but putting him out of the house wouldn't do any good. Please bear with me."

"That is a subject that we'll have to agree to disagree on," Kenneth said. "So let's make a pact from this day forth that we'll be open to the suggestions that Dr. Taylor and Reverend Nixon give us regarding Amir." Kenneth looked pleadingly at Beverly while she stared back at him with resignation in her soft, dark brown eyes.

Kenneth continued speaking. "We have to turn this situation over to God and be submissive to what He wants us to do. We are never really in control of our lives, our heavenly Father always is. With all that said, I think we'll be fine if we remember that."

"I know you're right, but I'm so afraid of what might happen to Amir if he's out in the world without a job or money. Jalin needs his daddy. Other people in this family will be impacted if you put our son out," Beverly said as she moved her body away from her husband. She laid down in the bed and Kenney followed suit. Beverly's gold nightgown flowed across the sea blue and pink floral comforter.

Kenny took Beverly's hand. "Lord, give us strength for what lies ahead. We don't know what's going to happen to Amir. We take comfort in knowing that you promised never to leave us alone any time, and I know that you won't. My wife is worried about our son. Please help her stop her worrying. We trust and love you, God, and know that you're the head of our life and you won't let us down. Amen."

"Amen," Beverly echoed. "Now get the Bible and the daily devotional guide." She pointed to Kenny's nightstand. "It's my turn to read tonight. Tomorrow is another day, and we'll face it when it comes."

Chapter Thirteen

Zora saved the Word document she had finished updating and looked across her desk at Jordan Brown, the tall, handsome star athlete of the academy's football team. Zora had scheduled an introductory meeting to learn Jordan's post-high school plans since he was graduating in June. She offered to help Jordan weed through the red tape of the college admissions process. She found him remarkably mature for his young age and enjoyed the discussion with him.

Zora smiled at the boy; then her smile faltered as she stared at Jordan's eyes. His boyish good looks coupled with a slim, lithe build and twinkling dark eyes. His hair was braided into an intricate pattern. Zora thought Jordan reminded her of someone from her past, but the idea was fleeting, and she quickly returned her attention to the present. "Okay, young man, we're done for now." She handed him a folder containing university documents she had printed out for him. When you get a chance, read these and schedule another meeting with me when you're done. How does that sound?"

Jordan stood up, grabbed his book bag from the floor, and shifted it from one hand to the other. "That sounds great, Dr. Taylor. Everyone keeps telling me how my college choice will affect my future and that I have to be careful. Even Reverend Nixon, my old mentor, says the same thing. I'm going to talk to him too,"

Jordan nodded. He strolled to the office door, opened it, turned around, and waved good-bye. "Have a good weekend."

"You too," Zora smiled at Jordan. After he left the room, Zora added paper to the HP printer sitting on a stand next to her desk and printed her notes from the meeting. When the printing was complete, Zora placed the documents inside a file she had created prior to her meeting with Jordan. Then she placed the file on the triple-tiered inbox on her desk for her secretary to file.

Zora's eyes wandered to the bonsai tree Calvin had given her as a welcome gift on her first day at the job. Her lips curved into a smile as she remembered her surprise at the minister's thoughtfulness. Zora touched the soil in the bottom of the pot, and it felt dry. She made a mental note to water it before she left work that afternoon.

The church had given Zora a stipend, which she supplemented with her own income to decorate her spacious, windowed office. She and Meesha went to the academy the week before Zora's start date and painted the office a warm olive green. The color created a cozy, inviting atmosphere that Zora hoped would put the students at ease.

Zora's many degrees were framed and hung on the wall closest to the door. A two-cushion, plume-colored microfiber couch and matching chair faced each other on opposite walls. A small, rectangular table and four chairs rested on the other wall. Zora's desk and a smaller file cabinet were placed near the window.

She buzzed her secretary. "Tiffany, how long do I have until my next appointment?"

"Half an hour, Dr. Taylor," the young woman answered. She adjusted the headset atop her head.

"Okay, let me know when Rolanda Harris, my next appointment arrives." Zora looked down at the file spread open on her desk.

"Will do, boss." The woman disconnected the call.

Zora placed the telephone receiver back into the base. She spun in the swivel chair, and when it stopped Zora was facing the window.

Friendship Christian Academy conducted classes for students in kindergarten through twelfth grade. The school had been founded seven years ago and was the brainchild of First Lady Laura Dudley. She had been employed as a chief area officer for Chicago Public Schools until she took an early retirement to work in the church and academy full time.

The school boasted small class sizes, and the teachers on staff were Christians committed to spiritual and academic excellence. Most of the students in the academy were members of the church. Every year, the church sponsored an open house in the community to recruit new students.

Zora smiled as she looked down at the copy of the questionnaire she and Calvin had created for the next couples' therapy session:

1) Name three things about your spouse that you consider pleasing in your eye and the Lord's.

2) Name three things about your spouse that would try the patience of Job.

3) Select a scripture that you think best describes the state of marriage or love.

*Be prepared to discuss all three in a dignified Christian manner.

Zora chuckled every time she looked at the paper and saw how Calvin put a nice, spiritual spin on the questionnaire. The second session was scheduled for that evening. It was four o'clock P.M., and Zora's workday ended in an hour. She usually stayed at school since it was located across the street from the church. She had put a hefty down payment on a condominium in Kenwood, an up-and-coming community adjacent to Hyde Park. The condo she'd purchased was one of the properties she'd visited when Calvin had driven her to the realty office. The church was located in Chatham, forty minutes from Kenwood, and it made sense for Zora to stay at school after work instead of traveling back and forth.

Zora and Reverend Nixon had developed a friendly relationship that Calvin felt had the potential to develop into something more substantial, if he had his way. Zora supposed their chemistry was because of the passion they shared for the sessions, although she admitted only to herself that she enjoyed Calvin's companionship and witty conversation. He had contributed great ideas for the sessions, and Zora was pleased that they were able to work so well together.

Zora had been celibate since high school. She had been in a life-altering situation during her teen years, and though she dated sporadically, Zora shied away from meaningful relationships with the opposite sex. Somehow Calvin had managed to break down the barriers around her heart, and that piqued her interest in him.

The telephone on her dark wooden desk buzzed. Zora picked up the receiver. "Yes, Tiffany?"

"Reverend Nixon is here, and he'd like to know if you're available." Tiffany couldn't keep the excitement out of her voice. She hoped the guidance counselor and the minister would make a love match. Tiffany thought they made a cute couple. Tiffany also surmised correctly that the minister had more than a professional interest in the good doctor. Reverend Nixon called Zora frequently at work, and Tiffany answered his calls. She assumed they weren't all business-related. The young secretary also didn't miss the soft look on Zora's face when she talked to or about Reverend Nixon.

Zora's left hand moved to her hair, and she hoped her lipstick was still intact. Zora unconsciously finger combed her unruly locks. "Sure. Send him in. Thank you, Tiffany."

Zora hung up the phone and tried to squash the somersaults pummeling her midsection. She stood up and smoothed down the slimming navy blue mid-length skirt she was wearing, and pulled a piece of dark lint from her white angora sweater. She sat back down in the chair. When she heard a loud rap at her office door, she said anxiously, "Come in."

"Good afternoon, Miss Zora. How are you doing this blessed day?" Calvin asked. The dimples in Calvin's cheeks seemed to play hide-and-seek with Zora. He walked over to Zora's desk. She stood up, and he engulfed her body in a quick hug.

"I'm doing well," Zora replied trying to keep her voice from trembling. She sat down, crossed her legs, and gestured toward the chair sitting in front of her desk. "Have a seat. What brings you here early today?" She glanced at her watch. "Therapy doesn't start for another few hours."

Calvin removed his coat and placed it on the back of the chair. A green and navy blue wool scarf was draped around his neck. He sat down. "I decided to play hooky from work." Calvin's orthodontist-straightened teeth gleamed as he smiled mischievously at Zora. "Actually, I had some errands to run and only worked half a day today. I thought I'd stop by the church to see if you'd like to have an early supper with me before the session starts."

"Well"—Zora brushed her hair off her face—"I wish you had said something earlier. I brought dinner with me. I'd planned to stay in and read a book or work until the session starts."

"I know whatever you brought for dinner can't taste as good as the Creole meal I have in mind. There's a good restaurant located in Lansing that I dine at from time to time, and it's not too far from the church. Surely, whatever you brought with you can wait for another day." Calvin learned forward in the chair as he presented his plan to Zora.

"Is that a fact?" Zora said playfully, though her stomach felt like it was doing backstrokes. "The weather is a little iffy today. You're welcome to share my dinner with me. I don't have anything as fancy as Creole cuisine; still, it's edible."

"Great," Calvin grinned. "That will be fine. Are you sure you have enough for both of us?"

Zora pushed her seat away from the desk. She walked over to the file cabinet and took out a plastic bag. "Definitely, I have more than enough. I always cook enough food to feed an army and freeze leftovers. I might be a bit biased, but I think I make the best chili this side of Texas. I have a package of oyster crackers and a thermos of lemonade. How does that grab you?

Calvin stood up. "I'll take you up on that chili. I know you won't be off work for a little while. I have some chores to do at the church." He glanced down at his watch. "I'll meet you back here in an hour or so."

Zora smiled. She picked up a pen off her desk. "You have a deal. See you later." Zora waved as Calvin left her office. She resumed working.

The young minister returned to Zora's office fifty-five minutes later. By then Tiffany had departed for the day. Calvin stood in the doorway watching Zora admiringly.

Zora had set up the table in her office for dinner. Two white Spode bowls along with silver spoons and crystal glasses adorned the table, which was covered with a lacy white tablecloth. Meesha had given her the upscale picnic basket as an office warming gift. Meesha advised her friend to be prepared for anything, even a dinner meeting. Packages of oyster crackers sat in the middle of the table. As Zora tidied her desk, she looked up to see Calvin staring at her. She smiled and motioned for him to come inside the office. Then she stood and walked over to the table. "Your timing is perfect. My tummy has notified me many times that it's time for me to eat," she remarked lightly.

Calvin's left hand was hidden behind his back as he walked over to the table. He presented Zora with a bouquet of pink, yellow, and white lilies.

Her eyes widened with pleasure. "Calvin, you shouldn't have." She took the bouquet from him, brought it to her nose, and sniffed. "They smell wonderful. Thank you," she said shyly.

She walked over to the cabinet and took a crystal vase out of the bottom drawer. "Give me a minute to fill the vase with water. I'll be right back." Zora left her office. She returned a few minutes later and put the flowers inside the vase. She set the flowers in the middle of the table, then stepped back and looked at the arrangement appreciatively. "Again, thank you. Lilies are one of my favorite flowers."

"It was my pleasure." He pulled out a chair for Zora, and she sat down. Calvin sat across the table from her in the other chair.

Zora carefully spooned chili into both the bowls, ever conscious of Calvin sitting a few feet away from her. He poured lemonade into the glasses. Calvin blessed the food.

Thirty minutes later they had completed the meal. Calvin wiped his mouth with a napkin. "Zora, the chili was great. You can add cooking to your long list of skills."

"Thank you, Calvin. I hate to admit this, but chili and spaghetti are my specialties. I'm not a gourmand, as you claim to be. But when it comes down to my favorites, I like to think that I can throw down with the best of them."

"Good job to the cook. I'm looking forward to the session tonight. What about you?" Calvin asked her as he leaned back in his chair.

"I think it will be interesting to say the least. I think we have a good group of people facing a myriad of issues. They run the gamut of ages and issues, and that usually makes for a lively discussion," Zora said. She took a sip of lemonade.

"I agree," Calvin replied. "The questions should generate dialogue." He glanced down at his watch. "Speaking of the meeting, we should probably go to the meeting room and begin setting up."

Zora waved her hand. "Why don't you go ahead? I want to rinse the dishes. I'll meet you there in a few minutes."

"Okay," Calvin replied as he stood up. "See you shortly."

Zora watched his retreating figure. She clasped her hands together and expelled a loud sigh. She stood up and began clearing off the table. Zora looked up to see Meesha standing at her door. "Hey, how are you doing?"

Meesha walked inside the office. "I'm okay. I had a difficult day at work, so I'm a little out of sorts." She unzipped her down coat. "And it's cold outdoors. Today just hasn't been my day," she complained as she took off her coat.

"Well, it can only get better at this point. We have a few minutes to chat before the session begins." Zora stacked the bowls on top of each other. "I'm going to the kitchen to rinse out these dishes, and then I'll be back." She avoided Meesha's probing eyes.

When Zora returned to her office, she put the bowls inside the top drawer of the cabinet. Meesha was sitting at the table eying the flowers. Zora walked over and sat with her friend.

"So, Dr. Taylor, tell me, who are the flowers from?" Meesha asked pointing at the floral arrangement. "Do you have an admirer I don't know about? Don't tell me you've been holding out on me?" Meesha couldn't resist teasing her friend.

"They are from Calvin." Zora elongated the *vin* in Reverend Nixon's name.

"Do I sense a courtship brewing?" Meesha's eyebrows rose dramatically as she stared at her friend.

"No, we're just friends," Zora replied evasively. She looked out the window instead of at Meesha.

"Please," Meesha sputtered, holding up her hand. "Tell that to someone else. I noticed the looks Reverend Nixon gave you during our planning sessions and at the meeting last week. Hmmm, this could be a love match in the making." She couldn't resist ribbing Zora about the minister. Meesha alone knew the issues Zora had when it came to dealing with the opposite sex.

"Now, you know you're wrong for saying that," Zora scolded her friend with a telltale red face. "There's nothing going on with me and Calvin."

"I think the lady doth protest too much," Meesha retorted as Zora walked over to her desk and began straightening it up. She put pens and pencils inside her desk drawer. She and Meesha chatted until Zora completed her end-of-day chores. Then they headed to the meeting room to prepare for the evening's session.

Chapter Fourteen

By 6:55 P.M., the group had filed into the meeting room with the exception of Edward. Meesha had called him a couple of times, and her calls went to voice mail.

At seven o'clock, Calvin called the meeting to order and said the opening prayer. Everyone took his seat around the circle, leaving a spot vacant for Edward in case he made it to the meeting.

Meesha uncrossed her legs, reached down, and took her tote bag from the floor. She removed the questionnaire from it. She had just put the bag back on the floor when Edward rushed into the room.

"Sorry I'm late," he said to the group as he took a brown fedora off his head and removed his outer garment. "Traffic was heavy coming from downtown." He glanced at his wife as he sat in the vacant seat next to hers. His cell phone rang. Edward pulled it out of his pocket, glanced at the phone, stood, and said, "Excuse me, I have to take to this call." He then left the room.

"How has everyone's week been thus far?" Zora asked by way of opening up the meeting. They all said the week had been going well. "Did everyone have a chance to finish the questions for this week's meeting?" Zora looked around the circle. Everyone nodded. "Did anyone have any problems with the assignment?" Zora asked. The group shook their heads.

"I . . . um . . . wondered if we could have worked on the questions together?" Brandon asked tentatively.

He had forgotten to take his hoodie off. Julia leaned over and whispered to him to remove it. "Sorry," he mumbled as he pushed it off his head.

"I swear, he acts like he doesn't have any home training sometimes," Julia complained helplessly to the group.

"You will have the opportunity to work together as the sessions progress," Zora said. "So who wants to go first?"

There weren't any volunteers. Heads were bowed as the group looked at the questionnaire one last time.

"Erin, why don't you start tonight's discussion?" Zora suggested.

Erin's voice squeaked as she said, "Me?"

"Yes, why not?" Zora smiled encouragingly at Erin.

"Well," Erin began as she looked down at her paper. "The things about Brandon that would try Job's patience is, one, he doesn't pick up behind himself. He leaves his clothes lying around like I'm his maid or something."

Julia humphed loudly when she heard Erin say that. She folded her arms across her chest.

"Secondly," Erin went on, pushing her braids out of her face, "he doesn't seem to be as happy as I am about the baby. Sometimes he won't go to the clinic with me." The young woman rubbed her tummy. "And last, he won't help me clean up our part of the house. You know what I mean, the bedroom or bathroom. And look at me."

Brandon's eyes grew large with astonishment. He looked at Erin as if she were an alien who had just been beamed down to earth. "Duh, I have a job, and I'm trying to make it in the music industry, and you want me to help you clean up? Please," he said snidely.

Zora glanced at Brandon. "Let's try to be courteous and hold all comments until later," she cautioned the young man.

"Man, I don't believe this," he muttered under his breath.

Julia pulled on her son's arm and shook her head warningly.

"Now, tell us, what's pleasing in God's sight about your husband," Zora asked Erin.

Erin smiled, glanced at Brandon, and said, "That's easy. He has a great sense of humor. He makes me laugh. He can make such silly faces. Sometimes I feel homesick, at least for my best friend from back home, and Brandon will do something silly to cheer me up. Secondly, he rubs my feet." She looked down at the floor. "My feet swell up if I stay on them too long because of the baby. And, last, even though I know his mama don't like me a lot" Erin stole a peek at Julia—"Brandon tries to explain to me why she doesn't, and he supports me."

Julia's mouth flew open; then she stared at her son and daughter-in-law with enmity in her eyes. "I know you didn't say that. Not here in public with all these people around." She pointed her finger in Erin's face.

Douglas suppressed a grin as he watched his family with interest. *At least they're talking about the problems. Thank God for that,* he thought. He leaned over and patted Julia's arm

"Julia," Zora firmly admonished the older woman, "please refrain from making comments." She turned her attention back to the younger woman. "Erin, you didn't give us a Bible verse that describes love or marriage. What do you have?"

"I'm sorry, ma'am," Erin drawled. "I don't know the Bible too well. I didn't go to church much back home.

I didn't like the church my mama and daddy went to.
I like going to service at Friendship though. I'm sorry,
I don't have a verse. I don't have a Bible." The young
woman dropped her head, ashamed.

"I understand," Zora nodded. "Next time ask for
help, okay?"

"Yes, ma'am." Erin said, clearly relieved.

"Okay," Zora said. Her eyes lit on Erin's husband.
"Let's move on. Mr. Brandon, what do you have for
us?"

Brandon pulled a crumpled piece of paper from his
pocket. Julia frowned at him. "What?" He asked his
mother, shrugging his shoulders. He looked down at
his list and said, "One good thing about Erin is that she
listens to me. I mean really listens. Two, she shares my
dream of me making it big as a rapper, unlike some
people." His eyes darted to his mother. "And her final
good trait is that she's gonna have my baby." Brandon
reached over and caressed Erin's belly.

"Boy . . ." Julia stopped herself from saying that's not
what Dr. Taylor meant.

Brandon continued speaking. "Her worst traits are
that she can't cook. I think she's a little lazy because
as my wife, Erin should clean up, and that includes
my stuff too. Last, she gets real emotional sometimes.
We'll watch a movie, and the next thing I know, she's
boo-hooing." He imitated Erin crying and everyone
laughed, even Erin.

"Okay," Zora said. "I know you have a Bible verse for
us. Let's hear it."

"Uh, my verse is taken from Ephesians 5:31: 'A man
leaves his father and mother and is joined to his wife,
and the two are united as one.'" Brandon looked at
Douglas, who smiled approvingly at his son, while Julia rolled her eyes. The young man took his wife's hand.

Julia thought, *Hmm, the operative word is leave. He and his wife are living at our house. Lord, give me patience tonight.*

"Very good," Zora said approvingly. "Good job. Now what do you two think that verse really means?"

"That a man should put his wife first in his life, even before his parents," Erin said smugly, glancing at Julia.

"After God, that is," Brandon chimed in.

Zora nodded. "Nice job. Erin, I have a Bible I'd like to give you tonight. You'll need it for the homework assignments."

"Thank you, Miss Zora," Erin said.

"Well, you could have borrowed one of ours," Julia couldn't help but tell her daughter-in-law. "There are plenty of Bibles at the house. Next time ask. Okay, Erin?"

Erin nodded and smiled, pleased with Zora's approval.

"Consider the Good Book my gift to Erin," Zora said. "Now who wants to be next?"

Kenny raised his hand in the air. "Me and Bev." The navy blue fleece shirt he had worn with a pair of jeans had ridden up over his stomach.

"That's fine." Zora wrote notes on a pad of paper that rested on her lap.

Beverly nervously twisted the straps of her brown leather purse. "I'll go first." She glanced at Kenny who nodded at her. "First of all, Kenny and I have been married a long time, and I can truly say that God has blessed me with a loving mate. So I was a little hard-pressed to find three things about him that would try the patience of Job."

"Say, who came up with that saying, trying the patience of Job?" Brandon asked Zora, interrupting Beverly. Julia looked at her son disapprovingly.

"Actually, Reverend Nixon did," Zora answered as she looked at the minister. "He thought it would be a good idea to inject some humor into the questions. I think that was a good idea."

The group nodded their agreement.

Meesha kept folding and unfolding her questionnaire apprehensively. Edward looked like he didn't want to be at the session and kept glancing at his watch.

"Well, like I was saying," Beverly continued, "Kenny is a good man. It was hard for me to come up with three things that irritate me, but I did my best." Beverly chuckled; then her expression became serious. She glanced down at the piece of paper she held in her hands. "Kenny can be so bullheaded about some subjects. He's stubborn with a capital 'S,' especially when it comes to our son, Amir. He complains too much about my spending habits, and sometimes his feet smell like they should be taken out with the garbage."

Everyone laughed at that last remark.

Beverly continued speaking when the laughter ceased. "I didn't have a hard time finding a scripture or verse that describes our marriage at all because I used part of the scripture to describe Kenny's good traits. My scripture is from a variation of First Corinthians thirteen, and it reads like this: 'Love is patient; love is kind and envies no one. Love is never boastful, nor conceited, nor rude; never selfish, not quick to take offense. There is nothing love cannot face; there is no limit to its faith, its hope, and endurance. In a word, there are three things that last forever: faith, hope, and love; but the greatest of them all is love.'

"Kenny's best traits are that he is patient, giving, and most of all, he shows his love for me." Beverly sighed and wiped her eyes. "When I read those words I think of my Kenny."

Kenneth's chest puffed out proudly. "I guess it's my turn," he announced. "Beverly is the best. She's supportive, and she has encouraged me to follow my dreams. I was offered a promotion at work and wasn't sure if I should take it. Beverly said that I should accept it, and picked up the slack at home when I had to work extra hours for a couple of months. My wife has provided us with a lovely home. I was an old bachelor when we got married, and my house reflected my unmarried state. Beverly turned my house into our home. Last, she has been a wonderful helpmate. We work together on most issues as a team."

Meesha peeked at Edward who gave Kenneth his undivided attention. Edward's interest was piqued when Kenneth mentioned his job.

"Good going, Kenny. Now on to the other traits," Zora interjected.

Kenneth licked his lips nervously. "I feel that Beverly has put the children's feelings over mine many times. I know how mothers are about their children, and at times she refuses to compromise when it comes to the kids. Bev will make a decision and run with it. Secondly, she spends too much money on trivial things. She has overdrawn our secondary checking account so often that I feel I should own stock in our bank. Last, I think she plays favorites between the children. I just want you to know, Bev, that I say these things out of love." Kenneth knew he was in for a tongue-lashing later.

Beverly looked away from her husband and put her left hand over her face to hide her embarrassment. On the one hand, she could understand Kenneth's thinking he was doing the right thing by opening up to the group. On the other hand, Beverly felt he was wrong to blurt out her shortcomings with no regard for her feelings. She looked down at the floor and spaced out. She zoned back in just in time to hear Kenneth begin discussing his Bible verse.

"My Bible verse was taken from John 15:9–12, and it reads like this: 'As the Father has loved me, so I have loved you; abide in my love. If you keep my command-ments, you will abide in my love; just as I have kept My Father's commandments and abide in His love. These things I have spoken to you so that My joy may be in you, and that your joy may be made full.'"

"Thank you, Kenneth and Beverly. Good job." Zora looked at Edward, "Mr. Morrison, would you care to share your thoughts with us?"

Edward exaggeratedly unfolded his sheet of paper. "I always like bad news before the good. The last thing you hear makes a lasting impression. Let me think. Things about Meesha that would try the patience of Job are: one, she nags too much. She's like a dog with a bone; she won't let go. Two, she isn't supportive of my job. And three, she can be too controlling at times."

Meesha had joined Beverly in the humiliation club, and she could hardly wait for her turn to speak.

He glanced down at the paper again. "Meesha's posi-tive attributes are that she has done an excellent job raising our children. Two, we have a lovely home. And last, she can burn in the kitchen. Meesha is a wonderful cook. The scripture I choose is from Ephesians 5:22–23: 'Wives submit yourselves unto your own husbands as unto the Lord.'" Edward had an arrogant sneer on his face as Meesha sat in her chair woodenly, as if she couldn't believe what she'd just heard.

Zora felt sorry for her friend. She knew the sessions were not going exactly as Meesha would have hoped, and Meesha looked like she was about to cry.

"Thank you, Edward," Zora said. "Why don't we take a break, then we'll come back and finish up with Meesha, Douglas, and Julia."

The group rose from their seats. The men congregated at the refreshments table, while Beverly and Julia went to the ladies' room. Brandon and Erin stood off to the side and spoke in low tones. Meesha sat in her seat fumbling in her tote bag, trying to regain her composure. She knew the women were probably in the bathroom gossiping about Edward's comments.

Everyone returned to his or her seat ten minutes later. "Meesha, you're up," Zora informed her friend.

"Okay." Meesha's smile was forced. She cleared her throat a couple of times. "One of Edward's positive traits is that he is a great provider; we never lack for material things. He's a good father, when he's around. Before he rose to his current status on the corporate ladder, Edward coached the Little League baseball team in our community. Lastly, he is extremely smart, and if I need an answer to a question, I can go to Edward, the walking encyclopedia.

"Edward's traits that leave much to be desired are he doesn't know how to balance his time in what I consider a healthy manner; he doesn't spend enough time with me or the children. He can be argumentative at times. Last, his arrogance or ego overshadows his good traits. My scripture was also taken from the book of Ephesians 5: 25: 'Husbands, love your wife, even as Christ also loved the church and gave himself for it.'"

Zora nodded at Douglas and Julia. Then Douglas nodded for Julia to go first.

Though Julia held the piece of paper in her hand, she didn't read from it. "Douglas is very gallant. He compliments me on a regular basis and opens doors for me. That includes the doors to our house, the car door, and when we enter or leave a building. My husband is business-oriented. He owns different diverse companies. He knows the art of compromise and communication. We rarely go to bed angry with each other. Douglas prefers to talk through our issues." Julia peered at her husband, and love shone in her eyes. "I used the same scripture as Beverly did. I guess great minds think alike." Julia looked at Beverly and tittered.

"Douglas's traits that try my patience are that he is too methodical sometimes. Douglas can analyze an issue to death. I think he babies Brandon at times. Last, I think he keeps things from me so I won't get upset about them. I think he tries to protect me from negative situations, and it's not necessary."

"Good points," Zora said. "Mr. Freeman, let's hear from you."

"Sure," Douglas said. He pushed his glasses back on his nose, as they had slipped down. "One of Julia's traits that can try Job's patience is that she can be a snob at times. Julia can be very opinionated, but if you can explain your position in a logical manner, she may come around to your way of thinking. I think Julia feels guilty about the death of our infant daughter. I wish she'd let go of the emotion and accept the good things we've experienced in life.

"When I saw Julia all those years ago, she was the most beautiful woman I'd ever seen in my life, and she still is. Her beauty, both inner and outer, is one of her best assets. She is giving of herself and volunteers her time for many charitable organizations. Last, she is my best friend. I can talk to her about anything because Julia is indeed my soul and helpmate. The scripture that comes to mind when I think about my lovely wife is Ecclesiastes 4:9–10, and it reads likes this: 'Two are better than one; because they have a good reward for their labour. For if they fall, the one will lift up his fellow: but woe to him that is alone when he falleth; for he hath not another to help him up.'"

It pained Meesha to the depths of her very soul to hear the other men and women praise their spouses for what she considered meaningful traits instead of frivolous ones as she and Edward had.

"Very good," Zora extolled the group fervently. "Everyone did a great job on the assignment. I hope during the upcoming week, everyone reflects on the state of their marriages and how you can apply the scriptures you shared tonight to help resolve issues you may face. We all know that God is the head of our life, but what we fail to realize sometimes is how important communicating is to a successful marriage. There is *no* me, but we. Let's talk a little about Brandon and Erin's situation now, and then go over our assignments for next week."

Calvin interjected, "Do you think this is a good time for everyone to break out into groups? I thought at some point I could talk to the men and you the women."

"Good idea, but not just yet. We'll split into gender groups in later sessions."

Brandon and Erin looked apprehensive as they waited for Zora to speak.

"Relax," Zora chided them as she crossed her legs. "I promise this part of the session will be painless. What I'd like is for one of the older couples to share a memorable experience from when they first got married."

Brandon and Erin leaned back in their seats and sighed with relief.

"Oh, I can contribute here," Beverly smiled at the young couple. "As supportive as Kenny was and has been throughout our marriage, I had a problem with my sister-in-law, Emma. She didn't like me. I think she was a little bit jealous of my and Kenny's relationship. I prayed to the Lord for guidance for eight months and nothing happened."

"Aw, Bev, did you have to go into that?" Kenneth groaned as he leaned back into the chair. "That stuff happened a million years ago."

"Of course I do. Remember, we're sharing," Beverly said triumphantly as if she was getting back at her husband for his earlier comments. "I think because I already had a child by another man when Kenny and I married that Emma thought I was a gold digger."

"No way. So what did you do?" Erin asked Beverly, rapt in the conversation as she rubbed her abdomen. Brandon listened intently. He knew his mother acted at times like there was an invisible "GD" for gold digger tattooed on Erin's forehead.

"I took the high road and smothered her with kindness," Beverly replied complacently.

"Wasn't that hard to do?" Erin asked. Her eyes darted to Julia. The older woman was taking a breath mint out of her purse, pretending to be busy as she listened skeptically to Beverly.

"At first it was because I wanted to get up in her face and ask her, What is your problem? I'd complain to Kenny, and he'd say to give her time and that she would come around."

"And did she?" Erin couldn't stop herself from asking Beverly.

"Not for a very long time. . . . I think it took nearly a year. Finally I took matters into my own hands and went to visit Emma alone without Kenny." Beverly paused speaking to count on her fingers. "It was about nine months after Kenny and I were married. Emma and I sat down and talked, and I professed my love for Kenny. I asked her if the two of us could spend time together so she could get to know me better. Later, I invited her to our house so she could show me how to prepare Kenny's favorite meals. We went shopping together and out to lunch, just the two of us, and eventually her feelings for me began to change.

"Emma admitted she had preconceived notions about me being a single parent. After that we became inseparable, and to this day Emma is my favorite in-law."

Julia and Erin exchanged glances. Julia shrugged as if to say, We'll see. And Douglas squeezed her arm encouragingly. He had advised Julia all week to open up during the meetings and to be kinder to their daughter-in-law.

"I told Douglas I would try to do better by Erin, and I will." I'm just disappointed with Brandon's choices in life. This is not what I had in mind for him," Julia sighed aloud. She suffered from the green-eyed monster and felt displaced by Erin as the main woman in her son's life.

"I know the feeling," Kenneth whispered under his breath. Beverly poked him in the ribs.

"There is a reason for things happening the way they do, and we don't always understand why, but as Christians we should be still and let the Spirit guide us," Calvin added.

"I know," Julia opened up. "But I have a tendency to associate White people with the Boers, who oppressed South Africa for so long. I remember how many of my relatives were killed, and then I see Erin in my house and I remember what happened all those years ago." Julia looked ashamed. "I guess I'll have to pray for more patience and try not to let my past ruin my future." She stood and walked over to Erin and stretched out her arms. The two women hugged as the group clapped their approval.

Brandon stood up and waved one of his arms in a circular motion. He whistled loudly and shrilly, and sat back down.

"Sister Freeman, I have some scriptures that I'll e-mail you to help you overcome those feelings. Immediately, Romans 15:7 comes to mind. 'Accept one another then, just as Christ accepted you, in order to bring praise to God,'" Calvin recited.

"And Galatians 3:28, 'There is neither Jew nor Greek, slave nor free, male nor female, for you are all one in Christ Jesus,'" Zora added.

Calvin looked at Zora admiringly. He wrote the verse in his notepad, then added a note to himself to send the verses to Julia.

"Man, sometimes I feel so inadequate," Brandon admitted, looking miserable. "I feel like a failure sometimes. My dad is so successful. He's provided well for me and my mom and now my wife. I love rapping, though, because I can express my feelings. It's such a release."

"But will rapping pay the rent?" Edward threw out to the young man.

"Why didn't you just stay in school and play ball? Wouldn't that have made your future?" Kenneth asked Brandon.

"My dad thought it would be best if we came back home since Erin's folks have pretty much disowned her. Erin's pregnancy is a high-risk one. We headed back to Chi-Town. I took a job at UPS, and I work gigs on the weekends. I believe if I continue rapping, one day it will pay the rent." Brandon opened up to the group.

"That's whacked. You should still be playing ball and going to school," Edward commented. He shook his head pityingly at Brandon.

Meesha opened her mouth to protest, but Zora beat her to the punch. "Edward, we are not here to judge; instead we're here to help one another, so please refrain from negative comments."

"Sorry. " Edward's cell phone rang. "I'm going out to take this call."

Meesha watched her husband's retreating figure and bobbed her head up and down slowly. She thought, *Some things never change.*

"It seems to me, young man, that you two did the right thing," Kenneth said. "So many young couples find themselves in your predicament, and they get rid of the baby, or the girl has the baby and then the boy is nowhere to be found. God in His infinite wisdom provided for you, Erin, and the baby. My sister, Emma, raised me after my parents died in a car accident. Emma is a lot older than I am, and though my parents were gone, God provided for me through my sister. Keep giving God the praises and stay prayerful. Listen to your mother and father. They've traveled the road you're on now, and believe me, Jesus will work it out."

Edward finally returned to the room. After he sat down, he leaned over and whispered to Meesha that he would have to travel out of town within the next week or so. He would also have to travel to Texas bi-monthly until the project wore down.

"That's all the time we have tonight," Zora interrupted Kenneth. "I think we're making substantial progress. Reverend Nixon will close the meeting with prayer. Then pick up your assignments; they're on the table."

The group stood up and clasped hands with the person standing next to them. Reverend Nixon bowed his head. "Father God, thank you for allowing us to come and meet together one more time. Lord, thank you for the meeting tonight. I hope something was said here tonight that would help encourage and lift us up, and lift you up as well. Until we meet again, Father, keep us safe from all harm and danger. In your son's name I pray, amen."

The group exchanged good-byes, stopped at the table and picked up the assignment, and then headed for home. After glancing at the first question on the sheet, some of the members could hardly wait until the next Couples' Therapy meeting. From the handout, it appeared the next session would be a treat.

Chapter Fifteen

The fourth meeting of Couples' Therapy was about to commence. Julia thanked Reverend Nixon for the scriptures he'd e-mailed her to study. She enthusiastically told him that the verses and prayer were helping her cope better with Brandon and Erin's situation. The verses the minister e-mailed her included Ephesians 2:14, 2 Corinthians 7:2, Psalm 133:1, and Matthew 7:12, which read simply, "Do to others what you would have them do to you."

Zora called the meeting to order. The mood of the group was genial and filled with laughter. Julia volunteered to begin the homework assignment, which was about songs that best described their feelings for their spouses.

"Being from Africa, my song choice was a no-brainer. I had to go with Sade's 'The Sweetest Taboo.' The song sums up my feelings for Douglas exactly. I know I'm not the easiest person in the world to live with. Still, Douglas has hung in there and has been there for me through thick and thin, kind of like the lyrics from the song," Julia ended shyly.

The other people in the room could see the love that just seemed to glow from her eyes when she looked at her husband.

Douglas, not to be outdone, asked Zora if he could go next.

"Not a problem," Zora laughed. "I think that's a good idea that husband and wives answer the question as a team, or one after the other."

"The choice for me was a little bit more difficult because I really love all genres of music. Finally, I narrowed it down to the master of romance, Luther Vandross. Luther has made so many wonderful songs. When Julia and I dated and then got married, the song for our first dance as husband and wife was 'Here and Now.' Whenever I hear that song today, it brings back memories of Julia and me dancing at our wedding reception. It is a fitting tribute to my Doll Baby," Douglas proclaimed.

Julia looked embarrassed but couldn't keep a grin from sneaking on her face. She and Douglas held hands.

"Aw, that's so sweet," Beverly gushed. "I think I want to go next. What do you think, Kenny?" She turned to glance at her husband.

He gestured for her to proceed.

"Me, I like oldies too, and I love my girl Aretha. She's done for soul what Luther did for romance. Ree-Ree has made a bunch of songs, but there's something about the song 'Day Dreaming.' The song speaks of living up to expectations, pretty much like I felt before Kenneth and I married. We may not agree on all things that we do, but I can truthfully say I love my man, and I know he loves me too." Beverly folded her hands primly in her lap. Kenneth reached over and squeezed her hand.

"I guess it has something to do with our age group because like Doug, Julia, and Beverly, I like the oldies, or dusties as we call them. It seems like we're paying homage to some of the greatest singers ever, and I'm not going to disappoint you. I have to go with my guy Al Green and his song 'I'm Still in Love With You.'"

He tried to sing the melody, and the group laughed as he slaughtered the song, crooning off key.

"See, that's why I'm a deacon and not in the choir," he quipped. "Seriously, Al is the man, and this song has stayed in my heart all these years. I'm still and will always be in love with Beverly Jean Howard.

"Aw, no. See, we can't go out like that," Brandon said loudly to his wife. "Miss Zora, can me and Erin go next?"

"The floor is all yours," Zora answered with an amused twinkle in her eye.

"Well, Erin and I didn't have a big wedding, and we didn't know each other too well before we got married. Thanks to my parents I grew up on ole skool music, as my generation calls it, and I kinda always liked the Temptations' song 'My Girl.' Me and Erin are still learning each other's ways, but I know we got nothing but love in our hearts for each other."

Erin burst into tears and buried her face in her hands. Beverly handed the young woman a tissue. Erin blew her red nose and sniffled.

"I'm sure it's those hormones working overtime because of the baby," Julia apologized affably.

The group nodded with understanding.

After Erin had calmed down, she apologized to the group. "I'm sorry, everybody. Every now and then Brandon says something totally sweet. I didn't grow up listening to R&B. My family liked gospel and C&W. They loved Elvis Presley songs. I had one African American friend; we met in high school. My parents didn't approve of me hanging out with her, but I sneaked and met her behind their backs. My friend Olivia loved music and dancing. Her dream was to be a dancer.

"Hanging out with Olivia, I fell in love with African American music. The song that comes to mind for me regarding how I feel about Brandon is by Lauryn Hill, and it's called 'Can't Take My Eyes Off of You.' The words to the song describe how I felt when I first laid eyes on him. Brandon is the finest man I have ever seen."

"Good going, Erin," Brandon said approvingly. He put his arm around the back of her chair.

The only couple left to give their choices was the Morrisons, Meesha and Edward. Meesha waited a few seconds for Edward to designate which one of them would go first. When he didn't, she jumped in. "I think our group has pretty good taste in music," she complimented the group. "I feel pressure to continue the roll we're on. I'm glad I chose Jennifer Holliday's and Jennifer Hudson's song, 'And I Am Telling You I'm Not Going.' The lyrics and the voices of the powerful women who sang the song transcend how I feel and felt about Edward on our wedding day and beyond." After Meesha finished explaining her choice, she was at a loss as to what her husband might select. For a change he looked like he was enjoying himself.

"Man, y'all took all the good singers," Edward complained good-naturedly. "But not all of them. I liked me some Barry White back in the day. Remember how we used to wear out his albums, Meesha?" He grinned at his wife.

Meesha nodded and then she became starry-eyed, reminiscing of times gone by. She knew which song Edward was going to select, and she soared with happiness.

"Yeah, this was me and Meesha's song, 'Never, Never Gonna Give You Up.' That was our wedding reception theme song."

For the next fifteen minutes, Zora explained to the group how to use scriptures to modify negative traits that could try the patience of Job. She also advised them to remember the fun times they shared while dating, and counseled them to perhaps go back to the place where they shared their first date.

Five minutes into the last portion of the session, Kenneth's cell phone sounded. He stood up and walked to the rear of the room, then answered the call and said loudly in a frantic voice, "Say what?"

Beverly stood and walked rapidly over to her husband. "What's wrong?" She wrung her hands together anxiously, waiting for Kenneth to get off the telephone.

"That was Tracey," Kenneth said with his voice dropped. "Amir has just been arrested. We've got to go." He and Beverly walked back to their seats and removed their coats from the backs of the chairs.

Beverly couldn't stop her body from shaking as she clumsily fastened her coat. Kenneth pulled on his jacket and zipped it. He said to Zora and Calvin, "We have an emergency at home. Hopefully we'll see you next week."

Calvin turned to Zora and said, "I'll walk them to the car." All eyes followed the trio as they departed from the room.

Midway to the car, Kenneth pressed the remote door opener. Beverly walked to her side of the car and opened the door. Kenneth got inside the car and rolled down the window.

"I pray that everything will work out well for you and your family," Calvin said to Kenneth and Beverly.

"Thank you, Reverend Nixon," the older man told the younger one. "Please keep us in your prayers. There's no telling what my son has gotten himself into." Kenneth rolled up the window and pulled out of the church parking lot.

When Calvin returned inside, he found Zora praying and assumed she planned to dismiss the group early. His assumption was correct.

After everyone had left for home, Calvin and Zora tidied the room. When they completed the chores, Calvin waited patiently for Zora to gather her possessions. He put on his coat and hat while she did the same. Fifteen minutes later, they were headed out the door.

Calvin stood shivering in the cold wind as he waited for Zora to get inside her car. She turned on the vehicle so it could warm up. She rolled down the window, and snowflakes drifted inside the car. Calvin turned up the collar of his coat and instructed her, "Be careful driving home tonight. The roads look a little slick. Sometimes the city is slow getting snowplows out to salt the streets."

"I will," Zora said and smiled as she changed the gear from park to drive.

Calvin said, "I'd like to call you this week, if you don't mind." He tucked his hands under his arms.

"Why would I mind?" Zora looked out the window at him quizzically. "You've called me before."

"You're right," Calvin agreed, "but usually when I call it's about the group. I'd like to call you on a personal level, to get to know you better."

"I don't know . . ." Zora hesitated as she chewed on her lower lip. "I'm not really interested in dating at this time."

"All I ask is that you give us a chance, Zora. I'm attracted to you, and I sense you feel the same way, although you're fighting the feeling."

Zora put the car back in park and tapped her foot nervously on the footboard; and then she accidentally revved the motor. Calvin held out his hands. He jumped away from the car. Zora tee-heed edgily and said, "Maybe . . . shoot . . . I don't know. Calvin, let me think about it. I'll give you a call tomorrow or in a few days. Please be patient with me. I've got to go. I have chores to do at home tonight."

Calvin's dimples flashed reassuringly at Zora. "Sure, I can do that. Be patient, I mean. I look forward to talking to you, Zora. Drive carefully." Then he walked to his car and waited for Zora to leave the parking lot.

She waved at him, then wiped her sweating forehead. Zora put the car in drive and drove slowly and carefully across the parking lot. She tried to stay focused on the road ahead of her, but her mind kept shifting to Calvin. Zora admitted to herself that the minister was correct in his assessment of her feelings. She was indeed attracted to him.

Calvin also drove home carefully, mindful of the road conditions. Before he left church, he put his cell phone's blue tooth device into his ear and dialed Reverend Dudley's telephone number.

The minister answered the call cheerfully. "Hi, Calvin. How are you feeling and how did the meeting go tonight?"

"I'm good, Pastor, and the meeting went quite well. I think the members of the group are becoming more comfortable with each other. They provide good feedback, and I like the ways the sessions are going so far."

"Great news. The Lord is using you and Sister Zora in a blessed way."

"Thank you, sir. The reason I'm calling is because Brother Kenneth and Sister Beverly had to leave the meeting early. Their son, Amir, was arrested tonight. The details as to what happened are sketchy. From what Kenneth told me there was some type of altercation at their house, and Amir was involved."

"I'm glad you called. I'm assuming they took Amir to the closest police station to their house. Laura and I will go there."

The first lady had been listening to her husband's side of the conversation. She rose from her seat and went to the powder room to comb her hair and freshen her makeup. When she returned to the living room, Reverend Dudley had his coat on and held up his wife's coat and helped her put it on.

"I guess you heard me talking to Calvin. Kenneth and Beverly are at the police station. Let's go there and see what we can do to help."

"Yes," Laura agreed. "Let me grab my purse, and I'll be ready."

The couple left several minutes later, concerned about what awaited them at the precinct. They were both certain that the situation couldn't be good. Reverend Dudley and Laura were aware Amir had been a handful for his parents since the onset of puberty, and they felt that tonight's situation was more of the same.

Chapter Sixteen

Kenny and Beverly sat on an uncomfortable, hard-wood bench inside the police station located at Seventieth Street and Cottage Grove Avenue. The building was crowded for a weekday evening. A cacophony of noise hung in the air. The floor was littered with debris, and many voices were raised in outrage. Some drunks' and drug users' speech was slurred to the point that their words were unrecognizable.

Beverly sat in her chair in a state of shock. She rested her elbows on her knees and her drooped head inside her hands. Kenny would occasionally rub her back and whisper words of encouragement to his wife, telling her not to worry. Beverly didn't hear a word her husband said. Her mind wandered back to her conversation with Tracey and the awful story she told her parents when Beverly called after she and Kenneth left church.

Keisha had come to the Howard house to pick up Jalin after her workday. Keisha returned to the house later for money that Amir had promised to give her but didn't. This led to an argument. A shoving match ensued in the dining room, and Amir shoved Keisha stronger than he intened. They were standing near the wood and glass cabinet which was old and fragile. As Keisha tried to break her fall, she fell forward, head-first, breaking panels of glass in the cabinet. Her face and hands suffered the brunt of her injuries She was cut badly. Shards of glass were sprinkled all over the carpeted floor along with blood.

Upon hearing the commotion, Tracey ran out of her bedroom to the dining room. When she saw Keisha's bloody face, the young woman was horrified and immediately called 911. A couple of police officers came to the house along with an ambulance. After the police took statements, Amir was cuffed and arrested for domestic violence.

Beverly raised her head. "I don't believe Amir put his hands on a woman. Keisha has to be lying. He knows a man doesn't hit or push a woman," she said to Kenny in a choked-up voice. Her left hand clutched her throat.

"Maybe you can't believe it, but I can. I've told you time and time again how the boy is out of control. Maybe now you'll believe me," Kenny replied as he stroked Beverly's back.

"No, I'll never believe our son is capable of violence. Keisha has to be making the whole story up. Where is your allegiance to our son? Who are you going to believe anyway? Your son or that little hoochie mama?" Beverly nearly screamed.

"Hon, let's try to refrain from the name-calling. Keisha is Jalin's mother, so it's not right to call her out of her name," Kenny said to his wife gently.

"You're right. Father, forgive me." Beverly looked upward; then she hopped out of her seat and stared down the long hallway at the doors separating her from her son. Beverly sat back down and asked Kenneth, "What's taking so long for them to get back to us? You are going to post bail for Amir, aren't you?"

"Well, I . . ." Kenny stammered. "I think we need to talk about it some more." He turned and faced his wife.

"What do you mean? Are you saying that you won't post bail?" Beverly's lips turned downward as she pulled away from Kenneth. "I don't believe you. Why wouldn't you? As far as I'm concerned, there is nothing to discuss. I want my baby out of here now." Beverly stomped her size six, brown-booted foot on the floor for emphasis.

The side of the room they were sitting on suddenly became quiet as people stared at the couple, sensing a showdown.

"Would you lower your voice, please?" Kenny said through clenched teeth. He reached for Beverly again. She folded her arms aggressively across her chest.

Beverly lowered her voice by a few decibels. "Kenneth Howard, you'd better bail my son out of jail. I know he must be going crazy, and feeling abandoned."

Kenny took Beverly's arm and led her out the room and into the long, winding hallway. "I think we should leave Amir here for a night or so. I think it might give him some time to reflect on his life and try to straighten it out."

Beverly looked at her husband coldly, and her voice dripped venom. "How could you even think of something like that? That's our son in there. Now is not the time for you to decide that you want to take a stand. You know what goes on in jails. I won't have it, Kenny," Beverly spat. She rolled her neck with a righteous attitude.

"Over the years, we have gotten Amir out of a few scrapes." Kenneth held out his hand. "When will it be time for him to face the music on his own? I disagree with you. I am not spending one red cent of my hard-earned money to get him out of jail. And that's final," Kenny proclaimed. "In fact, I suggest we leave here and come back to see him tomorrow."

"No," Beverly hissed, pointing her finger at Kenneth. "Amir is not staying here. I have money in the bank, and I'll get him out myself. In fact, I think that's what I'm going to do. We are definitely not on the same page on this issue—shoot, we're not even reading the same book. I think you've lost your mind."

"I have not lost my mind," Kenny said heatedly as he waved his arms in the air. "What you need to do is step back from the situation and pray for guidance. It's never good to make decisions in the heat of emotion. Don't you realize this may be Amir's last opportunity to straighten out his life and get himself together?" He looked at his wife and shook his head entreatingly.

"No. Under no circumstances is our son going to spend one night in this God-forsaken place. If I have to I'll bail him out myself. Why would you let me sit here all this time expecting him to come out when you planned to leave him here all along?" Beverly's body shook from feelings of devastation and betrayal.

"Because I was hoping you would come to your senses and realize it's the best place for Amir to be," Kenny retorted. He balled up his fists inside his jacket pockets. "You've spoiled him, Bev, and this is where he's ended up." He took one hand out of his jacket and swung it in an arc.

"Oh, so now it's my fault." Beverly pointed at her chest. "I don't want to have this conversation with you right now. I know if Tracey were in jail, you wouldn't hesitate to get her out. Now, you're playing favorites. Amir is my son, not yours, and I'm going to do what I can to get my son out of jail."

"I'm begging you, Beverly, please don't do that," Kenny said in an ominous tone.

Beverly had begun walking away from her husband but stopped dead in her tracks and peered back at him with loathing in her eyes. She put her hands on her hips and said, "Or what? If I do, what are you going to do?"

'Don't push me on this issue," Kenny warned as he held up his hand. His face was a mask of anger.

Beverly spun on her heels. "I'm going to get my son out of jail. You can do what you want."

Kenneth's face burned as he watched his wife walk around the corner. Beverly went into the room next door to stand in line to talk to the officer on duty about bailing out her son.

A man walked over to Kenneth and tapped him on the back. Then he asked Kenneth if he knew where a bail bondsman could be found. After replying that he didn't know, Kenneth muttered aloud, "Lord, help her because she truly knows not what she's doing." He glanced at his watch and rubbed his eyes. He knew it was going to be a long night. He decided to go outside the building to cool off. "I need some air."

When he was outdoors, Kenny pulled his cell phone out of his pocket and dialed his home number. Tracey answered the phone promptly. "Hi, Daddy. What's going on? How is Amir?" She nervously twisted the telephone cord in her hand.

"He's in a holding cell," Kenny replied grumpily. "Hey, have you heard anything about Keisha? And where is Jalin?" He walked to the front of the building and paced back and forth. The wind off Lake Michigan brought tears to his eyes.

"Keisha is still in the hospital. From what I could tell, her face and hands were cut pretty badly, and she'll be in the hospital for a while. Her sister Tangie told me that Keisha will probably need plastic surgery. Tangie promised she'd keep me updated on Keisha's condition. There's a lot of blood on the dining room floor and wall. Jalin is still here with me and Rhianna. I told Tangie that Jalin could stay here with us tonight since she'll be at the hospital," Tracey answered. "I guess it's going to take a long time to get Amir out of jail, right? How is Mom?"

Kenneth could hear Jalin and Rhianna yelling in the background. "Yes, it looks like it's going to take a while to get Amir out. I think he should stay in jail for a couple of nights and contemplate his situation. Of course, your mother thinks otherwise." Kenneth sighed. "She's going crazy as expected. The kids didn't see Amir and Keisha fighting, did they?"

"They were in the room with me, thank God," Tracey replied. "So they didn't see the actual fight. They knew something was up when the ambulance and the police came to the house"

"Did Jalin or Rhianna ask you about what happened?"

"Well, I talked to them. There is blood all over the dining room, and the police instructed me not to touch anything until they were done with their report. They also took a statement from me. All I could say was that I didn't actually see what happened." Tracey looked at the children. "Jalin, bring me the remote."

The little boy brought the remote control to his aunt.

"Now, go back and sit on the floor with Rhianna until I get off the telephone," Tracey instructed the boy.

"Jesus Christ. What did you say to the kids?" Kenneth asked.

"I just told them that there was an accident, and explained to Jalin that his mother was hurt and he was going to stay with us for a little while," Tracey said. "Rhianna, stop jumping on the bed," she told her daughter. "Dad, I'll talk to you later. I need to keep an eye on the children. I'll be up when you and Mom get home."

"Okay, call if you need us," Kenneth instructed his daughter. The two exchanged farewells, and Kenneth closed his cell phone. He shivered from the cold air biting his ankles and hurried back inside the police station.

He returned to the area where he and Beverly had been sitting and found not only his wife gone, but her coat also. Kenneth looked at a couple sitting a few seats from where he and Beverly had been sitting and asked them if they knew where Beverly had gone. The pair ignored him and began arguing. Kenny sat down and prayed his wife would return soon.

After nearly a half hour had elapsed and Beverly still hadn't returned to the waiting area, Kenneth decided to go to the front desk. He stretched when he stood up and walked to the desk.

"Say, my wife, her name is Beverly Howard, and we're here to see about my son, Amir Howard. Has she been here?" Kenneth asked the officer. He stuck his hands in his pockets.

"You mean you can't even keep up with your wife? Should we file a missing person report," the female officer dressed in a dark shirt and slacks asked Kenny with a smirk on her face. She laid down the pencil she had been holding.

"Yes—I mean, no." Kenny shook his head, frustrated. "She probably went to see if we could bail my son out of jail. Where would she have gone to do that?" Kenneth felt slightly annoyed. To his way of thinking it was bad enough Beverly had left him without saying where she was going, but then he had to deal with an officer who had jokes.

The officer went on to explain that bail could be posted only if his son had been to court and was actually charged with a crime. Then and only then could the Howards pursue posting bail. She added, "Sometimes the wheels of justice turn slowly. You and your wife will have to be patient. Your son will have his day in court probably tomorrow; if not then, he'll have to wait until Monday."

"Thank you." Kenneth returned to his seat. Five minutes later he spied Beverly looking for him. He hopped from his chair and walked to where Beverly stood. "Where have you been?" Kenneth asked. He stared down at his wife, who had an aggrieved expression on her face.

"I went to do what you wouldn't—to see what I could do for my child." Beverly's lips trembled as she clutched her arms across her upper body. "They still couldn't tell me anything definite about Amir."

Kenneth could see from the discouraged expression on his wife's face that she was quite distraught. He sighed. "Now, Beverly, you're not being rational. I don't dislike Amir; I care about him. In my heart, he's my child as much as Tracey is. I adopted him and gave him my name. I just want him to become the man I know he can be." Kenneth took Beverly's arm and led her to a seat. They both sat down.

Beverly moistened her lips and pulled her body away from her husband. "Parents are morally obligated to do anything and everything for their children. Amir may be a little misguided right now, but that's because you've put him under so much pressure to find a job and do right by Jalin," Beverly said haughtily.

Kenneth groaned audibly, and he took Beverly's cold hand and held it in his own. "Honey, I pray every night and even during the day that Amir will find himself and become a better father to Jalin and his other children."

"Hmmm," Beverly snorted as she snatched her hand from Kenneth's. "I think sometimes you want him to fail." She folded her arms across her heaving bosom.

"That's not true. I gave the children my all when they were growing up. But, Beverly, they are no longer children. Amir and Tracey are grown adults who are almost thirty years old. When does the support and giving end?" Kenneth shrugged his shoulders helplessly. He laid his hands across the back of the bench.

"You're missing the point, Kenneth Howard," Beverly replied, pointing her finger in her husband's face. "It never ends. Parents are always obligated to help their children."

Kenneth shook his head. "Bev, that's not how you and I were raised, and I don't intend to become an enabler for my children. If we don't take a stand now, how else will Amir and Tracey learn to stand on their own two feet and lead successful lives?"

"I don't know." Beverly broke down into tears. "I just don't know. Kenneth, I'm so scared. Amir could be charged with attempted murder or something. My God, how did this happen?" She raised tear-stained eyes to her husband.

Kenneth pulled Beverly into his arms. He murmured against her hair. "We'll get through this. I promise, honey. We just have to put our faith in the Lord. He hasn't failed us yet."

"Maybe we should call Pastor Dudley?" Beverly moaned as she laid her head on Kenneth's shoulder.

"Let's just remain prayerful and wait and see what happens. We'll call Reverend Dudley if we need too," Kenneth whispered, as he tried to comfort his wife. With a sinking feeling in the pit of his stomach, Kenneth realized that he and Beverly were probably in for a long night. "Bev, I meant to tell you . . ." Kenneth began.

The couple looked up to see Reverend Dudley and First Lady Laura. Kenneth waved them over to where he and Beverly were sitting.

Beverly closed her eyes as visions of assault charges or, even worse, attempted murder floated through her mind as she contemplated her son's fate. She looked around the room, then up and down, as if she could see through the walls. Her mouth barely moved as she sent a message to Amir that he wouldn't hear, at least not that night. She bade Amir to hold on. She vowed to do everything in her power to make things better.

Chapter Seventeen

Zora had just returned from the kitchen, where she had prepared hot chocolate. The warm cup heated her hands. She walked into the living room and placed the mug on a coaster atop the brass-and-smoked glass cocktail table. Then she settled comfortably on the velvety, deep purple sofa and tucked her legs under her body. Zora reached across the table, picked up the mug, blew on the dark, sugary liquid, and took a sip. She reached over the table, set the mug on it, and sighed out loud.

She listened to the adult choir of Friendship Church sing "Blessed Assurance" from the disc in the CD player that sat on a brass glass-shelved étagère tucked into a corner of the room. Zora's head bobbed as she hummed along with the choir. Her eyes roamed the room, proud of the space Meesha had helped her decorate.

The rooms inside the condominium located at Fifty-second and Drexel Boulevard were sizeable and had a modern design. A fire roared in the fireplace. Zora looked up and could see the stars twinkling from the skylight in the broad-beamed cathedral ceiling.

The living room walls were painted two-toned colors, beige and umber. African masks and paintings were lovingly placed on the walls. Gold throw pillows were scattered on the floor and atop two black leather chairs.

Zora's motive for asking Meesha to assist her in decorating the condominium was to take her friend's mind off her deteriorating marriage. So far, neither Meesha nor Edward were budging from their polar positions on their union.

Then Zora's thoughts flitted on her own issue—namely, a handsome minister at the church. Zora knew Calvin was going to ask her out on a date. Just thinking about it made her heartbeat accelerate rapidly out of control.

She wasn't sure she had room in her heart to allow a man to enter. Zora hadn't been involved in a serious relationship with a member of the opposite sex since her senior year of high school. Disaster had struck, and Zora had vowed never to entrust her heart to a man again. For most of her adult life, Zora had made good on her promise and kept men at an emotional distance. She accepted her fate to spend life alone without a spouse and children. Zora was content with her lot in life; that is, until she met Reverend Calvin Nixon. His caring, concern, and closeness caused Zora to rethink her position.

Zora often thanked God that she had met Meesha, and that they were roommates during Zora's first year of college and had become close friends. Growing up, Zora didn't have many close friends; she was a loner by nature. She knew her life would have been incredibly lonely had Meesha not been a part of it. Zora continued her musings. The CD continued to play. The cordless phone that sat on the end table rang.

Zora picked up the remote to the player and turned it off. Then she quickly scanned the caller ID unit. "Hello, Calvin. How are you doing?"

"I'm doing well. How about you? I just wanted to make sure you made it home safely." Zora could hear the care in Calvin's tone.

The sound of the minister's voice caused tremors to course through Zora's body. "I'm okay. I'm just enjoying a little downtime. I brought a stack of files home with me from work. I've already looked through a couple of them while I was listening to a CD of the choir. I bought the CD from the church store last Sunday," Zora babbled nervously.

"I'm glad to hear you're having a little R&R," Calvin remarked. "We all need a break from the rat race from time to time. I was also calling to see if you'd heard from Kenneth and Beverly."

"No, I haven't, and I'm starting to get a little concerned about them. I hope things turn out well for them and their son," Zora replied. She had been sitting upright and relaxed her body against the back of the couch.

"I haven't heard from them either. I've prayed for the Howard family. And I know that, God willing, they will be fine," Calvin added.

Zora's heartbeat had returned to normal. Suddenly she felt at odds with herself, like she usually did when Calvin was around or if he happened to call her. "Well, I guess I've been lazy enough," she proclaimed nonchalantly. "I should probably get off this phone and continue working on my files."

"Wait a minute," Calvin urged her. "I mean . . . What I'm trying to say is, How would you feel about going out on a date with me?" He stood in his kitchen at the counter turning vegetables inside a wok with a long-handled fork. The telephone was cradled in the crook of his neck.

"Oh, I don't know . . ." Zora replied helplessly. "I think we should continue our relationship as colleagues and friends. Why muddy the waters? You're a minister, and I know everything you do is examined under a microscope. Not too mention how many sisters in the church would love the chance to call themselves Mrs. Calvin Nixon." Zora tittered as she tapped her fingers on the arm of the sofa.

"Why don't you allow me to worry about that?" Calvin asked with a spark of tenderness in his voice. He placed cut up chicken strips into the wok. Calvin walked to the refrigerator and removed a bottle of water. He turned the temperature setting on the wok to low and then sat at the kitchen table.

"I . . . I," Zora gulped. "Calvin, you don't really know me that well. I know we've become close over the past few months because of the sessions, but I'm not in the market for a relationship. Not now or ever."

"Never is a mighty long time, Miss Zora," Calvin replied evenly. The sadness in Zora's voice seemed to slither through the telephone wire. He unscrewed the bottle of water.

"I know, but I made a promise to myself many moons ago not to become involved with the opposite sex. And so far I've stood my ground," Zora shot back, feeling defensive.

"I guess I can surmise from your statement that someone hurt you and hurt you badly," Calvin guessed.

"Yes, you're right, and I don't think I ever want to go back to that place. There are plenty of women at the church who would jump at the chance to date you. I may show a professional persona outwardly, but inside I'm dead. I don't have it in me to invest emotions in a man."

Calvin turned up the bottle and took a sip of water. "Maybe you just haven't met the right man. In this situation, like others, maybe you should let go and let God."

Zora laughed and Calvin joined her. "Somehow I don't think that saying applies to dating. Seriously, I still carry a lot of baggage from the past. I've moved on, but some experiences change the course of a person's life, and they can never forget them." Zora's whisper was so poignant that Calvin couldn't help but be moved.

"I think everyone has something that may have happened in their life, Zora, that he or she might not be proud of or obsess over." Calvin's voice was very tender and soothing to Zora's ear. "I've been guilty of that myself. And that, my dear, is why I adhere to Matthew 7:1–2: 'Judge not, that ye be not judged. For with what judgment ye judge, ye shall be judged: and with what measure ye mete, it shall be measured to you again.'"

"You seem to be such a good man, Calvin," Zora murmured as she scooted close to the back of the sofa. "I bet you grew up in the suburbs with a nuclear family. Your parents probably had the requisite two and a half children and a dog. I also bet you were an overachiever throughout school who probably did all the right things in the right season. If only I had met you years ago," she said morosely.

"You read me completely wrong," Calvin replied. The chicken filled his modern kitchen with an appetizing aroma. He stood up, walked to the counter, and stirred the food.

"Really?" Zora asked. She picked up a throw pillow from the end of the sofa and pressed it against her stomach.

"Really. For all intents and purposes, I am the product of a single-parent home," Calvin confessed. "My grandmother raised me and my brother, Phillip, until my father was able to raise us himself."

"Where was your mother?" Zora couldn't help asking the minister.

"My mother was diagnosed as being bipolar in her early teens. Everyone knew she had issues, and most people called her Crazy Monica. She had my brother when she was fifteen and then me at sixteen. We lived with my grandmother, or Ma'Deah. My father enlisted to escape the shame of having two children out of wedlock with the neighborhood kook, as my mother was called. When my father finally came out of denial long enough to admit my mother was mentally ill, he had just finished his first stint in the service. He had matured and stepped up to the plate. Dad took custody of me and Phil and raised us after that. So I'm a military brat."

"Wow, I never would have suspected that," Zora remarked. "You seem so . . ."

"Normal? Settled?" Calvin joshed with her. "My life is a testimony of God's mercy." He stood up, dimmed the light in the kitchen, turned off the wok, and walked down the hall to his home office. Calvin flipped on the light and sat down on the futon. Dinner could wait. Calvin hoped he would be able to persuade Zora to take a chance and agree to a date. The minister was sure by then that Zora was the woman God had chosen for him. The challenge would be convincing Zora to see things his way.

"Do you still see your mother?" Zora asked.

"I see her at least once a quarter. She and Ma'Deah live in Memphis. That's where my people are from. To my family's surprise, my mom had a baby when I was twenty years old. By the way, I'm thirty-eight. My sister Synclare is a blessing from God. Ma'Deah is still alive, and she helped my mom raise Synnie, as we call my sister. While Phil and I were embarrassed by our mother or saw her as a burden to bear while we were growing up, Synnie truly loves and accepts our mother. My sister is very kind and loving with Mom. Synnie grew up in a trailer park; Mom wouldn't accept money from me or Phil. Synnie is extremely smart. She's a gifted student and has been awarded scholarships to Howard, Spelman, and Harvard University. I am very proud of my little sister. She stays with me and Phil a couple of weeks during the summer.

Though Phil and I experienced many ups and downs with Mom when she would go off her meds, Synnie showed us how to love her as she is. Luckily, Mom has been on a medical cocktail that has been working well for years. She's settled down as much as she can, and I think her having Synnie in her life has helped her tremendously," Calvin said.

"That is indeed a wonderful testimony. I never would have guessed you faced such difficulties while growing up because you seem so normal," Zora observed.

"That just goes to show you that you can't judge a book by its cover," Calvin told Zora. "Tell me about your family." He pressed Zora.

"I was a product of a nuclear family," Zora confessed. "My mom is a well-known evangelist in the south Mobile area. My father is as active in church as Mom is, although he's not a minister. I have an older brother and younger sister. It seems like I missed the normal mother-daughter relationship because of my mother's calling," she said ruefully. "Looking back in retrospect, it is what it is."

"It's good you can look at it that way. I mentor young African American males at the church, and the hardest part of the job is trying to convince them that whatever happens in life is part of God's plan, and that the difficulties they experience are just temporary situations."

"You sound like you speak from experience," Zora commented.

"Definitely. There was a time when I walked in those boys' shoes. I was lucky to meet Reverend Dudley when I was a teenager. After my father retired from the service, we moved to Chicago. I had gotten into some trouble. I had a temper and was always spoiling for a fight. I had a chip on my shoulder because of the hateful things kids had said about my mother, and I fought to hide my pain. Reverend Dudley and my father didn't give up on me, and they helped turn my life around. I've tried my best to walk the Christian walk since then."

"And you're a stock broker too. Wow, Calvin. You are a true testament to God's goodness. My mother would say that you're blessed and highly favored," Zora said in a serious tone of voice. Her eyes strayed to the other folders she planned to work on that evening. "I've really got to go. I still have work to do. Maybe we can continue this conversation at another time . . ." Zora's voice trailed off.

"How about tomorrow? I know a nice Italian restaurant in Old Town on the north side of the city that has a jazz band. I just ask that you hear me out, Zora, and give us a chance," Calvin pleaded his case.

A million reasons why she shouldn't go out with Calvin whirled through Zora's head. She hesitated, knowing if she took that step she wouldn't be able to turn back. She gnawed on her lower lip and sighed. "I . . . uh . . . I don't feel very comfortable about us dating. Would you let me think about it? I promise you that I'll let you know my answer tomorrow morning."

"Sure." Calvin's voice masked the disappointment he felt. "Only if you keep your word and call me like you say you will. I hope you'll relax and enjoy the rest of the evening. In case you don't, I'm going to let you get back to work. Don't work too hard, and I'll talk to you in the morning."

"Good night, Calvin. Enjoy your evening," Zora said in closing.

"Back at you. Good night, Zora."

The two hung up the telephones.

A smile traversed Calvin's face as he walked back to his kitchen and turned on the wok again. *At least she didn't flatly turn me down. So maybe there's hope.*

After Calvin finished cooking the chicken, he ladled the meal onto a plate, set it on the table, then walked to the refrigerator and poured himself a glass of cranberry juice. Calvin sat at the table and bowed his head. "Father above, thank you for the blessings you bestowed on me today. Thank you for allowing me to see another day. I hope I did things that were pleasing in your sight. Lord, I know I only have to ask, and it will be done. Lord, please heal Zora. I know she is struggling with an issue. Please lay your healing hands on her tonight. Continue to rain your blessings on her. Thank you for a successful session tonight, Lord. I think we made some breakthroughs. Help and strengthen Beverly and Kenneth tonight along with the other members of the group and my church family. Amen." Calvin picked up a fork and began eating the tasty meal.

At Zora's house, she stared at the telephone while her mind raced a million miles a minute. *Lord, what did I just do? I know I didn't imply that I might go out with Calvin. What was I thinking? I can't do this.* She rose from the couch and paced the room, trying to stymie the panicky feeling that invaded her soul.

After minutes of pacing around the room and nibbling on her lower lip, Zora picked up the telephone and dialed Meesha's number. When Meesha answered the telephone, Zora asked, "Can you talk? Are you busy?"

Meesha didn't miss the tone of urgency in her friend's voice. "I just finished getting the kids in the bed. Edward isn't home, so yes, I'm all yours. What's wrong?"

"Calvin called me. He wants us to go on a date to-morrow," Zora answered in a shaky voice. She continued walking around the room while she talked on the phone.

"And what's wrong with that? It's about time you resumed life. I've sensed our assistant minister has been smitten with you for a while," Meesha scolded her friend.

"Girl, nobody uses the word smitten anymore," Zora complained. "What do you mean by what's wrong with that? Everything is."

"It's time for you to throw your old baggage away and embrace the blessings that God has in store for you with Calvin. He's a good man, and we both know he could have any woman he wants in the church. Zee, you should be honored that he choose you and vice versa, if you decide to date him." Meesha smiled. She was already planning a wedding in her head.

"We both know that I'm not worthy of Calvin or any other man," Zora moaned. Her eyes filled with tears. "No matter how much you think the past is just that, the past, it always seems to come back and haunt you."

"No, Zee, it hasn't come back to haunt you. You've kept the memory alive instead of burying it. It's time for you to share what happened to you with a special man. We're in our mid-thirties, and I know you want a family and children one day, no matter how hard you try to deny it. God loves you, and He's sent an incredible man your way. Now is the time to embrace the happiness God has in store for you," Meesha lectured her dear friend. She just prayed that Zora would listen to her.

"I want to so badly. Calvin has been a good friend, and I know any romantic relationship starts with friendship. He's been so kind to me since I've moved here. But I'm scared, Meesha, of opening my heart. What if he doesn't accept me and my baggage?"

"Stop worrying and trust the Lord. Calvin will accept you. You were young and immature. It's not like you committed a crime."

"Only the sin of fornication, and that's a big one, and I managed to get pregnant in the process. I had sex one time, and me, Fertile Myrtle, managed to get knocked up." Zora felt a sense of relief talking to her friend about what had happened to her at the age of seventeen. Tears dripped from her eyes as she thought of how she put her baby up for adoption.

"That was the past, Zee. Let it go, please. I pray every night that you will let it go and become the complete person God wants you to be." Meesha closed her eyes and said a quick prayer for her friend.

"That's easier said than done. I'm sure Calvin expects to marry a virgin. I can't even begin to think how I'd tell him that I'm not. If only I hadn't tried to be like regular kids and gone to that party. Then none of this would be happening."

"That's not true. Had it not been that incident, it might have been something else that could have been worse. What happened in your past was part of your destiny. Use it to strengthen yourself and help others. Who knows, Calvin might not expect you to be pure as the driven snow. None of us are spring chickens anymore. I feel that he'll accept you, past and all." Meesha gave it her all trying to sway Zora.

"You make him sound like a Superman," Zora replied, wiping her nose on the sleeve of her pajama top.

"He's a man of God, and he understands that people make mistakes. Go out with him and see what happens. I'll bet my entire paycheck you'll have a good time," Meesha urged Zora.

Zora snorted. "I tell you what, if things don't work out, I'm going to come calling on you to collect my money."

"Bring it on, girl. I can handle you."

Zora crinkled her nose. "I don't have a thing to wear."

"Now you sound like the Zee that I know and love. Why don't we meet tomorrow after work and go shopping."

"Who'll watch the kids?" Zora asked.

"They are spending the weekend with my parents. I'll drop them off there and meet you at the church. Then we can go to River Oaks Shopping Mall. It's not too far from the church. We can hop on the e-way and be there in no time."

"Okay. I'll call you tomorrow, assuming I tell Calvin yes."

"Girl, stop fronting. You and I both know you're going to call that man and tell him yes," Meesha retorted. "Have a good night, and don't worry, everything will work out the way God intends it to."

"You have a good night too, girlfriend," Zora replied. The two friends hung up the telephones.

Zora still felt unsettled. Though she'd given up her child for adoption over seventeen years ago, sometimes it seemed like yesterday. Her mother, who almost never allowed her daughter to attend house parties unless it was hosted by a member of the church, had relented and allowed Zora to attend a few graduation parties celebrating the end of high school.

Zora felt a heady sense of freedom that for once she could just be one of the gang and not the preacher's kid. She'd had a crush on the quarterback of the football team, Jeremy Stewart, since the beginning of the school year. His bulging muscles and dazzling smile overwhelmed the young, sheltered girl. She danced with him awkwardly in the dimly lit basement. He kept bringing her drinks. Zora didn't want to seem like a square, so she had more than her fair share of alcohol that night.

Jeremy led her to one of the bedrooms in the basement to talk, as he initially told her. In that room, the bed seemed like the natural place to be. Zora willingly gave her virginity to him because she thought she loved him. When she awakened from her drunken haze, Zora was disgusted by her behavior. Her head was pounding. She later called her mother to ask if she could spend the night with a girlfriend from church. Amania had a car. She came to pick up Zora from the party and consoled her sobbing friend throughout the night.

Zora was humiliated when Jeremy never called her as he promised. If they saw each other in public, Jeremy averted his eyes and scurried off, saying he was busy. Two month later, Zora's world shattered into a million splintered pieces when she discovered she was pregnant. She never had a chance to tell Jeremy about their predicament; he had already left for college.

Closing her eyes, Zora remembered the hurt and dismay on her mother's face when she told her about her situation. Annie Lee Taylor supported her daughter but was adamant that the baby be put up for adoption. Zora was sent to live with Annie's sister, Camille, in Rockford, Illinois, until she gave birth to her baby boy. Afterward Zora returned home for a few weeks to pack her remaining belongings and then headed back to Illinois to attend college.

Zora received counseling and eventually came to terms with her teenage pregnancy. She just couldn't shrug off the guilt that invaded her soul from letting her parents down. When laws were relaxed for adopted children and biological parents to have access to legal records, Zora was initially consumed by a raging fire to find the child she'd given up for adoption. Then after many weeks of prayer, Zora decided to drop the matter and satisfied herself with the thought that her son was safe and happy with a loving family.

The relationship between Zora and her mother became strained after the pregnancy, and Zora was still wearing her mantle of guilt. She decided to attend college as far away from home as possible, and other than the weather, Zora liked Illinois. After she received her master's degree, Zora returned to Alabama to live, but she and her mother couldn't quite capture the closeness the two had once shared. Zora later decided to move to Arizona.

Now, how do I explain all this to Calvin without him looking at me with horror or disbelief in his eyes? Will his knowing the truth change our relationship? He's held to a higher standard by the church and his peers. Lord, I am so unworthy. Zora sighed and looked upward. "Lord, please guide me and help me. I don't know what to do." Zora picked up the telephone and dialed her parents' home. "Hi, Mama, how are you and Daddy and everyone doing?"

Annie Lee replied that everyone was fine. Then she asked Zora how she was doing. She asked about Zora's job and the weather in Chicago.

"Mama, I need to talk to you about what happened when I was in high school . . . Do you have time?"

Annie Lee's face creased into a wide smile. This was the call she'd been praying for, for so long. "Always, Zora. I always have time for you."

Mother and daughter talked and cried together, and when the call was completed, each felt better, and Zora had a sense of closure.

Zora felt better mentally than she had in a long time after her conversation with her mother. She had opened up and told her mother of the shame she felt at giving birth to a child out of wedlock as the daughter of a minister. Zora also admitted to her mother how she really didn't want to give up her child for adoption. Zora hadn't ever disclosed that fact to her mother before.

Annie Lee in turn explained how she thought she was making the right decision at the time. She apologized to her daughter for not being more considerate of her feelings.

Zora prayed for God's guidance before she drifted off to sleep. A tiny part of her could hardly wait to talk to Calvin the following morning.

Chapter Eighteen

Reverend Dudley and First Lady Laura strode to where Beverly and Kenneth were sitting. Laura embraced Beverly while Kenneth and the minister shook hands.

After greetings were exchanged, Reverend Dudley asked the couple, "How are you two holding up?" Reverend Dudley and his wife removed their coats, laid them on the back of their chairs, and sat down.

Kenneth stole a look at Beverly and replied cryptically, "We're making it, Pastor, but barely. The situation isn't easy, and Bev and I are at odds as to what to do."

"Let's bow our heads," Reverend Dudley instructed. "Father above, keep your children wrapped in your loving arms. Bring Kenneth and Beverly together as they reflect on the best way to help Amir. Lord, give them strength, and let them know they are not alone. We know you're already on the case and handling the situation. Amen."

"Amen," the others said.

"Now, tell me what's going on," Reverend Dudley said.

Kenneth brought the minister and his wife up to speed about what had transpired.

Reverend Dudley promised to pray for Amir and Keisha. "I take it you haven't had a chance to talk to Amir yet?"

"That's correct," Kenneth answered. He glanced at Beverly, who looked emotionally spent. "I feel this would be the perfect opportunity for Amir to reflect on his life and try to turn things around. I think his staying in jail a couple of nights won't hurt him. He needs a healthy dose of tough love and, of course, Beverly disagrees."

"My baby is in a cell somewhere in this building." Beverly slumped dejectedly in her seat. "I just can't bear the thought of Amir being in jail. He doesn't belong there. Whatever happened between him and Keisha was an accident. All Keisha has to do is tell the police that, and then Amir can come home."

Everyone except for Beverly knew the situation wasn't that cut-and-dried.

"Have you two eaten? Are you hungry or thirsty?" Laura asked.

Kenneth and Beverly shook their heads and said they weren't hungry. Kenneth remarked he was thirsty.

"Beverly, why don't you and I go to the canteen and bring coffee back for everyone?" Laura suggested. She looked at Beverly expectantly.

"I can't leave," Beverly said obdurately as she waved her hand in the air. "What if the police tell us we can see Amir and I'm not here? I can't chance not seeing my son." She closed her eyes and rubbed them.

"If anyone comes looking for us, we'll wait for you to come back," Kenneth said just as forcibly. "Bev, why don't you go with the first lady? It will help take your mind off Amir if only for a few minutes. You need a break."

Laura placed her hand on Beverly's arm. "We won't be gone long, I promise."

Beverly looked as if she were going to shake off the first lady's hand; then she glanced at Kenneth and Reverend Dudley. "Okay, but Kenny, if they come looking for us, wait on me or come and get me."

Kenneth and Reverend Dudley stood as the women departed. Kenneth took Beverly's hand and squeezed it. After the women left, Kenneth and Reverend Dudley sat back down.

"How are you holding up, Kenneth?" the minister asked the deacon.

"I could be better. Bev is bent on rescuing Amir out of his latest escapade, and sometimes a person has to take his lumps and pay the piper. I think this is one of those times for Amir."

"Stay prayerful and keep talking to Beverly. I know your views are as far apart as heaven and earth right now. Try to understand Beverly's point of view. Right now she's like a mother hen trying to protect her chick," Reverend Dudley counseled Kenneth.

"Pastor, I understand what you're saying," Kenneth remarked bitterly. He chose his words carefully. "I feel Beverly's overprotecting Amir over the years has led him to where he is in life and tonight. He knows whenever he gets into trouble that Beverly, like a white knight, will ride to his rescue."

"That's what mothers do best." Reverend Dudley smiled and nodded his head. "Just keep praying and listen to the Spirit. God will offer a solution that will appeal to both of you. Reverend Nixon called me this evening and told me what had happened. He asked me to tell you that he's praying for you and Beverly."

"I'll have to thank him the next time I see him," Kenneth said. He folded his arms across his massive chest. "I love Beverly with all my heart, and I love Amir like a son, but he isn't right, Pastor. He has three kids by three baby mamas. The only one of his kids that he has a relationship with is Jalin, and that's because Beverly and I insisted he be close to one of his children. Amir can barely keep a job, and he lives in our basement. On top of that, he acts like he's the king of the castle and Beverly and Tracey are his maids."

Reverend Dudley nodded sympathetically at Kenneth, encouraging him to continue. He sensed correctly that his deacon needed to let off a little steam.

Kenneth went on. "I look at the future, and I see me and Beverly old and depending on our children for help. If we have to depend on Amir, then we're in trouble. He doesn't appear to have any direction in his life. I have a couple of friends who own their own businesses. They hired Amir as a favor to me in the past, and he blew every opportunity. He can't seem to keep a job for more than a few months, so he has no place to live except with us. Tracey is living with us too. She has money problems. Tracey filed bankruptcy last year due to her husband's gambling problem. She and her husband are finally divorced. Tracey is working to try to get back on her feet. Sometimes I feel like Beverly and I have failed our children. They don't seem to know how to make it as adults on their own."

"What they're undergoing is called a life lesson," Reverend Dudley said as he smiled at Kenneth. "We all face peaks and valleys during our life journey. Eventually, we're able to rebound. However, some people can't rebound as easily as others for different reasons or for inexplicable reasons. It can be due to youth, upbringing, or a lack of resources. Everyone doesn't get it immediately, how to lead a good productive life. For some people, it takes longer. God didn't bless Laura and me with children, so we might not have firsthand experience with childrearing, but we can certainly sympathize with you. Know that we're here if you need us."

"Thank you, Pastor. I appreciate your words and all the support you've given us in the past." Kenneth shook his had sadly. "I think Amir is a bad seed."

"Please don't think of your son in those terms. He may be misguided, but he's still a child of God, like you and me. Once his legal situation is resolved, we need to put our heads together and come up with a plan to help Amir along the way."

"I've been working on a plan with Amir since he was sixteen years old. This latest situation may work against him. He's had scrapes with the law before, so he may not get bail. Beverly thinks that because I don't want to bail Amir out of jail that I don't love him. She thinks I don't care about him because he's not my biological child. That's not true. I'm the only father he's ever known."

"Has Amir ever expressed a desire to see his biological father?"

"Not lately. And that's probably my fault. He wanted to see him," Kenneth closed his eyes in thought, "when he was around fifteen years old. His father was in jail, and I felt that wouldn't be a good environment for Amir to be around since he was already giving us problems."

"Is that when his problems started?" Reverend Dudley probed Kenneth gently.

"That's when they worsened. Amir has always had problems." Kenneth's eyes widened. "You don't think his not being around his biological father is the cause of Amir's problems, do you?

"It might be an underlining cause," the minister suggested. "Perhaps he felt abandoned by his father, and to make sure his mother would never forsake him, he acted out. Maybe Amir doesn't know how to gain affection without negative behavior."

Kenneth's eyes narrowed as he stroked his chin. "Perhaps you're right. I certainly can't rule it out."

"Kenny, keep Psalm 127:3 in mind, 'Children are a gift from the Lord; they are a reward from him.' I know some children are more challenging than others. Whatever you do, don't give up on Amir. I think Beverly is afraid that's what you're going to do, and the thought probably frightens her more than the situation with Amir."

"Maybe you're right, Pastor." Kenneth stroked his chin. "My father was from the South, very old school, and he would always quote Proverbs 13:24 to us. I know it by heart: 'He that spareth his rod hateth his son: but he that loveth him chasteneth him betimes.'"

"That's true, but discipline isn't always in the form of spankings. It sometimes means taking a stand, like punishment, extra chores, or loss of an activity they hold dear."

"I agree." Kenneth nodded his head vigorously. "Problem was, Beverly wouldn't allow me to spank Amir because he wasn't my son. When Tracey was growing up, Bev and I could look at her sternly and she'd cry. So we rarely had to discipline her."

"Your work is cut out for you," Reverend Dudley commented. "Still, you will get through this trial, Kenneth. Lean heavily on the Lord and stay prayerful. I suppose my better half is trying to cheer up your better half. Let's go see if we can find out what's happening with Amir. Hopefully you'll be able to tell Beverly whether she can see him tonight or not."

"I forgot that I had spoken to an officer earlier because Beverly and I were bickering. Amir won't be released tonight because he has to be arraigned first. They told us to come back or call in the morning," Kenneth informed Reverend Dudley. While they waited for the women to return, the men continued to talk.

Laura and Beverly were leaving the ladies' room. Beverly had just finished crying her heart out to the minister's wife. They walked to the canteen, bought four cups of coffee, and sat at one of the small round tables.

Beverly took a tissue out of her pocket and rubbed her eyes. "I'm sorry, Lady Laura. I just feel so helpless." She put the tissue back inside her pocket. "Amir's getting arrested and Kenny's refusing to bail him out has been more than I can bear."

"I know you're going through a lot, but it's not more than you can bear. God never puts more on us than we can endure. You have the Lord to lean on and others who will be praying for a favorable outcome for Amir and your family," the first lady offered, hoping to comfort Beverly.

Beverly's face looked ashen and bore tracks of her tears. She looked across the table at Laura. "I'm so frightened that Kenny might leave Amir here in jail. Nothing makes a parent feel worse than hearing that their child is in jail. I've failed Amir so miserably." Tears gushed from Beverly's eyes as she wept pitifully. She covered her face as her shoulders heaved convulsively.

Laura stood and moved to the chair closest to Beverly and pulled the sobbing woman in her arms. "It's going to be okay, dear," she said softly. "I know Kenny is going to do the right thing. Please don't worry, Beverly. Have faith in the Lord and allow Him to direct your path."

Several minutes later, Beverly composed herself. "If Kenny doesn't bail Amir out of jail, then I'm going to leave him and go stay with my sister, Babs. I can't stay in the same room, much less the same house, with Kenny knowing that he didn't get my son out of jail."

Laura looked dismayed. She put her hand on Beverly's arm. "Please don't be hasty about making decisions right now," she cautioned the visibly distraught woman. "This is an emotional time for you and Kenny right now. You don't want to cloud the issue by doing something you might later regret. Please pray and think the situation through."

"I can't promise you that I won't take matters into my own hands. Kenneth treats Amir badly because he isn't his biological son," Beverly complained. Her lips were drawn like she'd been sucking on lemons.

"I want you to really think about that statement, Bev." Laura dipped her head. "I remember Kenneth bringing Amir to father-son functions at the church, and I know Kenneth attended Amir's baseball games when he was in high school. I think that Kenneth has been there for Amir. What I need you to do is pray and think your situation through."

Beverly looked troubled. "I promise you that I will pray and ask for guidance from the Lord. But this situation is so difficult."

Laura said gently, "I understand. When times get difficult you have to lean on God more heavily. Let's go get more coffee for the men. These cups here are cold." She pointed to the table. "Maybe by the time we return to the waiting area, the officers will have given Kenneth more information about Amir."

Beverly rubbed her face. Laura stood up. The first lady picked up the cups, walked over to the trash bin, and dropped them inside. She then returned to the line to purchase replacement cups of coffee while Beverly checked her voice mail messages. The screen on Beverly's cell phone went blank, and the phone died because it needed charging. She dropped it into her purse just as Laura returned to the table. She and Beverly left the cafeteria and returned to the waiting area.

"Did you find out anything while we were gone?"

"Yes," Kenneth said, nodding his head. "I forgot to tell you that I had talked to an officer earlier. She said that Amir probably won't see the judge until tomorrow morning, and that we should call in the morning to make sure his case is on the docket. "

"Kenneth," Beverly's eyes flashed displeasure. She called her husband by his full name only when she was upset. "Why didn't you tell me that earlier? I had questions I wanted to ask the officer."

Kenneth raised his hands in the air helplessly. "There wasn't much more she could tell us, Bev. The main thing was finding out when Amir would see the judge, and she told me that. You disappeared, and then I forgot to tell you."

"I don't care what they told you." Beverly was aghast. "I wanted to find out for myself how Amir is doing and feeling. I know he must have been horrified when he found out he couldn't get out of jail. You are going to bail him out in the morning, aren't you?" Beverly held her breath.

Reverend Dudley cleared his throat and said, "Laura, we should probably be going. I have a trip to Michigan planned for tomorrow morning." He stood up, and his wife followed suit. The minister helped his spouse put on her coat.

He turned to Kenny and Beverly. "You two have my home and cell phone numbers. Don't hesitate to use them if you have to. I should be back from Michigan late tomorrow evening, and I'll call you then. I will keep your family in my prayers."

"Thank you for coming tonight," Beverly said after she hugged the first lady and Kenny shook Reverend Dudley's hand again.

Laura tied her black scarf/hat around her neck. "Please think about what we talked about, Bev." She squeezed Beverly's hand; then she and Rev. Dudley departed.

Beverly and Kenneth removed their coats from their seats. Beverly put on her purple down coat. As she zipped the garment, she cut her eyes sharply at her husband. "I'm going to ask this question one more time, Kenny. You are going to bail out Amir, aren't you?"

"If you don't mind, I'd like to discuss that in the car." Kenny put his orange and navy blue Chicago Bears skullcap on his head.

"No, I want to discuss it now," Beverly said through clenched teeth. She stood in a stance that suggested she wasn't leaving until she got an answer from him.

"I don't know, Bev." Kenny shrugged his shoulders. "I'm still praying over what to do."

Beverly took a step away from him. "Then you do what you have to do, and so will I." She walked toward a bank of telephones. Kenny trailed helplessly behind her.

"What do you mean?" Kenneth asked as he struggled to keep up with Beverly's rapid pace.

"Until you decide what you're going to do, I think it's best that I stay with my sister, Babs," Beverly snapped as she continued walking away from Kenny.

"And how are you going to get to Babs's house?" Kenny asked as he walked rapidly to keep pace with Beverly.

"I can call a cab, or call Babs and ask her to come get me. I am disappointed in you, Kenneth Howard," Beverly said in an acerbic tone of voice.

"I think you're trying to force me to bail out Amir," Kenneth muttered under his breath.

The couple had reached the bank of pay phones, and all of them were in use. Beverly stood in line behind six people, waiting for her turn.

"Why are you standing in line for a pay phone? Where's your cell phone? You know all of this isn't necessary." Kenny scratched the side of his head and then held up his hands. "You've made your point. I never said I wouldn't bail Amir out of jail. We need to talk about it. You don't have to try to manipulate me to make a point."

Beverly looked up at her husband. Her eyes widened in disbelief. "So you think I'm trying to manipulate you? Humph . . . I don't think so." She moved up in the line. "I don't need your money. I can get the money myself if I have to. I have resources."

"Why don't you come home with me? Or at least let me take you to Babs's house. This line is long. I think we need to put our feelings aside and decide what's best for Amir, not just now, but in the long run," Kenny said in a wheedling tone of voice.

Beverly moved up another space in line. "I already know what's best for Amir." She pointed her finger at Kenny. "You can go on home. I'll handle things from here on out."

Kenny fought back a wave of anger. He looked at his wife dubiously. "I think you're making a mistake, but I am not going to argue with you. I will see you later." He turned on his heels and headed for the exit.

Beverly watched her husband walk away; then she turned back around. *I don't need him anyway. He wasn't going to help Amir. My poor baby can't depend on anyone but me. I hope my sister is home, and that she'll come and get me. Otherwise I'm in trouble.* Beverly moved forward two steps and willed herself not to look in Kenny's direction. She knew when she'd walked in the door of the police station that the situation would prove to be trying, and her assumption was correct.

Her shoulders sagged with indecision. It was Beverly's turn to use the phone. She removed a calling card from her wallet, picked up the receiver, and then dialed her sister's house. The phone rang until the answering machine picked up the call.

Lord, I hope I'm making the right decision, she thought as a familiar hand covered her own, disconnecting the call. Beverly looked around to see Kenny standing behind her.

"Come on, Bev, let's go home." She hung up the receiver and followed her husband docilely out the building, and then down the street to their car.

They didn't speak as they fought their way through the blustery Chicago winds, which stung their faces. Tears streamed from Beverly's eyes at the thought of leaving her precious son behind bars for even one night.

Chapter Nineteen

After weeks of studying the scriptures that Reverend Nixon had provided her and reflecting on the therapy meetings, Julia softened her stance regarding her treatment of Erin, and a semblance of peace reigned in the Freeman household. Julia planned to leave work early that day so she could accompany Erin and Brandon to Erin's doctor appointment that afternoon. It was about 6:45 A.M., and Julia had another fifteen minutes to sleep. She inched closer to Douglas's side of the bed to snuggle close to her husband's warm body, and instead Julia found an empty space.

She sat up on her elbows after Douglas burst frantically into the room.

"Jules," he shouted, rushing over to the bed. "Get up. Something is terribly wrong with Erin."

Julia immediately sat upright in the bed, "What do you mean? What's wrong with her?" Her heart rate soared inside her chest.

"I don't have time to explain now. Please get up. We need to get her to the hospital as soon as possible." Douglas went to the walk-in closet and began shedding his robe and pajamas, and quickly put on his clothes.

Julia lay in the bed stunned. She swung one leg out of the bed and then the other. She pushed her hair off her face. "Should we call an ambulance? Maybe I should go check on her," she said timidly as her hands began to shake. Julia clasped them together.

"Just get dressed. Brandon is with her now, trying to calm her down. I don't think we have time to wait for an ambulance to arrive. Erin is having severe pains, and from the way Brandon described them, it doesn't sound like normal labor pains. As soon as you get dressed, we're going to the hospital," Douglas replied as Julia walked to the closet, pulling off her nightgown and then getting dressed.

Fifteen minutes later the couple rushed to the basement and found Erin fully clad, lying listlessly on the untidy peach sheets on the full-sized bed. Brandon looked up as his parents walked into the bedroom. His face was a mask of fright while Erin's face was scrunched up from pain.

Julia bent over her moaning daughter-in-law. "Where does it hurt?"

"My stomach feels like a belt is tied too tightly around it. I've been having pain since last night and some light bleeding," the pale young woman admitted. She screwed up her face and let out an agonizing wail.

"Why didn't you say something last night? You don't think you're in labor, do you?" Julia asked. "The baby isn't due for another month or so."

"I don't know, Mama Jules." A wince crossed Erin face. "I never had a baby before."

"I'm going to pull the car around to the front door. Brandon, help your wife up the stairs," Douglas ordered. He looked apprehensively at Erin. "You can walk, can't you?"

She nodded and gingerly maneuvered her massive body over to the edge of the bed.

Douglas said, "Jules, you and Brandon help her up the stairs. I'll be in the front." He looked at Erin again. "That is, if you think you can make it. Otherwise, we could call an ambulance," he suggested.

"No, don't do that," Erin said mournfully as she rubbed her back. She looked at the stairs, the height of which seemed as high as Mount Everest.

"I'll bring the car to the front while you and Brandon help her up the stairs," Julia suggested, wringing her hands helplessly together.

She raced up the stairs and out the back door to the garage. By the time, she drove to the front of the house, Brandon and Douglas were walking out the door supporting Erin's weight as best they could.

Julia pushed a button on the dashboard, which opened the trunk. She got out of the car, took a navy blue blanket out of it and spread the blanket along the backseat. Julia watched while Erin eased her body inside the vehicle. Julia hopped into the front passenger seat. Douglas pulled the car away from the curb and sped to Little Company of Mary Hospital.

Brandon looking frightened as he held his sobbing wife's hand. Julia kept craning her neck to look in the backseat. She was alarmed to see blood pooling under Erin's body. Julia whispered grimly to Douglas, "Hurry up."

Douglas exceeded the speed limit, and twenty minutes later the tires screamed on the pavement as he passed the red-and-white-striped emergency sign on the side of the hospital. Julia jumped out of the car and ran inside the building. She returned minutes later with hospital personnel. The aides quickly transferred Erin into a wheelchair as Brandon looked beseechingly from his parents to his wife.

"Go on with Erin. We'll be inside in a minute. I'm going to park the car," Douglas instructed his son. He drove down the street and around the block before he found a parking space.

He and Julia exited the car and walked toward the hospital. "What a morning," Douglas commented as he ran his hand over his head. "I hope Erin is going to be all right."

"I hope so too. Do you think we should call her parents? I mean, have Brandon call them?"

"Let's wait and see what happens first. There's no need to get everyone in an uproar until we know something definite."

"It's just too early." Julia shook her head. "I just hope the baby is okay."

"Erin and the baby will be fine. She's close to her eighth month," Douglas said as they walked into the hospital and headed to the emergency room.

Brandon fled from his seat when he saw his parents. "They took Erin back there." He pointed to the emergency room doors.

Douglas said kindly to his son as he gripped Brandon's arm, "Stay strong. Trust in the Lord. He will take care of Erin. Let's stay prayerful."

They sat tensely as they waited for someone on the medical staff to give them an update on Erin's status. After thirty minutes and numerous trips to the information desk, finally a doctor came to the waiting room and called Brandon's name.

The young man hurried from his seat and raised his hand. "I'm Brandon Freeman." He walked toward the doctor, and Douglas and Julia walked behind him.

"How is Erin, I mean my wife?" Brandon's words seemed to run together. He unconsciously clenched and unclenched his hands nervously.

"She's weak from blood loss, and we're still trying to stabilize her blood pressure. Her readings have been very erratic," the doctor answered. He looked tired as if he had been at work many hours. Stubble covered his brown chin. His clothing was wrinkled and marked with faint brown stains.

"Um, can I . . . I mean, can I see her?" Brandon's voice cracked as he rocked on the balls of his feet.

The doctor looked at Douglas and Julia. "Are you his parents?"

"Yes, we are," Douglas answered. "Has Erin's doctor been called?" Douglas put his arm around Julia's waist.

"Yes, we've called Dr. Livingstone, Erin's obstetrician. She should be here momentarily. She was already in the hospital dealing with another emergency. We're trying to get Erin comfortable." The doctor looked back at Brandon. "Yes, you can see her now."

"Will you come with me?" Brandon asked Julia as if he were a little boy. Terror still shone in his eyes.

"Why don't you go ahead with doctor"—Douglas glanced at the nametag clipped to the doctor's white coat—"Dr. Byrd, and then we'll join you in a minute. I need to call the office." He glanced down at Julia. "You can go with him now if you'd like, and I'll come back there after I'm done with my call."

Suddenly the doctor's pager sounded. He took it out of his pocket, looked down at it, and said to Brandon tersely, "Excuse me. Why don't you wait here? I'll have a nurse come back to take you to your wife's room." He jogged back to the doors and disappeared inside.

A nurse met the doctor as he entered the emergency area. "Dr. Byrd, the patient in cubicle two is in trouble. They both raced down the hallway. "She's hemorrhaging again."

Douglas looked at the closed door thoughtfully and wondered if Erin was in trouble. He suggested Julia and Brandon return to their seats and said he'd join them after he called his office. Douglas walked rapidly to the nearest exit.

Brandon's face was ashen and his eyes dilated with fear. "You don't think something bad happened to Erin, do you?" He swayed in his seat, feeling as if he were going to be physically ill.

Julia shook her head and took her son's arm. "Let's go sit down. I'm sure someone will be back shortly to take you to see Erin."

Brandon shivered and looked fearfully at the closed doors. Then he submissively followed his mother to a row of seats in the front of the waiting room.

Douglas returned several minutes later. He sat down and closed his eyes, while Julia fidgeted in her seat, praying the Lord would forgive her for every mean thing she had ever said to Erin.

Brandon leaned forward in the chair. His elbows were propped on his thighs, and his head was lowered. He was terrified about Erin and the baby's condition. The young man didn't love Erin with a deep, abiding love, but that was his baby Erin was struggling to bring into the world. He had gotten caught up with being a celebrity while attending college. It was a heady feeling to be the big man on campus, a part of the elite basketball squad. Many women, including Erin, threw themselves at him left and right. Erin was quite persistent in her dogged pursuit of Brandon.

The young man had gone to a party with a few members of the squad, knowing he needed to stay in the dorm and study for an English exam. Brandon let his guard down and had one drink. He became dizzy. To that day, Brandon never knew that he had been drugged. Erin volunteered to take him back to his dorm. The young man woke up later to find himself naked in the bed with Erin unclothed by his side. The pair dated a few times after the party, and then a month later Erin informed Brandon that she was pregnant and he was the father. Brandon wanted Erin to have an abortion, but she refused, and when his father caught wind of his failing grades, Douglas flew to Nashville immediately. When he learned his son was going to be a father, Douglas insisted the couple marry, saying he didn't want his grandchild born out of wedlock.

Julia pitched a fit when she learned the news. She berated Brandon for not using protection and hammered home how he could have been infected with HIV. Brandon and Erin married at a Nashville courthouse with Douglas and a hysterical Julia in attendance. Erin's pregnancy proved to be difficult, and her family disowned her once they found out Brandon was African American. Douglas decided to bring the couple back to Chicago with him and Julia. It was later decided that Brandon would work and attend night school while waiting for the birth of the baby. Instead, Brandon took at job with UPS and decided to try his hand at being a rapper.

Douglas had returned to the waiting area, and he and Julia were talking softly. Brandon lifted his head and said to his parents, "Mom, Pops, on the real, do you think Erin is going to be all right?"

Julia nodded receptively. "I'm sure everything is going to work out fine, son. It's not unusual for women to suffer complications while giving birth." Then Julia remembered her own experience, and her body quavered. "I just know that the doctor is going to come and talk to us soon. You'll see, they'll tell us that everything is fine." She patted her son's shoulder.

"God, I'm so scared," Brandon whispered. "Did I tell you that Erin wanted to name the baby Julian if we had a son? She decided to name the baby Juliana after you and her grandmother, Ana, when we found out she was having a girl."

Julia tried to smile, and her lips trembled. "No, I didn't know that. I know God is going to take care of our little girl. So try to calm down."

It seemed like an eternity had elapsed before Dr. Byrd returned to the waiting room. Douglas and Brandon rose from their seats. Julia could see from the doctor's expression that the news wasn't good. He shook his head regretfully from side to side. "Erin is not responding as well as we would have liked. We can't seem to get her pressure stabilized, so we're going to perform an emergency C-section. Dr. Livingstone is scrubbing as we speak."

Brandon's body sagged so heavily that Douglas grabbed his arm. "Can I see her?" the young man asked the doctor.

"Yes, I think you should." The doctor looked solemnly at the family. "Would you like to come back with your son?" he asked Julia and Douglas. "We usually allow only one or two persons at a time . . . We can waive the rule this time."

"Thank you. Yes, we'd like to come with our son," Douglas replied as the doctor led them to the emergency room.

"We're going to take her to the operating room in a few minutes, and from there she'll probably be moved to a regular labor room, if all goes well," he explained in a hushed tone of voice. He then led them to cubicle two.

Erin could barely raise her head when they walked in the room. She looked pale and licked her chapped lips. "I'm sorry, Mama Jules, for upsetting you," she apologized to Julia.

Julia walked beside the bed and pushed Erin's damp hair off her forehead. "Now, don't you worry about my feelings, young lady. You need to take care of yourself and get my grandbaby into the world." Julia tried smiling and nearly broke down.

Brandon walked to the other side of the bed and looked down at his wife. "How you feeling, Erin?"

"Not real good. Like your mama said, I gotta get this baby born. I'm going to be fine." She tried to smile, and her body went limp as her breathing became shallow. The blood pressure monitor began beeping like an impatient driver hitting his horn while stuck in traffic.

Julia looked on helplessly while Douglas ran from the room shouting for help. The nurse and doctor ran into the room. Dr. Livingstone took one look at the monitor and said, "Okay, folks, you've got to leave the room. We need to get her to the operating room, STAT.

"I'll be back, Erin," Brandon shouted as Douglas led him out of the room. "Hang in there, girl."

Erin smiled feebly and nodded as the nurses and doctor began dealing with the calamity. A nurse intercepted them as they walked back to the waiting room. "The maternity operating room is on the other side of the hospital. They're taking Erin there now. Why don't you and your family wait there? I'm praying for you and your family."

"Thank you," Douglas said with a quiet dignity that was his trademark. "I appreciate that, and yes we'll head over to the operating room now."

As the family walked to another wing of the hospital, each was quietly lost in thought. Julia and Douglas were overcome with memories of another pregnancy that went awry many years ago. Brandon walked woodenly, his steps heavy.

Upon the trio's arrival at the maternity ward, a nurse led them to a private waiting room. She informed them that the doctor would be in to see them as soon as there was news.

"I just don't understand how this could happen," Brandon said. "Erin is healthy. Why did this have to happen to us?" He sat slumped in his chair.

"Her pregnancy was a high-risk one, son," Douglas answered. "Didn't she tell you that?"

"She mentioned that, but I didn't really know what she meant." Brandon looked up at his parents with teary eyes. "I still don't know what it means."

"Her pressure has been unstable throughout the pregnancy. That's why I'd take her to her doctor appointments when I could. Her doctor talked to me about the possibility of a caesarean section the last time I was there with Erin," Douglas explained to his son, as he tried to comfort him. "The Lord will see us through this dilemma. Let's just lean on Him and remain positive."

Guilt singed Julia's heart. She stood up. "I'm going to the ladies' room. Come and get me if the doctor comes back before I return."

Douglas nodded then turned back to his son.

Julia stopped at the nurse's station and asked for directions to the bathroom. She thanked the nurse then made a left turn and walked down the hallway. As soon as she walked inside the bathroom stall, Julia locked the door, then broke down and cried. *Lord, what have I done? How could I turn my back on that child? All she wanted to do was please me. But I was too caught up in my own needs to pay any attention to hers. I even doubted if the baby she was carrying was my son's.*

She clasped her hands in front of her body and bowed her head. This time she talked to God out loud. "Lord, please take care of Erin and the baby. Forgive me for not being more sensitive to Erin's needs. I was selfish, and I just hope that Erin and the baby don't have to pay the price for my ugliness. Because that's how I've been acting, Lord, pure ugly." Julia raised her hands over her head as she rocked from side to side. "Father above, hear my cry. Please take care of Erin and the baby. God, I beseech you in the name of Jesus."

Julia walked out of the stall, stood in front of the mirror a few more minutes; then she turned on the water and waited for it to heat up. After washing her hands she tore a paper towel from the dispenser, dampened it, and wiped her face. She mouthed, "Lord, give us strength for what lies ahead." After tossing the paper towel in the garbage can, Julia walked out of the bathroom and back down the hallway to her men. She held fast to the thought that God would work it out. She vowed to be more helpful to Erin in the future. As Julia neared the waiting room, she saw the doctor talking to Brandon, and her son gasp. Julia knew then that the news couldn't be good. As her stomach zigzagged, Julia walked slowly inside the room.

Chapter Twenty

Friday morning, Meesha sat on the side of the bed inside her bedroom and watched Edward snap shut the gold lock on his suitcase. He had just finished packing for his trip to Dallas. He would return home on Tuesday or Wednesday evening.

Did you pack everything you need?" Meesha asked. "You know you always forget something when you travel."

Edward picked the suitcase up off the bed and sat it on the floor next to the door. He walked back over to the bed, leaned over, and picked up a Post-it note from the floor that had fallen from the nightstand. He hastily stuffed it inside his pants pocket. "I'm pretty sure I have everything. I created a checklist this time, and I've checked off everything as I packed." He waved the list at his wife, and then handed her a sheet of paper. "Here's my itinerary. You might have a hard time reaching me during the day and some evenings. I'll be in meetings most of the trip."

He turned and walked to the dresser, stood in front of the mirror, and tied his tie.

"That takes care of the day. Where will you be during the night?" Meesha asked him dryly, as her eyebrows arched upward.

"Don't start, Meesha," Edward said sharply. "Can't we just be civil for a change? You know how hard I work for the family. We should wrap up this project within the next couple of weeks, a month tops. When we do, we'll be one step closer to easy street."

"That may be how you see it," Meesha said, "but we both know that there will be other horizons for you to conquer. Shoot, I don't see an end to this madness. Now you're traveling to Texas too. It seems you're there more than you are here. One day you're going to wake up, Edward, and wish you had smelled the roses and not sacrificed so much of your time to your job and paid more attention to your family." She fidgeted with the scarf around her head.

Edward glared at Meesha. "I'm not going there with you this morning. I have important meetings to attend today, and I refuse to let you get inside my head and mess up my day." He put his watch on and picked up his suitcases. "I'm going to head out. My limousine should be pulling up right about now."

The doorbell rang. "That's probably the driver," Edward said. "Why don't you answer the door while I go tell the kids good-bye."

"Sure," Meesha said sarcastically. She folded her hands together and bowed, "Anything for the lord and master of the manor." She walked out of the room to answer the door.

Edward sighed, feeling that nothing he did was good enough for Meesha. He'd had it up to here with her nagging. Edward had been toying with the idea, unbeknownst to Meesha, that perhaps it was time for him to make some changes in his life. He was the man, and he had other options. Edward felt he needed a woman who appreciated what he did to get ahead and, most important, who knew how to keep her mouth shut some of the time. His eyes swept over the bedroom once more. He then departed the room and walked down the beige-carpeted hallway and stopped at Keon's bedroom first.

The little boy's room was a bit untidy, but not overly messy. Games were stacked carelessly from constant usage on a white shelf on the wall of his blue-painted room. Keon's prized computer sat on the left side of the wooden computer desk. His prized PS2 lay on the other side of the desk. Meesha had painted a mural of sports equipment that included balls, bats, a hockey stick, tennis rackets, and nets on one of the walls. Edward walked over to the bed, bent down, and kissed his son's forehead.

Keon opened his eyes and wiped them with his fists. "Hi, Daddy." He smiled sleepily. "You going away?"

"Yes, son. I'll be back early next week, and when I come back we're going to hang out together, just us men. I promise." Edward wiped a crumb from the corner of his son's eyes.

"Cross your heart and hope to die?" Keon looked hard at his father.

Edward was taken aback. "Sure."

"Daddy, you said that the last time you went out of town. I waited for you to go to a football game with me, but you had to go to work, so Mom had to take me. I wish you'd come to my games sometimes like the other daddies do." Keon turned away from Edward and curled his body into a ball.

Edward felt a shaft of guilt run throughout his body. "I promise you that we'll spend time together, and I'll go to your next game." He held up two fingers. "Don't give your mother any trouble, and I'll see you Tuesday or Wednesday."

"Kay, Daddy." Keon pulled the comforter over his head and went back to sleep.

Edward walked across the hall to Imani's girly room. Candy striped wallpaper covered the walls in her room. In the center of the room was a white canopy bed. Books and a ballerina doll collection were placed on the shelves. Black Raggedy Ann and Andy dolls lay atop her toy box. Ballerina posters were taped on the walls along with a mural of a black ballerina that Meesha had painted on the wall opposite Imani's bed.

When the little girl saw her father, she jumped out of the bed and ran into Edward's arms. She hugged and buried her nose in Edward's neck; then she peered at him sadly. "Daddy, do you have to go away?" Her small face dropped.

"Yes, I do, sweetie, but I won't be gone long, just for a couple of days." Edward squeezed his daughter close and inhaled her bubble gum bath scent.

Imani said dramatically, "I wish you weren't going. I miss you when you're gone. Are you going to bring something back?" she asked Edward hopefully.

"Don't I always?" he chuckled. "I will be back before you know it." He carried Imani back to the bed and laid her on top of the sheet and pulled the comforter over her body.

"Don't forget my dance recital is next Saturday, Daddy. You have to be back to see me dance my solo," she reminded Edward as she snuggled under the pink comforter.

"You know I wouldn't miss my baby dancing for the world. I'll be home soon, Princess. Mind your mom while I'm away." Edward glanced down at his watch. "I've got to go. I'll see you on Tuesday."

"Okay, Daddy. I'm going to miss you." She waved at her dad as he left the room.

"Me too, baby. Be good."

Edward rushed down the stairs and to the door. Meesha stood at the door, holding his coat and briefcase. She handed both of them to him.

He sat the case on the floor, put on the coat, and fastened the buttons.

Meesha said to Edward, "Have a safe trip, and don't forget Imani's recital is next Saturday. She'll die if you don't make it."

Edward grimaced. "She reminded me when I told her good-bye. I don't plan to miss it. Hey, I have to go. Take care of the kids and be careful." Edward began walking out the door.

"Aren't you forgetting something?" Meesha asked as she thrust her face toward Edward.

"Sorry," Edward mumbled and kissed the side of his wife's face. "I'll see you Tuesday or Wednesday evening."

"Good-bye, Edward," Meesha said somberly; then she closed and locked the door. She walked to the window and watched the driver take Edward's bags and stow them inside the trunk while Edward got inside the vehicle. A few minutes later, the car pulled away from the curb, and Edward was on his way to O'Hare airport.

Meesha walked back upstairs and checked on the children. She stopped in Keon's room and tucked the comforter over his shoulders. Then she returned to her and Edward's bedroom and put the items away that Edward had decided not to take with him. She placed his itinerary on the nightstand, and then Meesha got into the bed.

Meesha pondered why her relationship with Edward seemed to be on an endless downward spiral. She wondered if they would even be married this time next year. If she were a betting woman, her answer would be no. Meesha wondered where she went wrong and if she was incorrect to insist that her husband spend time with her and the children.

Meesha and Edward's bank account had never been healthier, and she could buy any material object her heart desired. Nonetheless, Meesha knew something vital had gone from her and Edward's relationship. Meesha longed for the days when they first bought the house and then brought the children home from the hospital. She reminisced back to her wedding day up until the present time.

"I tried to stifle my feelings for the sake of the children and to keep the peace. Perhaps I waited too long to make my feelings known," Meesha sobbed silently. "Lord, is my marriage over? Is this how it ends?" She put her hands over her eyes, and her shoulders heaved as she wept. Eventually she fell into an uneasy sleep.

Meesha's eyes flew open. She looked up to Imani pulling on her arm, concern gleaming in the little girl's eyes. "Mommy, you didn't wake up me and Keon. It's time for us to get up and get ready for school."

Meesha looked at the clock on the nightstand. "Goodness, you're right. Go get your brother up. I'm going to call my office and go to work late. I'll be in your rooms in a minute to pick out something for you to wear to school." Meesha was thankful that Imani was an early riser like her father.

"Okay." Imani ran out of the bedroom into her brother's room. Meesha could hear her daughter yelling at Keon to get out of bed.

Meesha sat on the side of the bed, wiggled her toes, and yawned. She felt lethargic, like she hadn't gotten enough sleep. Then she remembered Edward's slight when he left for Dallas. She sighed and got out of bed.

She walked down the hallway to Keon's room and found Imani still trying to rouse her brother from the bed. "Tell you what, Imani. Why don't you go wash up? I'll put out an outfit for you to wear to school today. Leave your brother to me. I'm going to fix a hot breakfast for you two this morning; no cereal. Then I'll drop you off at school."

"Yippee. I will, Mommy." The little girl departed and went into her bedroom. Edward had a bathroom built last year that was attached to Imani's bedroom.

"Keon Edward Morrison, it's time for you to rise and shine." Meesha began tickling Keon.

Laughing, he pulled away from his mother. "Okay, Mommy, I'm getting up." He scooted out of the bed to escape Meesha's tickling fingers and went outside the room to the hall bathroom.

Meesha quickly made up her son's bed. Then she walked over to his dresser drawer and removed jeans, a blue turtleneck, and a white and red sweatshirt. Next she laid a pair of heavy socks and underwear on top of Keon's bed.

"Hurry up, kids," Meesha yelled as she walked to Imani's room. She took a pair of red, bibbed corduroy pants and a pink top out of her daughter's closet along with underwear and socks.

Satisfied with her choices in the children's clothing, Meesha sped to her room, called her office, and was about to inform her secretary that she would be about an hour late to work that morning. Meesha changed her mind and told her assistant that she was going to take the day off. She felt out of sorts that morning. She decided to take the children to school and then come home for some much needed "me time." *God knows I need it*, Meesha thought.

She went to the bathroom, showered, dressed, and afterward headed to the kitchen. Meesha prepared oatmeal with raspberries, turkey bacon, and hot chocolate with whipped cream for the children. An hour later, she and the children departed the house. She dropped the children off at school and then returned home.

She put roasted coffee beans into the coffee maker and waited for her morning drink to brew. Then Meesha contemplated what to do with herself the rest of the day.

Though she tossed and turned during the night from indecision about how to respond to Rev. Nixon, Zora arrived at work on time that morning. She had a consultation scheduled in twenty minutes, one that she wasn't quite prepared for. She couldn't stop her eyes from straying to the beautiful floral arrangement of red and yellow tulips that sat on the left side of her desk. Tiffany had brought the vase and card from Calvin to her office a half hour ago.

Zora couldn't stop a grin from blossoming across her face as her telephone rang. She waited for Tiffany to answer the call and when she didn't after five rings, Zora picked up the receiver. "Hello, this is Zora Taylor. How may I help you?" she said in her most professional voice.

"Good morning, Zora. How are you this morning?" Calvin asked her.

"Good morning to you, Calvin. I feel blessed this morning. How are you?" Zora used her free hand to nervously twist a lock of her hair.

"Blessed and sanctified. How is your day going so far?" Calvin asked as he spun his chair around to face the window in his corner office.

"Not bad." Her eyes traveled to the butcher-block clock on the wall. "I have an appointment with one of the students soon."

"My day is going well, but it would be better if a certain guidance counselor would agree to have dinner with me tonight," Calvin replied solemnly with a twinkle in his eye. "You might have an inkling of who I'm talking about," he teased Zora.

"I think I might have an idea." Her voice dropped to a husky whisper.

"So what do you think, Ms. Taylor? Do you think I could have the honor of your presence tonight? I promise to have you home at a decent hour. The band playing tonight is simply awesome, and the food is quite appetizing." Calvin turned to his desk and scanned an e-mail that had popped into his inbox.

Zora closed her eyes for a minute. She inhaled deeply then exhaled. Her head told her that the right thing to do would be to turn down Calvin's invitation. Her heart told another story, and she couldn't deny the attraction she felt toward the minister.

"Tiffany just brought in the flowers you sent. They're lovely," she said, trying to change the subject.

"Well I'm glad you liked them. It was my pleasure to give them to you. Give me some credit, woman. That means I can do some things right," he ribbed Zora. Calvin closed an e-mail and opened another one, which he printed out. Then he turned his attention back to the conversation.

The moment had come for Zora to put up or shut up. She took a deep breath. "Yes, Calvin, I'll go out with you tonight. I mean I'd love to have dinner with you tonight."

"Great," Calvin's voice boomed jovially across the phone line. "I'll pick you up at seven o'clock. Is that time good for you?"

"That will be fine. Look, I have to go. I'll see you tonight."

"Okay. I'll be at your house at seven o'clock sharp, And, Zora, thank you. I promise you won't regret your decision." Calvin hung up the phone after he and Zora exchanged good-byes.

Zora held the phone to her chest and prayed that she had made the right decision. She buzzed Tiffany and asked her to send in Jordan for his session. Jordan was close to making a choice for college and wanted another opinion, so he requested a consultation with Zora.

Following Zora's appointment with Jordan, she debated what to do for lunch. She didn't have anything to wear for her date. It had been so long since she indulged in that social activity. Zora recalled that there was a strip mall located a few miles from the school. Though she and Meesha planned to go shopping after work, Zora decided to go to the mall in case Meesha's plans changed. She reached in her bottom desk drawer for her purse when her telephone buzzed.

After Zora pushed the talk button, Tiffany announced, "Dr. Taylor, Mrs. Morrison is here to see you. Is it okay if I send her in?"

"Sure, by all means," Zora said as she closed the drawer. Meesha walked into the room and over to Zora's desk. The women embraced; then Meesha sat in the chair in front of Zora's desk.

"Why aren't you at work?" Zora asked her friend, alarmed at Meesha's hollow eyes.

"I overslept and decided to stay home today," Meesha answered flippantly as she squirmed in her seat.

"Well, that's not like you. Is something wrong? Did you and Edward have another spat?" Zora asked her friend.

"No, I wouldn't call it an argument exactly. It was as if Edward wasn't there with me. He was in the room with me physically, but mentally he was somewhere else."

Zora tried to downplay Meesha's fears. "Well, there's nothing new about that. Edward has been driven and focused on taking care of business since we were in college."

Meesha paused and replied thoughtfully, "That's true, but something is different this time. When he left for his business trip this morning he forgot to kiss me good-bye. That has never happened before, no matter how bad things have gotten between us." She couldn't prevent the devastation she felt from Edward's actions from glimmering in her eyes.

Zora stood up and walked around her desk. She sat in the seat next to her friend. Zora patted Meesha's hand. "I'm sure that he's just preoccupied with work. He probably looks at this project as the culmination of everything that he's tried to attain, and his attention is honed in on the outcome of the trip."

Meesha wiped a tear from her eye. Zora leaned across her desk and handed her friend a tissue.

"I could almost believe you, but my wife's intuition is telling me a different story. Since Edward was promoted to director of sales a year ago, he's started changing. Now he's like a different person. He's hardly at home, and he's been traveling nonstop as if he doesn't want to be home with me and the children. I feel like I'm losing him, Zora. I think Edward could be cheating. I never thought I'd say those words, ever. In my heart"—she put her hand on her chest—"I feel like my husband is going to leave me. And I don't know what to do about it."

Meesha began sobbing loudly. Zora put her arm around her friend's shoulder as Meesha released her doubts and fears. She wept a while longer, then picked up the balled up pink tissue and blew her nose. "I feel so stupid, and even worse, I'm bringing you down with my troubles."

"That's not true," Zora protested, holding up her hand. "You can always talk to me. I will always be here for you as you have been for me in the past. I was just going to lunch. There's a deli in a strip mall not far from here. Let's have lunch together."

Meesha felt drained, and her movements were slow as the women prepared to leave, putting on their coats. After Zora locked her office, she informed Tiffany that she didn't have any afternoon appointments and wouldn't be returning to the office after lunch. Zora asked Tiffany to remain in the office for a few hours in case an emergency arose, then Tiffany could start her weekend early. Zora was determined to cheer up Meesha.

The women drove west on Ninety-fifth Street to a local deli. After finding a space in the busy parking lot, they went inside the restaurant, ordered food, and ate their lunch in an orange booth near the window. After talking over the meal, the friends drove to Evergreen Plaza. They found a great sale at Carson Pirie Scott & Co. Zora bought a couple of outfits for her date with Reverend Nixon. She was indecisive about which outfit she preferred. Meesha bought socks, undershirts, and tops for her children. Before Meesha and Zora headed home, Zora promised to share with Meesha the next morning details of her date with Reverend Nixon.

Chapter Twenty-one

Early Friday afternoon, Beverly sat at the kitchen table with a cup of coffee at her left hand. The thick Yellow Pages book was opened to the attorneys section. Beverly was searching for a lawyer to represent Amir. The young man had been arraigned that morning and charged with one count of domestic violence and battery. As soon as Beverly arrived home from court, she began looking for an attorney to represent her son.

Kenneth almost had to physically remove Beverly from the courtroom after Amir was charged. She yelled to the judge after his pronouncement, "You're wrong. It was only an accident."

The judge banged his gavel and said stridently, "Order in the court."

Beverly grabbed Amir's arm as he was being led from the courtroom and wouldn't let go until Kenneth separated his wife from their son. As Amir was being led out the door, he turned and looked at his mother with a pleading look on his face. Beverly shouted to Amir to be strong and told him she and Kenneth would find him the best lawyer that money could buy.

Beverly was distraught when she found out a bail hearing would be set for the following week due to the overcrowding of the docket. She expressed her disapproval with the court system as she and Kenneth rode home.

When Kenneth came downstairs to the kitchen, he had changed clothes for work. He poured himself a cup of coffee and sat across the table from Beverly. He silently watched her put a check mark by a lawyer's name, and then sipped his cup of coffee.

"How's it going?" he asked his wife. Beverly looked haggard. There were circles under her eyes, and her lips were pursed downward in a permanent frown.

"I've found a couple of neighborhood attorneys, and I'm going to call them later. I also plan to contact a bail bondsman today," Beverly replied without looking up at her husband. She turned a page in the book and peered at more attorneys' names.

"I wish I could stay home with you, but one of my employees is sick. So I have to go in because we're shorthanded. I'll probably work late," Kenneth said, shaking his head. He sat the cup on the table and stared at Beverly.

"That's okay. I want to do this myself. I logged on to my job's website and downloaded a leave of absence form. I'm going to take it to the office later, and then I'm going to call the jail to see if I can visit Amir today." Beverly was employed as a secretary for a local real estate firm.

"Don't you think you should have discussed taking a leave from work with me first?" Kenneth asked Beverly unsmilingly. He thought she had really gone over the edge, and Amir hadn't even gone to trial yet. He couldn't imagine what her mental state would be if Amir had to do time. Beverly's hand shook as she turned another page of the book.

"Truthfully, I didn't think you'd care either way, so I made the decision on my own," Beverly responded sarcastically. She picked up her coffee mug, took a sip, and frowned because the brew had become cold.

"Of course I care. If we're going to lose part of our income, then I want to know about it," Kenneth said in as neutral a tone of voice as he could manage. "I'm sure your leave will be an unpaid one. How long do you plan to be off work? I don't want to upset you or anything, hon, but what makes you think Amir will get bail? This is his third or fourth offense, so I don't think he's getting out any time soon."

"That's your opinion, Kenny, and I disagree with you. Amir has had minor scrapes with the law, nothing major. Anyway, I want to use the house as collateral for bail." Beverly glanced up at her husband and then dropped her head back down to the phone book.

"I don't think that's a good idea," Kenneth said after he drained the last of the coffee from the cup. He stood up, put the cup in the kitchen sink, and turned to face his wife.

"What do you mean that isn't a good idea? How else is Amir going to get out of jail?" Beverly's mouth dropped open. Her eyes flung daggers at Kenneth.

"Just what I said, Bev. I'm not risking my home and everything I've worked for my whole life on Amir. Who knows, he might decide to skip town or something."

Beverly looked wounded. "How can you say something like that? Amir would never do that to us. I am offended that you would think that about the boy you helped raise. If necessary, I'll call the mortgage company to see if we could get a second mortgage on the house. I plan to go see Keisha soon and ask her to talk to the district attorney and tell them that what happened was an accident."

"I have to leave for work soon." Kenneth glanced at his watch. "Before you do anything rash, let's talk about it. I think you should leave Keisha alone and let the law handle it. You don't want to be charged with witness tampering, now do you?" He smiled, trying to lighten the mood. Kenneth didn't want to tell her there would be no second mortgage. He knew she was spoiling for a fight.

"If you thought that was funny, it wasn't." Beverly gave Kenneth an ugly look. "After all, Keisha is my grandson's mother. Surely I am allowed to visit her and see how she's doing. Anyway, I just want to hear her version of what happened. We can discuss the money situation all you want, but I am going to do what I have to do to make sure my son gets out of jail."

"There's nothing wrong with calling her to see how she's doing. Tracey talked to her sister yesterday, and she said Keisha will probably need reconstructive surgery. I don't think you should bring up Amir. Wait for Keisha to bring up what happened," Kenneth advised Beverly.

"I'll think about it. . . . Now if that's all you have to say, then I need to get back to finding a lawyer for Amir. We can talk after you get home, but nothing you can say is going to stop me. If I have to arrange for a loan on my own, then I'll do that."

"Good luck with that." Kenneth opened the refrigerator door and removed a brown paper bag that contained a turkey sandwich on rye and a bunch of grapes. He also took a bottle of water from the shelf, and then closed the door. "I'll talk to you later."

Kenneth went to his and Beverly's bedroom, removed his wallet from the nightstand, stuffed it inside his pocket, and walked back into the kitchen. He walked over to Beverly and leaned down to kiss the top of her head. After he stood up, Kenneth looked at Beverly with a worried expression, as if he wanted to say something. He thought better of it and departed for work.

I don't understand Kenneth. Beverly closed her eyes and massaged the pressure point between them. She could feel a stress headache coming on. In her mind, Beverly thought Kenneth was being unreasonable about not mortgaging the house. He knew there wasn't any other option to get Amir out of jail. Beverly felt if Tracey were in trouble, Kenneth wouldn't hesitate to do everything in his power to help their daughter. Beverly couldn't understand why everyone was against Amir, even her relatives.

She blamed Amir's negative behavior on his father, Zeke. He had deserted the family when Amir was a baby. Beverly's mother had advised her daughter not to marry Zeke, but Beverly didn't heed her advice. Many a day she wished that she had. Beverly shook her head. If she had listened to her mother, she would not have had Amir. "Excuse me, Lord, for my harsh thoughts. Take care of my boy. Lord, please make it right for him," Beverly said aloud.

An hour later, Beverly had called five attorneys. One turned her down outright, and the others said they'd call her back on Monday. Beverly felt disconsolate one minute and angry the next. It seemed the deck was stacked against Amir. She called the jail to see if she could visit Amir, and was told that he was still being processed and to call back tomorrow. After she hung up the telephone, Beverly burst into tears. Nothing was going the way she hoped.

She sobbed for a few minutes, wiped her eyes, and used a napkin to blow her nose. Then she stood up, walked to the refrigerator, and removed a chicken from the freezer to cook for dinner. Beverly looked beaten; then she straightened her body and thought, *Satan is busy, but I'm not going to let him win.* She put her mug in the sink and rinsed it along with the cup Kenneth had used.

Beverly went upstairs to shower and dress, then began what she thought could be a long, but she hoped productive, day. An hour later, Beverly was seated in the office of her supervisor, Nancy Banks. The older woman double-checked the form to see if Beverly had signed it in all the necessary places. Sure enough, Beverly had missed a line. Nancy slid the paper across the desk to Beverly to sign.

After Beverly signed the final line on the form, she picked up her purse off the floor next to her chair. "Thank you for being so understanding. I know my being gone puts the office in a bind. To me, family comes first, and I have to do what I can for Amir."

Nancy, a no-nonsense, rail-thin woman with blue steel wool hair, nodded sympathetically at Beverly. "I understand. Believe me, I would do the same thing in your place. I hope all goes well with your son. I could only get your leave approved for a month, so I hope that's enough time for you to handle everything. If anything changes with your situation, let me know as soon as possible. The timing isn't great, but I'll do what I can."

"I appreciate it, Nancy. I can't believe this is happening to Amir. I think his ex-girlfriend is trying to get back at him because Amir broke up with her. You know how some of these girls are; they're just gold diggers," Beverly said self-righteously. She stood up, and put on her coat and gloves.

"Times are definitely different now than when we were coming up," Nancy commented. "Take care of yourself, Beverly, and try not to worry too much. Things will work out one way or the other."

"You're right about that. I'll call you next week," Beverly replied; then she left the office. As she walked out of the building, Beverly calculated her next move, which was a trip to the bank. There was a branch located on Stony Island Avenue, not far from her job, so she decided to go there.

Twenty minutes later, she was ushered into a personal banker's office, where Beverly quickly explained her reason for the visit. The banker accessed Kenneth and Beverly's account on her computer. Beverly informed the banker that she was looking to borrow a minimum of $20,000.

The banker entered data into her computer, and within a few minutes she told Beverly that her and Kenneth's accounts were in good standing. She reached into a desk drawer and gave Beverly an application.

"Do I have to apply for the loan with my husband?" Beverly's voice trembled as she tapped her foot on the floor. "Can't I get the loan myself?"

"You can certainly submit the application for yourself. Looking at your payroll information from your direct deposit data, I don't think you would qualify for a loan of that amount on your own unless you had an asset for collateral. Would you like to apply for a loan using collateral?"

"No, not really," Beverly admitted. She looked down at the floor.

"Then I suggest you apply for the loan with your husband. Or you and your husband could apply for a second mortgage. Why don't you take the papers with you, think about how you'd like to proceed, and call me back on Monday? You can submit the loan application online if you have access to a computer." She took a business card out of the holder on her desk and handed it to Beverly.

"Thank you. I guess I'll do that. If we took a second mortgage on the house, would that loan be approved quickly, without any problems?" Beverly asked as she stood up.

"Yes, that's correct. Your house is nearly paid for"—she looked at the PC monitor—"and you could always refinance the house."

Beverly nodded. The suggestions were good, except Kenny wouldn't approve of them. "Thank you, Mrs. Jones. I'll be in touch."

"Thank you, Mrs. Howard. Please feel free to call me if you have questions. I look forward to talking to you soon." Mrs. Jones stood and walked Beverly to the door.

Beverly exited the building to find the snow falling thickly and drifting into mounds. A brisk wind took her breath away, and Beverly put her hood on her head. Her eyes stung as she walked to her car. Nothing was going her way that day. Beverly felt like a failure as she got into the vehicle. It seemed she could do nothing to help Amir and that Satan was putting up roadblocks at every turn.

Beverly's mood brightened after she decided to go to the hospital to visit Keisha. She presumed that all she had to do was talk to Jalin's mother, and all of Amir's problems would disappear like a puff of smoke. Though the morning hadn't gone as she planned, she knew things weren't over until the fat lady sang. Beverly might be down, but she wasn't out. She still had a few tricks up her sleeve. During the drive to the hospital, Beverly decided to pick up a plant for Keisha. She remembered that there was a floral shop on Ninety-fifth Street in Oak Lawn.

While Beverly was plotting her next move, Kenneth was on his lunch break at work. He assisted a member of his staff who had been waiting on an irate customer. Then when Kenneth returned to his office, he logged on to the Internet. He wasn't fond of the World Wide Web, but he admitted it had its uses, and this was one of those times. Kenneth typed data with two fingers into the Goggle search box. *Maybe I can do something to help Amir, something that money can't buy.*

He waited a few minutes for the screen to return with selections. After a few seconds, a row of names was displayed. Kenneth sent the page to the printer on the credenza behind his desk. He glanced at the clock on his desk and noted that he had ten minutes before his break would be over. Kenneth balled up the paper bag that had contained his lunch and put it in the trash can near his feet. Then he screwed the cap back on his bottle of water and sat it on top of his desk.

When the printer stopped, Kenneth turned his chair, took the pages from the machine, and sat them on his desk. He opened the bottom drawer, removed a folder, and put the papers inside the folder. "Lord, I hope you will help Amir. Father, guide me as I try to help my family."

Chapter Twenty-two

The morning had come and gone. Julia, Douglas, and Brandon still found themselves at the hospital. Their faces were downcast, drooping with sadness, while their bodies wilted from the tension surrounding the day. Dr. Livingstone had informed the family that Erin had delivered a baby girl. The infant weighed a little over six pounds and was doing fine. Sadly, Erin had slipped into a light coma and had suffered a minor heart attack during the surgery.

The hospital staff categorized Erin's condition as serious. She had been stabilized to the point where she had been moved from recovery to a room on the maternity floor. Dr. Livingstone somberly informed the Freeman family that the next twenty-four hours were critical to Erin's recovery and that she would be monitored carefully by the nursing staff.

With all the chaos that had transpired that day, the family had yet to see the baby. A nurse had just come into the waiting room and informed them that they could see the baby whenever they were ready. Erin had filled out a visitor's list when she registered at the hospital. Douglas suggested Brandon stay the night with Erin. Julia emphasized that they would be only a phone call away and would return to the hospital if needed.

The trio trudged down the hallway and around two corners to the nursery where the newborn babies were housed. Their eyes swept hungrily through the heavy glass window separating visitors from the babies. There were five infants lying in the cribs. An African American girl and boy lay side by side. There were two Caucasian babies, two girls, and the last infant appeared to be a Hispanic boy bundled in a blue blanket.

A nurse walked into the room and spied the Freemans. She walked to the window and asked which baby they wanted to see. Brandon swallowed hard and said in a gravelly voice, "Baby Girl Freeman. I'm her father."

"We have gowns that you can put over your clothes. Why don't you come in?" The nurse ushered them into a small waiting room.

The nurse checked the ID bracelets that had been administered to them, and showed them where the dressing gowns were located. Minutes later, they waited for the nurse to bring Baby Girl Freeman into the room.

In no time, Brandon stared down at his first child, who was wrapped in a pink receiving blanket, while Julia looked at Brandon and the baby with tears misting in her eyes. Douglas smiled with pride.

Brandon clumsily held the sleeping infant in his arms as Julia instructed her son to keep his hand under the baby's head. Brandon awkwardly removed the pink skull cap from the baby's head and cradled her to his chest.

The baby squirmed, opened her eyes, looked up at Brandon, and then closed her eyes.

"Oh, snap," Brandon shrieked as he thrust the baby at Julia. She nearly dropped the child as she took the infant from her son's arms.

"What's wrong?" Douglas asked Brandon, alarmed at his son's pallid face.

"This is not my baby, that's what's wrong," Brandon shot back. "This baby has blond hair. Her ears are funny shaped like my teammate Rich's ears. Erin lied to me."

The young man was visibly shaken. His hands curled into fists as he cut his eyes sharply and scowled at the baby again.

Juliana opened her eyes and began mewling as if she could sense the tension around her. With his mouth open and his breathing so heavy he sounded like he was panting, Brandon glanced at his mother holding the baby and fled from the room.

"If you had asked me, I would have sworn things couldn't get any worse, and look what has happened," Julia said to Douglas. "What are we going to do?"

The baby howled.

"I'll go look for Brandon. You stay here with the baby." Douglas left to find his son.

Julia peered at the baby's face, and she didn't see a trace of Brandon in the child, nor Erin for that matter. Julia couldn't help but wonder whether Brandon was right and Erin had lied about him being the father. She didn't want to stay with the infant knowing the baby might not be their grandchild.

Julia looked for the nurse. She was in a room adjacent to the nursery. Julia walked toward the room. When she went inside, Julia gave the baby to the nurse and told her that she'd return later. She went to the hallway to wait for Douglas.

Douglas returned fifteen minutes later and told Julia that he didn't see hide nor hair of Brandon, and he was going to drive around the hospital and look for him.

"This is a disaster, Doug. I want to go with you to look for Brandon. I don't want to stay at the hospital with Erin. Humph, she's a liar and a tramp." Julia's hands were on her hips, and she looked furious.

"She also may be on her deathbed. Stay with her, Doll," Douglas pleaded with his wife. "I'll go look for Brandon and then call you. Whatever way this plays out, remember it's part of God's plan." He hugged her. "Try not to worry. God willing, we'll get to the bottom of this."

"Humph, that's easy for you to say." Julia tapped her foot nervously and glared at Douglas. "I will stay, not because I want to, but because I know it's the right thing to do."

"That's true. Try not to dwell on what just happened. Keep an eye on Erin. I'll call you as soon as I can." Douglas leaned down and kissed Julia's forehead, then he pulled her into his arms before leaving to go look for their son.

Julia ran her hand over her head and went back into the nursery. She wanted to see for herself if Brandon had overreacted about the infant. She had merely glanced at the infant after Brandon had given her the baby. She needed to scan the baby from the top of her head to the bottom of her feet with grandmotherly x-ray vision.

The nurse was friendly. She smiled and asked Julia if Juliana was her first grandchild.

Julia closed her eyes, grimaced, and replied, "Yes, she is. This has been a terrible day for my family. The baby's mother had a heart attack, and I'm here pulling double duty trying to keep an eye on both of them."

"Oh, I'm sorry to hear that. Why don't you go back to your daughter-in-law's ward and talk to the duty nurse? The census is low on the floor tonight, and I'm sure we can accommodate you with a room, and then the baby can stay with you if you'd like."

Julia was torn with indecision. She didn't want to bond with the baby and then find out the child wasn't Brandon's. Finally, she answered, "Okay. I'll see what I can find out."

"Great. After you talk to the nurse, I'm sure someone will give me a call. Hopefully I'll bring your granddaughter to you soon."

"Thank you," Julia replied as she walked back toward the maternity rooms. She stopped at the nursing station and inquired about staying in the hospital for the night.

"Your daughter-in-law has a double room. We can put you there if you'd like or we can put you in a vacant room. We all wish your daughter-in-law a speedy recovery."

"Thank you. I'd prefer a separate room if one is available." Julia answered with a grim look on her face. She tried not to roll her eyes.

"Give us about half an hour or so. After you come back, we'll get you settled. Then we'll have the baby brought from the nursery to the room."

"That's fine. I'm going downstairs in a bit to stretch my legs," Julia replied before returning to the waiting room. When she plopped down in the seat, she leaned her head back and closed her eyes. Julia felt ill will toward Erin. No matter what Douglas had said, Julia had a feeling Brandon was correct and that the baby wasn't his child.

Meanwhile, two floors below the maternity ward, Beverly had entered the hospital. She stood at the information desk and requested a pass to Keisha's room. After the attendant gave Beverly the pass and pointed out the elevator to take to Keisha's floor, Beverly was on her way. During the short ride, Beverly rehearsed in her mind what she would say to Keisha. Beverly exited the elevator and followed the sign leading to Keisha's room.

She tiptoed inside the room and found Keisha lying in the bed. The left side of the young woman's face was heavily bandaged. Beverly's knees buckled, and she gasped aloud. Keisha was a very attractive, curvaceous young woman. Part of her face was wrapped like a mummy, and the other side of her face bore deep scratches from the glass.

Keisha heard Beverly's gasp and opened her eyes. "Oh, Mrs. Howard, I didn't expect to see you here." Keisha's voice was a bit muffled from the bandages covering her face. Her lips were still slightly swollen but not as bad as before.

Beverly walked over to the bed and laid the plant she'd bought on the table beside Keisha's bed. "How are you feeling? I brought you a plant from my family and Jalin."

"Thank you," Keisha replied shyly. She didn't have a relationship with Beverly. She was closer to Tracey since their children were almost the same age.

"So how are you feeling? I didn't realize your injuries were so severe."

Keisha's left hand flew to her face. "The nurse won't give me a mirror. Do I look that bad?"

"No, not too bad," Beverly lied as she took off her coat and sat in a chair next to the bed. "Seeing the bandages threw me off. How long does the doctor think it will take before you heal fully?"

"Well, the cuts were so deep that I will probably have to have plastic surgery, maybe more than one surgery. So my recovery time could take months," Keisha told Beverly woefully.

Beverly's heart dropped to her feet. If Keisha appeared in court looking as she did that day, there was no doubt in Beverly's mind that Amir would be found guilty of the domestic violence charge.

"I am so sorry to hear that," Beverly stammered. "Jalin is more than welcome to stay with us while you're recovering. I'm sure you realize that Amir didn't mean to hurt you, and I hope you told the police that what happened was an accident."

Keisha shifted her body and sat upright in the bed. She flinched from the pain and held her head down for a few seconds. "Mrs. Howard, I appreciate you coming to see me, and for everything you and your family do for Jalin. I can't lie and say that what happened to me was an accident because Amir had been shoving me around for a long time. That's the main reason we broke up. When Amir loses his temper, he either yells at me or shoves me. I got hurt badly this time. My mother warned me that this might happen."

Beverly fell back against the chair she was sitting in. She felt like the wind had been taken from her sails. Her hand gripped the sides of the chair. Beverly opened her mouth mutely as she tried to find words to say to the young woman. "I didn't know that. It was my understanding that Amir broke up with you, not the other way around."

"He had no reason to break up with me," Keisha retorted crossly. "I got tired of putting up with Amir's selfish ways. The time came when I couldn't take care of Jalin and Amir. I ain't got it like that. When we lived together, I asked Amir a lot of times to find a job and help out. He would promise to, but never did. I couldn't talk to you about the way Amir was acting because I always felt like you looked down on me and thought I wasn't good enough for Amir because I grew up in the projects. And he is your son, so I knew you would take his side.

"I grew up in the ghetto, and I didn't know how to take care of a baby. My mama could tell me everything I wanted to know about a man, but she couldn't tell me jack about taking care of a baby. If I didn't have my sister, I don't know what I would have done." Keisha shook her head. "I applied for a Link card and medical care for Jalin. I also took parenting classes. I wanted to better my life."

Beverly's heart tumbled with each word that Keisha said.

"I didn't want my son to grow up and think it was okay for a man to shove a woman around, and sit in the house all day eating my food and running up my bills while I worked and went to school. I took some computer classes last year, and I thought I was getting my life together. Things were going good in my life until Amir shoved me. Now I feel like I'm back at square one." A tear trickled down her face and soaked the edge of the bandage.

"I didn't know that," Beverly said softly, feeling helpless. She felt sorry for the young woman in the bed and for Jalin. "I am so sorry I misjudged you, Keisha." Beverly tried to apologize to the young woman.

Keisha looked sad. "My people might not have a lot of money, but they've always had my back. One way or the other I'm going to make it, Mrs. Howard. But I'm not going to lie for Amir. I've made too many excuses for him in the past. When I woke up in the hospital with my face messed up, I knew I had made the right choice by asking him to leave my house. The doctor told me that I was lucky that the glass didn't pierce my head or get in my eyes, or I could have died. I can't lie for Amir. I'm not pressing charges against him; the district attorney decided to do that. I found out they can do it without my permission."

Beverly sat in the chair next to the bed, and as Keisha's story unfolded, the older woman began sobbing openly. "My God, I didn't realize things were so bad between you and Amir." She wailed, throwing her hands in the air.

"Please don't cry." Keisha hated to see Beverly so distraught. She licked her lips and tried to find words to comfort Beverly. "Amir is not a bad person. I think he just has demons he can't face, and he tries to drown the demons by drinking and doing drugs. I don't hate him. I wish him well and hope he'll do better by Jalin and his other children."

Beverly, for the first time in many years, was ashamed of her son's behavior; more so she was in awe at Keisha's attempts to better her life. The young woman retained her grace even under fire. Beverly knew if the situation were reversed, she probably would have called security and asked them to remove Keisha from her room. Beverly unconsciously rubbed her eyes. Her hands made an upward motion over her closed eyes, like invisible blinders were being removed. Keisha looked at Beverly sympathetically with her hands folded across her chest.

Finally, Beverly gathered her emotions. She stood up, walked over to the bed, and looked down at the young woman sitting in the bed. "Keisha, I am so sorry for everything that you have endured. I am so ashamed of Amir's behavior. Please try to forgive him, and if there is anything I can do to help you or Jalin, please don't hesitate to call me. I know you and Tracey are close, and I'd like us to spend time together in the future."

"Thank you, Mrs. Howard," Keisha whispered. She held out her hand to the older woman. Beverly clasped Keisha's hand tightly.

"I'm going home. I'll call you or come back to see you tomorrow if that's okay with you."

"Yes," Keisha smiled. "I hope Jalin has been acting good. My sister Tangie wanted to keep him at her house because of the circumstances. I told her that Jalin is used to being with your family and that I know he's in good hands."

"No, thank you, Keisha. Talking to you has been a real eye opener for me. God sent me here. I came here for my own selfish reasons, but I know now you had to tell me things I needed to hear. I'll make sure Jalin talks to you tonight and every night he stays at my house. You take care of yourself, and if you need anything, please call my husband, Tracey, or me. Will you do that?"

"Yes, I will. Kiss my baby for me." Keisha waved to Beverly as she walked out the door.

Beverly's eyes were full of unshed tears. Her head felt like it was literally spinning like a globe from her talk with Keisha. She wanted to deny everything Keisha had told her, but in her heart she knew the young woman spoke the truth. Beverly literally felt heartsick as she plodded slowly to the elevator. Her stomach lurched when she thought about how she planned to go behind Kenny's back to secure the loan if necessary. She was prepared to forge his signature on the loan paper if that's what it took to get Amir out of jail.

Beverly stepped out of the elevator, and tears began to pour from her eyes. She walked slowly to the waiting room near the entrance of the hospital and almost fell upon a chair in the rear of the room. She covered her face and prayed that she wouldn't see anyone she knew. She took a tissue out of her purse and wiped her eyes. Beverly felt a gentle tap on her arm; when she looked up and saw Julia, she burst into tears.

"Beverly," Julia said anxiously as she knelt down on the side of the chair. "What's wrong?"

"Everything," Beverly sobbed. "I've been such a fool." She wept while Julia stood beside the chair patting her shoulder.

After Beverly calmed down, Julia suggested they go to the cafeteria for coffee. Beverly's cell phone sounded. She knew it was Kenneth and let the call go to voice mail. "Coffee sounds good. I haven't eaten since breakfast. Can we stop in the ladies' room first? I know I must look a mess."

"No more than I do. I've been at the hospital since early this morning."

Beverly stood up, and the women asked the attendant at the information desk where the restroom was located. Ten minutes later, they were sitting at a table in the cafeteria sipping coffee.

Beverly held the warm cup in her cold hands. "I had an eye-opening experience today. Amir shoved his baby's mama, and she was hurt badly. I insisted everything that happened was her fault and learned I was wrong, dead wrong." She went on to explain everything to Julia that happened.

"Goodness, and I thought I had a bad day," Julia commiserated with Beverly. She explained how Erin went into early labor then suffered a heart attack and how the baby in the maternity ward looked White.

"It sounds like we both had one of those days," Beverly commented remorsefully after Julia spilled her tale of woe.

"I've had better days, that's for sure," Julia added just as ruefully. "I'm worried about Brandon. He was so insistent that the baby isn't his. You know what, I didn't look at her that closely. After Brandon left the hospital, Douglas insisted I stay here while he looked for Brandon. I wish it had been the other way around, and I was the one looking for my son."

"So you don't know for sure who the baby's father is?" Beverly asked. "Well, a paternity test can be done, and you can find out for sure."

"No, I don't know who the father of the baby is. I always suspected that Erin was deceptive. Her condition isn't good, and she's legally married to Brandon. This could turn into a real debacle if she doesn't survive."

"I thought the same thing about Keisha," Beverly admitted. "Until I saw with my own eyes that she's going to make it. I suspect if she's called to testify, the jury or judge will take one look at her face and sentence Amir to prison and throw away the key. Her face took the brunt of the glass and looks like it."

"That's tough," Julia agreed, "but as Douglas says, the Lord will work out both our situations. All I know for sure is that this is out of my hands. There is nothing I can do to make things better for Brandon like I used to do when he was a child."

"I agree with you. I can't kiss the boo-boos away for Amir like I used to do when he was little. I feel so helpless because I know the outcome for Amir is not going to be a good one."

"Who's to say?" Julia tried to comfort Beverly. "Maybe the circumstances will help Amir to change his life. I noticed in our sessions that when Kenneth would make comments about Amir, you never denied what he said." Julia squeezed Beverly's hand. "Maybe something good will come from his situation."

"If you had said those words to me yesterday, I would have argued with you, but today I just feel numb, like I don't know my son. I have been so blind about him for so long. It's a wonder Kenny hasn't left me. I've put Amir's issues over Tracey's, and I hope she can forgive me."

"I think you did what any mother would do to protect her child, but at some point we have to let them go. They have to make their own mistakes, learn and grow from them."

"I know you're right Julia. Still, it hurts to know how bad I treated other members of my family. My sisters tried to tell me I was enabling Amir, and I told them to mind their business," Beverly moaned.

"We've all been guilty of one sin or another; none of us are perfect. I have been a handful for Douglas many times, and he never complains, at least not to me. I thank God every day for my husband. Any other man would have sent me back to Africa a long time ago," Julia said jokingly.

"I said some mean things, very unchristian-like things to Kenneth over the past few weeks. And I still have to face Amir and let him know that he'll have to face the music without me or his father bailing him out. He's going to hate me. I've been the only person who he could depend on his entire life." Beverly covered her face with her hands.

"That's going to be hard, I'm not going to lie to you, but know that you are doing the right thing and God is with you every step of the way. Pray and remember that, and this too shall pass," Julia advised Beverly.

The women finished their coffee and gathered their belongings to prepare to leave.

"I hope things work out for Brandon and Erin," Beverly whispered. "I will keep your family in my prayers."

"I feel the same about Amir and will keep all of you in my prayers. I guess I'd better go upstairs and check out little Juliana." Julia pushed her hair off her face.

"Good luck and God's blessing to you," Beverly said as she put on her coat.

They walked to the entrance and hugged before Beverly left the building.

"Call me if you need anything," Julia urged Beverly. They saved each other's cell phone numbers in their phones.

"Same to you," Beverly smiled weakly. "I may take you up on that. Tomorrow I plan to visit Amir, and I don't look forward to seeing him." She shivered.

"You will be fine. God is going to be with you, and if I know Kenneth, he'll be there beside you too," Julia said wisely.

"Thanks, Julia, for listening to me. I needed some-one, and there you were."

"I think it's called divine intervention. God brought us together for a reason, to console and help each other. Don't forget to call me if you need to."

Beverly headed out the door, and Julia headed back upstairs to Erin's room. Each woman felt uncertain about what the next day would bring.

Chapter Twenty-three

At 6:15 P.M., Zora stood inside her stylish master bedroom wracked with indecision as she held up a hanger with a three-piece burnt orange pantsuit in one hand and one with a navy blue two-piece pantsuit in the other. *Decisions, decisions*, she thought. She peered at the clock on the nightstand and saw she had about forty-five minutes before Calvin would arrive for their date. She blew a strand of hair out of her face. She looked at the two outfits once more and decided to wear the orange one. In her haste to finish shopping, Zora forgot to buy a blouse to match the navy suit. She laid the three-piece suit on the bed, rushed over to the walk-in closet, and hung the blue suit on the rack. Then Zora made a mad dash to the bathroom to shower.

Thirty-five minutes later, Zora was dressed and sitting on the side of her bed, pulling her calf-length burgundy leather boots over her feet when the doorbell chimed. She smiled, knowing she should have realized Calvin would arrive early. She went into the foyer, pressed the intercom button, and when she heard Calvin's voice she buzzed him in.

Zora opened the door, and Calvin stood before her. A few snow flakes covered his face. She resisted an urge to brush the flakes off him. She swept her hand in an arcing motion, smiled, and said, "Welcome to my humble abode."

Calvin took a leather fedora off his head before walking inside the condo. Zora reached out and took his hat from his hand; then she opened the closet door and put it on top of a shelf. "Can I take your coat?" she asked Calvin.

He saw a wooden bench in the foyer and asked, "Why don't I put it here? It's a bit damp."

"That will be fine," Zora said softly as butterflies flitted inside her stomach. She watched Calvin fold his coat and lay it on the bench. "Follow me." Then Zora led him into her living room.

Calvin's eyes darted around the room, and he smiled his approval. "I like what you've done here. I remember coming here to look at the condo with you. You've decorated your home very nicely." He sat on the love seat while Zora sat on the matching sofa.

"Thank you. Meesha helped me pick out the colors, and we actually painted the rooms ourselves. Would you like a tour?"

Calvin nodded. Zora stood and gave him what she called the fifty-cent tour. They returned to the living room twenty minutes later.

"I—" they both said at the same time and laughed.

Calvin said courteously, "Why don't you go first."

"I was just wondering about the weather and travel conditions. I've been peeking outside since I returned home. Meesha and I went shopping earlier this afternoon, and the snow was starting to come down heavily then. Do you think we should postpone dinner?" She tried not to stare at Calvin. He looked so handsome. He had obviously gone to the barbershop. Calvin was dressed in a dark suit with a cream-colored shirt and gold tie.

"I was thinking along those same lines," he admitted. "I cancelled our dinner reservation in Old Town. I thought the weather was too bad to go downtown. So I logged on to the Internet before I came here and did a little checking. I found an Italian restaurant not far from here near the Museum of Science and Industry. I remembered you telling me that Italian cuisine is one of your favorites. My BMW has four-wheel drive, so traveling in the neighborhood shouldn't be a problem. What do you think?"

"I think you improvise very well." Zora grinned at Calvin. "Meesha recommended a restaurant called Piccolo Mondo. She said the food is very appetizing there. Do you think it's close to here? I still don't have a good feel yet for how far or close locations are from my house. I'll venture out more once winter is over."

Calvin chuckled and nodded his head. "Great minds do think alike. I was going to suggest we go to Piccolo Mondo, the same place Meesha told you about. It's a few miles from here on east Fifty-sixth Street."

Zora shook her head, smiled, and then stood up. "Well, let's go then. I'm kind of hungry. I had a light lunch."

She removed her coat from the closet, and soon they were on their way. Calvin held her arm as they walked to his car, which was parked around the block. The sidewalks were slightly slippery.

Twenty minutes later, they arrived at the restaurant. "Well, it's not crowded," Calvin observed as he pulled into a parking spot. "We're in luck. It looks like the snow kept people home tonight."

"The outside is unpretentious. I hope the food is good," Zora observed as Calvin held the door open for her. They walked inside and were surprised by the stylish interior. A store with various products was set up near the entrance of the restaurant. The couple began to browse, but before long they were being seated at a booth. The host presented them with menus before he exited the table.

There was a comfortable silence between the pair as they read the dinner choices. Calvin closed his menu and said, "I think I'll have calamari for an appetizer and Linguine Con Vongole for my entrée. What would you like?"

"I thought about having the linguine too. I think I'll have bruschetta for my appetizer and Pollo Marsala for my entrée," Zora said as she closed the menu.

Calvin relayed the dinner choices to the waiter when he returned and asked him to bring a bottle of red wine after checking with Zora first. The waiter departed after saying the appetizers would be up shortly.

"The restaurant has received good reviews," Calvin said. "It certainly smells good in here."

"I agree. Meesha likes this place, so it can't be bad. Reviews are subjective anyway. I am game for trying new places regardless of professional reviews," Zora told Calvin.

"I feel the same way," he admitted. "I like dining out from time to time. I'm also a great cook. I've taken a couple of classes. I'll have to invite you over to my place for dinner one day."

Zora didn't respond verbally although she smiled her approval.

"I meant to tell you earlier that you look very beautiful tonight. That outfit becomes you." Calvin's eyes beamed his approval.

"Thank you," Zora said. "You look handsome yourself," she complimented the minister.

They chatted about their jobs, upcoming events, new movie releases, the church, and then the Couples' Therapy group.

Calvin remarked, "Our session members are experiencing crises. Reverend Dudley called me this afternoon to tell me that Erin went into early labor and suffered a heart attack. He planned to go to the hospital this evening to see her," Calvin said.

"I'm sorry to hear that," Zora replied. "I know Beverly and Kenneth are going through a tough time with their son. I pray all goes well with Erin. She seems like a nice young woman. I guess we'll have to check and see if anyone will be available for the meeting next week."

"That's true," Calvin agreed. The waiter returned to the table with their appetizers, a bottle of Merlot, and two goblets. He set the plates and goblets on the table. Then he uncorked the bottle of wine, filled both glasses, and informed the couple that he'd return shortly with their meals.

Calvin blessed the food. The couple picked up their forks and knives and began eating the appetizers.

"Um, this is good," Zora said after she tasted the bruschetta. She quickly cut and ate another portion.

"So is mine. Would you like to share?" Calvin asked her after he dipped a piece of calamari in the red sauce and ate it.

Zora nodded. "Don't mind if I do." Calvin held up the dish while Zora took a few pieces of calamari and spooned some of the red sauce on her plate. "You're more than welcome to sample mine." Zora passed the plate containing the bruschetta to Calvin.

The waiter brought the entrees to the table thirty minutes later. They continued conversing, and soon they were done with the meal. The restaurant began filling up with customers.

"It must have stopped snowing," Calvin observed after he took a sip of wine.

"Good," Zora replied. She pushed her chair away from the table and wiped her mouth with the napkin. "The food was fantastic. I'll definitely come back and eat here again, now that I know where the restaurant is located."

"I agree with you; the meal was quite good. Would you like dessert?" Calvin asked Zora.

"Goodness, gracious no." Zora held up her hands after she laid the napkin on the side of the table. "I don't have room for dessert. The food portions were healthy. I'll have to work off the calories I put on when I get home tonight."

"From where I'm sitting, you look just fine," Calvin complimented Zora.

"Thank you, Calvin. Believe me when I say that I have to work to maintain my weight. I love food, but in moderation. I can't eat like this all the time."

Calvin glanced at his watch. "It's still early. Are you game for hitting a jazz club? It's not flashy or anything like that. The name of the club is the Checkerboard Lounge. It's located in Hyde Park, and I know the musicians who play there. They are excellent."

Zora frowned. "The church doesn't have a problem with you going to jazz clubs?" she asked Calvin. The waiter had brought two cups of espresso to the table, and she sipped from her cup.

"Friendship Church is progressive. I enjoy jazz. When I was in college I played in a jazz band to supplement my income. I was awarded a scholarship to the University of Illinois in Champaign and needed every dime I could get my hands on. Now I try to get out once or twice a month to support local musicians since I walked in their shoes at one time. It's not like I'm taking you to a strip club or something like that."

"I didn't know that you play an instrument. What do you play? My mother's church doesn't approve of secular music, that's why I asked. Personally, I like it. I have a small collection of jazz at home," Zora confided to Calvin. She put her cup on the table.

"I play the keyboard. Not to brag on myself, but I'm not bad at all. Your mother's church is like a lot of organized religious groups, quite a few have restrictions. That's one of the reasons why I like our church and Reverend Dudley. He's open-minded and fair while staying true to the tenets of the Christian faith. The fact that the board approved the therapy shows how progressive our church is. Times and people have changed, so the church has to be somewhat creative in how we minister to people." Calvin was clearly on a soapbox and enjoying himself.

"Preach, Pastor." Zora clapped her hands together softly. "I hear you, and I agree with you. People today are dealing with tumultuous times, so anything the church can do to draw people to God, I say go right ahead. My mother is an evangelist, and her teachings are more restrictive than Reverend Dudley's, though the core tenets are the same."

"So, pretty lady, are you up for listening to a good jazz set at the Checkerboard Lounge? I promise I won't keep you out late." Calvin motioned for the waiter to bring the check. The waiter scurried over to the table and left the leather casing on the table. Calvin quickly scanned it and put his American Express Platinum card inside it.

"Sure, I've enjoyed the evening so far. Let's go for it," Zora said excitedly. She drained the last drop of the espresso from her cup. Then she removed her coat from the back of her chair. Calvin jumped up from his seat to assist her.

The waiter returned with the approved card transaction, and Calvin signed the slip. He stood up and put on his coat. On the way to the car, the couple stopped at the desk in the front of the restaurant and took peppermints from a crystal bowl, opened them, and popped them into their mouths.

Calvin and Zora walked outside the restaurant to the parking lot and to his car. Thus far, the evening had been a success, and the couple had enjoyed themselves immensely. Zora knew her worrying had been for naught. She could hardly wait to go to the jazz club. She hadn't been to one ever in her life. When Zora dated in the past, she tended to go to movies, plays, and restaurants. She sensed hanging out with Calvin wouldn't be dull. He was full of surprises, and the conversation between them had flowed as easily as water from a faucet.

While Zora was enjoying her evening with Calvin, the same couldn't be said of Meesha. The children were in bed, and she had just put on a pot of hot water for orange tea. As the water boiled, Meesha went into her home office to log on to the Internet and check her e-mail account. The snow had been coming down steadily most of the day, and she was glad the teenaged boy who lived next door shoveled when Edward was out of town. Meesha didn't have many e-mails, and after powering off her computer, she went downstairs to the basement and removed a couple of loads of clothes from the dryer and put them into the clothes basket.

She turned off the jet under the teapot, went into the bedroom and quickly sorted the clothing while the water cooled. After completing that chore, Meesha went downstairs to the kitchen and poured herself a cup of tea. When she returned to her bedroom, Meesha sipped the tea and then set the cup on the nightstand. She began folding clothes and divided the items into neat piles by owner. Meesha glanced at the telephone on the nightstand, willing it to ring. She had called Edward a couple of times that evening, and obviously he had been busy because the calls had been routed to voice mail.

Meesha felt unsettled because she hadn't talked to her husband since he'd left for the airport that morning, yet another deviation from Edward's usual behavior. She dropped a sock on the bed, removed the telephone from its charger on the nightstand and hesitantly dialed Edward's cell phone number. Before the call could be connected, Meesha pressed the off button and put the phone back in the charger. She made a silent vow to wait for Edward to call her.

After she'd put the clothing inside the drawers, Meesha sat on the bed and sipped the tea. She set the cup back on the nightstand and swung her body into the middle of the bed. Meesha wondered how the members of the therapy group were faring and quickly said a prayer for all of them.

After she completed her prayers, Meesha pondered Zora's date with Reverend Nixon, and she hoped her friend was enjoying herself.

"I know what I can do." An idea formed in Meesha's head, and she eagerly rose from the bed and returned to her home office. She quickly powered on the computer again and accessed Hotwire.com, where she did a quick search for airfares and departure times to Dallas. Meesha was aware that flying at the last minute could be costly. She quickly scanned Southwest Airlines' website for last-minute deals. Meesha whistled shrilly upon discovering the airfare roundtrip was close to six hundred dollars.

Well, she thought, *Edward is always talking about how hard he works for us. Maybe it's time for me to reap some of those benefits.* She ran back upstairs and took her wallet out of her purse to use her credit card. Meesha booked a reservation for Saturday evening, the following day. She knew her parents would be more than happy to spoil their grandchildren for a weekend even with short notice.

After she had made the reservation, Meesha turned off the light in the office and returned upstairs. She decided to draw a bath using her favorite bath salts and soaked in the tub, releasing some tension. Feeling refreshed after her languid soak and dressing for bed, Meesha picked up the telephone and called Regina. "Hey, girl. How are you doing? Am I interrupting anything?"

"Heck, no," Reggie replied. "I rented movies this evening, and I'm watching *Love Jones*. What's up with you?" She picked up the remote control unit for the DVD player and pressed the button to pause the movie.

"Nothing, I'm just relaxing. The kids are in bed. I just finished doing laundry, I cleaned the house, and now I'm done with chores for today."

"Cool, I plan to do chores in the morning. I'm going to clean and, of course, run errands. How are the children doing?"

"They're fine," Meesha replied. She told Regina about her shopping expedition with Zora.

"So, what are you doing this weekend?" Regina asked a few minutes later. She put a few kernels of popcorn in her mouth.

"Well, I made a reservation to go to Dallas tomorrow afternoon. I want to spend time with Edward. If the mountain won't come to Mohammed, then Mohammed has to go to the mountain," Meesha joked. She picked up her television remote and turned on the local news.

"Alrighty now, Ms. Meesha is gonna go get her man." Regina laughed; then her tone became serious. "Do you really think that's a good idea though?"

"I see nothing wrong with going out of town to surprise my husband and spend time with him," Meesha replied, unperturbed. She hoped her hair stylist could fit her into her schedule tomorrow morning. "Maybe being away from home in a different setting will help us resolve our issues."

"Do you want me to agree with you or tell you what I really think?" Regina asked her friend bluntly. She pressed the stop button on the remote control.

Meesha sighed and hesitated for a moment. "I want you to be honest . . . I think."

"I think your going to Dallas without talking to Edward first is a big mistake. He is so anal, and he doesn't like surprises. Going there without talking to him first could make the situation worse."

Meesha assumed that's what Regina would tell her. Regina and Zora had always kept it real with her, even when she didn't want to hear their opinions. In the back of her mind, Meesha was also aware that Zora would probably agree with Regina.

"I know what you're saying, but it sounds so ugly to hear it verbally. In the past, you would have told me to go with Edward without a second thought and volunteered to keep the children." Meesha's head dropped. She felt depressed.

"You're right, girlfriend, I would have told you that back then. But this is now, and things aren't right between you and Edward. Maybe you need to give him space," Regina suggested diplomatically.

Tears singed Meesha's eyes. "I hear you, but I can't just stand by and let my marriage fall apart."

"Then you have to make a decision, Meesha, and you knew it might come to making a choice as to whether you can love Edward unconditionally with his good and bad traits, or let him go." Regina wiped her hands and mouth on a napkin.

"That sounds so final," Meesha replied after a moment of silence. "I don't know. We took those vows that said until death do us part, and I meant what I said, but I am at the end of my rope. I feel like a single parent. There's too much on my plate. I run back and forth between work and the children's activities, their school, and sometimes I get tired."

"I know what you're saying, Meesha, but that goes with the territory of raising children. If you leave Edward, I don't see him helping you out any more than he does now. You will really become a single parent. Is that what you want? What about the children and their feelings? If Edward is making the money he says he is, you could probably stop working if you wanted to," Regina recommended.

"The children will be devastated. Still, it isn't good for them to be in a house filled with so much tension. I love my job. All I've wanted to do since I was a teenager is to help people and families. What was the purpose of me getting a degree if I don't use it?"

"It served a purpose before you had children," Regina answered gently. She knew Meesha was at a crossroads regarding her marriage, and she wanted to help her friend make a decision that would benefit her entire family. "Life doesn't stand still, Meesh; you know that. The degree served a purpose to help you find a job, which in turn helped you and Edward use your income to buy a home to raise your children. There is nothing wrong with change because nothing in this life stays the same."

"I never thought about it that way," Meesha said reflectively. "I don't want to quit my job. I never saw myself as a stay-at-home mom. I have flexibility on my job to attend the children's events, but sometimes life becomes overwhelming. I feel like I'm in the marriage alone."

"Maybe you should check into working from home one or two days a week, or take a leave of absence and assess what you want to do," Regina suggested. "Instead of focusing on what you want Edward to do, maybe you should figure out what exactly it is that Meesha wants. Your children are growing up. You'll look up and wonder where the time went. So before you run off to Dallas and confront Edward, maybe you should look at your options and take it from there."

"You are so wise; that's why you're my best friend. You're right. I need to do some soul-searching. I still plan to go to Dallas and talk to Edward. I already bought a ticket. I'm going to call him and let him know that I'm coming. Hey, maybe you could go with me?" Meesha asked coyly.

"Now, why do I need to do that?" Regina asked Meesha. "You're going to save your marriage. I don't need to be involved with that. Plus, I have a date tomorrow. Do you know how long it's been since I've been on a date?" Regina tended to have problems sustaining long-term relationships through no fault of her own. As an only child, she lived at home with her elderly parents to care for them in their old age. Most men were put off that she still lived home and that she put her parents' needs before her own. Regina never gave up hope that she would one day meet *the one*.

"Reggie, I am happy you have a date, and yes, I know it's been a while, but I need you for sister support, in case things go wrong for me," Meesha whined." I'm nearly at the point where I realize that Edward isn't going to change. I remember my mama telling me when I was younger, when she called herself schooling me about men, how they don't change. Now I see what she meant. I just need to figure out what I want and how it plays into Edward's plan. If I can't deal with it, then I'll have to walk away. It will be the hardest thing I would have to endure since I've been in a relationship with Edward, which is since my junior year of college. Please, Reggie, would you go with me tomorrow? If you don't have the money, then I'll pay your fare. Please," Meesha pleaded with her friend.

"I'll go with you because Lord knows I may need you to reciprocate for me one day. I'll see if my cousin Bettina can stay with my parents this weekend." She looked at her open closet door and saw her suitcases stacked in the rear. "How long do you plan to stay there? What am I supposed to do if you and Edward resolve your differences? I'll be a third wheel."

"Thank you so much. We'll come back Sunday. You don't know how much this means to me. If Edward and I can come to a meeting of the minds, then I'll treat you to a spa day. He's staying in a five-star hotel, so you'll get the works. Let me get off the phone and make reservations for you. The flight leaves at noon tomorrow. I'll see if my dad can take us to the airport. We're leaving from Midway."

"Okay, call me in the morning or e-mail me the details. What can I say except, Dallas here we come," Regina joked. "See you tomorrow."

When the friends ended the conversation, Meesha called her parents to see if they could keep her children through Tuesday. After her mother gave her the go-ahead and cautioned her to be prepared for anything with Edward, Meesha removed her suitcase from the closet. She laid it on the bench at the end of the bed, then walked to her dresser and began taking items from the drawers and putting them into the suitcase.

She prayed as she packed and asked God to give her strength for whatever lay ahead, and she asked for His intervention to save her marriage.

Chapter Twenty-four

By late Friday evening, Julia had checked on Erin off and on since Brandon and Douglas left the hospital. Reverend Dudley and First Lady Laura had stopped by the hospital to pray for Erin. And Julia had called her husband periodically to check on Brandon's whereabouts; much to her chagrin, her son was still MIA.

After talking with Beverly earlier that afternoon, Julia had been full of bravado, but deep inside her heart she had no desire to bond with a baby who might not be her grandchild and one who appeared to be, from the outside, one hundred percent White.

Julia went to the cafeteria for coffee, and she made a decision to just get the deed done and check Juliana out for herself. Julia talked to Douglas before she went back inside the maternity unit. After she arrived, Julia stopped at the nurse's station to tell them that she was in for the night. The nurse put Julia in a room across the hall from Erin's. The room was situated away from new mothers bonding with their babies. Julia informed the nurse that she could now bring Juliana to her room.

The last time Julia entered Erin's room, her daughter-in-law lay prone on the bed, with her arms straight at her sides. Machines were attached to her body. Julia sat next to Erin's bed for a few minutes; then she went into her room.

Julia put her purse in the bottom drawer of the nightstand next to the bed covered with sharply creased white linen. Julia took her shoes off and rubbed her feet. She stretched her hand over her head and rolled her neck a couple of times. Julia picked up the remote control unit to the wall-mounted television and turned it on.

She washed her hands, but when she sat still in the chair next to the bed, she dozed off. A knock at the door awakened her. Julia stood up as the nurse wheeled the baby into the room.

"She's all yours," the nurse told Julia with a smile. "I put a bottle on the side of the crib in case she gets hungry." The nurse pointed out the intercom on the side of the bed and explained to Julia how to use it. "Let us know if you need anything else," the nurse said as she walked to the door.

"Um, would it be okay if I took the baby into her mother's room?" Julia asked as her eyes wandered toward the crib.

"Definitely, I think that's a good idea," the nurse agreed and then left the room.

Julia wandered over to the crib that sat on the left side of the bed and stared down at the sleeping infant for a long time. After several minutes had elapsed, Julia picked up Juliana and held her in her arms. She inhaled the sweet baby scent emanating from the child's body. Julia walked to the bed and sat down. She cradled the baby in her arms, and then she gently laid Juliana on the bed.

Her eyes scanned the baby's body from top to bottom like an MRI machine. Julia removed the pink cap from the baby's head to find a sprinkling of blond curls. *Hmmm, I wonder who she got that hair from. She definitely doesn't have Brandon's mouth or nose*, Julia thought. She gently bent Juliana's ear and checked to see if the coloring of the baby's ear was darker than the rest of her body, and it wasn't.

Juliana's arms flailed as she kicked her legs, and her mouth gaped open into a yawn. The baby opened her eyes and peered at Julia. The older woman was startled, and Julia inhaled sharply when she saw the color of the child's eyes: a brilliant emerald green.

"Dear Lord, have mercy on us," she cried. "Brandon was right. This baby is not a Freeman. Blond hair and green eyes? No way."

The baby, as if sensing Julia's distress, began to cry softly, and then her sobs built into a loud crescendo. Julia put her hands over her ears and shook her head wildly from side to side as if to drown out the sounds.

"Bebe, please be quiet," Julia said over and over as if the words were a litany. Her African accent had returned thick and heavy. Finally, she couldn't stand the sounds any longer, and she picked up Juliana, placed the child on her shoulder, and patted her back. Instantly the baby quieted.

"My grandmother always said that blood knows blood, and I know as sure as my name is Julia Marie Freeman that this is not my son's child. Oh, Erin, what have you done to my family?" Tears rolled down Julia's cheeks.

Juliana began fussing again, and soon she began mewling. "Are you hungry?" Julia stood up and removed the bottle from the side of the crib. After Julia finished feeding Juliana, she burped the baby and changed her diaper. Soon Juliana was asleep again, and Julia laid her back into the crib. Afterward, she walked over to bed and laid down on it.

"I wish I could shake Erin awake," Julia fumed. "All this time, she knew that baby's wasn't Brandon's child. Oh, Doug, why did you make Brandon marry that tramp? You should have left well enough alone. The situation would have worked itself out. That witch made a fool out of all of us, and you had the nerve to make me go to those darn sessions. Lord, I just can't bear it. Why, Lord? Why us?" Julia wept audibly, and then she turned on her side, and like Juliana, she drifted to sleep.

Douglas sat in his reclining chair in the dark living room of the Freeman house with his eyes closed. He'd been praying for Erin, Brandon, and the baby all day.

Douglas's spirit was disturbed. He had called Erin's family in Tennessee earlier, and he was shocked and disheartened by the blatant racial animosity the Wheatleys displayed toward him and his family. The Freemans were called everything but children of God. Douglas could still hear Shirley Wheatley's nasal twang as he replayed their conversation in his head.

Douglas felt he'd made the correct decision by calling Erin's family after she had lapsed into a coma. He had found the number in Erin's cell phone after he returned home.

Shirley told Douglas in no uncertain terms that she no longer had a daughter and that Erin was dead to her since she married *that Negro*, though she used another n-word. When Douglas told Erin's mother that she had given birth to a girl and was near death, the irrational woman told Douglas in a chilling tone of voice, "It's a sin against God to mix the races. She got what was coming to her." Douglas took the receiver away from his ear to make sure he had dialed the correct number. Shirley informed Douglas that he should never dial her number again, and she said the same applied to Erin. Shirley slammed the telephone into the receiver with such force that Douglas's ear rang for a short time.

Douglas felt nothing but sympathy for Erin and admired her for breaking free of her racist heritage. He could only imagine how she felt being cut off from family. Shadows danced on the living room wall from the television. Douglas sighed and looked at the telephone, wishing it would ring. Douglas wondered how things were going for his daughter-in-law at the hospital. He knew Julia would call him if Erin's condition worsened.

The hour was growing late. Douglas rested his head along the back of the chair and snored softly. He awakened when he heard a car door slam and later a commotion at the front door. He turned on the table lamp, sprang from his chair, and walked over to the windows and peeked out the curtains. He went to the door and flung it open to find Brandon fumbling for his keys.

Douglas stepped back. He folded his arms across his chest as Brandon walked into the house. The older man's face morphed into a scowl when he caught a whiff of what he assumed to be marijuana and alcohol wafting from his son's clothing. Douglas closed the door firmly.

Brandon caught sight of his father's glare and aggressively raised his chin a notch. "Pops," he nodded to his father with glazed, reddened eyes.

"Boy, where have you been? Do you know how worried your mother and I have been about you?" Douglas chided his son.

"I was out with my boys kickin' it. I didn't know I had a curfew and had to be home at a certain time." Brandon sneered . He wisely stepped away from his father and placed his arms across his puffed-out chest.

"Did you forget about the crisis at the hospital? How could you just leave knowing that Erin was in critical condition? Your actions have been irresponsible, and don't you ever come to me and your mother's house reeking of that . . . that stuff," Douglas roared.

"I give less than a hoot about Erin. She pinned the pregnancy on me, knowing I wasn't the father. I don't care if she lives or dies," Brandon said, not meeting his father's eyes.

Douglas grabbed his son's shirt with a tight grip. "Don't you ever let me hear you talk like that again about anyone—ever! Do you understand me?" he growled at his son.

Brandon's body sagged as Douglas released his shirt, and he nodded his head submissively at his father.

"Now have a seat." Douglas pointed to the chair across the room from his chair. Brandon walked over to the seat and dropped his body unceremoniously into it.

"First of all, don't you ever come to my house smelling like you've been inside a crack house or something. It's disrespectful, and I don't appreciate it. You know that using drugs doesn't solve anything, except maybe give you a temporary reprieve from your demons. You wanted to be a man and lay up with a woman knowing she wasn't your wife, and because of your recklessness you are now facing some dire consequences."

"You sound like you're on her side." Brandon's voice cracked as he spoke.

"No, I'm on the right side, and if Erin was wrong in saying you're the baby's father, the truth will come to light. You're playing Russian roulette when you have unprotected sex. That's why it's best to remain celibate until you find a woman worthy of being your wife and you put a ring on her finger."

"Please, Pops," Brandon said contempously as his lip curled. He waved his hand dismissively in the air. "This is the new millennium. That's how it was back in your time. It's a new day, and no one waits until they're married to have sex." Brandon looked at his father skeptically. "Can you honestly say Mom is the only woman you ever had sex with?"

"It might be a new era, but human nature has and will always be the same. I have loved two women, and I had two children with the only woman I took vows with, you and your sister, Nia. I was raised in church by honest, God-fearing parents, and whoever I've had relations with is not the issue now."

"See, that's what I'm talking about. Old people always want to tell you what to do like they forget they were our age once. I noticed how you dodged my question, Pops," Brandon retorted. He flung out his arm in frustration.

"Okay," Douglas nodded. "You want to go there? Yes, I had relations with other women. Not many. I've only been in love with two women my entire life. One was a woman named Susan, and she left me for another man. I was crushed and realized that indulging in sex before marriage is a sin. I wanted to save you from some heartbreak I experienced. I think all parents want that for their children."

"I knew you were being hypocritical, telling me what to do while you did the same thing I'm doing," Brandon observed smugly. He felt vindicated in his assumptions that his father wanted him to do as he said, not as he did.

"Son, a wise man learns from the mistakes of others without being judgmental. This new millennium has spawned the worst outbreak of a disease that has annihilated a good number of all races, and especially the African American community. I can admit a wrong. Can you? I was brought up to respect women, and having unprotected sex with a woman just to say you're a man is an overt lack of respect for yourself and the young woman.

"Unlike in your generation, AIDS didn't exist in mine. Do you realize how many people, including African American babies, are infected with HIV because some guy wanted to be the man? The numbers are staggering. Do you have to be added to the statistics to realize your wake-up call? Still, through it all, God loves us and is still in the blessing business."

Brandon dropped his head. "No, that's not what I want. Still, I don't want to be clowned either. Erin played me; heck, she played all of us, especially you."

Douglas thumped the side of his chair loudly. "Didn't you hear a word I said? Doing the right thing means you don't worry about being played because you've handled your responsibilities like a man. I am giving you a little leeway because you're young and have many life lessons to learn. I would suggest you refrain from using that stuff. It won't help in the long run, and it's illegal. Secondly, if you're so sure that Juliana isn't your child, then we can have a paternity test administered immediately, which we planned to do anyway. Today might seem like the end of the world for you, but it was a test—God's test—and you'll have to buckle down and stay prayerful as the truth unfolds."

"Pops, I don't normally smoke anything. I need my voice for rapping, and there's still enough of an athlete in me to know I don't want to put illegal substances in my body. But I was mad, mad as all get out. When I left the hospital, I walked to a store down the street, ducked inside, and called Will to come get me. He did, and we went to his house. A few of the fellas stopped by; the next thing I know dude is rolling a blunt, and I took a few hits of it. I knew what I was doing was wrong, but I was just so mad at Erin. I'm sorry, Sir. I didn't mean to disrespect your house by coming home this way."

Douglas shook his head bleakly. "Drinking or smoking won't help resolve your problems. Son, you're going to have to grow up faster since you thought with your little head and not your big one. Erin's condition is still not good. We both know a biracial child can look more like one race than the other one, or look pure White. Why are you so sure Juliana isn't your child?" Brandon asked his son gently.

Brandon's eyes filled with tears, and he swallowed hard before answering his father. "Because she looks like Richard Duncan. He lived in my dorm, down the hall from me, and he was on the basketball team too. He had a reputation as a real stud. The guys said he would sleep with anyone." Brandon made quotation marks with his fingers.

"And?" Douglas probed. He leaned forward in his seat.

"Rich has blond hair and green eyes just like Erin's baby. I'd heard rumors about them, and I even asked Erin about them, and she said they were just that, rumors."

"Did you ever talk to him about it?" Douglas asked after he settled back into his seat.

Brandon had a faraway look in his eyes as if he were reliving the conversation. "I did, and he hotly denied having a relationship with Erin. His face turned red, and I had a feeling he was lying. Both he and Erin stuck to their stories."

"Why didn't you tell me that when I insisted you and Erin get married? I asked you multiple times if you thought someone else could be the baby's father. You told me no." Douglas was distressed upon hearing his son's revelation.

"I didn't want you to think I was weak or a chump," Brandon confessed. Tears pooled in his eyes and spilled over. He covered his face and sobbed. "I realize now that I should have told you the truth. I messed up, Pops."

Douglas stood up, walked over to his son, and placed his hand on Brandon's shoulder. "I wish you had told me the truth too." He shook his head unhappily. "At this point, we can't change the past. We can only look to the future. I promise you, Brandon, that we will get to the bottom of this. Still, I warn you that if you had unprotected sex with Erin around the time the baby was conceived, then there's a chance that you are the baby's father, regardless of how she looks." Douglas stood by his son's side until the young man's nerves had settled. "Why don't you go to bed and get some rest? Your mother is staying at the hospital tonight. Get yourself cleaned up. We'll go to the hospital early in the morning."

"Thanks, Pops. I'm sorry for the way I acted today and for everything that's happened." Brandon stood up, and Douglas pulled his son into his arms and hugged him tightly.

"This situation is going to work out according to God's script, and not yours, because the Lord has the situation under control."

Brandon went to the basement to bed, and Douglas returned to his recliner. He leaned against the back of the chair and closed his eyes. "Heavenly Father, thank you for bringing my son home safely tonight. I refuse to fret about everything that has happened today; instead I'll wait on your will to become clear. Lord, give Brandon strength for what lies ahead. Let Julia be a comfort to Erin and the baby. Show us the way, Lord. I beg you, show us the way." Douglas picked up the remote from the side of his chair and powered the television off. He turned off the light as he was leaving the living room. When he arrived upstairs to his and Julia's bedroom, Douglas lay on the bed, then picked up the telephone to call his wife. He informed Julia that Brandon had returned home and told her he was proud of her for spending the night with Erin and the baby.

In the wee hours of Saturday morning, a nurse walked into Julia's room. "Mrs. Freeman?" the nurse shook Julia's shoulder to awake the sleeping woman. "Your daughter-in-law has come out of the coma. She's still very weak, and she's indicated that she'd like to see you. Would you come to her room as soon as you can?"

Julia was slightly disoriented as she swam to consciousness, pushing away the cobwebs of sleepiness. Then she remembered she was at the hospital and sat upright in the bed. "Is she okay? I mean, Is she coherent?" She pushed her hair off her face.

"Her speech is a bit slurred, but she made it clear to us that she wants to see you."

"Okay, give me a minute. I'll be right there. Um, should I leave the baby here or can I take her with me?" Julia rubbed her eyes and then slid her feet into her shoes.

"Yes, you can bring the baby with you." The nurse answered portentously as if she were trying to telegraph Julia a silent message before she went to see Erin.

The nurse's somber tone of voice troubled Julia and caused her heart to buck wildly within her chest. She wrapped the receiving blanket around Juliana, who was still asleep, then walked across the hall.

Erin's eyes were closed when Julia walked into the room and over to the bed. Julia wasn't sure if she should try to awaken her daughter-in-law, so she sat quietly in the chair on the side of the bed.

Juliana awakened and began squirming and fretting. Erin's eyes flew open, and she tried to turn her body to look for the baby. Julia quickly stood up and brought the baby to the side of the bed. She held Juliana near the young woman's face so Erin could see her child. Erin's face crumbled painfully, then a tear seeped down her left cheek. She tried to speak and couldn't because her throat clogged up with emotion.

Julia's eyes were luminous with unshed tears. She laid the baby in the crook of Erin's arm and held her there. "Shhh, don't try to speak. Everything is going to be fine."

Erin's voice was very low and slightly slurred as she spoke, "I am so sorry, Mama Jules, for any trouble I caused your family. I never wanted that to happen . . ." She paused as if to catch her breath, which was becoming shallow. "I never knew what a real family was until I married Brandon and came to live with you and Papa Doug. I love you, all of y'all. You have been so good to me."

"It's okay, Erin. I understand," Julia moaned. "I really do. Please save your strength. You need it to raise your baby." Julia's voice became thick and cracked.

Erin shook her head sadly "No, ma'am, I think the Lord is going to take me home with Him. But I've got to try to right some wrongs I done. Tell Brandon he was the best, and I'm sorry for . . ." Erin's body went limp, and the machines attached to her body began to beep piercingly.

Juliana's eyes were screwed shut as her little mouth gaped open and she let loose a yell that Julia had never heard from a newborn baby. It was as if the child had discerned something momentous was happening. Nurses and doctors swarmed into the room and over to the bed. The doctor yelled instructions to a nurse, who pulled a cart into the room.

"I'm sorry, ma'am. You'll have to leave now," one of nurses instructed Julia firmly. "We'll take care of her." She steered Julia and the baby out of the room.

Julia could tell from the urgent voices coming from Erin's room that the doctor's ministrations weren't doing any good. For a few minutes, Julia stood outside the door cradling the baby in her shaking arms. Finally, she went into her room, and sank into the chair and crooned a lullaby to the baby softly. Her head swayed from left to right.

She couldn't rid herself of the thought that Erin was fighting for her life and losing. Julia felt imprisoned by coils of fear that were wound around her heart. She held on to the baby tightly and prayed that Jesus would work it out. Forty-five minutes later, simultaneously, the doctor stepped into the room with a professional mask of sorrow on his face, and the telephone rang.

Chapter Twenty-five

Kenneth fretted as he sat on the sofa in the den. He was extremely worried about Beverly. She hadn't been herself since she'd returned home late that evening. Beverly had been uncommunicative, and she lay on the bed in the couple's darkened bedroom with a towel over her eyes. Kenneth asked Beverly repeatedly if anything was wrong, and each time she replied no. Finally, Beverly told Kenneth she just wanted peace, and he didn't press her anymore.

When Beverly didn't come down for dinner, Kenneth went upstairs and asked her if she was hungry. Beverly replied no, listlessly. Kenneth left her alone, and after discussing dinner options with Tracey, he ordered a large sausage and cheese pizza for the family.

The house was silent as a tomb. Rhianna and Jalin went to bed early, so the house had been unnaturally quiet most of the evening. Kenneth had just finished watching a Wesley Snipes action movie when he decided to call it a day. He made sure the house was locked up and turned off all the lights before retiring for the night.

When he went to his and Beverly's bedroom, he found his wife lying on her side on top of the comforter and facing the wall. She still had on the clothes she'd worn that day. Kenneth shook Beverly's shoulder until she woke up.

"Bev, you still have your clothes on, and it's after midnight. Do you need me to help you change into your nightgown? Are you sick? What's wrong?" Kenneth was becoming more concerned by the minute by Beverly's odd behavior. His sober expression signaled his worry.

Beverly looked into her husband's caring face, and tears gushed from her eyes. "Kenny, I've been such a fool." She moaned as she sat up and clutched his midsection. "Please forgive me."

"Hey, what is this about?" Kenneth sat down next to Beverly. He tipped her head to the side and looked at his wife with a perplexed expression on his face, not sure what she meant.

"I went to the hospital to see Keisha," she told him contritely. "I know you told me not to go, but I did anyway." Her mind still spun from her conversation with Jalin's mother.

"Well, that's nothing new. There have been many times you haven't listened to me. What did Keisha say to throw you into a tailspin?" Kenneth knew it had to be painful from his wife's uncharacteristic behavior.

"God, I don't know where to begin." She relayed her talk with Keisha to Kenneth. When she finished, she waited for her husband to say, "I told you so," but Kenneth was unusually quiet. "Well, I know you have something to say. Let me have it."

"No, I don't have anything to say except I'm sorry you had to find out about Amir that way. Tracey and I have known this for years." Kenneth began hesitantly.

"And you didn't think I should know about it?" Beverly's temper flared. "Why not? I'm Amir's mother. How could you keep that kind of information from me?"

"Because you wouldn't have believed us." Kenneth cleared his throat. "I just prayed that one day you would see Amir for who he is and try to help him. I don't think anyone can help him change except you."

"Fat chance of that. I'm the reason he's the way he is today. Isn't that what you've told me for years and years?" Beverly said in a low tone of voice.

"I'm guilty as charged. Still, I knew if you could ever look at Amir and see him for who he really is, that you would realize he needs help. Who better than you to help him?"

"I just don't know, Kenny. The things Keisha said about Amir were so heartbreaking. I could hardly believe she was talking about my son. How did Amir get so messed up? I don't understand. We gave him the best of everything. That's why I chose to work, so he and Tracey could have things that I didn't have when I was growing up. There were nine children in my family, and we were dirt poor. I wanted better for my family." Beverly looked miserable as tears dripped from her eyes.

"That's a noble task you took upon yourself, but you seem to forget, Bev, that though your family was poor, they are some of the most caring and generous people I know. You shouldn't be ashamed of how you were raised. It made you want to do better with your life, and you did. Having material things doesn't make a person better than someone who doesn't."

"A part of me knows you're right, but the other part is still ashamed of my family. When I was growing up my family never went out to dinner, not even to McDonald's. My mother always shopped in secondhand stores, and I wore hand-me-downs. There were times when the utilities were shut off. I vowed no child of mine would go through that."

"The unpleasant things you endured as a child made you stronger as a person, but also skewed your view of life. You know at the end of the day life is about the love you have within your heart for your fellow man that comes from Christ. You have gone overboard with Amir, but it's not too late for him to turn this thing around if that's what he wants. We can both want it for him so badly, but at the end of the day, if he doesn't want change himself, then all the wanting in the world doesn't mean a thing."

Beverly's face drooped disconsolately. "He's almost thirty years old. It might be too late for him to change."

"That's not true. We can do all things through Christ who strengthens us. You know I'm here for you and Amir. As much as I fuss about him, I can't help but love him because he's a part of you. I talked to Pastor, and he said he'll see what he can do to help Amir once his legal problem is resolved."

"If Keisha has to testify, then Amir will go to jail. She was horribly disfigured by the glass. Her face is cut up bad. If a judge or jury sees her, then it's over for Amir," Beverly announced dejectedly.

"Does Keisha plan to testify against Amir? Did she say that?" Kenneth asked.

"She didn't say," Beverly admitted. "But what if she gets a subpoena to testify? Keisha told me that this is not the first time Amir has shoved her. What if she gets on the witness stand and says that?"

"Then Amir will have to accept the consequences of his actions, whatever they may be. Did you have any luck finding a lawyer today? Maybe we need to consult with someone who can answer those questions."

"One lawyer turned me down outright. He said Amir's case was too small for him to try. Another told me bluntly that he wasn't a magician and don't expect him to perform miracles because more than likely Amir will have to do time. I have an appointment with a lawyer on the southwest side Monday. I feel so helpless." Beverly face's fell. She rubbed her eyes.

"You should never feel that way. Whatever happens is what was supposed to. Where is your faith, Bev? God will see us through this trial," Kenneth said kindly as Beverly snuggled into his body.

"I went to the bank this morning to see if I could get a loan by myself, and the banker implied my income alone wasn't high enough. She said we wouldn't have a problem getting money if we apply together. I don't know how to tell you this"—Beverly nervously licked her lips—"but I was going to forge your name to the loan papers if that's what it took to get Amir out of jail. I knew you would never agree to us taking out a loan."

"That's why we need to consult a lawyer. We don't even know if Amir can get bail because of his record. I'm disappointed that you would do something like that to get Amir out of jail. You know as well as I do that when you do something the wrong way or based on a lie, nothing good will come of it."

"I realize that now," Beverly groaned. "It took Keisha to show me how wrong I've been about so many things. I never thought she was good enough for Amir, and she had the nerve to call me out on it to my face." Beverly tittered and shook her head in amazement. "She isn't as bad as I thought she was, and better than some of Amir's other baby mamas."

"No, she isn't bad at all. I've gotten to know her fairly well since I pick up Jalin on my way home from work when he spends weekends with us. We still have to communicate even if we don't agree about the subject. We've learned that from our sessions. You've got to stop judging a book by its cover and give people a chance on their own merits." Kenneth stroked the top of Beverly's head.

Beverly sighed audibly. "Yes, I know that. I also realize that I don't have a right to impose my will on anyone except you, the kids, and the grandchildren."

Kenneth frowned.

"Just kidding. I plan to ask Tracey to go out to breakfast with me in the morning. I need to apologize to her for the way I've put Amir's needs over hers. You were right, I've played favorites. It's a wonder she wants to be around me."

"She understands now, since she's an adult, how a parent can favor one child over the other. She didn't when she was growing up. I guess it was normal that she became a daddy's girl after it was apparent to everyone with eyes that Amir was a mama's boy," Kenneth admitted. "She will be thrilled to have breakfast and talk with you tomorrow. I guess I'll be stuck with the little rug rats. That's no problem since I'm taking them to the UniverSoul Circus tomorrow anyway. That's how Tracey was able to get them to go to bed early." Kenneth laughed. "I guess me and the kids will make a day of it."

"Thank you, Kenny, for putting up with me all these years. And forgive me for putting the kids'. . . I mean Amir's problems over yours and Tracey's. I've learned some painful truths about myself from the sessions and my talk with Keisha. I was wrong, and I hope you can find it in your heart to forgive me." She took his hand from her shoulder and kissed it.

"I love you, Beverly Jean Howard." Kenneth planted a loud kiss on her cheek, which always made Beverly smile. "I always have, and I always will. I just didn't like the way things went down in this house sometimes. But it's a part of life, and I wouldn't have it any other way. Your being a part of my life is mandatory. I'll go with you Monday to the lawyer's office, and we'll take it from there."

"Thank you, love." Beverly put her hands on the sides of Kenneth's face and kissed him passionately. They lay on the bed intertwined. Then Beverly said, "Oh, I forgot to tell you that I ran into Julia at the hospital. Erin is in a bad way. It doesn't look good."

"I'm sorry to hear that. I don't know her outside of the therapy sessions, but she seems to love being a part of the Freeman family. You could see how much she loves Brandon, Douglas, and Julia. We'll have to say a prayer for them."

"I already have. It had to be God who brought me and Julia together today." Beverly nodded her head. "I was glad to be there for Julia. She was very upset. She thinks the baby isn't Brandon's, and Erin had a heart attack. This is a difficult time for her family."

Kenneth bowed his head and took his wife's hand. "Father above, please watch over and take care of the Freeman family tonight. They are in need of your tender mercy. Lord, watch over and heal Erin. Thank you for the new baby born today. Keep your hand on her and help her to grow strong. Father, please continue to bless my family. Help us find a solution for Amir, and, Lord, thank you for putting new understanding in Beverly's mind and heart. Forgive us of our sins and shortcomings. Help us to be better people and better Christians. These blessings I ask in Jesus' name. Amen."

"Amen," Beverly echoed. "You are a good man, Kenny. I thank God for bringing us together."

"You're not too bad yourself, Mrs. Howard. Why don't you get ready for bed; it's already one o'clock in the morning. We have a long day ahead. It will be time to get up before we know it."

At the same time Beverly and Kenneth were having
their discussion, the telephone rang in the master bedroom of the Morrison house, startling Meesha awake.
Her heart beat in rapid palpitations. She put her hand
to her chest and snatched the phone out of the cradle
expecting the worse.

"Meesha, it's me, Edward. Did I wake you?" He
sounded tense, as if he expected harsh words from his
wife.

"Uh, yes, I was asleep. I'm glad you called. What
took you so long?" She looked at the clock and couldn't
believe how late the hour was. She nestled against the
fluffy down pillows.

"I've been busy since almost as soon as I debarked
the plane. The company had a car waiting for me and
the other associates who came down here with me. We
were whisked away to corporate headquarters and later to dinner, so it's been a long day." Edward yawned.

"Did you have a good flight?" Meesha asked like a
dutiful wife. She pulled the sheet over her shoulders.

"There was a little turbulence, but overall the flight
was fine. How are the kids?"

"They're asleep. They had a good day. It's Friday, so
they stayed up a little later than normal. Keon played
on his PS2, and Imani practiced her dance routine."

"Good," Edward remarked as he tried to stifle another yawn. "How was your day? What did you do?" He
stretched his body out lengthwise on the bed.

"I went shopping with Zora earlier. Actually, I overslept this morning and took the day off work. So Zora
and I went to lunch and then to the mall."

"Good, you need to relax and get out more. Well, I
didn't want anything else. I just wanted to tell you that
I made it here safely and tomorrow, no, it's Saturday
already, so today will be just as intense as yesterday.

The project is moving along well, so things should ease up somewhat in the future."

"Good. God knows you've invested all of your time with it." Meesha regretted her words as soon as they slipped out of her mouth. She should have left well enough alone.

"Whatever. I'll let you go. I need to get some rest. Take care and kiss the kids for me," Edward said.

"You too," Meesha replied. "Good night." After the call ended, she leaned over and placed the telephone back into the charger. She analyzed her conversation with Edward. *We were so formal with each other. What was that about? Edward never said he loved me. In the past, he'd always say that and how he missed me. In reality, I bet Edward is glad that he's away from home. I have a little surprise planned for you, darling. We're going to get this marriage back on track or go our separate ways. See you later, Mr. Edward Morrison.*

Meesha shivered as she lay in the dark bedroom. Her mind continued to wander. Would Edward be pleased by her appearance tomorrow afternoon or annoyed? She decided not to tell Edward she was coming to Dallas. She had a feeling he would be averse to the idea, and her women's intuition told her to go. "Oh well, by this time tomorrow I'll know the answer to all my questions and more." Meesha sat upright in the bed, leaned over, and removed the clock from the nightstand. Then she set the alarm for eight o'clock the following morning. She burrowed inside the covers and went back to sleep.

Chapter Twenty-six

Saturday morning dawned clear and crisp in Chicago. The city is known for its fickle temperature. Luckily for the residents, snow wasn't in the forecast for that day. Instead, meteorologists predicted the temperature would hover around zero.

Beverly tiptoed into Tracey's room, mindful not to awaken Rhianna and Jalin. The children were nestled next to Tracey in the full bed Tracey had slept in since childhood.

Tracey looked up groggily when she saw her mother gesture for her to come outside the room. The young woman put on her robe and stepped outside the door.

"Mom, what's wrong? Did something happen with Amir?" Tracey rubbed her eyes and put her hand over her mouth as she yawned.

"No, there's nothing new with Amir. I wanted to know if you would have breakfast with me this morning. I thought we could go to IHOP. Your father said he would watch the children."

"Why? Did I do something wrong?" Tracey looked at her mother warily. She leaned against the wall.

"No, nothing is wrong. I just wanted to spend some mother-daughter time with you. I thought breakfast would be nice. Perhaps we could go to the mall or something . . ." Beverly's voice trailed off as she watched the expressions on her daughter's face.

Tracey initially looked curious about Beverly's request, then dubious, as if her mother had a hidden agenda. She hoped her mother wasn't planning on asking her to contribute money to bail out Amir because she didn't have a penny to spare.

"I guess so." Tracey's eyes darted up and then down to the floor. "I was going to meet my friend Katrina at Borders bookstore this afternoon. I'll call her and see if we can move the time back. Sure, Mom, I'll have breakfast with you."

"It's seven o'clock. I thought we could leave in an hour or so before the restaurant gets crowded. Is that a good time for you?"

"That's fine, if you're sure Dad is okay with keeping the kids." Tracey looked at her parents' closed bedroom door.

"We talked last night, so I don't think he'll have a problem babysitting. I know the kids are looking forward to going to the circus. I think he plans to take them to McDonald's for breakfast and then to the circus."

"Fine, I'll be ready to go in an hour." Tracey slipped back into the room.

Beverly was mildly distressed at Tracey's reaction. She realized she had no one but herself to blame for making Amir the center of her life. She knew Tracey loved her, and Beverly hoped Tracey knew that she loved her in return. Then Beverly smiled to herself. *Thank God*, she thought. *God gives us a chance to make it right*. She planned to go to jail to visit Amir, and for the first time in many years, Beverly didn't look forward to her time with Amir, and that was a strange feeling for her.

Beverly and Tracey had a good chat over breakfast and were able to clear the air about issues Tracey hadn't shared with her mother. Tracey volunteered to go to the jail with Beverly. She told her daughter no thanks and that she needed to see Amir alone. A few hours later, Beverly waved good-bye to Tracey after she dropped her daughter off at the mall to meet her friend. Beverly called Kenneth's cell phone and left him a message that she was headed to Twenty-sixth and California streets to visit Amir.

Beverly turned on the radio and listened to gospel music as she drove north to the county jail. She arrived at her destination a short time later. In no time, she found a parking space relatively close to the building. She exited her car and trudged rapidly down the two blocks to the building south of the downtown area. Beverly's hands were inside her pocket, and she averted her face to dodge the cold wind.

An hour elapsed before Beverly had been processed and checked into the visitor waiting area. She had been searched and asked to show her ID multiple times. A decent crowd of people was gathered in the midsized room to see their loved ones. Finally, the visitors were told the inmates would be coming out in ten minutes. Beverly glanced at her watch and looked around the room. It was utilitarian in appearance—gray cinder block walls, tables and chairs in neat rows, and an assortment of vending machines resting on a wall. Beverly felt uncomfortable being there, realizing she was in the last place she ever expected to be visiting Amir.

At last, the prisoners streamed into the room. Amir's eyes lit up when he spied Beverly. He sauntered over to his mother, leaned down, kissed her cheek, and sat in the empty chair across the table from her.

"Hi, Mom. Man, am I glad to see you. Have you found me a lawyer yet? How come the old man ain't here with you? Let me guess; he didn't want to be bothered." Questions spilled rapidly from the young man's mouth.

Beverly's eyes drank in the sight of her son. Amir was dressed in the standard orange jumpsuit that prisoners wore, and his hair was disheveled. The braids were frizzy like they needed to be re-done. Flashbacks of Amir's life flickered in Beverly's mind—the high hopes she had for him at birth when she first laid eyes on his face, the brilliant future she envisioned for him, the trials and tribulations she had endured with him in recent years. "How are you doing, son?" Beverly deadpanned. "I'm good." She was being sarcastic.

"Sorry." Amir looked chastened like a young boy. He flashed his mother a wide smile. "How you feeling, Mom?" He held out his hands. "I know you're disappointed with me, and I know it must be killing you to see me in a place like this. I want you to know that everything that happened was a mistake. Keisha getting hurt was an accident. I didn't have nothing to do with what happened. She slipped and fell into the china cabinet. I told the police that's what happened."

Beverly had a sudden urge to smack Amir's face because she knew he was lying. She'd listened to enough of his stories over the years. When Amir lied, he swallowed rapidly and licked his lips, as he was doing then. Beverly's left arm began to rise from her lap; she quickly dropped it back down. "Why don't you ask me how Jalin is doing? Or Tracey, Rhianna, and your dad?" Beverly asked her son, trying hard to mask the anger she felt at his selfishness. She thought about how it had always been about him.

"My bad. How is the little fella doing and everybody else?" Amir sensed his mother was not in a good mood. He realized he was too dependent on Beverly's good nature to get on her bad side.

"Thank you. Everyone is doing well except Jalin. He misses his mom, and he was traumatized by what happened to her, and rightfully so. Keisha is still in the hospital, so he's been staying at our house. Rhianna and Jalin have been having nightmares from the glass and blood that was in the dining room. They've been sleeping with Tracy ever since," Beverly said sadly as she shook her head.

"I don't understand why Jalin is still with y'all anyway. You guys shouldn't have to be bothered with keeping him. It was Keisha's fault that she got hurt." Amir's expression turned from repentance to anger. His nostrils flared like a stallion's.

"Amir, stop it. Just please stop." Beverly's voice rose a few octaves. "I went to see Keisha yesterday, and she told me what happened. You pushed her. Why would you do something like that to your son's mother? You've never seen Kenneth lay a hand on me, and to do that to your son's mother is plain wrong. Shoot, it's unconscionable."

"Why are you taking her side?" Amir complained. His lips tightened in annoyance. "She shouldn'a been bothering me. I asked her to leave. All she does is complain about what I'm not doing for Jalin. She know I ain't got a job. I barely touched her."

"When and if you see her face, you'll see what you did was more than a little push. Half of her face was badly injured, and she'll probably have to undergo many surgeries. I just wish you'd be honest and admit you injured her and express remorse for what you did. Instead, you're blaming her instead of yourself."

"Whoa," Amir held up his hand. "Where is this coming from? You know I don't hit women. The situation got out of hand."

"Keisha told me that you've shoved her more than once. I don't believe you asked her to leave and she wouldn't. And if she didn't, then you should have walked away from her and the situation." Beverly ran her hand through her hair in frustration.

"Mom, this is me, your boy, Amir." The young man was astounded that his mother was taking Keisha's side against him. "You know me. I ain't perfect or nothing. Stuff always seems to happen to me. I don't know why. I try to do right."

"So now you're the victim?" Beverly asked. She couldn't believe what she was hearing.

"Yeah. Just being a Black man makes me a victim. If it ain't the law, then it's a woman. Somebody is always up in your face talking smack. I've been gone, what, a few days and already Dad has poisoned you against me. I bet that's where all of this stuff is coming from."

"Kenneth has been nothing but good to you. He has taken care of you for most of your life. So I'd appreciate your not talking about him like that. Kenneth has nothing to do with how I'm feeling right now. I wanted to hide under a rock when Keisha told me what happened. You need to stay focused on how you're going to defend yourself when your day in court comes around."

Beverly leaned across the table and pointed her finger at Amir. "If you went to court tomorrow, there is no doubt in my mind that the judge and jury would throw you in prison and throw away the key." Beverly's voice was heated, and her chest heaved rapidly.

"Do we have to talk about that now?" Amir turned away from his mother as if to tune out their conversation. He looked around the room then back at his mother. "What's happening with the lawyer? You got one for me, didn't you? I don't want to be bothered with no public defender. I could do a better job defending myself than they can." Amir sounded as if he was entitled to the best money could buy regardless of his family's financial situation.

"I've made some calls. Some of them don't want to be bothered with your case since you have prior offenses. They think you'll have to do time."

Amir nodded at another prisoner who had been watching Amir and Beverly.

"Are you listening to me?" Beverly exploded with displeasure. She felt old, tired, and defeated. She wondered if today was an omen of her future, visiting Amir in jail in her old age.

"Huh? Sorry," Amir mumbled as he scratched his itchy scalp. "Look, Mom." He held up his hands. "I know you're not happy with me right now. On the real, I am sorry about Keisha getting hurt. But not sorry enough to do time for something that was her fault anyway. She shoulda left the house when I asked her to," Amir said smugly. "End of story."

Although Beverly had been visiting Amir for less than an hour, it felt like she had been there all day. She knew she wasn't going to get through to her son, not that day. Beverly opened her purse, which lay on her lap, and took her gloves out and put them on her hands. "Amir, I'm tired. I think I'll just go home. I'll see you in court this week. I'll pray that everything turns out well for you. Maybe Kenneth is right. Maybe I've babied you too much and you feel like you can do whatever you want. Your way of thinking has got to stop today." She stood up and prepared to leave.

Beverly's statement and her slumped posture held Amir's attention. He stood and put his hand on Beverly's arm to stop her from leaving. "What do you mean?" Amir blustered. "Come on, Mom. You know I was just talking. Of course I'm sorry about Keisha, and

I'm sorrier that you and Tracey got stuck keeping Ja-lin. If I could take that day back, I would. I'm going to straighten up as soon as I get out of jail. I'm gonna find a job and take care of my children. I promise you on my honor." Amir put his hand over his chest.

"Do you know how many times you've told me that?" Beverly hissed. Her voice shook. "And you've never made good on your promises, not one time. It's getting late, and I'm ready to go home." She leaned toward Amir and kissed the side of his face. "I'll see you Wednesday."

"Before you go, can you put some money in my account?" Amir asked Beverly without batting an eye. He put his arm around her shoulders. "It don't have to be much. I also meant to ask you if you could set it up so I can call home collect. One of the guys here was telling me about that. He said there's some type of phone agency that you can do that with, as long as you have a credit card. I need to connect with you. Sometimes I feel so isolated here, and then other times I feel like the walls are closing in." He pulled at the collar of his shirt.

"I'll think about it." Beverly buttoned her coat. "I've got to go. God willing, we'll have a lawyer to represent you, and maybe the judge will allow us to post bail."

"Thanks, Mom." Amir smiled and hugged Beverly again. "I knew I could count on you. Nobody in the world has been there for me except you. If you could leave me a c-note, that would be great. That should tide me over for a week or so."

Beverly and Amir embraced. One of the guards escorted Amir back to his cell.

When Beverly exited the visitor's area, she asked the guard at the desk how to put money in Amir's account. The guard told her how and where. Beverly went to another office and left fifty dollars for Amir's use instead of the hundred he had requested.

Thirty minutes later, Beverly had arrived home. She was glad she had the house to herself. After she hung up her coat in the closet, Beverly raced upstairs. She threw herself on the bed and bawled like a baby.

As ashamed as she was of Amir, she felt even worse about herself because she knew she had created the monster she'd seen at the jail. "Lord, forgive me. I didn't know what I was doing. I thought I was raising him the right way. I was so wrong." Beverly covered her face as tears leaked between her fingers. "What am I going to do? Help me, Father. Please show me the way." She prayed until her voice became hoarse.

Her head hurt. It felt like someone was pounding her skull. The telephone rang. Beverly looked at the caller ID unit and didn't recognize the number. She almost let the call go to voice mail and then picked up the receiver. "Hello," she said tentatively.

"Beverly? Hello, this is Zeke." Never in a million years did Beverly expect Amir's father to call her.

"Zeke? What . . . I mean, why are you calling me? How did you get my number?" Beverly stammered as she sat upright in the bed. Her body trembled uncontrollably as if she had a virus. Beverly's face whitened as her mouth gaped open.

"I got a call from your husband, Kenneth. He tracked me down on the Internet and called me. Can you believe that? He told me that Amir is in trouble. Tell me what I can do to help," Zeke informed his stunned ex-wife.

For a brief moment, Beverly was upset with Kenneth, but the thought flickered and died. She knew Kenny did what he thought was the right thing. Beverly cushioned the telephone against her neck and wrapped her arms around her body as she rocked back and forth. "Let me think about this. I haven't heard from you since Amir was three years old, and now he's twenty-eight. In all this time, you've never checked on either of us, nor sent me one red cent for child support. Now you have the nerve to call here like we saw you just yesterday?" The words spewed spitefully from Beverly's mouth. All the frustration she felt during her visit with Amir rained on his father.

Zeke, to his credit, just let Beverly vent until she ran out of steam. "I'm sorry Lee-Lee," he began. He knew the long-overdue call wasn't going to be easy.

"Don't you dare call me that," Beverly said in a chilling tone of voice. "You walked out on me and your son. By my reckoning, you lost that right more years ago than I care to count. Now, I have no problem with you wanting to help your son. It's about time you stepped up to the plate."

"All I want to do is help Amir. I'm sorry if I spoke out of line. Old habits die hard," Zeke tried to explain.

Has the entire world gone nuts? Beverly wondered. She rolled her eyes upward and exhaled loudly.

"I mean it. Your old man is a good one. There aren't many men who would call their woman's ex. I guess he must be pretty secure in his relationship with you," Zeke said. He planned to apologize to Beverly for walking out on her and Amir.

"Yada, yada, yada," Beverly muttered impatiently. "Let me tell you about Amir." Beverly began telling Zeke about their son. Tracey came home and peeked in Beverly's bedroom. She saw her mother engaged in an intense conversation and backed out of the room.

An hour later, the call began winding down. Beverly heard the back door open and close. Jalin and Rhianna excitedly relayed the highlights of their day at the circus to Tracey in the kitchen while Kenneth looked on.

Beverly gave Zeke information regarding the bail hearing. The two terminated the call. Beverly sat on the side of the bed with her knees pulled to her chest in wonderment. *Who would have thought?*

Eventually, Kenneth came upstairs. He took one look at his wife's distraught face and hurried to the bed. He knelt down in front of Beverly, took her hands in his, and said, "You can do all things through Him. Trust in Him, Bev. The Lord will take care of us and Amir. Let go and let God. Turn this burden over to Him." He went into the bathroom attached to their bedroom, and moistened a towel and brought it back to her.

Beverly wiped her face and sat the towel on the nightstand. She looked over at Kenneth. "I talked to Zeke," Beverly said with amazement in her voice. "Let me tell you about my conversation with him, and my visit with Amir." Kenneth and Beverly held hands as she relayed the day's events to her husband.

Another one of the sessions' couples was experiencing a crisis. Julia's felt sorely aggrieved. She knew Douglas was calling her when the doctor walked into the room. So Julia let the call go to voice mail. Her body went hot and then cold. She knew the conversation was going to be difficult. She was just glad that Brandon had his father to comfort him.

The telephone rang twice; then Douglas picked up like he'd been waiting for her call. "Doll, how are things going at the hospital?"

"Douglas," Julia's voice segued into a long whimper. Her knees felt weak and her body languid. She nervously tapped her foot on the floor.

"I know, Jules," Douglas said sorrowfully. "She's gone, isn't she?"

"Yes, she left this earth around forty-five minutes ago. The doctor tried to revive her, but his attempts were in vain." Julia sobbed softly as tears rained down her face.

"God rest her soul. I'm sorry to hear that. I liked Erin. My heart goes out to the baby, who will grow up without a mother. I'll tell Brandon, and then we'll come to the hospital. How is the baby doing?"

"The baby is fine. I feel like crap, Doug, and I didn't think I would. She talked to me at the end."

"We'll talk about it when Brandon and I get there. Stay strong, my darling. We'll be there as soon as we can. Can you do that for me?"

"Hurry up, Doug," Julia urged her husband. She swallowed hard a couple of times. Her voice was drowning in tears.

"Brandon and I will be there soon. Hang on."

When Douglas and Brandon arrived at the hospital, they found Julia sitting in the chair in her room, holding Juliana with a mournful look on her face. Julia rocked the motherless baby in her arms.

Brandon looked spaced out. His steps were jerky as he walked into the room. To Brandon it seemed like Julia was in a far-off place. When he finally managed to walk to the chair, the young man's legs gave out. He fell to his knees, moaned loudly, and buried his head at Julia's side.

She held the baby tightly in one arm and with her free hand Julia stroked Brandon's head. Douglas removed the baby from his wife's arm. Julia reached down and encircled Brandon's shuddering body in her arms. "It's going to be all right, my boy. I promise you."

The tension in the room must have crept over to Juliana. She woke up, looked up at Douglas, scrunched her face and waved her tiny fist in the air. She let out a healthy cry. Douglas smiled and stroked the baby's Downy-soft cheek. Her tiny hand found Douglas's finger, and she held onto as if for dear life. Douglas smiled. "You're a strong one," he declared. "You will be fine."

Brandon was utterly spent. His eyes were nearly swollen shut, and the young man breathed heavily from his mouth as if his nasal pages were swollen. Brandon cleared his throat a couple of times, and his voice sounded raspy when he finally spoke. "I can't believe this is happening to us. It's all my fault; everything that has happened is my fault," the young man groaned.

"Now, boy, don't you talk like that." Julia sharply reprimanded her son. "It's one of those things that happen that none of us could foresee. I feel terrible about Erin. I wish she had lived to see her child grow up. I wish I had treated her better. As much as I'd like to, I can't undo the past. But I can try to be a better person in the future."

A nurse came into the room. "I see you've made it here, Mr. Freeman. On behalf of the staff here at the hospital, I'd like to offer my condolences to you and your family. There's still time. Would you like to see your wife before we move her?"

Brandon visibly recoiled and shook his head vigorously as he held up his shaking hands. "No, I don't want to see her. I'd rather remember her the way she was."

"That's your choice." She looked at Douglas. "What about you, sir?"

"Yes, I think I will." He looked at Julia and held out his hand. "Would you come with me?" Douglas requested of his wife. He put the baby into the crib.

Julia and Douglas followed the nurse out of the room.

The room was quiet save the sound of the baby gurgling in the crib. Then she cried loudly. Brandon put his hands over his ears. He didn't want to hear or see any reminders of Erin's deception. Then he thought about the events of the day, and he began hyperventilating. Brandon tried to stifle his moans as tears gushed from his eyes like oil spewing from an oil derrick.

When Julia and Douglas returned to the room they found Brandon with his head between his knees and the baby crying uncontrollably. Douglas went to his son while Julia picked up the baby.

A few minutes later Julia laid the baby back into the crib. Brandon left the room, saying he needed some air. Douglas said to Julia, "I'm going to talk to the doctor to see if they can perform the paternity test. I don't think Brandon can take much more. We might as well start the procedure ASAP."

Julia nodded. "I agree with you. This is such a critical time for Brandon. Let's try to expedite the test regardless of the cost. Hopefully with our love and support, and help from above, Brandon will recover. What are we going to do about the baby? She's going to be released from the hospital today. Brandon had such an adverse reaction to her." Julia looked worried.

"We don't have a choice except to take her home with us," Douglas replied soberly. "The baby is legally Brandon's. We'll probably have to hire a lawyer to sort through the red tape, depending on the test results."

Julia's sympathies were torn between her son and Juliana. "Maybe Erin's folks will take custody of the child. We should call them when we arrive home to tell them what's happened."

"Erin's family keeping the baby is not an option."
Douglas sighed. "I talked to Erin's mother yesterday,
and she made it clear that her family wants nothing to
do with us or the baby."

"My, God," Julia moaned. Her hand flew to her throat.
"How can someone act that way about their child? I
guess you're right, and we'll have to take Juliana home
with us. We don't even have a room prepared for her
yet. She came earlier than we thought she would. And
we had planned to move them to an apartment." Julia
clicked her teeth.

Douglas took charge. "I'm going to talk to someone
on the staff about getting Erin's body released to a
funeral home so we can make arrangements. We also
need to know what ultimately happened here today. I
suspect Erin's hypertension was the cause of her death.
There's a lot going on, and I know we'll get through this
by the grace of God."

Brandon stepped into the room. He asked his parents, "What were you talking about?"

Douglas told Brandon what he and Julia decided to
do about the baby, and Brandon's body tensed. "I don't
want her in the house with us. She's too much of a reminder of how Erin played me."

"Son, I know you're hurting," Douglas told his son
sympathetically. "But there are decisions that need
to be made, and because you're Erin's husband, everything goes through you. Your mother and I will
help you as much as we can. We need to take care of
some immediate issues so that we can get home. Your
mother has been here since yesterday morning, and I
know she's tired. We need to go home so she can get
some rest."

Julia nodded in agreement. "You're right. I'm so
tired I feel like I could sleep for a week. I'll see what

I can do about getting the baby released. And we'll go from there."

Brandon glared at the baby and threw his hands in the air. "Okay, whatever. I'm going downstairs." He stalked to the elevator, leaving his parents to deal with the hospital staff.

Chapter Twenty-seven

Meesha and Regina arrived at the Dallas airport late Saturday evening to sixty degree temperatures, a welcome change from the Windy City. The flight arriving on time was an added bonus. After the women retrieved their baggage, Meesha became plagued with doubts about surprising Edward. By now, Meesha wished she had stayed home and waited for Jesus to work it out instead of taking matters into her own hands.

The women sat in the backseat of a Yellow Cab traveling on the expressway to the Marriot Hotel in downtown Dallas, where Edward was staying. Meesha nervously nibbled at a hangnail on her left hand. Regina glanced at her friend and groaned. "What's wrong, Meesh? Please don't tell me that you're having second thoughts?"

"I am a little apprehensive about seeing Edward. I don't know what I'm walking into," Meesha replied. She tapped her foot, feeling agitated.

"You're going to surprise your husband, that's what you're walking into. I still don't think this was the best way to handle your problems, but we're here now. Everything is going to work out the way it's supposed to, even if you don't like the results."

"Don't remind me," Meesha begged her friend. She reached into her jacket pocket and took out her cell phone. Meesha punched in Edward's cell phone number. It rang five times before going to voice mail. Meesha didn't bother to leave a message.

The taxi driver pulled in front of the hotel. He shifted to park and turned to the backseat. "That's fifty dollars," he announced.

Meesha took her wallet from her purse and handed the driver three crisp twenty dollar bills and told him to keep the change. He asked Meesha if she wanted a receipt, and she declined.

The driver exited the cab, opened the door for Meesha and Regina, then walked to the back of the vehicle and removed their luggage from the trunk. A hotel employee arrived with a cart to put the suitcases on.

"Thank you, ma'am." The driver got inside the taxi, and drove away.

"Well, let's go in," Meesha said, shivering. She and Regina walked inside the hotel and to the reception desk. In a matter of minutes, Regina had checked in and received her room key. Meesha pulled out her driver's license to identify herself as Edward's wife. She even had her marriage license as backup documentation. The check-in process took longer for Meesha than it did for Regina. Finally, she received a key to Edward's room. She crammed her possessions back inside her purse.

The women followed the bellhop to the elevator, and soon they were inside Regina's spacious double room. Meesha decided to stow her bags in Regina's room temporarily. She presented the young man with a generous tip as Regina scoped out the room and went into the bathroom. When she returned to the bedroom area, she whistled and said, "The room is very nice." She walked across the room and sat in a chair at the table and kicked off her shoes. "So what are you going to do now?" Reggie asked Meesha.

"I guess I'll go up to Edward's room and check it out. I'll be back here in a few minutes." She walked toward the door.

"What's his room number? Are you sure you want to go now?" Regina asked her friend. She couldn't help but notice the look of uneasiness on Meesha's face.

"He's in room 1127. And yes, I want to get the deed over with." Meesha sounded braver than she felt, but Regina wasn't fooled.

"Okay, I'll be here if you need me." She walked to the dresser and removed her purse from on top of it. Regina took out her spare room key and handed it to Meesha. "Take this in case I'm not here when you get back. I'll pray everything works the way you want."

Meesha flashed her friend a shaky smile. "I'll be fine. Don't worry about me." She departed from the room and walked down the hallway to the elevator. She pushed the up arrow, and the elevator car arrived. Meesha's hand shook as she pushed the button to the eleventh floor.

She stepped out of the elevator and, following the sign on the wall, went to her left and walked past a few doors until she stood in front of room 1127. She took the room key out of her purse and inserted it into the lock. The red light turned green, allowing Meesha access to the room. Meesha took a deep breath and stepped inside.

She felt giddy and light-headed. Her smile was bright as a hundred watt bulb when she noticed the suite was immaculate. Then Meesha's smile abruptly dimmed. The suite looked like Edward hadn't been staying there. Meesha marched into the bedroom and to the closet. She flung the door open and gasped audibly because none of Edward's possessions were inside the closet. Meesha distinctly remembered Edward packing two bags for the trip. Meesha walked slowly to the bathroom and found a few hotel toiletry items on the sink countertop.

Meesha's stood in the bathroom as her eyes traveled from the bathroom to the opened closet. Her body twitched slightly when her cell phone rang. She removed it from her pocket. Meesha glanced at caller ID. *Speak of the devil*, she thought. It was the culprit himself, Edward. Meesha longed to call Edward a few choice names. She suppressed the urge and pressed the button to answer the call. Her voice was pleasant when she said, "Hello, Edward. How are you doing? How is work coming along?"

"My nose has been to the grindstone all morning. I barely got any sleep last night. Despite that, things are going great here. I wish you were here to see the end result of all my hard work. You might be proud of me for a change. I feel like I've really made a difference," Edward boasted as he put his finger over his mouth and shook his head so the person in the room with him wouldn't make a sound.

"I wish I was in Dallas with you too," Meesha gritted her teeth. "What do you think about me taking a few days off work and coming down there to join you?"

"Oh, no, you don't need to do that." Edward sounded flustered. "The conference is intense. We're working long hours, and I wouldn't be able to spend much time with you anyway. I promise you that we'll have our own celebration when I come home." His voice took on a cajoling tone. "Look, I have to run, Meesha. I'll try to call you tonight, but I can't make any promises. The president of the company is taking the executive staff to dinner tonight to celebrate the successful software installation. If I don't talk to you tonight, I'll call you first thing in the morning, I promise. We'll talk when I get home. We'll straighten things out."

Meesha could hear a female voice in the background, urging Edward to get off the phone. "Who is that?" Meesha asked snidely.

"That's Ashley, one of the California associates. The next session is about to start. I'll talk to you later." Edward pressed the end button and disconnected the call. A fine sheen of sweat covered his brow. "I asked you to be quiet, Mac. I was talking to my wife."

Mackenzie Livingston put her hands on her hips and rolled her head on her neck. "No, what you told me is that your wife wanted a divorce. Why did you call me Ashley? I don't have time to play games with you, Edward. You need to come clean to you wife so we can get on with our lives," Mackenzie huffed. "I'm tired of our relationship being a secret."

"Come on, baby," Edward urged the young woman. "If Meesha got a whiff that I'm having an affair and that I plan to leave her, she will take me to the cleaners and back. She doesn't know about the money I have stashed. I'd like to move some of my assets around before I talk to her. It's best we keep things on the down low for a minute. I promise"—Edward held up two fingers—"scout's honor, that I'll divorce her soon. Just give me a little time." He grabbed Mackenzie's hand, and she pulled away from his grasp. "Come on, don't be like that. You're the only woman for me. I have to play the game until I can get things settled with me and Meesha." He had a scowl on his face when he said his wife's name.

Mackenzie smiled sweetly at Edward. She pulled his tie toward her and kissed his lips ardently. Then she reached up and wiped the lipstick stain off his mouth with her finger. "I guess I can be a little bit more patient. Just don't try to play me, Edward." She fluffed her blond tresses, and the two sprang apart and walked down the hallway and into the meeting room together. They sat seats apart from each other.

Meesha, meanwhile, frowned at the phone before she snapped it shut. "I don't believe him. I know Edward is lying to me. He hasn't been in this room since he got here on Friday. My Mama didn't raise no fool."

She started to sit on the bed, then detoured and sat on a chair in the room. "Ugh." She frowned at the largest object in the room. "There's no telling what's been going on in that bed."

Like an intricate puzzle, the answers to Edward's behavior fell into place. Meesha knew for certain that her husband was having an affair. She fumbled in her purse, tears blinding her eyes, until she found Edward's itinerary. Then she put the paper on the table and walked to the bathroom to get a tissue.

Meesha looked at her reflection in the large mirror. She wanted to rail on Edward and hurt him so he could suffer the way she was suffering. She removed a tissue from a tissue holder on the countertop and blew her nose. She dropped the tissue on the floor instead of the garbage can. When she bent to pick up the tissue, Meesha's eyes zeroed in on a few strands of hair on the floor. Meesha bent down and picked them up. The hairs were long and blond. She stared at them for a long time, and then she turned on the faucet and watched the hairs disappear down the drain. Then Meesha returned to the sitting room.

"I have two choices, Lord. I can wait for him to come back to this room, which he probably isn't coming back to, or I can go confront him at his meeting." She rocked on her heels, torn with indecision. "I know the civil thing would be to wait for him to return to the room and we sit down and talk rationally. Another part of me wants to hurt him so bad, and I know that's wrong. He has some nerve trying to pin our problems on me when he knew he had stepped out of the marriage. If he thinks he's going to get away with treating me that way, he has another thing coming."

Meesha shed a few tears for love lost. Then she picked her purse up off the table and went downstairs to hail a cab. Edward had a lot of explaining to do.

Regina was in the lobby headed to the spa when she saw Meesha exiting the elevator. "Hey, Meesh," she yelled and walked over to her friend. "Where are you going?"

Meesha stopped walking and turned around when she heard Regina's voice, "I'm going to find Edward."

Regina was alarmed by Meesha's too-calm appearance and the tears trickling down her face. "What's the matter? Did you talk to Edward already, and he left? I guess things didn't go well. Wait a minute, do you mean you're going to look for Edward because he wasn't upstairs?"

"No, he isn't in his room," Meesha answered calmly. Then her face crumpled. She clutched her midsection and moaned, "Oh, Reggie, I hurt. I hurt so bad. Edward is messing around. He's here with a woman."

Alarm sprang into Reggie's eyes. "I'm so sorry. But where are you going?" She pulled Meesha's arm.

"I'm going to that meeting to confront his butt. I brought my copy of his itinerary with me, so I know where he is," Meesha said in an unyielding voice. She pulled away from Reggie.

"Please don't," Reggie pleaded as she grabbed Meesha's arm again. "Don't do it that way. Wait for him to come back to the hotel and then confront him. Are you sure he's having an affair? You could be wrong," Reggie said hopefully.

"I'm one hundred percent sure, and I want to hurt him. I really want to slap him over and over and ask him what he was thinking, how he could do this to me and the children." Meesha's body sagged, and her knees buckled. She almost lost her balance.

Regina put her arm around Meesha's waist and steered her to the elevator. "Let's go to my room and talk. You don't want to confront him like that. Please don't go to the meeting and start a scene. That's not the way to handle this."

Finally, Meesha nodded meekly and allowed Regina to guide her toward the elevator. Before long they were in Regina's room. Meesha sat on a chair while Regina sat on the bed. Meesha told Regina what she had discovered in Edward's room.

"I don't know what to say . . . I'm speechless. If Edward wanted out of the marriage, then he should have talked to you about it. His behavior is way out of line. I feel like smacking him myself." Regina waved her fist in the air angrily.

"I can't believe it myself," Meesha said. "I knew he had changed, but it never dawned on me that it was because of a woman. I even asked Edward if there was someone else, and he denied it."

"Do you want something to drink? Water or something? I can order something from room service," Regina offered helplessly as she wrung her hands together. Pain and devastation were evident on Meesha's face.

"I don't want anything to drink nor am I hungry. I just want to confront Edward and see what he has to say." Meesha smacked her left fist inside her right hand. "Reggie, what am I going to do? I love him. I don't want a divorce. I wish I had never come here," she moaned, covering her face.

"It doesn't seem like it now, but it's better that you found out the truth since Edward was too much of a coward to come clean with you. I am so disappointed in him. He could have handled things differently."

"Am I so much of a monster that he couldn't come and talk to me and discuss our marriage like an adult?" Meesha looked at Regina.

"No, Edward is tripping. He feels like he can do whatever he wants without any consequences. Be glad that we're here so you can see him for who he really is, and that I came with you."

"I guess you're right, but my heart feels like it's being ripped apart." Meesha began sobbing again.

Regina rose from the bed and walked over to the chair. She patted her friend's back, urging Meesha, "Let it out, girl. Get all of the grief out of your system. I don't trust Edward. If he lied about messing around, then there's no telling what else he might be lying about. You need to get yourself together so you can confront him. The element of surprise is in your favor. Think about your children and how he's tearing your family apart, and be strong. Don't let him catch you in a vulnerable state. Edward will try to sweet talk and suck you in. Let it out, Meesha, so you can handle your business."

Meesha threw her hands helplessly up in the air. "I don't want him to go," she whined. "I love him. Edward is my world. I don't want him to leave me. I want my life back."

Regina thought to herself how sometimes she was glad that she wasn't married. Women invested time, emotions, and energy into relationships, and for what? To be discarded like yesterday's paper. She waited for Meesha to pull herself together. Regina knew her friend might be down now, but Meesha wouldn't take Edward's actions lightly. And when she rebounded, Edward had better watch out.

Regina offered Meesha one of the beds in the room. After Meesha lay down, Regina told her she was going downstairs to the drug store, and she asked Meesha if she wanted her to bring her anything back. Meesha shook her head and burrowed under the covers. She then pulled the sheet and comforter over her head and bawled like a baby.

Regina left the room and walked toward the bank of elevators. Her heart went out to her friend. She remembered when Meesha proposed couples' therapy and how her friend had mentioned the high number of divorced African American couples. Regina hated to see her friend become one of those statistics. She pressed the down button for the elevator and sighed heavily as she got on the empty car. "Lord, help my sister. Stop by my room and give her strength for what lies ahead. Take the sorrow and pain from her heart. Meesha's going to blame herself. Help her to see her marriage and Edward for what they really are. I ask that you be with her and bless her, Father. Amen."

Chapter Twenty-eight

Zora had called Meesha a couple of times since she woke up that morning. It was now five o'clock in the afternoon. All of Zora's calls had gone straight to voice mail. She hoped her friend was doing well. Zora had had a glow on her face ever since she arrived home from her date with Calvin. She'd had a fantastic time with the minister at dinner and at the jazz club. Zora hadn't had that much fun ever in her life.

She and Calvin had shared great conversation, and to her delight he really listened to her. They didn't always agree on all subjects, but each was respectful of the other's opinion. He knew a couple of the band members at the Checkerboard Lounge, and when the musicians asked him to sit in on a session, Calvin complied.

Zora swayed in her seat to the beat of the music while Calvin showed her his talent for the keyboard. He played quite well, and she knew every time she heard Billy Joel's song "Just the Way You Are" that she would always remember her evening with Calvin. Like the crowd, she cheered loudly when Calvin rose from his seat and took a bow.

When he brought her home in the early A.M. hour, Calvin was quite the gentleman. He wasn't all over her like an octopus with groping hands everywhere. Not that Zora expected him to behave that way. He merely gave her a quick hug and told her how much he enjoyed the evening. Calvin kissed her cheek after securing a promise from Zora that they would go out again. He whistled as he walked with pep in his step down the street to his car.

Zora smiled to herself. She'd gone grocery shopping and to the cleaners, and then cleaned the house, so she was at loose ends. She decided to catch up on some paperwork she'd brought home with her Friday after cutting her day short to hang out with Meesha. She also planned to send out e-mails to cancel the Thursday therapy meeting.

She walked into her home office and took a small stack of folders from her Louis Vuitton briefcase. She walked to her desk, laid the folders on the top of it, twirled the chair around, and sat down.

Zora powered on her laptop computer and opened the first folder. She scanned the file and wrote notes on a yellow, lined notepad. When she was finished with the file, Zora tore the page out of the pad and put it inside the folder. Next Zora picked up Jordan Brown's folder. As she read, Zora mused that he was a good kid. His grades were excellent. Jordan had played football since his youth in Pop Warner leagues, and now he played the wide receiver position. Jordan also had a part-time job tutoring students at the school.

The young man had received scholarships from Howard, Morehouse, and other universities across the country, but he was leaning toward attending Howard. *I know Jordan's parents must be proud of him. He is the poster child of a successful male teenager,* Zora thought.

She made a few notes and then leaned back in her chair, picked up the folder, and looked at it again. Zora noticed his birthday was in February. *The same month as my son's,* she thought. Then she knocked the thought out of her mind. There were several essays inside the file that Jordan had written, and Zora began reading them. She smiled to herself, thinking the young man's writing ability wasn't shabby either. It was no wonder the colleges had recruited him hard and heavy. He was that rare mix of athlete and intellect.

Zora turned the pages of the biographic essay that the young man had written. Then her body went rigid, and the paper she held slid from her hand to the floor. Zora slumped against the back of her seat, and her hands flew to her mouth. Suddenly a vision of who Jordan reminded her of thundered through her mind.

Zora's heart rate sped up so quickly that she felt like she was having a heart attack. She put her hand to her heart as if to slow down the beats. She then removed the picture of Jordan from the folder. Zora blinked rapidly as her teardrops dripped upon the young man's face. "No," she whispered. "It can't be. Lord, is this some type of cruel joke you're playing on me? Why? Why now when I was just beginning to enjoy life?" She dropped the picture back into the folder and closed it. Zora rose from her seat and walked unsteadily into the kitchen.

She stood at the kitchen window looking outside blindly. Then she walked to the refrigerator and took out a bottle of water. Zora tried to screw the cap off, but her trembling hands wouldn't cooperate. She put the bottle on the table.

The telephone rang, and she could hear Calvin speaking on the answering machine from the other room. Zora's legs were heavy as logs, and she couldn't move from her seat if she wanted to. Therefore, Zora didn't answer the telephone. When she regained her composure, Zora walked into the living room to the answering machine. She pressed the button to erase the message. "I'm done. What I just read in that file is a message from God. What was I thinking?" She lightly hit the side of her head. "I'm not good for anyone, much less a man of God. Maybe I should go back home. Oh, Lord, how could this happen? I know that Jordan is my son. Mine and Jeremy's." She slid to her knees and pounded the floor as she wept bitter tears.

Zora closed her eyes and sat there as memories played in her mind. Hours elapsed, and she blinked rapidly when she discovered that dusk had fallen, and the only light in the room was from the streetlight outside.

She rose from the floor and walked to her office, hoping that what she had read was a bad dream. Zora turned on the light on her desk, she dropped her head down and buried it in her arms, shocked that she had found her son, the son whose life she vowed to never to become a part of.

Jordan's file lay open on her desk, and Zora couldn't stop herself from re-reading the rest of his essay. The young man indicated that he planned to pursue a master's degree in sociology and become an advocate for foster children. He explained how he had been put up for adoption at birth, and the adoption fell through. He became a part of the system and was raised by multiple foster parents. He didn't have any horror stories to relay and thanked each family who opened up their homes and hearts to him. Jordan especially praised his current foster parents, Thomas and Lillian Gibson. Jordan had been living with them for ten years, since he was seven years old. The Gibsons were members of Christian Fellowship Church, and it was there that Jordan began his relationship with God. He ended the essay by saying how he'd like to meet his biological parents one day.

Zora had to put the paper down a couple of times because she felt overwhelmed with memories of yesterday. In addition to that, her eyes were too watery to read the print. She thanked God for taking care of her son as she had asked for the past seventeen years during her nightly prayers. Zora removed a tissue from a box on her desk and wiped her face.

For the first time since she'd signed the adoption papers, Zora felt torn about whether she should make her presence known to Jordan. She picked up her cell phone and called Meesha again and still didn't receive an answer. Zora needed someone to talk to about this latest development. Meesha was the obvious choice since she was the only one outside of Zora's immediate family who was privy to Zora's secret.

For a brief moment, Zora wished that she had known Calvin longer because he was so easy to talk to, but she couldn't predict what his reaction might be. It took many years for Zora to move beyond the fact that she was a young, sheltered girl, a minister's daughter, who'd given herself freely to Jeremy, albeit plied with drink.

Zora sat in the office for another hour, reading and re-reading Jordan's story until her head throbbed and her eyes hurt. Zora wished Meesha would answer her phone, and she decided to try calling her one more time.

Meesha awakened from the nightmare in Dallas. She looked at her cell phone and saw that Zora was calling. She groaned as she realized she was in Dallas and her life had become like the lyrics to Anita Baker's song "Fairy Tales."

Regina lay on the other bed with one foot crossed over the other, reading a book. The television was on, and the volume was low. Regina turned to see Meesha sit up on the side of the bed with her head hung low. Then Meesha turned to look at Regina, and Regina knew her friend was ready to do battle with Edward. Regina knew that after Meesha handled her business, her friend would return to the room with invisible scars etched deep in her psyche.

Regina felt as awful as Meesha did. She tried to put off the inevitable and tried coaxing Meesha into going to dinner with her, but Meesha flatly refused with a stony look on her face. She informed Regina that she was going back to Edward's room to wait for him to return, even if it took all night.

"Call me if you need me," Regina told Meesha with resignation in her voice after her pleadings for Meesha to eat fell on deaf ears.

"I'm fine," Meesha told Regina with a sickly grin on her face. "Or I'll be better once I confront Edward. And yes, I'll call you if I need you, but I don't think that will be necessary." Meesha walked out of Regina's room and took the elevator to the eleventh floor.

Meesha walked into the room and flipped on the light switch near the door. The door closed almost soundlessly behind her. She sat down on the sofa in the sitting room and thought, *What a waste of money since Edward isn't staying here anyway. I guess it doesn't really matter since the company paid for the room.*

She stood up and walked to the kitchenette area. A mini refrigerator sat next to the sink. Meesha opened it to find a bottle of Moët and Chandon champagne inside. That was a clear indication that Edward planned to celebrate his good fortune with someone other than his wife.

The room telephone rang in rapid succession. Meesha wondered who would be calling. She walked back to the sitting room to answer it. She noticed there were pieces of chocolate placed on the pillows of the king-sized bed.

A hotel restaurant employee called to verify Edward's dinner order. Edward had requested the meal be delivered to the room at eight o'clock. Meesha told him yes, to bring it on.

Meesha held up her wrist and looked at the slim designer watch that Edward had given her for Christmas. It was seven o'clock, and if she knew her husband, he would be making an appearance any minute now.

She dimmed the light and sat on the sofa in the sitting room, waiting for Edward's return. She felt bereft; her stomach clenched like her best friend had died, which was true in a sense. Edward had been that, and she mourned the demise of her marriage.

Meesha didn't have long to wait, at seven thirty she heard the lock on the door engage then disengage. The front door swung open and then closed. There was heavy breathing from Edward and a woman as they kissed each other passionately inside the door. Before Meesha shut her leaking eyes, she could make out Edward's and the woman's shapes, which looked like one. Her heart skipped a beat and then careened out of control.

Finally, the couple walked into the sitting room still holding each other. Meesha balled her fist and quietly sucked her breath. She had a strong urge to hit Edward and pull out the unseen woman's hair.

Edward pressed the light switch on the table a few feet from his wife. He didn't see Meesha because his back was to her, but Mackenzie did. Her eyes grew round as the moon, and her mouth dropped into an O as she fumbled trying to button her blouse.

"Edward," she shrieked. "There's someone in the room." Mackenzie gave Edward a dirty look; then she backed up toward the door.

Edward turned around. His eyes fluttered upward when he saw Meesha sitting on the sofa. He zipped his pants and buttoned a few buttons on his shirt. His face became pale when he saw his wife's murderous expression. Her lips were tight, and her eyes were narrow slits. Her breathing was labored. "Meesha, what are you doing here?" Edward asked weakly. He stepped away from Mackenzie.

"The question is, What is she doing here?" Meesha pointed her finger at Mackenzie. The young woman was the epitome of a White woman. She looked like she wore size zero clothing, and she had long, flowing blond tresses and blue eyes.

Mackenzie made a beeline for the door, flung it open, and exited the room.

"I can explain; she's nothing, just a friend." Edward tried to think of a lie to appease his wife and failed. Lipstick stains covered his face.

"I would say she's more than nothing or just a friend to you. You two were in the process of undressing each other, and her lipstick is all over your face. That makes her something. I can think of a few words I could use to call her, but I won't go there." Meesha walked over to Edward and pointed her finger in his chest. "Why couldn't you be a man and tell me what you really wanted? I asked you over and over for months what was going on with you, and you blamed all our problems on me. All you had to do was say you wanted out. I didn't deserve to find out like this." Meesha shook her head sorrowfully.

"You want the truth, Meesha? Well the truth is I've outgrown you." Edward's words spewed coldly from his mouth. His eyes flashed his anger and embarrassment at being caught. He thought, *She should have stayed in her place.* Edward walked to the kitchenette, picked a napkin up off the counter, wet it, and wiped his face. "All you do is nag, nag, nag." Edward twisted his lips. "Nothing I do is ever good enough for you. You complain about everything, and I'm tired of your nagging and of you. I deserve better, a woman who loves and supports me, and Mackenzie does all of that for me."

"If you felt that way, then you should have said something." Meesha felt light-headed, as if she was about to faint. She couldn't believe what she was hearing. "Why did you go to the sessions with me and pretend like you wanted to work on our marriage? You are a lot of things, Edward—arrogant, vain, opinionated. I never thought I'd add liar and cheat to that list."

"That's your opinion. I've asked you to ease up, and you wouldn't. Who wants to come home every day and listen to complaints? I went to therapy to shut you up. The only reason I'm still at home is the children. I held out as long as I could. They're young, and they'll adjust and learn to cope. You can keep the house." Edward eyed Meesha distastefully.

"So, it's come to this." Meesha shook her head sadly from side to side and flung out her arms. "You're willing to throw away our marriage because you wouldn't spend time with your family and I complained about it? So you turned to a White girl?" Meesha looked at Edward as if he were a stranger. "She doesn't look like she's any more than twenty-two years old. What's wrong with you, Edward? Are you suffering from male menopause?" Meesha sneered. The person standing before her barely resembled the man she promised to love until death us do part.

"I'm not suffering from anything except for a noose around my neck that's choking the life from me," Edward growled. "Mackenzie is twenty-five, not twenty-two. She respects me and encourages me to be the best I can be. She is who I choose to be by my side as I continue to climb the corporate ladder." He grabbed

Meesha by the shoulders and turned her toward a full-length mirror on the wall. "Look at yourself."

Meesha looked at herself and gasped at what she saw. She felt like the hands of time had turned back, and she had morphed into the chubby child she had been all of her childhood with low self-esteem issues. She shrugged her shoulders and said, "Sorry, Edward, you're not going to break me down. There's nothing wrong with me."

Edward dropped his hands from Meesha's shoulders and tsked. He said pompously, "Sure, there is. You need to lose weight for starters. Your clothes are too conservative for my taste. When a man reaches a certain financial status, he needs to have a dime-piece on his arm, and let's face it, Meesha, you're far from a dime-piece."

Meesha exhaled loudly, whirled around, and slapped Edward's face as hard as she could. Edward reeled backward and touched the side of his face.

"I am the mother of your children, and don't you ever forget that," Meesha yelled frantically. "You've gotten yourself a taste of that White girl and think you're all that." Her body vibrated with anger as she shouted, "I was the one who was there beside you, behind you, and in front of you as you climbed that ladder. I took care of your children while you went back to school and got your MBA. I also paid the bills so you could go to school full-time. I typed up your papers for school and even corrected them. So don't try to diminish what I've done for you," Meesha spat.

There was a tap at the door. Edward walked over to it and answered it. A waiter stood there with a cart of food. "Your order, sir." He pointed to the cart as he looked curiously at Edward and Meesha. He could hear their raised voices as he walked down the hallway.

Edward hesitated for a moment, then said, "Bring it in." He stood aside to give the waiter room to wheel in the food cart. After the waiter had placed the food on the table, Edward signed the check, and reached inside his pants pocket and gave the man a tip.

"Enjoy your meals," the waiter said before departing.

Edward thrust his hands in his pockets and looked down at Meesha who had sat on the couch with a woebegone look on her face. "Look, Meesha. I'm not trying to hurt you or really place blame on who did what. The marriage is over and done. There's not enough therapy in the world to make someone stay where they don't want to be. I'll always have love for you in my heart because of the kids and our history. However, I'm not in love with you. Mackenzie can relate to my life now and understands the pressure I face at work."

Meesha held up her hand. "Do me a favor and stop talking about Mackenzie. I'm not interested in hearing about your relationship with that. . . that home wrecker. Why did you tell me on the phone that you wished I could be here with you? I think you wanted to have your cake and eat it too. This farce of a marriage could have gone on indefinitely."

"I had to say something. What did you expect me to say?"

Meesha shot back, "I expected you to be honest with me. You owed me that much." She wiped the tears from her eyes.

"When we get back home, let's try to be civil for the kids' sake," Edward said. He looked at the ornate gold clock hanging on the wall. "Look, I'm going to clear out of here. You can stay here as long as you like, and we can talk when I return from my trip."

Meesha looked at him like he'd sprouted three heads. She stood on shaking legs, and her body felt like she'd been beaten black and blue. "I don't think so. I can find somewhere to stay on my own. I suggest you find a place to live; you're no longer wanted in our... no, make that my house. See you in court, Edward. Don't think I don't know about the accounts you set up in your name. I know how to pick a lock, and I know what you have, and I will get my fair share." Meesha grabbed her purse off the table in a dignified manner and walked out the door.

Meesha strolled down the hallway slowly to the elevator. She glanced back at Edward's room and imagined he was on the telephone laughing it up with Mackenzie. Meesha was thankful when the elevator arrived and it was empty. She thrust out her hand and held on to one wall for support. She held her midsection with her other hand as sobs tore from her throat. She didn't press the button for her floor for a few seconds. She could barely see. After several attempts, she managed to push the button for the seventh floor.

The ding of the bell awakened her from her daze. Meesha stepped out of the elevator and walked to Regina's room. She groped in her purse for the cardkey, and all her belongs spilled out of the purse. Meesha knelt down, grabbed a handful of items, and stuffed them back into her purse. When she finished, she rested her body against the wall next to the door.

Regina opened the door, and her breath caught in her throat when she saw Meesha. Regina grabbed her friend's hand and led Meesha into the room. Then she engulfed Meesha in her arms while her friend cried as if her world had come crashing to an end.

Chapter Twenty-nine

Wednesday morning at nine o'clock, Beverly and Kenneth sat inside the courtroom waiting for Amir's bail hearing to begin. Beverly was fidgety and kept looking at the door to the room Amir would be brought into the courtroom from.

At long last her son appeared with his hands cuffed behind his back, and wearing the suit, shirt, and tie Beverly had given the lawyer she and Kenneth retained for Amir's defense. She nodded encouragingly at her firstborn child. The braids had been taken out of Amir's hair, and he had gotten a haircut. Beverly thought he looked one hundred percent better. The bad boy thug look was gone.

Beverly hired the attorney two days ago. He didn't promise any miracles, and he had looked at Amir's paperwork only the previous day. He said he'd do the best he could.

Kenneth and Beverly had talked Sunday after church, and he finally convinced his wife that they didn't have money for both a lawyer and bail. They applied for a loan to pay the lawyer, but decided not to use their house as collateral for Amir's bail.

Beverly had talked to Zeke a few more times since their initial conversation. He told her that he had finally gotten his life together and he didn't have much, but he and his family would contribute what he could for Amir. Beverly's mood improved immensely after hearing that, and she realized God had answered her prayers, at least one of them.

Thirty minutes later the bailiff announced to the courtroom, "The State of Illinois vs. Amir Howard." After the charges were read, Amir's attorney, David Logan, requested bail be set.

The prosecutor shot up out of his seat like a rocket and strenuously objected, citing Amir's prior convictions. "Your Honor, the accused, Amir Howard, has an extensive criminal background. He's been in and out of court before. We feel he has exhausted any rights to leniency because of his prior convictions. His latest charge, however, is more serious. We move to deny bail because we think he could be a flight risk if bail is granted."

The white-haired judge looked down at the papers in front of him and peered out of the glasses that were nearly sliding off his nose. "Mr. Howard," he said, "please stand."

Amir and his lawyer rose from their wooden chairs and faced the judge.

"I thought you looked familiar." The judge glanced down at the papers before him and up again. "You've been in my courtroom before. I advised you to get yourself together the last time you were here. It looks like you didn't take my advice. You may sit back down."

Attorney Logan remained standing and said, "With all due respect, Your Honor, what happened to the victim was merely an unfortunate accident. My client wishes to clear his name, and I can assure the court that Mr. Howard is not a flight risk. I ask that you grant bail. His parents are in attendance." He pointed to Beverly and Kenneth. "They have assured me that the defendant can safely be turned over to their care. My client has not been involved in any violent crimes.

There is no legal reason for the state not to accept our request for bail."

"I object, Your Honor," the district attorney said. "The injuries suffered by the victim are so severe that she may have to undergo several extensive surgical procedures. The very basis of this crime personifies violence. The defendant has been in scrapes with the law before. We need to send a strong message to repeat offenders that this type of behavior won't be tolerated."

The judge thumbed through Amir's file. "Attorney Logan, I agree with the state. I warned Mr. Freeman not to show his face again in my courtroom or any other. He chose to disregard my advice. He has run the gamut of charges, from shoplifting to car robbery, disturbing the peace, late child support payments, and now this latest charge, domestic battery." He looked at Amir. "Son, you need to clean up your act." Then the judge turned his attention back to Attorney Logan. "I see Mr. Howard's trial is set to begin in three months, and considering the overcrowding of the docket, I think your client has come out ahead. I will apply the time served to his sentence if he's found guilty of the charge. There will be no bail set. It is so ordered." The older man struck his gavel on the top of the bench.

Beverly moaned aloud and swayed in her seat. Kenneth put his arm around her shoulders. Amir stood and shrugged his shoulders helplessly at his mother as he was led from the courtroom. Beverly and Kenneth walked outside the room and waited to talk with Amir's lawyer.

"That didn't go well at all," Beverly observed as she sat on a bench outside the courtroom, looking forlorn.

"Attorney Logan cautioned us not to get our hopes up because bail might be denied. We'll just have to take things as they come, Bev, and pray that Amir realizes the error of his ways and makes a change."

Beverly opened her mouth to defend Amir as she had done so many times in the past; then she closed it, thinking, *Old habits really die hard*. She took Kenneth's hand, and he squeezed it.

Attorney Logan walked over to the couple. "Hello, Mr. and Mrs. Howard." He shook the couple's hands.

"So what are Amir's chances for getting off?" Kenneth laid it on the table.

"My educated guess is that he's going to have to do some time. I went to the hospital yesterday evening to take a statement from the victim. I thought she might be helpful in getting bail set. She informed me that she didn't wish to lie to the court. And that she wished Amir well."

Beverly nodded and chewed her lip. She expected that would be Keisha's position.

"Sentencing in cases like this depends on the severity of the victim's injury, and Ms. Williams' injuries are very severe. I think Amir is looking at about five years, maximum. Luckily, the three months he'll serve until his trial will be applied to his sentence. With good behavior, he can be out in maybe three or four years. That's my best guess."

"That's longer than I thought," Beverly noted. "I thought he might get off with a year or so, and maybe he would be paroled or placed under house arrest."

"If this was Amir's first offense, then those might have been an option, but not with his record. It also doesn't help that he has been in Judge Willingham's courtroom before. Amir getting off lightly is not going to happen. That would be a miracle, Mrs. Howard."

Kenneth took his checkbook out of his pants pocket and gave a check to Attorney Logan. "I guess that's it for now."

The lawyer opened his briefcase and put the check inside it. "Okay, I have another trial starting soon. I'll be in touch with you if anything changes. Have a nice day."

Kenneth and Beverly watched him walk away. "I don't see how he could say, 'Have a good day,' considering Amir couldn't get bail and he'll probably have to do time," Beverly said. "I can't bear the thought, Kenny. It's tearing me apart."

Kenneth wanted to say that Amir brought this on himself. Instead, he just nodded. He stood up and waited for Beverly to rise, and then they departed the courthouse. Kenneth drove south to their home.

"Kenny," Beverly said, "before we go home, I want to stop at Julia and Douglas's house. We should pay our condolences. I want to make sure Julia is okay. She looked so sad when I saw her in the hospital."

"I agree. That's a good idea," Kenneth said as he looked out the review mirror, moved to the left lane, turned, and headed to the Freemans' house.

Twenty minutes later, the couple stood on the front steps of the house after Kenneth rang the doorbell. Douglas answered the door and greeted them with a muted smile, "Come on in. Thank you for stopping by."

Kenneth and Beverly walked inside the house. After Douglas took their coats, he led the couple to the spacious living room, where a few people sat chatting quietly. Douglas introduced the man and woman as his brother and sister-in-law and the other two persons as Julia's cousins. After the introductions were made, Kenneth and Beverly sat on a light blue, floral, three-cushioned sofa. Beverly scanned the room and the adjoining room and thought the house looked elegant, like Julia. She liked the color schemes.

Douglas sat in his recliner and informed the Howards that Reverend Dudley and Mrs. Dudley had just left the house, and that he and Julia were nearly done finalizing Erin's service. Douglas looked at the doorway and saw Julia entering the room. He stood up.

Kenneth stood too. He hugged Julia, and Beverly did the same. "I'm so sorry," Beverly said softly as she pat Julia's back.

Julia looked haggard; bags and dark circles were under her eyes. She sat on the end of the sofa. "Me too," she responded. "We're trying to remain prayerful. I just got the baby to go to sleep."

"Can I see her?" Beverly asked eagerly.

The relatives stood up and told Douglas they were leaving and would return later in the day.

"Sure," Julia told Beverly. After the relatives departed, she said, "Follow me." The women walked upstairs to the nursery.

"Please excuse the room," Julia apologized. "We put it together haphazardly. The plan was that after Erin recovered from having the baby, we were going to surprise the kids with a two-bedroom apartment in one of the buildings Doug and his brother own."

"The room looks just fine," Beverly commented. She gazed around the room as she and Julia walked to the white canopied baby crib. The room was Spartan; there was only a crib, dresser, and changing table in the room.

Julia stood on one side of the crib and Beverly on the other.

"Oh, Julia, she is so precious," Beverly exclaimed as she looked down in the crib. "She looks like a little angel."

Juliana wore a pink onesie, and she was lying on her side. Her left hand was under her head as if she was posing for a picture.

"That she is. Juliana is a good baby. She doesn't keep us up at night crying. There are no signs of colic, which Brandon had when he was born. She mainly cries when she's hungry or needs her diaper changed. I thank God for that because it could have been worse," Julia said as she leaned into the crib and caressed the baby's arm.

"That is indeed a blessing. It seems as though you have bonded well with the baby. I remember how you weren't looking forward to being a grandmother at all." Beverly tilted her head and put a finger on the side of her face. "You said something about being too young to be a grandparent." Beverly laughed quietly and Julia joined her.

Juliana began squirming and let out a little cry. She stretched her little arms and kicked her legs in the air. Julia picked the baby up from the crib and rocked her tenderly.

"How is Brandon doing?" Beverly asked.

Julia walked to the dressing table, laid Juliana on it, and changed the baby's diaper.

"He's doing fair. He's overwhelmed by everything that has happened. He is adamant that Juliana is not his child. He acts like she doesn't exist, so that complicates matters." She tossed the soiled diaper and wipe into the trash can and sprinkled talcum on the infant's bottom. She deftly fastened the strips on the side of the diaper. Julia talked to the baby as she completed the chore. Then she laid Juliana back into the crib.

"That's too bad," Beverly commented as she looked around the room. "What does the baby need? I'd like to buy her a gift. I don't see a mobile on the crib. How about I buy her that?"

"Anything you want to get will be appreciated. I went to the mall yesterday and got most of her basic needs." Julia exhaled loudly. "It's been a long time since I had to care for a baby. I took a short leave of absence from work until everything is settled."

"I'm off work on a leave myself," Beverly said. She brought Julia up to speed as to what was happening to Amir. Beverly candidly told Julia everything that had transpired, including the epiphany she'd experienced after visting Keisha at the hospital. "It was like a blindfold had been removed from my eyes. I was able to see Amir as he really is and, I'm sorry to say, I didn't like what I saw." She looked down at the floor. "That's a terrible thing for a mother to say about her child."

"Well, perhaps Kenneth is correct, maybe Amir needs time to reflect on his focus on his life and what he wants to do. Maybe his being locked up will help Amir change his ways," Julia said tactfully.

"I hope so." Beverly looked at Julia. "I've gotten my spending under control. It was like once I faced the truth about Amir, I lost my urge to shop 'till I dropped." She laughed.

"We had a paternity test done at the hospital before Juliana was released. Douglas had to pay a hefty amount to get the result back quickly. We should know the results by the end of the week. Brandon was furious about the cost. He said it was a waste of time and money because anybody with eyes could see that the baby wasn't his."

"Hmmm, what are you going to do if the baby isn't Brandon's?" Beverly asked, her eyebrow arched upward. "You've bonded with her, and you had a relationship with Erin. It will be hard for you to give her up. Do you think Erin's folks will want to raise the baby?"

"No. They pretty much disowned her. Doug called her parents to tell them Erin had passed. Her mother hung up the telephone and never called back."

"That's terrible. Poor Erin and poor Juliana." Beverly looked over at the crib.

Julia ran her hand over her head. "I don't know what we're going to do if Brandon isn't the father. Although Doug hasn't said anything, I know he wouldn't mind Juliana living here with us. Brandon would have a fit if we kept her. I think the baby being here brings back memories of Erin. He really hasn't mourned her properly. Once he saw the baby, it was over for him."

"Girl, we both just have to fall on our knees in prayer that everything will work out according to the will of our Father. I've been on my knees in prayer so much that my bones are aching," Beverly said, laughing.

"You're right. I worry about Brandon so much that sometimes I forget to pray. I just don't know what we're going to do." Julia sighed.

The doorbell rang, interrupting the intimate conversation.

"I know people have been in and out of here, so we're going to leave. Call me if you need anything or if you just want to talk. I'm a phone call away. I can run errands for you, anything that you need."

"Thanks, I appreciate your offer. Don't be surprised if I take you up on it," Julia said graciously.

"I will pray for you, Douglas, and Brandon." Beverly hugged Julia, and they walked out of the room.

Reverend Nixon sat in the living room talking with the men. He stood up when Julia and Beverly entered the room and greeted them. Afterward he said, "Ladies, I'd like to pray for your families. Where is Brandon?" He looked at Douglas.

"He's downstairs," Douglas answered. "I'll see if I can get him to come up." Douglas went downstairs and returned with a sullen-looking Brandon.

"Shall we join hands?" Reverend Nixon asked. The group took the hand of the person standing next to them and bowed their heads.

"Heavenly Father, in the midst of our pain, we still give you the glory. Though we are suffering right now, we know that you are here with us and that the pain and sorrow shall pass. Please stop by here today and bring healing to the Freeman and Howard families. We don't understand why things happen the way they do. We have to trust your judgment and know that you will make it all right.

"Lord, bless the new baby that was born and give Douglas, Julia, and Brandon strength as they take care of her daily needs. Father, please erase the burden on Brandon's heart so the healing can begin. Let him know that he is not alone that he has a friend in you that he can call on day or night.

"Most gracious Father on high, guide Kenneth and Beverly as they help their son, Amir. We all know that there is no problem you can't solve, nor any sorrow you can't heal. Please Lord, be with and comfort them during these trying times. These blessings I ask in your son's name. Amen."

"Amen," everyone said. Julia and Beverly quickly wiped their eyes.

"Can I be excused?" Brandon asked, looking down at the floor.

"I'd like to talk to you for a few minutes," Reverend Nixon said to the young man.

Brandon looked up and rolled his eyes. "Can't it wait until another day?"

"Brandon," Julia warned her son.

"It's okay," Reverend Nixon reassured Julia. "I promise you, Brandon, that what I have to say won't take long. Just give me a few minutes."

Brandon didn't say anything for a few minutes. Then he said grudgingly, "Whatever."

"Brandon," Julia raised her voice slightly, "Reverend Nixon is trying to help you. Please show him some respect."

"I'm sorry," he mumbled. "We can talk in the kitchen." He started down the hallway with Reverend Nixon following behind him.

They stood at the kitchen table. Brandon's arms were folded defensively across his chest. He looked at the minister warily.

"I know you're going through a tough time, son," Calvin began, "I just wanted to say if there's anything I can do for you, to let me know."

"Humph." Brandon shrugged his shoulders and cut his eyes sharply at the minister. "Tough doesn't even begin to describe what I'm going through."

"I've talked to your dad, and he told me what happened. We humans don't always understand why things happen the way they do, but take heart in knowing that it's part of God's plan. Life isn't easy, and I know you feel that at nineteen years old you should still be in school, living a normal, carefree life, but that's not what was planned for you. There is a lesson to be learned, and one day it will be clear to you what it is."

"I'd like to know why myself," Brandon blustered. "None of what happened makes any sense to me. I do know that my father made me marry a whore. That's what Erin was, and I was the fall guy. I was the one who got caught." He pointed to his chest.

Reverend Nixon patted the young man's arm. "We are all God's children regardless of our circumstances in life. God had a plan for bringing Erin and her baby into your life. I know this situation is difficult and you're angry. Turn the anger over to God. I learned the hard way that you can't live a full life with hate in your heart. God has subjected me to many trials and tests during my life, some of which I didn't handle as graciously as I could have. The good thing is that God is forgiving, and I did eventually learn from those trials. I promise you, Brandon, life will get better. Your relatives, friends, and church family will be praying for you."

"Is that it?" Brandon asked. He looked impatiently at the basement door.

"That's all for now. I will keep you in my prayers. Take care, young man, and know that you are not alone."

"Got it," Brandon said brusquely as he walked to the basement door, opened it, and went downstairs. When Reverend Nixon returned to the living room, Beverly and Kenneth had departed.

"Reverend Nixon, Julia and I want to know if you would read a scripture and pray at Erin's memorial service," Douglas requested of the minister.

"Of course, I will," Reverend Nixon assured the couple. "I would be honored."

"Thank you." Julia smiled gratefully. "I'm going to check on the little one. She should be waking up soon and ready to eat." Julia told Reverend Nixon good-bye and went to the baby's room.

"I don't know if Brandon was rude to you or not; if he was, I apologize," Douglas sighed wearily. "I don't know what I'm going to do with that boy."

"He's just a kid going through a hard time, no harm done. I understand," Reverend Nixon reassured the older man holding out his hands. "He's going through a situation that would be difficult for someone twice his age. Just continue to pray and be there for him, and in time Brandon will recover."

"Thank you. I appreciate your stopping by to see us. The church members have been supportive. Many of the sisters from the church have been coming by all week with food. We've gotten a lot of calls and sympathy cards."

"That's what we do as a family," Reverend Nixon remarked, nodding his head. "We come together and help each other in any way we can. I'm going now. Please call me if you need anything. I'll call Reverend Dudley this evening, and we'll shore up the program for the service."

Douglas and Reverend Nixon walked to the door together. Douglas removed Rev. Nixon's coat from the foyer closet and handed it to the minister. They shook hands and Reverend Nixon departed. After Douglas locked the door, he went to join Julia in the baby's room. The couple stood at the crib watching Juliana fast asleep with her thumb in her mouth.

Douglas and Julia both thought, *Are you our grandchild or not?* Friday couldn't come soon enough as far as they were concerned. The answer to that question would be revealed, and Juliana's paternity would be laid to rest. Then the doorbell rang. Douglas took Julia's hand, and they both trudged wearily downstairs.

Chapter Thirty

Earlier that day a light mist of rain sprinkled the city of Chicago, but now it was coming down harder. Calvin put up his umbrella as he walked briskly to his car after leaving the Freeman house. He sat indecisively for a moment in the car as rain poured down from the sky.

Calvin turned on the engine and decided to head north to Zora's house. He was mildly concerned because he hadn't talked to Zora since their date Friday night. She wasn't returning his calls and hadn't come to church on Sunday.

The minister was sure that Zora was the woman he was destined to marry. After he left her house that night, he felt the bond between the two of them had strengthened and that she had enjoyed the date.

Twenty minutes later, Calvin stood in the foyer of Zora's building ringing her doorbell. Zora didn't respond. He took his cell phone from his pocket and dialed Zora's home number. The telephone rang five times before his call was routed to voice mail.

Calvin called Zora's cell phone and had the same result, no answer. He decided she was busy and departed the building.

Upstairs in Zora's apartment, she stood in a corner of the room behind the drapery and watched Calvin leave. He looked up toward her window before he walked down the street to his car.

For a brief moment, Zora wanted to fling the door open and run down the stairs and out the door after

Calvin, but she stood rooted to the spot near the window until she could no longer see Calvin's figure. She walked to the sofa and plopped down on it.

Zora wasn't sure what to do. She had called Tiffany on Monday and told her secretary that she had an emergency and needed to take a couple of days off work. Tiffany promised Zora that she would rearrange her schedule and hold down the fort until her boss returned.

Zora's cell phone, which lay on the cocktail table beside the sofa, began to vibrate. Zora picked up the phone and saw it was Calvin again. She pressed the ignore button. When the phone stopped ringing, Zora quickly dialed Calvin's home number and got his voice mail. She said in a low, controlled voice. "Hi, Calvin, it's me. I'm sorry for not returning your calls. Look, I had a good time with you Friday night, but I can't see you anymore. It just won't work. Let's keep our relationship at a business level. I wish you the best, and I hope my decision won't interfere with our work at church. So please don't call me unless it's related to the sessions. Good-bye, Calvin." Tears streamed from her eyes as Zora hung up the telephone.

The cell phone rang and Zora saw that it was Meesha. In the midst of her trouble, Zora realized she still hadn't talked to Meesha. Zora quickly pressed the talk button. "Meesha, where have you been?" Zora asked, greeting her friend.

"To hell and back," Meesha answered wretchedly as she gripped the telephone receiver so tightly that her knuckles ached. "It's over between me and Edward." Her mouth twisted when Meesha said those words, and her voice broke when she said Edward's name.

"Oh, no," Zora cried. She sat upright and shook her head dejectedly. "What happened?"

Meesha gave Zora a recap of her weekend. "You were right. I tried to control the situation by forcing Edward to attend the sessions, and all my efforts were for naught."

"Don't blame yourself," Zora told her friend ardently. "You were trying to fix your marriage. In the long run it takes two to work on a marriage, and Edward apparently had a different agenda."

"You're right about that," Meesha replied sarcastically. "A totally new program that doesn't include me. Girl, he tried to break me down, but I wasn't having it. You should have seen that pale scarecrow he replaced me with. She beat a quick path out of the hotel room when she saw me."

"I know you don't want to hear this yet, but you're better off without him."

"My head knows it, but it will take my heart a little longer to catch up. He's coming here this afternoon so we can talk to the children. They know something is up. Imani asked me this morning if me and her daddy were getting a divorce. She looked so sad. It took all I had in me to stay composed."

"I think you should make an appointment for the kids to see a therapist. You have to stay strong, and as long as you and Edward provide the kids with love and support, they will eventually be fine."

"I suppose you're right." Meesha tugged on her ear. "I never really thought it would come to this, a divorce. Edward started changing after he got his last promotion. Saturday, I barely knew him as the man I married. He pretty much told me that I was a has-been and how I didn't fit the mold as a corporate wife."

"Well, knowing you the way I do, I know that you told him where he could go. Edward is chasing a pot of gold. And we both know that all that glitters ain't gold. He'll regret his decision one day."

"I guess you're right. It doesn't seem that way now. By the way, how did your date with Reverend Nixon go? Did you have a good time? What did you do?" Meesha changed the subject.

"It went well," Zora answered truthfully. "I had a wonderful time. We went to dinner and then a jazz club. Calvin is a great man, and he'll make some lucky woman a great husband. But I can't see him again. I just left him a message telling him that."

"Oh, no," Meesha exclaimed. "Why did you do that?"

Zora told Meesha about her findings regarding Jordan Brown.

"That's great! You found your son. I am so pleased for you. Are you going to contact him? Wait a minute, what does that have to do with Reverend Nixon? One thing has nothing to do with the other."

"I disagree," Zora interjected. "It's one thing for me to tell Calvin about my pregnancy and hope that he doesn't hold it against me. It's another matter altogether for that child to be a member of the church, a young man Calvin has mentored. How weird is that? I've come to the conclusion that my role in life is to help children and couples. God didn't mean for me to be a wife and mother," Zora replied loftily.

Meesha snorted and waved her hand in the air. "God has nothing to do with your decision; that's you being scared of life. You're afraid of happiness and enjoying life to its fullest. Now you're pushing Reverend Nixon away like you've done other men over the years. You're making an assumption without talking to him first. And you know that's not right."

"He's a minister." Zora's voice rose shrilly. "Sorry, I didn't mean to shout. He's different, Meesha. We're not just talking about any man. We're talking about a man of God. He's held to a higher standard."

"Girl, please," Meesha scoffed. "At the end of the day, he's just a man. When we all get to heaven, God is not going to give ministers a gold star just because they were ministers. We will all be judged according to our works. So don't give me that lame excuse about Reverend Nixon being different because we're all God's children."

Zora didn't say anything for a few minutes. She let Meesha's words digest. She opened her mouth to protest and closed it. "I guess you're right, but something within me can't accept what you're saying."

"That's because you won't let go of the guilt," Meesha shot back. "You wear it like an invisible cloak around your body. You were young; you made a mistake. Your parents kept you sheltered, but at some point you have to take that cloak off and throw it away—no, burn it so it never envelopes you again. You counsel children, and you know how unhealthy it is keep dwelling on things that happened in the past. For your own sake and happiness, let it go."

"Maybe you're right." Zora sounded confused. "I don't know what to do. Jordan wrote in his bio that he wants to meet his birth parents one day. My body shook, and I cried when I read those words. I gave him up assuming he would be adopted by a good family, and instead he grew up in the foster care system. His life could have been worse. The horror stories I've read and talked to children about . . . I feel terrible. I thought I was doing the right thing, and that didn't work out the way I thought it would." Zora's eyes became moist again.

"You did what you thought was right at the time. The Lord still took care of Jordan and kept him from hurt, harm, and danger. You have nothing to feel ashamed about. Maybe you should connect with Jordan, especially since he's open to meeting his biological parents. I think the Lord is handing you two gifts and a second chance. You would be a fool if you didn't take advantage of this opportunity. Stop shutting people out of your life. Embrace where you came from and the possibility of good things in the future."

"Maybe you're right," Zora conceded. "I don't know. I will definitely think about what you said. Maybe I need counseling." She chuckled nervously.

"Perhaps you do. Think about your life before Reverend Nixon came courting and then reflect on it now. Do you want to go back to being that lonely person?" Meesha asked her friend.

"I wasn't lonely," Zora protested. Then she snapped her mouth shut. She knew her friend was correct in her assessment of Zora's life.

"Sure, you were," Meesha scolded the young woman. "You were letting life pass you by. Once you begin analyzing your life, you'll see that I am correct. On the other hand, I have to let Edward go." Her voice cracked. "I love him and I always will. But he made it painfully clear that he doesn't want to be with me. When he told me about his feelings for Mackenzie, I felt like he had stabbed me in the heart." Meesha's hand unconsciously touched her chest. "My situation is different from yours. Still, it's better to love than not love at all."

"It's amazing you have that attitude." Zora shook her head in astonishment. "Under the circumstances you could be bashing Edward and all men in general. Instead, you're encouraging me to embrace life and Reverend Nixon."

"Life is too short. Let me rephrase that: tomorrow is not promised, and one should live every day as if it was their last one. I could mourn the loss of my marriage and wallow in unhappiness, but I can think of two reasons why that won't last very long: Imani and Keon. I have to be there to comfort them. That's what really kills me about all of this."

"Actually, I think you're ahead of the game. I think when Edward decided to put his career first and you had to step up to the plate and see to the kids' every need, God was preparing you for what was ahead."

"Hmmm. You're probably right. I didn't think of it that way."

"You have your parents and Edward's mother to help you. Don't forget me and Regina. You have a strong support base. That's more than a lot of women can say."

"You're right, further blessings from God. I know I'll be okay. I just feel like a fool and a failure. Just call me the F&F woman."

"You're a strong, beautiful Black woman who did what you could to hold your marriage together. Sometimes things work out, and other times they don't."

"You need to take your own words to heart and implement them in your own life," Meesha advised her friend.

"You're right. I guess I went from friend to counselor mode."

"Then physician, heal thyself," Meesha quipped. "Look, I've got to go. I saw you had called me over the weekend. I just needed some time alone when I came back from Dallas. I called to tell you that I'm making it. My body feels like someone has beaten me, and my heart is bruised, but in time this too shall pass."

"I'll stay in touch," Zora told her friend. "We can console each other."

"No, there's nothing for me to console you about. You just need to make up your mind to talk to Reverend Nixon and reach out to Jordan."

"I'll think about all of that," Zora replied carefully. Hope expanded in her heart from the possibilities Meesha had mentioned.

"I've got to get off this phone. Edward will be here soon. I need to pull myself together to deal with him and the children."

"Thanks for calling, Meesh, and for the pep talk. If you need me, just call," Zora offered as the women's conversation wound down.

"Same here. Take care of yourself," Meesha replied.

Meesha held the receiver to her chest and hung up the phone as the doorbell rang. She got up from the chair to open the door. "Oh, it's you. You're early." Her hand flew to her head to smooth her hair. She stepped backward so that her husband could enter the house.

"I wasn't far from here, so I figured I'd come by and get more of my stuff," Edward said stiffly as he walked into the house. He looked down at his wrist. "I know the children will be home soon, so I figured I'd get my belongings and talk to them at the same time. Then I'll be on my way." He was wearing a dark blue parka, jeans, and a sweatshirt, and he carried packing boxes in his arms.

"Whatever," Meesha said sarcastically. Edward walked up the stairs to the bedroom, and she followed him.

"You don't have to follow me around and watch me like I'm a child. I just plan on getting some of my clothing and computer hardware and software." Edward was annoyed that Meesha was in the room with him. He sat some of the boxes on the bed and the others on the floor.

"Trust me, Edward"—Meesha thrust her chin up— "I know that you're not my child. I just wanted to talk to you about what we're going to say to the children when they get home from school," Meesha said as she stood in the doorway watching her husband complete his chore. She looked on as Edward opened a dresser drawer and dumped the contents into a box unceremoniously.

"We'll tell them the truth as gently as possible," Edward replied impatiently. He walked to the closet and opened the door. "Children are the best survivors in the world. In time, and it may take a minute, they will accept our divorce. By the way, I've retained a lawyer. I suggest you do the same. There's no reason why this situation has to drag on."

Edward put his hand on his chin and looked at the dresser. He walked over to it, and removed his shaving kit from the top and put it into one of the boxes. He sat the now-full box on the floor and put the lid on it.

"You sure didn't waste any time." Meesha looked at her husband with a mixture of revulsion and pain in her eyes. "You're right about one thing, the children will be all right one way or the other. But tell me, are you so whipped and selfish that you can't even make the children a priority during this time? I swear, I don't know you anymore."

Though it seemed like a lifetime had elapsed for Meesha, it had been less than a week since her confrontation with Edward.

Meesha turned toward the steps. She could hear the front door opening and closing. Her mother had kept the children to give Meesha time alone.

The sound of running feet resounded on the stairway. Imani and Keon rushed into the bedroom. They ran to their mother and hugged her, wet jackets and all from the rain. Meesha helped them take their garments off and put the sodden jackets on the side of the bathtub adjoining the bedroom. The children turned their attention to their father. Edward paused his packing and stood next to the bed looking at his children.

Imani looked at her father and frowned. "Daddy, what are you doing?" she asked him as she crossed her arms over her chest and stared at him with a frown on her face.

"Don't I get a hug?" Edward held out his arms, and Imani walked to him reluctantly while Keon stood next to his mother and stared at his father.

"Your father and I need to talk to you and Keon," Meesha said. "Why don't we go downstairs and talk in the living room?"

"Hello," Sabrina yelled up the bottom of stairs.

"Coming, Mom," Meesha replied. Keon looked at his father fearfully and took his mother's hand, while Imani stood next to Edward and stared up at him with a sorrowful look on her face.

"I'm going to tell my mother good-bye," Meesha said to Edward and Imani. "I'll see you downstairs." She left the room with Keon on her heels.

"Keon, why don't you go to the living room and wait for me, your sister, and Dad?" The little boy obeyed his mother. Meesha turned to Sabrina. "Thanks for keeping the children for me, Mom. You don't know how much I appreciate it," Meesha told her mother after they exchanged greetings.

"That's what grandparents are for." She gazed at her daughter from head to toe with a critical eye. "Are you sure that you're feeling all right? You look tired."

"I feel drained, but that's to be expected under the circumstances." Meesha looked down at the floor. "Edward is here, and we're going to talk to the children about the divorce," Meesha whispered to her mother.

Sabrina looked bewildered. "I feel like you two are rushing into this. Maybe you and Edward should just separate for a while before you start making life-changing decisions that affect your children."

"Trust me on this one, Mom. It's time." Meesha couldn't keep the hurt she was feeling out of her voice.

"I hear you, but I don't understand," Sabrina commented. She switched her purse from one hand to the other. "I need to head home. Your father has been feeling a little under the weather. Call me if you need me." She took her daughter in her arms and held her tightly.

Edward and Imani were walking down the stairs. Sabrina and Meesha looked at them.

"Edward." Sabrina nodded at her son-in-law. Edward greeted Sabrina. She wanted to give him an old-fashioned tongue-lashing, but wisely kept quiet. She told everyone good-bye and left the house.

The Morrison family walked into the living room. Meesha sat on the sofa between the children while Edward sat on a chair across from them.

"I'm scared, Mommy." Imani burrowed into Meesha's side while tears trickled down Keon's face.

Meesha hugged Imani and told her daughter she had nothing to be afraid of. She then sat the child upright. She looked at Edward, and he shrugged his shoulders helplessly. "Your father and I want to talk to you," Meesha began.

"I know what you're going to say," Imani cried. "You and Daddy are getting a divorce, aren't you?" she said accusingly. She looked at her mother then her father.

"Yes, we are. But not because of anything you or your brother did," Meesha assured her daughter.

"Then whose fault is it? Are you sure I didn't do something wrong?" Imani looked up and asked her mother.

"No," Meesha replied firmly as she put her arms around both her children and squeezed them to her. "It's no one's fault. Sometimes these things happen. Your father and I love you two very much. That will never change. Right, Edward?"

"Yes, Princess. Your mother is right. It's no one's fault. I'm moving to another house, but I'll be back to see you. You two can stay with me on the weekends."

"I don't understand." Keon's lower lip trembled. "You live in our house now, and we don't see you. How are we gonna see you if you don't live here? You don't love me, Mommy, and Imani anymore." Keon's body shuddered, and he looked down at the floor as he wept.

"That's not true," Edward protested. "I love all of you. I always will," Edward tried to reassure his children. "Sometimes mommies and daddies don't live in the same house. That's what a divorce means. I promise I'm going to spend time with you and your sister."

Imani stared at her father with fear in her eyes. "Are you saying you don't love Mommy?"

"No, that's not what I'm saying. I love Mommy. Mommy and I just can't live together anymore." Edward tried to smile at the two unhappy faces that stared at him accusingly.

Imani rose from the sofa and ran to her father. She threw herself into his lap and flung her arms around his neck. "Daddy, I don't want you to go. I want you to stay here with us."

Meesha looked down and brushed away a tear from her eye as she rubbed Keon's arm. She knew telling her children about the separation would be difficult and that they would take it badly. She just hadn't imagined just how painful it would actually be. Meesha thought she had taken all the pain she could endure when she discovered Edward's infidelity. This situation was much worse because her children were suffering, and nothing affected Meesha more aversely than seeing her children hurting.

"I promise you that nothing will change except Daddy will live in another house, and we'll live here. Like

Daddy said, things happen sometimes. Remember when you twisted your ankle, Imani? And, Keon, when you hurt your knee playing baseball? How you cried and didn't think the pain would ever go away?" Meesha asked her children.

Imani and Keon nodded at the memory.

"Then one day you felt better, and the pain went away until it didn't hurt anymore. That's kind of how the situation will be with me and Daddy. One day you won't hurt as much as you do today. We'll still be a family but won't live in the same house," Meesha tried to explain to her children.

Keon looked up at his mother. "But in the books you read to me, the mommy, children, and daddy live in the same house. I don't understand how Daddy can live in another house." Keon looked confused.

"There are families who don't live in the same house." Meesha leaned down and kissed her son's damp cheek. "We'll go to the bookstore and get books that talk about other families."

"I know what happens when mommies and daddies get divorced." Imani's voice wobbled as her nose ran. "Lisa, my friend at school, told me her parents got a divorce, and then Lisa's father married another lady and they had a baby. Lisa doesn't like the baby. She says the baby gets all of her daddy's time, and he never has time for her anymore." Edward gave Imani a tissue from his pocket. The little girl jumped off her father's lap and ran to the sofa and sat at her mother's side.

"That doesn't always happen," Meesha said. She hadn't thought of that, but she knew Imani was right. There was a possibility that Edward and his girlfriend would marry and have children.

"You're getting too far ahead of yourself, Princess," Edward answered softly. "Your mother and I aren't thinking about that now. Our main concern is you and your brother's happiness and well-being." He had a flash of his future life with the children united with their mother against him and how he might have to play a secondary role in their lives. The thought struck a chord in his heart.

"How can you leaving us make us happy?" Keon asked Edward stubbornly. The little boy was having a difficult time trying to grasp the concept of divorce and how it would affect his life.

"I'm not leaving you and your sister, or your mother. Things happen in life that you are too young to understand. I'm sorry if you and your sister are hurting," Edward tried to explain the situation to his children. He stood up. "Look, I've got to finish packing. We'll talk again before I leave."

Meesha cursed Edward in her heart and called him a traitor. She was appalled that he was the one who had torn apart their family unit, and now he was running for cover. She wished she'd handled the situation differently and Edward could stay at home for a while and help the children adjust to his leaving. But she was so angry that she let her emotions overrule her common sense. As usual, she was the one left to handle a problem alone. Meesha couldn't believe that all Edward was concerned about was returning to Mackenzie.

Edward walked quickly up the stairs while Meesha held her children in her arms as they sobbed quietly. *This is what my life has become. Father, give me strength.* She reassured her daughter and son, "We will be fine. I promise you."

Chapter Thirty-one

Zora turned off the light in her office, walked out of the room, closed the door, and locked it. She had gotten a few calls from the couples begging her not to cancel the Thursday night meeting since the previous one had been called off. So she complied with the requests and didn't cancel the meeting.

As she walked through the walkway connecting the school to the church, she felt heartened at the thought that maybe the sessions had helped the couples. Then her heart took a nosedive. A week had elapsed since Zora left the message for Calvin requesting that they limit their communication to professional matters. He had only e-mailed her once, asking if she planned to hold or cancel the upcoming week's meeting.

When Zora arrived at the meeting room, the door was unlocked, so she opened it and went inside. She put a piece of paper on each chair and then sat down in her seat. She opened her tote bag to remove a package of cookies she had picked up from the bakery on her way to work and looked up to see Calvin enter the room. He nodded at Zora and removed his coat.

"Calvin," Zora began tentatively as she stood up and walked to the table to sit the cookies on it. "I want to apologize for not giving you an explanation for what happened. I've been going through a major dilemma, and I needed private time to think it through."

"I assumed as much, Zora. I just wish that you had shared your problem with me. I thought I had proved myself to be a good listener. And no matter what the problem is, I would never judge you. I consider you a friend." His cell phone rang, interrupting the conversation. Calvin walked out of the room to take the call.

Zora's face reddened. She wished that she had handled the situation differently and regretted how she had treated Calvin.

Douglas, Kenneth, and Beverly walked into the room. Zora stood up to greet them. They took their seats around the circle. Calvin returned to the room and joined them.

The minister asked the couples to stand and opened the session with prayer. "Gracious Father, we thank you for another opportunity to come together. We have suffered trials and tribulations over the past few weeks. Still, we can hold our heads high because you've been with us each step of the way. Some of our shoulders have been slumped as we try to figure out why things happen the way they do. Father, we can take comfort in knowing that you never put more on us than we can bear.

"Father, we know that in time the pain and heartache will pass. Until that day, we will continue trusting in your infinite wisdom. Stop by here tonight, Lord. Someone needs you. These blessings I ask in your son's name. Amen."

The group returned to their seats.

"Doug, thank you for coming tonight. I know I speak for everyone when I say our prayers go out to you, Julia, and Brandon," Zora said as she opened the meeting.

"Thank you," Douglas replied. "Julia and I appreciate your kindness and prayers. Continue to pray for my family. Julia couldn't make it this evening. She stayed home to care for Juliana. That's the name Erin chose for the baby. And Brandon is still trying to cope with all that has happened."

"Thanks for the update," Zora was telling Douglas as Meesha rushed into the room.

"I'm sorry," Meesha apologized. "Traffic was heavier than usual when I left work, and I had to drop my children off at my mother's house. Luckily, my parents only live a few miles from me." She sat in her seat and removed her coat and scarf.

"We just began the meeting," Zora smiled at her friend. "I thought instead of following an agenda tonight that we would just share what has been going on in our lives and offer any assistance we can. How does that sound?"

The group nodded in agreement and looked at each other to see who would speak first.

"I'll go first," Douglas said. "The past week hasn't been an easy one for my family. We lost Erin, and we miss her terribly. Sometimes people take others for granted and don't realize the part they play in our lives until it's too late. Brandon has also been on a tear because he doesn't think the baby is his. So there's been a lot of tension in the house. On a positive note, Julia has bonded well with the baby. I think she feels guilty for the way she treated Erin after the kids got married. I believe her caring for the baby is Julia's way of making amends for her actions."

Zora and Calvin nodded their agreement of Douglas's observations.

Beverly spoke next. "I think you're a very kind, caring man, Douglas. Just hang in there and continue to be strong for your family, the way Kenny has been for ours. Give Julia my love and tell her to call me if she needs anything. My son, Amir, wasn't given bail, and he'll be in jail for at least ninety days before his trial begins. I realize now that going to prison will be a part of Amir's destiny. He will either get his life together since he has to think over his actions, or he'll continue to make bad decisions the rest of his life. Reverend Dudley has been visiting Amir in jail, and the talks seem to be helping Amir a bit.

"Kenny got in touch with Amir's biological father, and he's been talking to Amir too. So I hope that Kenny, Reverend Dudley, and Amir's father can persuade Amir to change his ways," Beverly reported.

"That's good news, Beverly, Amir's biological father being back in his life. Keep us posted on how that works out for Amir," Zora said.

"I'm happy to say that Beverly has lightened up on her shopping sprees." Kenneth looked at his wife favorably. "I knew our life had changed for the better when she didn't go on a binge after Amir's arraignment. Beverly has also made an effort to become closer to Tracey. Our daughter felt like her mother favored Amir over her. Mother and daughter have had a chance to cement their bond. I've been stuck with the grandchildren, but I don't mind it because it's for a good cause. Keeping up with the grands will either keep me young or wear me out," Kenny said and let out a hearty roar of laughter.

"Good work, Beverly. Keep it up," Zora told the older woman.

"I guess it's my turn," Meesha said. She folded her hands primly together on her lap. "Edward and I are separated and are headed for divorce court. I know it's for the best, but still it hurts. I have been Mrs. Morrison for a long time. I have two small, confused children that I'm trying to take care of."

"I'm sorry to hear that." Beverly reached across Kenneth and squeezed Meesha's hand.

"As people and Christians, we have to be prepared to come out of our comfort zone sometime and know that life changes. We should know that God is with us and that He will never leave us alone. If we let Him, God will lead and guide us." As Zora spoke, she felt hypocritical because she hadn't been applying her advice to her own life. "This may be a little unorthodox, but since we're sharing, I think I will too."

Calvin turned to look at Zora with surprise in his eyes and said, "Amen." Then his gaze softened, and he silently urged Zora to continue speaking while Meesha nodded her support.

"I made a horrible mistake in my teenage years, one that altered my life. I knew that God had forgiven me, but I could never quite forgive myself. I isolated myself away from life. I could function well, but not on a personal level. I would shut down. Well, last week I came face-to-face, I mean smack-dab, with my past, and it threw me for a loop. I pushed away someone who proved to be a good friend and who had my best interest at heart. I should have handled the situation better, and I hope that person will, in time, forgive me." Zora looked at Meesha whose bright smile telegraphed, *Good job*.

Calvin smiled to himself as he turned a page in his Bible.

"Oh, come on, Doc, we know you mean the minister sitting to your left," Beverly said with a twinkle in her eyes. "I'm not so old that I didn't see what was developing between you two. Julia and I thought it was cute. Life is too short. Live each day to its fullest," she urged Zora.

"I will," Zora promised. She made up her mind in that instant to reach out to Jordan and talk to Calvin. If the minister couldn't cope with her past, then it would be his loss. Zora had a feeling he would though.

"Tomorrow will be a trying time for my family. For those of you who didn't know, Erin's memorial service is in the morning, and Brandon should have the DNA test result by then. I know that all things will work to the glory of God. I'm not worried about myself or Julia, but I am concerned about Brandon. This is the first major adversity he's suffered in his life, and it's been tough for him."

"Give him time," Calvin urged the older man. "There are not many nineteen-year-olds whose spouses have passed and left them with a child whose paternity is in question. I plan to talk to Brandon on a regular basis until he gets through the crisis."

"Good. Sometimes I feel like I'm talked out. I converse with him, and I know he's listening to me, but his mind and body seem to be in another place. I won't give up on him. I think it will help Brandon to talk with someone other than myself and Julia," Douglas said gratefully. "Thank you, Reverend Nixon."

"That's a good idea, Reverend Nixon. Talking to and praying for Brandon will, in time, uplift his spirit. The hurt he's feeling is too fresh. In time life will get better for him." Zora crossed her legs.

"That's what I've been telling my children to help them adjust to Edward not being home," Meesha added. "They slept with me the first few nights after Edward left. They looked so sad that I couldn't leave them alone. Imani actually smiled today, a tiny one, so we're making small progress. I plan to make an appointment with a therapist for them soon."

"I hear you." Beverly bobbed her head. "We may need counseling for Jalin. He's been wetting the bed and crying out for his mother at night. He's acting out, and we know it's because he misses her. The doctors are optimistic that Keisha's heavy bandages will be removed next week. She thinks he may become traumatized if he sees her with the bandages on her face. So we're abiding by her wishes. Kenny and I were debating whether to take Jalin to see his father. Dr. Taylor and Reverend Nixon, what do you think? Is Jalin too young to comprehend being at jail? Would taking him affect him later in life?"

"How old is he?" Reverend Nixon inquired.

"He's four years old. He's a little tough guy sometimes. Jalin can be mischievous, just like his father, but he can be a sweetie too," Beverly said proudly.

"There is nothing sweet about Jalin. He's all boy," Kenny said as he puffed out his chest.

"Has he asked about his father?" Zora asked.

"Not really. Amir didn't really spend a lot of time with him. We take care of him more than Amir ever did," Kenneth said.

"In that case, I'd say hold off on taking him to visit his father. If he asks for Amir, then we'll re-visit this topic," Reverend Nixon advised the couple.

"I was hoping Amir seeing his son would give him incentive to get his life together." Beverly sighed as she shrugged her shoulders.

"We can provide all the resources people need to change their lives, but until they make that decision for themselves, it doesn't mean a thing. A person has to want to make a change because of a need deep within," Zora added. "I totally agree with Reverend Nixon's assessment. Wait and see if Amir expresses a desire to see his son. If that happens, then you will know a change is occurring within your son. There are other things you can do to encourage Amir besides taking his son to see him in jail. I think the visits from his biological father and Reverend Dudley are a good start."

"Thank you," Beverly said. "My daughter and sisters said the same thing."

The group continued talking until the hour had elapsed. A few minutes later, Zora brought the meeting to a close, and then Calvin said the parting prayer. The group, with the exception of Douglas, who had departed before the meeting concluded, stayed and chatted for a few minutes. Everyone said they planned to attend Erin's service the following morning.

Finally, the room was empty except for Calvin and Zora. They began tidying the room as was their usual custom following a meeting.

Zora was in a quandary; she didn't want to part with Calvin on bad terms. She inspected the room one last time while Calvin shut his briefcase. Zora put on her gloves and retrieved her tote bag and purse from the table.

"Are you ready to go?" Calvin asked Zora with a stoic expression on his face.

She nodded, and they walked out of the room quietly together. Reverend Nixon locked the door to the room; then he and Zora walked out of the church to the parking lot. Calvin escorted Zora to her car, which he always did at the conclusion of a meeting, and waited while she got inside the vehicle. She started the car, then rolled down the window and gestured for Calvin to come inside the car. She had to wait for her car to warm up, so she thought that would be a good time to clear the air with Calvin.

He got inside the car, closed the door, and rubbed his hands together from the cold temperature. Then he turned to look at Zora expectantly. His eyes silently urged her to tell him her story.

"Calvin," she began, "I owe you a huge apology. I should have handled things differently. I am so used to being alone without having to answer to or explain my actions to anyone, and being that way had become second nature to me. I learned some shocking news that really floored me and tested my faith. Please accept my sincere apology." Her voice quivered.

"Zora," Calvin said tenderly. He took her hand as she turned the heater on to the low setting "I thought we were closer than that. I knew you had been hurt, although you've never opened up about what actually happened. I was not upset with you, just a little hurt that you couldn't confide in me about what was bothering you. I prayed that the Lord would help you resolve your issue and that in time you would come around." He grinned at Zora. "I haven't given up on you and hoped we could pick up where we left off."

Zora's eyes brimmed with tears, and she touched one of her eyes with a bent knuckle. "You are truly a man of God, Reverend Calvin Nixon. Sometimes I don't know what I did to deserve such a good friend. I had an epiphany a few Saturdays ago, and I'd like to share it with you."

Zora explained what had happened seventeen years ago in a small town in Alabama. Calvin listened attentively and nodded encouragingly at Zora. His hurt mirrored Zora's as she told her story. He didn't interrupt her and listened intently.

The couple sat in the parking lot of the church for close to an hour. When Zora finished speaking, she peeked at Calvin quickly to gauge his reaction to her confession.

"None of us are perfect, Zora. You were a kid experiencing your first major crush. I am sorry that Jeremy let you down. Like you, he was just a kid. As I listened to you speak, I surmised that you have never forgiven yourself for what happened. It's time to let go, leave the guilt behind, and come into your own. You are a strong, smart, beautiful Black woman with a heart of gold, and you need to see yourself for who you are." He adjusted the rearview mirror and gentled pulled Zora's face toward the mirror.

"You are a child of an omnipotent, powerful and, most of all, forgiving God. Let God heal you, Zora, so that you can live," Calvin urged the woman he knew God had sent to be his wife.

"Oh, God," Zora cried. She dropped her head in her hands and wept. Calvin put his arm around the top of her seat and stroked Zora's shoulder as she sobbed.

She finally managed to compose herself and fumbled in her pocket for something to wipe her eyes with.

Calvin reached inside his jacket pocked and pulled out a handkerchief. He handed it to Zora, and she wiped her eyes. "Where do you want to go from here? Do you want to make inquiries about your child and reach out to him?"

"This is the part of my story where I feel the Lord played a grand joke on me, or either it was my destiny to come here to put closure on my situation. My baby is here." She pointed across the street. "He's a member of the church and attends the academy."

"Our God is an awesome God. The Lord moves in mysterious ways, His wonders to behold," Calvin commented. "Are you sure?"

"My heart and spirit say yes." She took a deep breath and exhaled. "Jordan Brown is my son."

"You're sure?" Calvin reiterated as his mouth dropped and his eyes widened in amazement.

"As sure as I can be without a DNA test," Zora nodded. "I was reading Jordan's bio two Saturdays ago when my world crashed. I had a meeting scheduled with him that upcoming week, which I ended up canceling. I knew as I continued reading the essay he'd written that Jordan is my child. He bears a resemblance to Jeremy. When I first saw him, I thought he reminded me of someone, but exactly who eluded me.

"Jordan's bio stated that he was raised in the foster care system. His birthday is the same day as my child's. At first, I was elated. I thought maybe this was one of the reasons God called me to Illinois. Then as time went on, guilt crept in, and I felt like I had let him down. I was under the impression that he had been adopted after he was born, and I took comfort in knowing that he had been given to a good home and raised by caring, God-fearing parents. Instead, his upbringing was the worst-case scenario I could imagine."

"You're not God, Zora," Calvin chided her. "You took all the measures you could to give your child a good start in life. God had other plans. He sent Jordan on a detour, which eventually led him back to you. Life doesn't always go as we plan. You know our Father doesn't put more on us than we can bear. Jordan is a fine young man. You have nothing to feel guilty or ashamed of."

"I know that he's going to think that I abandoned him. I have counseled many children, some in foster care as well as adopted children, and they always feel a sense of abandonment. I wrestled with myself about contacting him, but I don't know at this point if doing so would prove helpful or harmful." Zora's voice trailed off doubtfully. She fidgeted in the seat.

"Jordan is one of the most grounded young men I know. I think I told you that I was his mentor. He has a good head on his shoulders and a gentle nature. I don't think you have anything to worry about."

"Has he ever said anything to you about learning the identity of his biological parents?" Zora asked. Unconsciously, she held her breath until Calvin answered.

"Sure, he has. He and I have talked about what type of people his parents might have been and about the circumstances that may have led to his being placed in foster care. For a while when Jordan was thirteen, he became obsessed with learning who his parents were. I told him all things happen in God's time. How ironic is it that I'm telling his mother the same thing." Calvin laughed. "Lighten up, Zora, things will turn out well."

"I guess you're right." Zora gave Calvin a trembling smile. "I'm not sure how to proceed though. I know it would be better if we have DNA tests performed, though I know it's not necessary, and then go from there. What do you think?" she asked Calvin anxiously.

"I think that's a great plan, and we should continue this conversation over some coffee. We can go to Starbucks up the street and come up with a strategy. What a blessing and happy ending to find your child and to experience the good works of the Lord."

"Are you sure you're not disappointed to find out I have a sordid past?" The words slipped from Zora's mouth. She nervously bit her lower lip as she waited for Calvin to reply.

"I am fine with who you are, Zora Taylor. That goes without question. No one is perfect, and we all have regrets in life, those shoulda-woulda-coulda moments. I just hope you realize that I have admiration for you, and I'm your friend. I don't care what happened in the past or happens in the future, please don't shut me out again. Share with me. Can you do that?"

Zora leaned toward Calvin and nodded her head; then she kissed him tenderly on the lips. "Thank you, Calvin. I promise never to shut you out again when I face a problem. Starbucks sounds good." She looked at the clock on the dashboard and then back at the minister. "We can't stay out too late this evening. Erin's service is in the morning."

"I promise to have you home at a reasonable hour." Calvin held up his hand and said, "I missed talking to you, and we need to make up for lost time." He unlocked the car door. "Give me a few minutes for my car to warm up; then I'll meet you at the Starbucks on Eighty-seventh Street near the Dan Ryan." He leaned over, kissed her cheek, then rushed out of Zora's car and sprinted to his own. Five minutes later, they pulled out of the parking lot of the church with grins as wide as the Mississippi River on both their faces. Zora realized as she drove to Starbucks that she loved Reverend Nixon.

Chapter Thirty-two

The sky was cloudy and gray the day of Erin's memorial service. High winds whipped around the corners of Chicago. Julia, Douglas, a reluctant Brandon, and other members of the Freeman family had just arrived at the church in a long, shiny black Lincoln Town Car limousine.

Julia and Douglas wore somber expressions on their faces as they exited the car, while Brandon looked as though he wished he was any place but at the church. Julia reached up and held her black hat firmly in place for fear the winds would carry it off like a kite. Douglas took Julia's arm, and they walked into the church with Brandon following slowly behind them. The young man looked as if he wanted to bolt.

The family decided Erin's service would be private. Douglas and Julia stood in the foyer of the church greeting relatives and friends as they walked inside. A few of Brandon's friends swarmed around him.

Latrell played "What a Friend We Have in Jesus" softly from inside the sanctuary. Reverend Dudley exited his office having noted the arrival of the limousine. He joined the family in the foyer clad in a flowing black robe. He greeted each family member and asked Douglas if they were ready to begin the service. Douglas nodded.

Reverend Dudley instructed the people milling in the foyer to line up in twos behind Julia and Douglas, who stood on each side of their son.

"Do I have to . . . ?" Brandon began saying. Douglas told his son yes, emphatically.

Reverend Dudley signaled to an usher to open the main sanctuary doors, and the family walked inside the auditorium behind the minister. They sat in the first row of the middle aisle while the usher led Reverend Dudley to the pulpit.

Julia placed her purse on her lap and glanced around the sanctuary. Fifty or so people were in attendance, mostly relatives, some church members including the therapy participants, and a few of Brandon's friends. Although Douglas left the Wheatley family a message about Erin's service, none of her family came to the funeral.

Reverend Nixon walked to the podium and opened his Bible. He adjusted the microphone then read the entire chapter of Psalm 121. "I will lift up mine eyes to the hills, from whence cometh my help. My help cometh from the Lord, which made heaven and earth. He will not suffer thy foot to be moved: he that keepeth thee will not slumber. Behold, he that keepeth Israel shall neither slumber nor sleep. The Lord is thy keeper: the Lord is thy shade upon thy right hand. The sun shall not smite thee by day nor the moon by night. The Lord shall preserve thee from all evil: he shall preserve thy soul. The Lord shall preserve thy going out and thy coming in from this time forth, and even for ever-more." When he finished the scripture, the congregation said amen. Reverend Nixon prayed fervently and then returned to his seat.

The memorial service began with Nichole Singleton singing a heart-wrenching rendition of "His Eyes Is on the Sparrow." As the service progressed, Julia kept dabbing at her eyes while Douglas kept a watchful eye on his son. Brandon was restless and jiggled his legs nonstop. He kept his head bowed and refused to look at the bronze coffin sitting at the front of the church surrounded by a sparse collection of floral arrangements. The morning had taken on a surreal air to Brandon. He could hardly wait until the service ended so they could go to the cemetery and he could go home.

An hour later, the memorial service had concluded. Reverend Nixon nodded to the funeral home staff to prepare the body for the final viewing. As people filed by the coffin, they stopped by the pew to shake the family's hands and offer condolences. Before long, the time had come for Julia, Douglas, and Brandon to say farewell to Erin.

Douglas was sitting at the end of the pew. He stood up, stepped out, and waited for Brandon and Julia to exit the row. They walked to the front of the church. All eyes in the building were glued on the family.

Douglas walked to the coffin first. With his back to the congregation, he leaned down and said, "Erin, good-bye. I am grateful to the Lord for bringing you into our lives and that you were a part of our family. I'll see you again one day."

Douglas had his arm around Julia's shoulders as she whispered to her deceased daughter-in-law, "I promise you that your baby will be taken care of. I know you are at peace." Douglas walked Julia back to her seat.

Douglas stood with his son. Brandon stared at Erin, and he thought she looked so pale and fake. She was wearing a blue dress, and her hands were crossed against her chest. The braids she usually wore were gone, and her hair flowed over her shoulders.

Brandon barely recognized his wife. He gazed at her for a long moment. His legs felt weak, and anger bubbled in his heart toward Erin for what he perceived as a lie perpetrated against him. He looked at his father and signaled he was done. They walked back to their seats.

Two hours later, Erin had been interred in the family plot at the cemetery, and the Freeman family had returned home. The house was full of people since Douglas and Julia decided to have the repast at their residence instead of the church.

The kitchen and dining room tables, as well as the kitchen counters were crammed with food donations. Several church members served the food from a table set up in the dining room. Hams, fried chicken, smoked turkey, greens, green beans, fried corn, candied yams, macaroni and cheese, casseroles, and salads were served. Many cakes, pies, and cobblers sat on top of the dining room buffet.

Though Douglas asked Brandon to spend time with the visitors upstairs, Brandon balked at the idea, so he and his friends talked and ate in the basement. The majority of the Freeman relatives had converged upon the dining room and breakfast nook off the kitchen, while Douglas and several of the other men were seated in the living room. Beverly, Meesha, Regina, and Zora were sitting on folding chairs in the master bedroom while Julia sat in a chaise next to the bed. One of the church members had come into the room multiple times to ask Julia if she was hungry, and each time Julia declined.

"You need to eat something, Julia," Meesha admonished the older woman. "You don't want to get sick. Did you have anything for breakfast?"

"My stomach has been in knots all day. I'm really not hungry. I had coffee this morning," Julia answered. Her eyes were closed and her legs crossed at the ankles as she leaned back against the seat.

"Well, before I leave here today I want to see you eat something," Beverly told Julia. "I thought Brandon held up well today."

"He did," Julia concurred. "It was a major battle just getting him out of the house this morning to go to the memorial service. Last night he insisted he wasn't going." Julia looked weary.

"He's young, and the situation has been difficult for him," Zora said wisely

"That's still no excuse for him to act like he had taken leave of his senses. I had to literally threaten him with bodily harm before he agreed to go to the service. I thought the service was nice. Reverend Nixon spoke well of Erin. Originally Reverend Dudley was going to deliver the eulogy, but after Douglas and I thought further, we asked Reverend Nixon to do it since he knew Erin better."

The women agreed Reverend Nixon had done a great job.

"We got the paternity test results today. It came in the mail," Julia whispered. "We'll read it later."

"You're good." Beverly shook her head. "Nothing could have kept me from reading it, full house or not."

"Douglas and I thought it would be better to look at the results with Brandon this evening after everyone has gone home. I found it eerie that we would have the results the day of Erin's service," Julia confided to the women, who hung on to her every word.

"I agree with you," Regina commented. "How is the baby doing?"

As if on cue, Juliana let out a yowl and then began crying in earnest.

"Do you want me to get her for you?" Beverly stood up.

"Thanks. Would you?" Julia asked as she sat erect in the seat.

"Sure." Beverly departed the room and returned minutes later carrying the baby.

Julia opened her arms, and Beverly gave her the child.

"She's a little beauty," the women cooed as they watched Julia calm the baby down.

"It looks like Juliana is attached to you," Meesha observed as Julia and the baby smiled at each other.

"Yes, she is." Julia looked up at the women and smiled. "Having Juliana here has been a blessing. I couldn't have children after my second pregnancy. I had suffered a still-birth and then had a hysterectomy. I had forgotten how nice it is to have a baby in the house."

"Except when they wake up for those midnight or early morning feedings," Meesha reminded Julia.

"You're right about that," Julia agreed. Juliana had fallen asleep, and Julia laid the baby against her chest. Juliana's head rested on the older woman's shoulder.

"I think she just wanted to be with you," Regina observed.

The women thought the baby probably wasn't Brandon's child and wondered what would happen to her if the paternity test proved that.

"Do you plan to keep the baby regardless of the test results? If you've gotten this attached to her, it will be difficult letting her go," Zora said.

"I'm going to cross that bridge when I get to it," Julia said nonchalantly. "We've been focused so on getting the test results back for Brandon's sanity that we haven't thought beyond that. I can't bear the thought of Juliana not being here. I have no idea where she might end up."

"She would almost certainly become a ward of the state and placed into foster care. I don't think she would be there long. She would be scooped up in a minute," Regina said.

"Especially if she's White," Meesha added. "White babies are adopted quickly. It's our children who usually languish in the system."

Zora felt guilty and pushed the thought away. She realized her situation was different.

"Do you think you could effectively raise a White child?" Beverly couldn't resist asking Julia.

"If you had asked me a few months ago, I would have positively said no. All of you know I was biased against Erin, but when all was said and done, I saw her as a person. The color of her skin didn't matter after a while. Still, I don't know if I'm the right person to raise a White child. Perhaps she needs to be with someone of her own race. I'm still thinking on it."

"I know your decision will be the right one for you and your family, including the baby," Meesha nodded. "I wish your family well, and will keep you all in my prayers."

"Julia," Beverly said as she rose from the bed, "can I fix you a plate now? I promise I won't put much on it. Kenny and I have to leave soon. Please?" she entreated.

"Yes, but please don't put a lot on the plate. A few slices of turkey and a little salad will be good." Julia nodded her head.

Meesha, Zora, and Regina stood up too.

"We're going to head home also." Meesha spoke for the group. They marched over to Julia and kissed her cheek. "Call any of us if you need anything." Meesha and the two ladies began their departure from the room.

"I appreciate all of you taking off work today to be with us," Julia said. "The sessions have brought us closer together. Take care of yourselves. I know there's tons of food out there. If you want to take something home with you, feel free."

The women left the room. Julia got up from her seat and took Juliana back to the nursery. Julia shed a few tears for Erin and her motherless child. She put a blanket over Juliana's legs.

As Zora was putting on her coat, Reverend Nixon walked into the foyer. Meesha and Regina moved discretely away from Zora to give the couple privacy to talk. "I'll call you later," Calvin said to Zora.

"Why don't you come to my house after you leave here?" Zora suggested.

"Good idea. I'll see you later." Calvin felt elated. He closed and locked the door after the women departed.

Three hours later, the house was deserted except for two of Douglas's brothers and their wives. The sisters-in-law were in the kitchen putting away the food. They brought Tupperware dishes to take food home with them at Julia's urging. One sister-in-law had cleaned the kitchen. The relatives told Douglas and Julia before leaving that they'd check on them later. Then they left, and only the Freemans remained in the house. Brandon's friends had departed too.

Douglas and Julia walked into the living room and sat side by side on the sofa. Julia rubbed her neck and announced, "It's been a long day—no, week—and I'm tired."

Douglas rubbed her back. "I guess we shouldn't put off reading the test results any longer," he suggested. "Let's call Brandon from downstairs and get this over with." He loosened his tie and pulled it off his neck.

"Mom, Pops," Brandon yelled from the basement. "Would you come down here? There's something I want you to hear."

Julia rose wearily from the sofa; then she and Douglas walked downstairs to the basement. They walked into Brandon and Erin's room and found Brandon sitting on a chair fiddling with a cassette player.

The young man's body trembled, and his voice was thick with emotion. "Erin left me a message on tape. I thought you guys should hear it. Then we can read the test results." He turned on the player.

Erin's thick drawl filled the space. She sounded like she was in the room with them. "Hey, Brandon, it's me. I recorded this message for you after the doctor told me a few months ago that I may have complications during labor because of my high blood pressure. If you're listening to this message, then that means I'm gone. I fully intend to erase this message if everything goes well. I couldn't go to my grave without you knowing the truth.

"I want to thank you for being the best husband in the world under the circumstances. I know you didn't really want to marry me and that Papa Doug made you. Tell him and Mama Jules that I love them. They have been better parents to me than my own flesh and blood." Erin paused for a moment; then she said in a hushed voice, "Brandon, I'm sorry. There is a good chance that you might not be Juliana's father. I should have told you that in the beginning, but I wanted to leave Tennessee and see something of the world.

"I was born and raised in a four-room shack in the foothills of the Appalachian Mountains. My parents can barely read or write, and they attend a fundamentalist church where mixing races is a big sin along with a lotta others. I barely got through school. The kids I went to school with considered me trash and looked down on me. I was judged harshly because of my raggedy clothes and worn-down shoes. People didn't take the time to get to know me. I had one friend that my folks didn't know about. I hung out with her. Her name is Olivia Davis. She was a couple of years older than me. We went to high school together.

"As soon as I turned eighteen and finished high school, I escaped the mountains and moved to Nashville with Olivia. We were an odd pair. Olivia's parents were kind to me, and Livy introduced me to the Black culture. She is the sister I never had. I called her last week and asked her if she would keep the baby if she turned out to be Rich's child and not yours, if anything happened to me. She told me that I should tell you all the truth, but I was scared to. If you don't want to keep my baby, please call Livy. Her number is programmed in my cell phone.

"I am sorry for any shame I brought upon your family. Please forgive me, if you can find it in your heart. Please take care of Juliana. I want you to keep her. I love all of y'all."

The tape ended. Douglas, Julia, and even Brandon couldn't hold back their tears. Julia sat down and cried. It tore her heart apart to realize how much Erin loved her family and how bad she had been to the girl.

Brandon kept opening and closing his mouth as tears ran down his face.

The family went upstairs. Douglas walked to his and Julia's bedroom to retrieve the envelope while Julia and Brandon went to the living room. Everyone was anxious to find out once and for all just who Juliana Freeman's father was.

Chapter Thirty-three

When Beverly and Kenneth returned home, Beverly immediately took a nap. She was mentally and physically exhausted from the events of the day. When Beverly awakened she felt sad for Julia and wondered how her friend was doing. The house felt a little cool since the temperature outside had plunged below zero. Beverly rubbed her arms. She stood up, stretched, and walked downstairs.

Kenneth was asleep on the sofa in the den. Beverly kissed his forehead. She then walked into the dining room and pressed the up arrow on the thermostat. A few seconds later, the furnace roared on.

Tracey had left a note for her parents stating that she had taken the children to McDonald's to burn off their energy.

Beverly was in the kitchen washing dishes when the telephone rang. "You have a collect call from the Cook County Jail," an automated voice announced. Beverly accepted the call from Amir. "Hello, son. How are you doing today?"

"How do you think I'm doing, Mom?" Amir asked Beverly sarcastically. "I'm in jail. I hate being in this place."

"I didn't mean to sound insensitive," Beverly replied. "I know you hate being there, and I hate that you're there." Beverly had a feeling that Amir wanted to indulge in a pity party. She felt too drained to participate and didn't feel like listening to the onslaught of complaints that would be forthcoming from her son.

"You should see what they feed us here. It's no joke. I wish I had one of your Sunday meals. That would do me some good," Amir commented.

"Well, you know I can't bring food to the jail. I promise you that when you come home, I'll prepare a big meal for you," Beverly told her son.

"I'ma hold you to that. Oh, I mean to tell you that Attorney Logan came to see me today. He said he's been talking to the state about offering me a plea deal. I told him no because that would be admitting I did something wrong, and what happened to Keisha was an accident."

"You don't understand, Amir. If the jury sees Keisha's face, things could be bad for you. There's a chance that you might have to do even more time than Attorney Logan thinks," Beverly replied ominously. She rubbed her forehead. Sometimes she thought Amir didn't get it.

"Yeah, yeah, whatever," Amir said in a tone of voice that indicated he was tired of Beverly's dire predictions.

"What type of plea deal is your lawyer trying to get for you?"

"Well, he wants me to plead guilty and get a three-year sentence, and I'd have to take anger management classes. He said something about house arrest for a while."

"What's wrong with that?" Beverly asked. "You need to find another way to manage your temper anyway. Attorney Logan said you could get up to five years in prison. You should reconsider your decision not to accept the plea. Three years isn't so long, especially with the time you've served applied."

"That's easy for you to say. Right now, I'm in a jail. Things could change drastically in the big house. Not that I'm scared or anything; I know how to handle myself," Amir bragged.

"You have a valid point," Beverly admitted painfully. "Still, you can use the time wisely. You can take courses. You could get your degree or training after you figure out what you want to do with your life. You're not getting any younger, Amir. Now is the time to get it right."

"Who's going to hire a convicted felon? All the education in the world ain't going change my status," Amir reasoned.

"The city has programs to help felons find jobs. Tracey researched it on the Internet." Beverly changed the subject and asked, "Has Zeke been to see you?"

"Yeah, he was here yesterday. He's kind of an interesting dude, different from Dad. He left money in my account, and we talked for a minute."

"Good, he told me he wants to be involved in your life. Maybe he means it this time."

"We'll see," Amir replied. "He told me he did some time back in the day for robbery. We were kind of vibing."

"Good. Maybe he can get through to you since Kenny and I can't." Beverly yawned and stretched her arm over her head.

"Look, I gotta go. One of the brothers wants to use the phone. I just kind of missed being at home. I even miss Dad, and I never thought that would happen," Amir joked.

"I'm sure you do. I'll talk to you tomorrow or the next day, Amir. I love you, son, and I am praying hard that God will be merciful to you and you will take the opportunity He's given you to get your life together. Think about the plea and take care."

"Okay, Mom. Talk to you later. Tell everyone I said hello."

"I will," Beverly promised. She hung up the telephone, pleased with her conversation with Amir. She returned to her bedroom and decided to give herself a manicure. She washed her hands in the bathroom. When she returned to the bedroom, Beverly took her nail kit off the top of her dresser.

Kenneth walked into the room a few seconds later and looked at his wife sitting Indian style on the bed with her hands outstretched. "You should have woken me up. I didn't mean to sleep that long." He stretched his body across the bed.

"Sorry, I figured you needed your rest." Beverly shook the bottle of base coat polish, opened it, and began applying it to her fingers. "Today was a long, emotional day. I feel for Julia. I don't know what she and Doug are going to do about the baby if she's not Brandon's child. I don't see any of the Freemans in that baby."

"I agree with you. She definitely looks White. You can never tell, though. Maybe she took after Erin's side of the family." Kenneth positioned his hands behind his head.

"Even if she does, we should be able to see some of Brandon's, Doug's, or Julia's features in her. I didn't see anything." Beverly began applying the base coat to her other hand.

"Whatever the outcome of the paternity test, I'm sure the Freemans will cope with the results. Doug is levelheaded, and I think Erin's passing has thrown Julia for a loop. I've never seen her so subdued."

"Death does that to people sometimes," Beverly mused. "Julia has a strong attachment to Juliana. It's going to be difficult for her to give that baby up."

"That's true. Still, they'll do what they have to do. I think Doug and Julia would probably raise the child. Brandon, on the other hand, is a different story. I never saw him with the baby anytime we were at their house." Kenneth picked up the remote control unit from the nightstand and turned to the cable guide to see what was airing on television.

Beverly blew her nails and waved her hands in the air. She opened the bottle of coral fingernail polish and with measured strokes applied the polish to her left hand. Beverly paused and shut her eyes. "Lord, bless Julia, Doug, and Brandon. Give them peace, Lord. Guide them as they make the decision about the baby."

While Beverly was praying for her friends, over at the Freeman house Brandon handed the envelope from the lab to Douglas, "Why don't you read it, Pops?"

Douglas stared at his son as he turned the envelope around in his hands. "The test concerns you and your wife. Are you sure you don't want to open it?"

"No, I don't. Just tell us what it says." Brandon sat next to Julia on the sofa. She sat stiffly with her head bowed and her hands clasped together. Frown lines were etched in the center of her forehead.

Douglas slit the envelope open with his fingernail as he sat in his recliner. He removed the letter from the envelope and slowly opened it. His eyes widened, and he blinked quickly after he read the results. Douglas shook his head. "The baby isn't yours, Brandon. The test is 99.5 percent accurate. I'm sorry, son."

"Yes." Brandon jumped up from his seat and thrust his fist into the air. "See, I told you I wasn't that kid's father," Brandon whooped. "Well, we knew there was a chance that I wasn't Erin's baby's daddy. So, that's that." Brandon acted as if the news didn't affect him, though the light in his eyes dimmed a bit. "I think we should call Erin's friend Olivia tomorrow and have her come to get the baby."

"Are you sure that's what you want to do?" Douglas answered. "Legally the baby is yours."

"I'm positive. I was talking to Tim this afternoon about what would happen if the baby wasn't mine, and he said I should get a lawyer after I got the test results. You know he's a law major. There's a legal procedure I can do to declare myself not to be the father. So I want to do that."

Julia rubbed her throat and swallowed a couple of times. "You still want to go that route after hearing Erin's tape?"

"Yes. Why would I want a reminder of Erin's pinning a lie on me?" He frowned at his mother. He sat back down on the sofa and had a big smile on his face.

"If you decide to go to court, that would be the same as announcing to the world that you're not the baby's father. Are you prepared for that?" Julia asked her son. She put her hand on Brandon's arm.

"I sure am. I've been thinking about what I want to do with my life. I can get back on track and put this mess behind me. I feel like I dodged a bullet." Brandon wiped his brow; then he looked at his parents. "What's the matter with you two?" Then he shook his head. "You want to keep the baby, don't you?" He glared at Julia.

"I . . . I . . . wouldn't mind it. I think it's a compliment to you and our family that Erin wants us to raise the baby. I feel it would be the right thing to do, to honor her last wishes. I admit I wasn't fond of Erin when she came here, nor about her being pregnant. But I've grown to love the baby, and I feel it would be the right thing to do, to keep her since that's what Erin wanted."

"Well, maybe you and Dad should adopt her." Brandon threw his hands in the air. "I was kidding. I don't want any part of her." He snapped his mouth shut.

"Remember, she's just an innocent baby in this," Douglas reminded his son. "You and your mother have valid points. I can understand where you're both coming from. I think we should think about the situation prayerfully over the weekend. Let's not be hasty about making a decision."

"You're on Mom's side like always," Brandon spat. "You should be glad I'm not saddled with a baby at my age. Maybe I'll go back to school. I look at the test results as God giving me another chance. Erin's kid to me is a non-factor. I feel nothing for her."

Juliana cried, and Julia jumped from her seat. "I'll go see about her. Brandon, I'm disappointed with your decision. Would you at least think about it over the weekend like your father asked?"

"It makes me no difference today, Monday, or years from now. Nothing will change my feelings about that baby. I'm your son. She's not your daughter or your granddaughter. Your loyalty should be to me." Brandon looked hurt as Julia went upstairs to the nursery.

"You're right," Douglas replied. "You will always be our first priority, but there's nothing wrong with helping others."

"Then you and Mom help her. Buy the kid a one-way ticket to Tennessee, and we can put this behind us. Can I be excused? I want to call Tim." Brandon jiggled his left knee.

Douglas nodded. "You can, but we'll have to eventually finish this conversation. Pray for guidance, Brandon, and we'll talk about this again on Monday."

Brandon stood up. "Fine, but I'm not changing my mind. I think I'll go to Tim's house and hang out with the fellas for a while. We can celebrate my freedom."

"Don't come home in the condition you were in last week," Douglas warned his son.

"No chance of that. I'm celebrating. I'll see you later." Brandon left the room and returned to the basement. Fifteen minutes later, he departed to go to Tim's house.

Douglas continued to sit at the table in thought. Julia yelled from upstairs, "Doug, would you warm up a bottle for Juliana? She's hungry."

"Yes." Douglas walked into the kitchen and took a four-ounce bottle of formula from the refrigerator. He put it in the microwave, set the timer, and waited for the milk to warm. The microwave beeped, signaling it was done.

Douglas took the bottle out of the microwave and went upstairs to the nursery. Julia was sitting in the rocking chair trying to soothe the fussy baby. He gave her the bottle, took a cloth diaper from the dressing table, and put it on his wife's shoulder. Juliana looked up at him and flashed him a toothless smile; then she resumed sucking the bottle greedily.

Douglas leaned against the wall and watched his wife feed the baby. Julia put the baby on her shoulder, then burped the infant. Juliana's eyes grew heavy and she fell asleep. Julia stood up and put her back into her frilly baby bed.

Julia and Doug walked out of the nursery and downstairs to the living room. After they settled on the sofa, Julia turned to Douglas and declared in an emotion-filled voice, "I want to keep the baby, Doug. I know Brandon is against the idea. But in time, he'll come around."

"I know you want to keep the baby, Julia. I have eyes, and I've watched you become attached to that baby more each day. But Brandon is right. Juliana's staying here would be a reminder of Erin, and do we really want to subject him to that?"

"I thought about that," Julia admitted. "If Brandon goes back to school, he wouldn't be here most of the time anyway. As he gets older he'll understand the situation better."

"We've still got to live with him in the meantime, Jules. This is an unusual and serious predicament. We're not getting any younger. Are you prepared to take on the responsibilities and care for a baby for the next eighteen years? I know Erin's tape moved you. It moved me too, but we still have to finish raising Brandon. Let's not forget we're not talking about a biracial child anymore; Juliana is White. There are a lot of factors to be considered."

"Brandon is over eighteen," Julia pointed out, "and our time with him grows shorter each day. The hardest part of raising him is done. At this point, we're providing him with guidance and money more than anything else. And as far as raising a White child, I can do it. The circumstances are personal. It's not like we've selected a child from an adoption agency."

"That's true," Douglas admitted as he pulled Julia into his arms. "You've come a long way, and I'm proud of you. Still, we have to consider our son's wishes. He's been through a lot the past year. I suggest we pray and allow God to guide us. I want you to remember, Juliana isn't Nia, and she can't replace our daughter. Perhaps we should call Reverend Dudley and have him come here and talk to us as a family. Or maybe even Dr. Taylor and Reverend Nixon."

"I know Juliana isn't Nia. I agree we should talk to Dr. Taylor and Reverend Nixon and get their opinion."

"Let's do that, though I don't see Brandon changing his mind. In the meantime, one of us should call Olivia tomorrow and tell her what's happened and see if her offer still stands to raise Juliana."

Julia looked at the wooden grandfather clock in the corner of the living room. "It's only eight o'clock, why don't we call her now? We can find out what she's thinking and maybe that will help us with our decision."

"Okay." Douglas stood up. "I'll go get Erin's cell phone from downstairs, and we can call her."

Douglas returned to the living room minutes later. He sat down next to Julia and handed her the phone. "Why don't you call her?"

"I will." Julia scanned Erin's contacts list. She found Olivia's number and then initiated the call. The phone rang a couple of times before a cheerful voice came on the line. "Hi, Erin, how are you doing? Did you have the baby?"

"Hello, Olivia. You don't know me. I'm Julia Freeman, Erin's mother-in-law." Julia licked her lips.

"Hi, Mrs. Freeman," Olivia replied. "Erin has told me a lot about you and your family. Where is Erin?"

"Well, I'm calling with bad news. Erin passed away last week. We would have called you sooner, but we just learned about you today."

"Oh, no!" Olivia exclaimed. She dropped the telephone. She picked it up and put it to her ear. "I am so sorry to hear that." Olivia sniffled. "What happened?"

"She developed complications during the labor." Julia explained what had transpired over the past week.

"I wish I had known. I would have come there. I assume you've had the service already?"

"Yes," Julia answered. "It was today. I wish we had known about you sooner too. Olivia, another reason I called you is about the baby. Erin left us a message that if necessary you would take custody of the baby. My husband and I want to know if the offer still stands."

"Oh," Olivia's voice dropped. "The baby must not be your Brandon's."

"That's correct. We received the DNA test results today, and the baby is definitely not Brandon's." Julia went into more detail as to the nature of the call.

"Well, I'm not comfortable discussing this over the telephone. Would it be okay if I fly to Chicago and meet you in person?" Olivia asked Julia.

"That would be great." Julia bobbed her head up and down. "Are you sure? We could come down there if you'd like."

"I'm positive. I work for an airline, and I can be there by Monday evening if that's okay."

"That's fine. Excuse me if I'm being forward," Julia said. "Are you the same age as Erin?"

"No, I'm a couple of years older than she was. I'm married and have a son."

Julia felt slightly relieved. "Why don't I give you our address and telephone number, and you can call us with the flight information. One of us will meet you at the airport, and you can stay here if you'd like."

"That would be wonderful, ma'am. Thank you for calling me. Give me a moment to find a pen." Olivia returned to the telephone a few minutes later. Julia gave her the information. Olivia promised to call Julia Sunday with her flight details.

Julia clicked off the phone. "Well, I feel better after talking to Olivia. She seems pretty well grounded, at least over the phone."

"Good. Now I believe I saw a pan of peach cobbler in the refrigerator left from this afternoon. Why don't I fix us a bowl and then we can relax?"

"Okay, I'll meet you upstairs," Julia told Douglas. He went into the kitchen. She turned out the light in the living room and went upstairs. Julia stopped in the nursery first; then she went to her and Douglas's bedroom.

Julia sat on the side of the bed with her head in her hands. Julia's mind whirled with indecision. She wasn't sure if she could give Juliana away to anyone because the baby was a part of her life, like Nia had been.

Chapter Thirty-four

Two weeks had elapsed, and the group planned to meet for the last time on Friday instead of the usual Thursday. The group felt a sense of loss. In eight weeks friendships had been forged, as well as a romance.

Spring was in the air, trees and lawns were beginning to turn green, and birds were retuning from their migration spots and chirping morning songs. The temperature had reached a record high of sixty-five degrees, and the sun emitted warm rays.

Zora was in a tizzy that morning at work. She had tossed and turned the entire night after talking to her mother, who was ecstatic about her daughter's news. Annie told her daughter that she could hardly wait to meet her grandson.

Zora bore little resemblance to her usually calm, scholarly self that morning. She had misplaced her favorite fountain pen, hit her knee on her desk drawer, and lost her train of thought multiple times. She had one appointment scheduled that day, and it was with Jordan Brown. Calvin planned to sit in on the session. Reverend Dudley was at the church and on standby if needed. Zora looked at the clock at the bottom of her PC monitor and saw the meeting was scheduled to begin in ten minutes.

She had given Tiffany the day off from work. Zora practiced in her mind a million times what she planned to say to Jordan. She had consulted with the state of

Illinois, Jordan's foster parents, a lawyer, and God. All signs pointed to go. Zora was lost in thought when she heard a tap at her office door. "Come in," she said.

Reverend Nixon walked into the room. He closed the door and walked to Zora's desk. She stood up, and he enveloped her in an encouraging hug. "Everything is going to work out. Don't worry."

They chatted as the minister sat in the chair across from Zora's desk and tried to allay her fears. He said a quick prayer, and then there was another knock at Zora's door. Jordan walked inside the room. His foster parents sat in the waiting area outside Zora's office.

Reverend Nixon sprung from his seat and shook the young man's hand. Zora remained seated at her desk. Her knees felt as limp as overcooked noodles, and she didn't think her limbs would support her body. She smiled at Jordan, pointed to the chair next to Reverend Nixon's, and asked the young man to have a seat.

The three conversed for a few minutes. Then Jordan quipped nervously, "I must be special. The big guns want to talk to me about my college choice."

"That you are," Zora said in a subdued tone of voice. Then she stopped talking, expelled a loud breath, and gathered herself. "Actually, that's not the only reason you're here, Jordan."

"It's not?" Jordan cocked his head to the side and peered at Zora.

Zora remembered the movement as being one of Jeremy's. "No, not quite." She folded and unfolded her hands. "I read your bio a little while ago and read that you were adopted. In your essay you expressed how you would like to one day meet your biological parents." Zora took a deep breath and croaked out, "I'm your mother."

Jordan stared at Zora for a long minute. His body went limp, and he grabbed the handles of his chair. "Are you sure?" he asked as his voice cracked.

"I'm positive. Do you remember going with your foster parents to your doctor's office a couple of weeks ago for a physical? The doctor took a mouth swab and used that for the DNA test. We got the test results back last week. You are my child." Zora's voice trembled as her eyes filled with tears.

Jordan turned to look at Reverend Nixon and asked, "You're not my father, are you?"

Reverend Nixon held up his hands. "No, but I hope any future son I may have grows up to be as fine a young man as you are."

"I don't know what to say . . . I planned to look for my biological parents one day." Jordan looked at Zora uncertainly.

"If I had never read your bio, I don't think I would have ever looked for you," Zora replied in a shaky voice. She told Jordan how he came into being seventeen years ago. When she finished speaking, her eyes were awash with tears and so were Jordan's. Reverend Nixon cleared his throat loudly.

"What I'd like to do, if it's okay with you," Zora said to Jordan with a tremulous smile, "is spend time getting to know you. One day, I hope we can have a parent-child relationship. Right now, I'd like us to become friends and see where it takes us."

"I think that's a great idea," Jordan said as he wiped his sweating palms on the side of his dark khaki pants. "I'm stunned," Jordan said as he stared at Zora.

"I plan to get in touch with your biological father. I believe he still lives in Alabama, and I'll see if he wants to be a part of your life. I want to do everything humanly possible to make up for what you've had to endure these years."

"Dr. Taylor, I haven't had a bad life. It's just been different and at times interesting. You don't have anything to make up for. What happened was one of those things. I'd love to spend time with you. My graduation is in a few months and then I go to college in June, so I'm ready when you are."

Zora stood up. She walked around her desk and held out her arms to her son. Jordan walked a few steps toward Zora, and the two embraced as tears poured down their faces.

Reverend Nixon quietly left the room. He closed the door and told Jordan's foster parents that the talk had gone well. He offered to buy them lunch while Zora and Jordan continued to talk.

"What happened with Jordan and Dr. Taylor is a blessing from God," Jordan's foster mother commented as she put on her leather coat. "I am so happy for Jordan. He's a good boy, and after his rocky start in life, he deserves all the blessings God sees fit to give him."

"I couldn't agree with you more." Calvin nodded at the woman. "Let's go find something to eat while mother and son spend some quality time together."

Zora sat in the chair that Reverend Nixon had vacated next to her son. She clutched Jordan's hand as he peppered her with questions about her life and his father.

When the afternoon rolled around, Zora couldn't keep a grin off her face. She had decided to hold the last session at her apartment instead of church and have a potluck supper.

She had just put chopped salad ingredients into a large bowl when her doorbell rang. She went into the foyer and pressed the intercom button. Meesha was downstairs; Zora buzzed her friend up.

Zora unlocked the door, and Meesha walked in carrying a bag from Jewel Food Store. Meesha followed Zora to the kitchen and laid the bag on the counter.

"Hi, Mommy," Meesha said with a wide smile across her face. The friends hugged.

"You can put your coat on the bed in my room," Zora instructed Meesha.

Meesha returned to the kitchen and asked Zora, "What do you need me to do?"

"You can set the dining room table. What did you bring?"

"I brought three rotisserie chickens and some French bread. I hope that's okay."

"That's great. Some people don't eat red meat. I broiled beef short ribs, so we have choices." The women chatted and continued their tasks.

A half hour later, the dining room table was just about set. Meesha was taking silverware out of the buffet and laying it on the table when the doorbell rang again.

"That's probably Calvin, I mean Reverend Nixon," Zora said as she opened the oven door and took the pan of ribs out of it. "Would you get the door for me?" she asked Meesha.

Reverend Nixon walked inside the condo carrying two coolers stacked on top of each other. "Good evening, Meesha. Where should I put these?"

"In the kitchen. Follow me." She instructed the minister to put the coolers on each side of the pantry door.

Calvin went back to his car and returned with beverages. He took off his jacket, and Meesha hung it in the hall closet. Calvin walked over to Zora, who was checking the ribs with a long-handled fork. He greeted her and said, "Do you need help?"

"No, why don't you relax? Everyone should be here soon. You can buzz them in as they arrive."

Calvin nodded and went into the den and put a CD he had bought Zora into the CD player. Then he waited for the group.

Twenty minutes later, everyone had arrived, and the women were in the kitchen transferring the food into bowls and platters.

"Your place is so eclectic," Beverly told Zora as she took a bottle of salad dressing out of the pantry. "You and Julia have beautiful homes. I've been talking to Kenny about giving our house a makeover."

"Thank you, Beverly. Meesha and I decorated my house together, and a lot of the credit goes to Meesha." Zora took serving utensils out of the cabinet drawer.

Beverly had brought a pan of macaroni and cheese and a pan of green beans, while Julia came bearing a red velvet cake, mixed greens, and potato salad.

Reverend Nixon, Douglas, Kenneth, and Brandon were in the den watching television.

"I'm glad Brandon decided to come to the last session," Zora told Julia.

"Believe it or not, I think he and Erin enjoyed the sessions. Doug and I, for once, didn't get any lip from him. He just asked what time and said he would be here. I think his talks with Reverend Nixon are bringing him around."

"Okay, ladies. I think we're done. Let's call the men and dig in," Zora said to the women. They walked into the dining room after inspecting the kitchen one final time to make sure the serving dishes had spoons and forks inside them. The men joined the women, and Zora then directed everyone to the kitchen to prepare their plates.

In no time, everyone was seated around the table with laden plates in front of them. Reverend Nixon bowed his head and blessed the food. Soon the group was chowing down.

"The food is great." Douglas complimented the women after he chewed and swallowed a piece of beef.

"You put on a great spread," Kenneth added. He broke a piece of buttered French bread and consumed it.

The lively dinner conversation consisted of the weather, current events, and politics. Kenneth mentioned that he'd heard a young, African American Illinois senator was planning on running for president.

The group put a dent in the food. The women removed the plates and eating utensils from the table, and took them to the kitchen. Zora put on coffee while Meesha took cups, saucers, cream, and sugar to the dining room. Then, after the coffee brewed, she and Zora took a couple of carafes of the brew to the dining room and returned to their seats.

"Thank you for opening your house to us," Julia told Zora after she took a sip of coffee. That was very thoughtful of you."

Douglas passed his wife a thin slice of strawberry cheesecake, while he had a hardy helping of red velvet cake to go with his coffee.

"It was my pleasure," Zora preened. She sat at the head of her table, and Rev. Nixon sat at the other end. "I don't entertain very often, so this was a good opportunity for me to get my feet wet. I thought a relaxed setting would be a good way to close our sessions. By the way, I want to thank you for participating. I think the sessions went well, and I hope you enjoyed the experience as much as I did and that you have a greater appreciation for group therapy."

Douglas said, "I definitely do. I would recommend it to anyone having marital issues."

Reverend Nixon grinned. "I have to admit I thought what we were doing was cutting-edge for a Baptist church. The sessions progressed very well. I propose a toast to our esteemed Dr. Taylor for a job well done."

Everyone raised their cups and said, "Here, here."

"Thank you, everyone," Zora said modestly. "We couldn't have accomplished our goal without the assistance of Reverend Nixon. I think he helped balance the sessions nicely, thereby allowing us to have observations from the female and male perspectives. My goal was to open communication between the couples and give you different techniques to resolve issues that arise, as well as give you a nudge to remember what attracted you to your spouses."

"That you did." Kenneth raised his cup. "I know if Bev and I hadn't participated in the sessions, our marriage might not have survived Amir's incarceration."

"Speaking of Amir," Beverly interjected. "He decided to accept the plea deal the state offered. He was sentenced to four years but could be out as early as two and a half years with good behavior. Since he's no longer drinking or doing drugs, his mind is clearer, and he's calmed down considerably. Amir is even taking a few classes. Reverend Dudley is going to put him in touch with an organization that helps felons find jobs after he serves his time. I've also gotten a handle on my spending habits. I slip up sometimes, but overall I'm doing better."

"That's wonderful news," Julia said enthusiastically.

The group clapped.

"Tracey has finally saved up enough money to move out of our house," Kenneth informed everyone. "Actually, she and Keisha, Jalin's mother, are going to rent an apartment together. They plan to move into the new place by the middle of April. As much as I complained about the children being home, I'm going to miss Rhianna and Jalin being in the house with us. They were my little buddies."

"Oh, I have plenty of chores planned to occupy Kenny's time." Beverly threw back her head and laughed. "I want to redecorate the house, and Saturday night will be our date night. I used to make all the decisions in the house regarding the kids, and now I'm willing to share with Kenny."

Brandon, who had been quiet up until that time, spoke up. "I am returning to Tennessee State for the summer session. I don't know what I was thinking about being a rapper. I think I was just overwhelmed by being a husband and father." His voice choked. "Pops hired a trainer to work with me, and I plan to try out for the basketball team as a walk on. I've had conversations with the coach, and he has agreed to my trying out. So things have gotten better for me. I may not be married anymore, but I learned some good things from the group that I plan to use in the future to keep my next relationship fresh."

"Very good." Reverend Nixon grinned at the young man. Brandon had finally let go of some of his anger. The minister, as he had promised, talked to Brandon on a weekly basis. The two men had gone to the gym a couple of times to shoot hoops.

"Douglas and I ended up giving the baby to Erin's friend Olivia after the paternity test showed Brandon wasn't Juliana's father," Julia reported. "Olivia is a delightful young woman. She is in the process of adopting Juliana, and she promises to stay in contact with us. Erin had an insurance policy, and Olivia was the beneficiary. She e-mailed us pictures of the baby last week." Julia rummaged through her purse for a mini photo album. She thrust it into the air. "I have pictures. Olivia is going to let us keep the baby during the summer and split holidays with us."

Brandon leaned back in his chair and added, "I still don't want anything to do with the baby. But I realize that I can't stop my parents from seeing her. So I'm good with that."

"We think he'll change his mind as time goes by," Julia said.

"You all remember how horrified Julia was by Erin's looks and behavior, and to her credit, she doubted the baby was Brandon's child. Living in our house was like living in the Wild West sometimes. I'm happy to say my Jules has done a one hundred-eighty-degree turnaround, and I know our experiences with Erin, Juliana, and the sessions had a lot to do with the change in her mindset." Douglas looked at his wife admiringly.

"That and finally realizing we are all God's children, we just come in different colors, shapes, and sizes," Julia added. "The scriptures Reverend Nixon e-mailed me helped tremendously. Even though Juliana won't live with us like I wanted, we still get to share in her life. When I call Olivia, I talk to Juliana and she just coos," Julia said humbly. "I feel like a real grandmother."

"I wish I could say that my story had a happy ending like the rest of you, but that isn't the case. I have filed for a divorce from Edward. I feel like a failure sometimes, but I don't have much time to feel sorry for myself. My time is spent making sure my children are adjusting to the changes in their lives."

"That happens sometimes, Meesha, even to Christians. You did what you could to keep your marriage intact. You and the children will be fine, and if it's God's plan and your own, you will meet a man one day who will love and appreciate you," Zora commented.

"I realize that. I'm blessed. My parents, Edward's mother, and Reggie have helped pick up the slack. If I had to raise the children alone, I would probably be crazy. It's best that Edward and I parted, though I never imagined a time when we wouldn't be together. Edward plans to marry as soon as the divorce is finalized."

"The Lord will take care of him," Kenny muttered. "You are in a better place, and if there's anything Bev and I can do to help, please let us know."

"Ditto for me and Julia," Douglas added.

"I think we should meet as a group once a year to keep up with the latest happenings in each other's lives," Beverly suggested. "Julia and I have become friends, and I always thought she was a snob. It just goes to show you can't judge a book by its cover."

Julia looked down for a minute; then she looked up and smiled brightly. "Oh, I was a snob all right. But now I'm a true woman of God."

Everyone laughed and clapped.

"I kind of alluded to a major change in my life a few meetings ago," Zora said shyly. She looked across the table at Reverend Nixon who dipped his head encouragingly at her.

"I know what it is." Beverly clapped her hands together and said gleefully, "You and Reverend Nixon are getting married."

"No," Zora blushed. "Not that. I had a child out of wedlock when I was a teenager and put him up for adoption. Well, I found him. As a certain minister told me, God works in mysterious ways, His wonders to behold. My son is a member of our church. He's Jordan Brown, and I'm happy to say we've been spending time together getting to know each other."

A babble rose from the table as everyone congratulated Zora.

"Hey, I know Jordan. He's got mad skills," Brandon said. "Cool, Dr. Taylor."

"You're going to be a wonderful mother," Julia told Zora.

"Getting to know my son has been pure joy. I am so blessed. I thank God every day for putting Jordan in my life."

"I still say that I'm right," Beverly insisted. "I know there's something going on between you and Reverend Nixon." She looked to her right at the minister.

"Okay, we can't keep anything from you all. Zora and I have been dating for a while. We're going to take it slow. One day in the not-too-distant future, I plan to make her my wife," Calvin announced as Zora blushed.

"We knew it," Beverly and Julia exclaimed triumphantly. The women gave each other high-fives.

"This is so exciting," Beverly exclaimed. "The couples after us will never be able to top the things we have accomplished."

Meesha gave a *Mona Lisa* smile and thought, *Everything worked out for everyone except for me.* Meesha realized her intentions for forming the ministry were selfish. But she was glad everything worked out for the other couples.

"I need to run downstairs to my car," Reverend Nixon told the group. He stood up and walked away from the table. "I have a message from Reverend Dudley." He left the condominium, went outside to his car, and returned with his briefcase.

He opened it and removed an envelope. "Reverend Dudley sends his congratulations. He also asked me to read this letter to you:

"'On behalf, of myself, and the official board of Christian Friendship Missionary Baptist Church I'd like to congratulate each of you for completing the debut session of Couples' Therapy. I have been in touch with each of you and the feedback you've provided has been very insightful. May God continue to bless all of you.

"I would like to commend Dr. Taylor and Reverend Nixon for a job well done. We have a long waiting list of members wanting to participate in the sessions, and that speaks very highly of your dedication and professionalism to the ministry. I can't leave out Sister Meesha Morrison and the Helping Hands Club because without Sister Morrison's vision, the program would not exist.

"'In closing, I'd like to leave you with these scriptures to ponder and urge you to keep the techniques you've learned during the sessions to preserve your marriage. Genesis 2:23–24 reads: *"And Adam said, This is the bone of my bones, and flesh of my flesh: she shall be called Woman, because she was taken out of Man. Therefore shall a man leave his father and his mother, and shall cleave unto his wife: and they shall be one flesh."*

"'Secondly, Proverbs 31:11–12: *"The heart of her husband doth safely trust in her, so that the he shall have no need of spoil. She will do him good and not evil all the days of her life."*

"'Sincerely,

"'Reverend Lawrence Dudley.'"

The group together raised their crystal goblets filled with sparkling cider and said in unison, "Amen."

Reader's Group Guide Questions

1. Should churches offer couples' support groups to their membership as a ministry?

2. Was Meesha correct in forcing Edward to attend the sessions?

3. Zora faced demons of her own. Do you think she was an effective therapist?

4. Should Zora have looked for her child after the adoption laws were relaxed?

5. Did Beverly enable Amir?

6. Should Keisha have pressed charges against Amir?

7. Was Douglas correct in making Brandon marry Erin?

8. Were Erin's motives pure for marrying Brandon? Do you feel she really loved him?

9. Did Beverly show favoritism between her children?

10.   Do you feel Kenneth loved and accepted Amir as his son?

Reader's Group Guide Questions

11. Are parents obligated to always help their children regardless of the child's age?

12. Was Regina a true friend to Meesha or should she have stayed out of her friend's business?

13. Was Edward's justification for his affair acceptable? Can one spouse outgrow the other?

14. Do you think family members are more open with accepting people of different races into their family?

15. Should Julia and Douglas have adopted Juliana regardless of Brandon's feelings?

16. Was Beverly correct in going behind Douglas's back to secure bail money for Amir?

17. What demons do you think Amir faced? What made him act the way he did?

18. Was Zora professional in sharing her issue with the group?

19. Do you think couples' therapy support was more effective using male and female facilitators?

20. Who were your favorite and least favorite characters and why?

About the Author

Michelle Larks was born and raised in Chicago, Illinois, and currently resides in a western suburb. Michelle was educated in the Chicago public school system and attended the University of Illinois at Chicago Circle Campus.

In 2000, Michelle submitted a poem titled "Land of the Free, Home of the Brave," to the International Poets Society as part of a series compilation. In 2003 she self-published *A Myriad of Emotions*, a compilation of poetry, essays, and a short story that was produced through Ebony Energy Publishing. The project garnered her Author of the Month honors from the Literary World website in March 2003.

Michelle originally self-published *Crisis Mode* in March 2004 with AuthorHouse. She re-released the book in May 2005 through her own publishing company, F&M Enterprises. *Crisis Mode* is a compilation of four short stories that delve into societal issues, including an unplanned pregnancy, spousal abuse, mental illness, aging parents, and mother-daughter issues. *Crisis Mode* was selected Book of the Month by Literary World in March 2004. BlackRefer.com named *Crisis Mode* best novella of the year in 2006. The RawSistaz website named the book one of its top twenty picks for 2004.

Michelle's first full-length novel, an eBook titled *Mirrored Image*, was released by Ocean's Mist Press in

About the Author

February 2006. Michelle followed that up with *Who's Your Daddy* in May of the same year. Michelle was offered a contract with Urban Christian Books in the summer of 2006. *Keeping Misery Company* was released in 2007, *The Legacies* in 2008, *Til Debt Do Us Part* in 2009, and *Faith* in 2010.

Michelle is married and the mother of two adult daughters.

Urban Christian His Glory Book Club!

Established in January 2007, *UC His Glory Book Club* is another way to introduce **Urban Christian** and its authors. We are an online book club supporting Urban Christian authors by purchasing, reading, and providing written reviews of the authors' books. *UC His Glory Book Club* welcomes both men and women of the literary world who have a passion for reading Christian-based fiction.

UC His Glory Book Club is the brainchild of Joylynn Jossel, author and Executive Editor of Urban Christian and Kendra Norman-Bellamy, author and copy editor for Urban Christian. The book club will provide support, positive feedback, encouragement, and a forum whereby members can openly discuss and review the literary works of Urban Christian authors. In the future, we anticipate broadening our spectrum of services to include online author chats, author spotlights, interviews with your favorite Urban Christian author(s), special online groups for *UC His Glory Book Club* members, ability to post reviews on the website and amazon.com, membership ID cards, *UC His Glory* Yahoo! Group and much more.

Even though there will be no membership fees attached to becoming a member of *UC His Glory Book Club*, we do expect our members to be active, committed, and to follow the guidelines of the book club.

UC His Glory Book Club members pledge to:

- Follow the guidelines of *UC His Glory Book Club*.
- Provide input, opinions, and reviews that build up, rather than tear down.
- Commit to purchasing, reading, and discussing featured book(s) of the month.
- Respect the Christian beliefs of *UC His Glory Book Club*.
- Believe that Jesus is the Christ, Son of the Living God.

We look forward to the online fellowship.

Many Blessings to You!

Shelia E. Lipsey
President
UC His Glory Book Club

**Visit the official Urban Christian His Glory Book Club website at www.uchisglorybookclub.net

Notes

Notes